As a journalist Polly has written for many publications, including *You* magazine, the *Sunday Times*, *Marie Claire*, the *Independent* and *In Style*. Polly is married with one child and lives in London.

'Delighting in the absurdities of modern motherhood's glossy myths – having it all, while wearing expensive designer clothing unmarked by baby sick – Williams is also keenly aware of how lonesome and disorientating the whole experience can be, and isn't afraid to expose the funny, painful truth'
Daily Mail

'The dilemmas of millennial motherhood, and her witty, empathetic story will strike a chord with anyone who knows it's not as easy as Gwynnie and co make it look'
Glamour

'A sharply written debut novel about the trials of playing hip happy families'
Tatler

'Funny and honest, this is a refreshingly thoughtful take on the hushed-up trials of making the transition to parenthood'
You magazine

'Read this: written with the lightest of touches and serious intent. A funny, smart and honest account of modern motherhood'
In Style

'Witty, moving, beautifully written'
Wendy Holden

The Rise and Fall of a Yummy Mummy

Polly Williams

sphere

SPHERE

First published in Great Britain in 2006 by Time Warner Books
This paperback edition published in 2006 by Sphere

Copyright © Polly Williams 2006

The moral right of the author has been asserted.

A CIP catalogue record for this book is available
from the British Library.

ISBN-13: 978-0-7515-3744-4
ISBN-10: 0-7515-3744-6

Typeset in Sabon by M Rules
Printed and bound in Great Britain by
Clays Ltd, St Ives plc

Sphere
An imprint of
Little, Brown Book Group
Brettenham House
Lancaster Place
London WC2E 7EN

A member of the Hachette Livre Group of Companies

www.littlebrown.co.uk

For Ben

Acknowledgements

A huge heartfelt thank you to everyone who helped get this book from my head to the shelves, especially my mother, Julia Williams, who made writing it possible, my husband Ben Chase, my agent Lizzy Kremer at David Higham Associates, my editor Jo Dickinson and the great team at Time Warner. Big kiss also to Lucy Johnston for being my Mario, Ed Williams for his tech-wizardry and my grandmother, Muriel Sutton, for insisting that I write and always asking, 'Is it done yet, dear?'

Prologue

As catastrophes go, it was a quiet one. You wouldn't have known that my world had imploded. I didn't talk about what happened, I stitched it up inside. A single girl might have sulked over a few cocktails before dieting defiantly and declaring 'Next!'. My affairs were more complicated. I was eight months pregnant. And Joe remained the proud expectant dad. He'd still trace my hard bump with fascinated fingers, kiss the heat off my bruised breasts. I was his, impregnated, fat and cosseted. But I wasn't enough.

It was an unseasonably warm autumn. An 'Indian summer' the breakfast TV weatherman crowed as if he'd divined it himself. That particular September morning I was awoken early by the baby pushing out its tiny palms like pastry cutters under the skin. Too tired to feel enchanted, I gracelessly levered myself out of my enormous bed. (Bought for sex when I was single. Look where it got me.) Pulling up the blind, residential Kilburn revealed itself in slices. The taste of next door's bacon slithered in through the gap in the window frame.

Another day, hungry, drunk on hormones. Another day being Amy Crane, celebrated Pregnant Person. Strangers smiled at me then. Needless to say, they don't any more. My mother says that this is because I sport a scowl. I say I'm just squintily short sighted and don't like wearing glasses. And in any case, Mum knows how to extract a scowl better than anyone.

Joe smack-kissed my tummy. 'Must go,' he said. 'Meeting. Out of the office. You have a lovely day.' He was dressed in a tan linen suit, an artfully crumpled good one. Birkenstocks. All dangerously Soho. But his great size and unselfconscious lollop – his head arrives a few inches before the rest of him, not because of a stoop, but rather due to an eagerness to get behind his Apple Mac – stop him from looking camp. The door slammed. Clump, clump down the steps – he used to jump every other one, doesn't now – and then the dry drag of his sandals on the pavement. Why is it that things sound different in the sunshine? You can hear the weather.

I lay back on the bed but a pile of bricks weighed down on my spine. Besides, croissants called. Five, perhaps six. Barely touched the sides. The best thing about being pregnant was the licence to eat with complete impunity, like a naturally thin person. Once I gave birth it transpired that the baby only accounted for a fraction of my pregnancy weight. Only Joe thought this funny.

Beep! A text. Joe.

Mt regents pk boat lake caf 12

Sweet. We hadn't arranged anything. But it was the first week of my maternity leave and Joe guessed I didn't know what to do with myself. After years of moaning about the nine-to-five I felt vaguely lost without its scaffolding. My intention to use that precious last bit of 'free' time productively – art galleries, foreign film matinees and girlie lunches –

had yet to be realised. No, I preferred cool, private, unsociable baths. I needed to wash all the time that summer. Pregnancy made me secrete hot sticky female stuff, like sex juice, but not. That was the last thing on my mind.

Flumping in, I displaced half the bath water. An archipelago of fleshy islands that broke the filmy surface, my shape barely human, nothing like those neat celebrity pods you see in magazines. After drying myself down – each pat indenting my waterlogged skin like a footprint – I squeezed into a tube of maternity Lycra and covered the mud splatter of pregnancy pigmentation marks on my forehead with a layer of thick foundation. A squirt of useless non-toxic deodorant and I was off, thudding forth on cracked heels.

The tube made me anxious. I knew I'd be the last person to escape through the cramped emergency exits should an emergency arise. I'd never felt so vulnerable. Protesting at the flood of adrenaline, the baby corkscrewed inside. The carriage smelt. The man sitting next to me scratched his scalp noisily. Then he sniffed his finger and I thought I might swoon with disgust. Surfacing at Baker Street I breathed deeply between cars to avoid asphyxiating my baby with exhaust fumes and, following the loop of the lake, walked through Regent's Park, slowly, like I was wearing one of those Hollywood fat suits.

Chinese ducks with calligrapher-drawn faces, moorhens, drab brown females and a heron, one leg bent back as though assuming a particularly punishing yoga pose. Bucolic, for the city. I waddled breathlessly up a small arched bridge to get a better view. To my right, through the horse chestnuts, rose the bronze dome of the Regent's Park Mosque. Behind the willow tree, to my left, was the boating lake, bobbing sky blue rowing boats. On the other side of the bridge, the café. My phone beeped.

3

Snt messg 2 wrng phone. srry. wrk thing. canclled. spk ltr.

Sent while I was underground. Great. I leant my cargo against the wooden handrail and considered a compensation prize from the café. Bagels? Magnum? A flapjack would be nice. Suddenly I heard a laugh, nasal, screechy, like a parakeet. I looked to my left. And that's when I saw him, from behind, in the umbrella of shadow cast by a willow tree. If I'd looked two seconds later, or shut my eyes in rapture over flapjacks, I would have missed him. I really wish I had. But he is unmistakable from behind, even at a distance. Who was he with? Cursing my short sight, stomach on spin cycle, I gripped the handrail of the bridge. Damn my impressionist vision! Then they walked away, into the light. And what I saw ruined everything. So I ran. Not terribly fast, obviously.

One

It's just as well that I stopped caring whether men looked at me after that because now they don't, not even a quick double-take. I can weave through crowds without the slightest sexual ripple. Like a woman in her sixties perhaps, or in a burka. Of course, there's no reason why anyone would look. I'm no longer a blooming Pregnant Person. Nor am I sideshow ugly, comically obese or in any way beautiful or striking. No, I'm five-foot-four-and-a-half inches, thirty-one years old, ten-stone-six, with dyed blonde hair (two-inch mousy roots) and washed-out-denim eyes. The lashes I used to get tinted are now pale as a pig's. After years of blasting my salary on blow-dries and beauty counters, my monthly grooming budget – mostly products for thinning hair and breast pads – now amounts to little more than the price of a Chanel nail varnish. No, I'm not one of those women who pinged back to their pre-baby selves, not in any way. I'm irreparably changed. And I dress accordingly. Today: three-year-old Nike Airs, drawstring M&S khakis and a blue T-shirt that slips off my shoulders to reveal feeding-bra straps sprouting elastic. My other clothes, from my pre-baby life, no longer fit.

So no wolf-whistles and, a little more crushingly, no competitive size-ups by other women. (It's funny the things you miss.) Only the care-in-the-community loons and charity chuggers note my passing. Which made the following incident all the more extraordinary.

Last Wednesday, on the Salusbury Road, Queen's Park, 3.15 p.m. Handsome and surf-dirt blond, he was wheeling a hand-painted, rainbow-striped mountain bike along the pavement. Taut brown legs scissoring in neon yellow cycle shorts, he was muscular, short, built like a hammer. I'd just nipped into the pub, pretended that I was looking for someone so that the landlord thought I was a customer before stealing into the Ladies. My bladder isn't quite what it was. On my way out I walked straight into him, grazing my knee on his pedal. I said sorry. He said sorry. He flirted his eyes up, then down and grinned shyly. Jolting with embarrassment, I walked away, a sharp trot, past the Queen's Park dads – accessorised with baby slings and expensive trainers – browsing the estate agent's windows, the cappuccino drinkers at the pavement café and the low plateaux of jostling heads that made up a crowd of school children. I was aware, even then, that the fleeting flush of attention changed the way I walked. My spine lengthened in a supermodelish kind of way. My head craned up so that I looked straight ahead, on an eye level with others, rather than at the unfolding grey landscape of pavement. Of course, with hindsight, this exacerbated the situation. It took me until I had passed the third avenue (about six minutes) before I realised I had four sheets of white loo paper flagged to the sole of my left trainer.

No such delusions today. A twig is caught in the back right wheel of the pram, ticking time with each rotation as I walk along Brondesbury Road (unnoticed). It's breezy but unusually warm, like the low setting on the hairdryer I haven't used for

6

months. Blossom, dense as broccoli on the trees. Shit, there I go again, already thinking about food and it's only six o'clock. There's a buzz of people escaping work, impatient to get home before the last of the sunshine slopes off into the chill of the May evening. I love London like this. It reminds me of when I was single. That exciting smell of spring – cigarettes, beer, camellia blossom, low-hung pollution – is the smell of libido rising, the promise of skimpy dresses, damp knickers and brown feet. It means everything when you're single. Now what does it mean? A parasol on Evie's pram. A tooth. Solids.

'Honey, you're home!' Joe's attempt at an American accent.

He opens the door as I twiddle the key, so I fall forward. He catches me. Whoa! I get a double-take flash – I've been getting these a lot recently, still a little startled that this life is mine – and see Joe distinctly, as if for the first time. Not bad looking, not at all. A big man. Over six foot, coat hanger shoulders, a smile wide enough to glimpse the mercury fillings in his molars. Eyes, Atlantic blue, feathered with ink-black lashes. He's by far the most attractive one in this relationship now. The power has shifted.

Joe stumbles, tripping on a plastic brick. While this would make me curse, he tuts affectionately. He loves our baby's imposition, the clues to her six-month-old existence. A contented father. A good catch. Still, most women would have confronted him, I know that. But if you absolutely can't risk losing, you don't play, do you?

'Got off early,' he says.

'That makes a change.' Joe is usually home late. He runs his business hours infuriatingly erratically. I never know where he is from one day to the next, which leaves me wondering.

He ruffs up his sleeves exposing wide freckled forearms. 'Thought I'd come and see what mischief you two got up to when I'm not here.'

'Now you know. Wild Bacchanalian sex orgies, blizzards of cocaine . . .'

Joe grins shyly. 'Er, I've got something for you. A present.'

'Oh fab. No birthday required.' My last present involved a travel bottle steriliser and a recent photograph of me which he'd doctored in Photoshop, removing the bags under my eyes and my post-partum chins. (He didn't understand why I was offended.)

Joe peers into the pram. 'Asleep, good.' He wheels it into a nook of the hall and swivels it to face the wall. 'Amy . . .'

Joe lunges for my hand and folds it into his, digging his fingers into my palm. When we first met I loved his big hands, like the Green Cross Code man, the way they made mine look so pretty and doll-like. We haven't held hands for a long time.

'I just want you to know that . . .'

I brace myself. What have I done wrong now?

'. . . You're an amazing mother. Maybe I don't say it enough.'

We stare at each other, slightly embarrassed. We don't operate in this gear. We don't do soppiness. Life with a baby requires practicality, organisation, a delegation of tasks. Romance is too time consuming and susceptible to awkward misunderstandings.

'But there *has* to be more to our relationship than parenting.' He looks down, slightly embarrassed by his own sincerity. 'We must not forget about us, Joe and Amy *the couple*. It's been tough. But a happy couple make the best parents.'

I recognise this line from the 'The Shock of the New' chapter of his well-thumbed baby manual.

Joe whips out a bag from behind his back. 'So I got you this.' The box is nipple pink and long and flat with the words Agent Provocateur scrawled across it in bordello writing.

'Wow, thanks.' Paroled from his grip, I open the box and peel away the layers of tissue paper. Oh! A froth of pale pink and black lace. A bra! After all my industrial strength maternity bras I'm stunned by its gossamer lack of substance, its defiance of function. 'Oh Joe, so beautiful.'

'Obviously you can't wear it yet, it's got underwiring,' he says authoritatively. 'Something nice for when you finish breastfeeding. I intended to just get you the knickers but it matched and the lady in the shop said . . .'

'Shush, I'm impressed.' Joe's never bought me lingerie before. But it hadn't been needed. Didn't matter what knickers I was wearing, they came off. But that was before my life was measured out in fluid ounces.

'I did my homework,' he says quietly, eyes fever bright.

I try not to dwell on the nature of his homework. There is more! I rummage into the tissue paper. Lacy knickers! 'How pretty!' How alien. (I still wear my maternity knickers a lot. They're very comfortable.) I hold the knickers up. Oh Christ! The gusset splits in two. A ribbon-seamed hole where my bottom should be hidden. 'My bum isn't up to this.'

'Don't be silly, you've got a great bum. Put them on. Go on. Evie's asleep.' Joe's big frame is silhouetted against the wall lamp. He is the shape of a men's lavatory graphic.

'Later. After supper.'

'You always say that. Let's seize the moment . . .'

I flip through my excuses. Tired? It's only six thirty. Period? Duh! I'm breastfeeding. There are none. Apart from the obvious, and I can't go there. So I carry my pretty pink box upstairs and peel off my big nude pants (where did I get these from? why?!) and M&S maternity bra. Gawd! My

9

matted triangle of pubic hair is like an illustration from a seventies print of *The Joy of Sex*. I haven't trimmed it since, well . . . I can't remember. I grab the sharpest thing I can find, a pair of blunt nail scissors, and snip manically at my pubic mop until it resembles a badly mown lawn, then pull the underwear on in a fast, functional way, as if I were in a changing room full of lithe teenagers slithering into size sixes.

Lo! The bra manages to compensate for my lost oomph with some clever architecture, but the knickers pinch the pancake of flesh that folds over my wonky caesarean scar, my 'crooked smile' as Joe calls it. (My bikini line clearly wasn't the surgeon's priority.) Pubes spike out of the lace. When I open my legs there's a draught. And when I turn? Oh dear. A hole showing my bum cheek cleavage, tied with a bow. A bow! God. I don't look sexy. I look ludicrous. I look like a reader's wife.

'What're you doing in there?'

I can't walk down the stairs like this, bottom wobbling, so exposed. What if Joe compares me to other women? (*His* other women?) And more to the point, why is he doing this? This is humiliating, sadistic behaviour.

'Wah, wahhhhh, wahhhhh . . .'

Impeccable timing. Saved! I throw on my towelling dressing gown (towelling is milk-absorbent, my silk one is ruined) and stomp downstairs. Joe has Evie in his arms and paces the stripped wood floor in the living room, singing 'The Wheels on The Bus' under his breath. The answerphone light blinks. Two messages. Thankful for something to do, I depress the button.

'*Hi-yahhh!* Sue here. I'm organising a group rendez on Monday, 10.30 at Teaz Time, Willesden Lane. All the girls should be there. Oh, by the way, Oliver has a new tooth! It's the sweetest. *Bye now!*'

10

Every development of Oliver's is 'the sweetest'. Sue is the sweetest too. Sue is what's known as An Amazing Friend. There's nothing she likes better than discussing birth stories. She phones all the time, offers information on inoculations, commiserates about the disturbed nights, offers to take the baby for a couple of hours, an offer which, to my knowledge, nobody has taken up because you don't want to get into an exchange situation with her. You don't want to be beholden somehow.

Beep beep beep.

'Amy, Alice. Done our duty, we're going dancing. I'll pick you up Friday at eight. Glad rags on! Call me if a problem. Later.'

Alice! My new friend Alice. We were 'put in touch' by Sophie, a workmate at Nest PR – where I worked in my pre-baby past life – because we live close-by and both have babies (although Alice's is almost a year older, so in baby terms, a different species). I think Sophie thought I might be lonely. Having a baby is like belonging to an exclusive dating club, or being Jewish. You get introduced. Just not to women you want to date. Most of them you've got nothing in common with bar exhaustion, which limits conversation rather. But it was different with Alice. We met a few weeks ago at the Porchester Baths, Bayswater, by the shallow end with our babes in armbands like Bertie Bassets. She said she'd be the one in the bikini. It was lip-gloss pink with shells on the ties. In a pool filled with mothers in M&S navy swimming costumes with low-cut legs, Alice stood out.

'How rude is she? So bloody presumptuous.' Joe is angry because I've ruined the mood by opting to press the telephone's buttons, not his. But then I don't seem to do that anymore, with or without expensive underwear.

'Oh it's fine. She's a bit of a character.'

11

'But she hardly knows you! What makes her think you'd want to go out dancing when you've got a six-month-old baby and you're not getting any sleep and you're breastfeeding? The whole point of you two meeting up was to have someone to go to play groups and things with, not—'

'Sadly, I've got absolutely nothing to wear. Any half decent items of clothing are three sizes too small.'

'Exactly,' Joe says, visibly relieved. 'Besides, Evie's too little. I really don't think you'd enjoy it.'

This gets me. Joe presuming what I'd enjoy! Like everything at the moment, my instinct is just to oppose him. Pulling in the opposite direction is a way of creating space in our newly shrunken life.

'On second thoughts,' I clear my throat, 'maybe a night out would do me good. I haven't been out for months. I must have *something* that won't get me turned away at the door.' Joe's face sags with disappointment. 'You'll be fine here with Evie, won't you?'

Joe looks doubtful. It's all very well me living under a six o'clock curfew, different for him. 'I was planning . . .'

I push hair out of my eyes to give Joe a don't-go-there glare. As my arm shifts, the towelling dressing gown gapes open to reveal a frothy flash of pink lace. Joe stares, shocked. My newly packaged flesh seems wildly inappropriate here, in the chilly hall, caught in the crossfire of the unsaid. He looks away, ignores it.

'. . . We were hoping to go out for dinner this Friday. Remember? You did ask your mum if she could babysit?'

'I did. She can't,' I lie.

Later that evening, after Evie's bath and putting her to bed – listening to her scream, getting up, stroking her head, trying to remember what that supernova nanny preached on TV, letting her scream and feeling horribly guilty – I collapse on the sofa. Joe sits down heavily next to me, beer in hand. A repeat of *ER* is on. I'm so tired I can't follow it. I just watch the mouths move, like bad dubbing. Joe's ham hand worms its way under the towelling, on my knee.

'Darling, you look so sexy in this.' He rubs his hand between my legs.

Nothing. I feel nothing. It's like trying to strike a damp match. I curl up, squishing his hand and restricting its movement. 'Not now, I'm so tired.'

'Suppose you must be,' he says, hand quickly retreating to the easy predictability of the TV remote control.

Gussetless on the sofa, sleep seduces instead.

Two

Alice leans back in a battered leather armchair, scarved in cigarette smoke.

'No one tells you this, Amy, but the less you see your baby, the less you miss her when she's not there. It's just like sex,' she says, tugging down the V of her top to show more cleavage. 'That's how working mothers cope. A natural independence develops. Those women who bleat on that it hurts the baby?' She swirls the ice cubes in her glass. 'Hysterical womb worshippers. Babies are hardy creatures, they adapt. So don't let Joe make you feel guilty about going out. Evie will be fine. Young babies are about as loyal as cats.'

Evie. Milky Evie, sweet and warm as a pudding. Is she coping with a mama-shaped hole in her evening? Probably. Do I miss her? Well, actually, at this moment, shamefully . . . no.

'What are you drinking? Water! How about a champagne cocktail?' Alice orders before I answer.

Alice makes me feel much better about everything actually. She's not like the other mothers – like Sue – from my National Childbirth Trust group, that weird institution that all middle-class mothers are too scared not to sign up to in the run up to The Birth. (That the real trauma begins after this event never makes the white-board.) At the NCT you don't meet teenage mothers. Or single ones. Or lesbian ones. Well, not in north west London. You meet the coupled-off mothers, the thirtysomethings relieved that they got their eggs fertilised before the biological alarm clock chimed their ovaries into pumpkins, the ones who talk about massaging their perineum with organic nut oils, the ones who think they'll give birth 'naturally' in pools and end up begging for drugs, cut to pieces. Or the ones like Sue who do my head in by flopping out their great pendulous blue-veined breasts at every opportunity. I once got squirted. You know, when that first gush of milk sprays into the baby's surprised mouth like a garden sprinkler. Well, the baby turned away. I didn't.

Like me, Alice is thirty-one. Alfie, her little boy, is eighteen months, so she's almost out of babyworld, although it seems unlikely she was ever in it. You'd never know she was a mother. Her belly is as flat as a changing mat. She's wearing tailored long shorts cut so low you can tell she's had a Brazilian (her pubic bone is *tanned*), a studded belt, tight green cashmere cardigan and heels like chopsticks. A huge bangle, woven leather and silver, slides up and down her slim forearm. And her face belongs to a thirties film star, the kind who had fast affairs and faster ripostes: rosebud lips and wide-set eyes framed by a cloud of butter-blonde curls. No, you'd never look at Alice and think, stress incontinence.

'Managed to get out much since Evie was born?' Late evening sunshine slices through the window. Alice squints. Her eyes are absinthe green.

'Uh, not really. Not together. I mean Joe still goes out quite a lot.'

'Sadly, babies don't really cramp daddies' style, not in the same way. If anything, parenthood gives them the opportunity to behave like single men again, going out and about unaccompanied. It can turn into one long stag party if you're not careful.'

'Well, I'm breastfeeding. It's strategically difficult to do things as a couple. Mum babysits occasionally. But Joe's parents haven't been much use, being six feet under.' Alice snorts. I feel bad going for a cheap laugh. Joe's parents died in a Corsican pedallo accident in the early nineties. 'Still, we've got some great friends in the country, Kate and Pete. Been there a couple of times, shown Evie what a cow looks like. That sort of thing.'

'Now friends in the country are good, especially hospitable ones with beautiful houses,' says Alice, conducting the conversation with a pretzel. 'But in-laws, bad. You're well out of it. In my experience their purpose is to make you fat and miserable. All those "helpful" meals they cook, to "give you a break". Pah! About as relaxing as a meal with your old headmistress.' Alice puts the half-eaten pretzel in the ashtray, as if finishing it off might just tip her calorific daily allowance over the edge, and lights another cigarette. Incorrect to say, but shit, it does look sexy, the smoke curling from her partly open glossed mouth like an exhalation of desire. 'The problem is, once you have their grandchild any mother or mother-in-law thinks she's got an access-all-areas pass to your life.'

I laugh, thinking of my mum; her invasive offers of 'help' – the plant potting, washing up, toy delivery – just thinly disguised reasons to visit Evie. I think she probably loves Evie more than she loves me. Which is quite understandable. So do I.

'All you really want them to do is take over in the morning while you get some sleep, make tea and disappear again. But

16

they don't. Which is why we all end up spending a fortune on maternity nurses.'

Do *we*? Not anyone I know.

Alice rolls her shoulders. 'Ah, so stiff. Must do some Pilates, been slacking.'

I'm not entirely sure what Pilates is. I've seen it written about in magazines but skipped the articles, not being the fitness-trend type.

'A very precise workout that sorts everything out with little sweating,' Alice explains, catching my ignorance. 'Not to be confused with yoga, not if you're a purist. But Josh . . .' Alice laughs to herself. 'Josh, my instructor, ain't no purist. So it's confused with yoga.'

'Where do you . . . ?'

'A little studio in NW10. Hey, you should come along.' A smile curls her lips. 'But less of boring old Pilates. The big question is,' Alice camps up a perfect arch of eyebrow, 'how is your lurve life?'

A gulp of water torrents out of my left nostril. I can't believe she's asked me that! I wipe my nose with my sleeve. A waitress clinks down our cocktails. Without being asked, Alice slips her credit card into the girl's hand, slick as a poker player. 'A tab,' she nods, swinging one leg over the other. So long and lean it's vaguely pornographic, the leg protrudes out into the communal space around our table so people must manoeuvre around it, becoming the unconscious focus point of the bar. During pauses in conversation, those spacey moments when you have to look away to avoid intimacy, both men and women's eyes fall on the leg rather than their wine glasses or blank mobile phones (turned off, it's private members in here).

'I remember the first time. Like being fucked by a cheese grater! That's breastfeeding for you. It changes the chemistry

17

of it. Turns a black run into a dry slope.' She doesn't lower her voice. At an adjacent table a man's hooded eyes flick up from his beer glass.

'I don't know,' I say, daring myself to confess. 'We haven't done it . . . not yet. Well, it's been months actually.' There, outed! I search Alice's face for a reaction. To my relief, she's unfazed. Everyone else who talks about this issue – mostly GPs and other mothers – just keep banging on about contraception and how easy it is to get pregnant when you're breastfeeding, which makes me feel worse. 'I'm beginning to feel like a bit of a freak.'

'You're so *not* a freak,' Alice says, perhaps too insistently, like I need strong defence. 'I doubt any of your new mum friends are swinging from the nursery mobiles.'

'No, no, they're all at it. Did I mention Sue at NCT?'

As Alice nods, the gleam on her hair shifts and slips like a halo. My hair has no light-reflecting qualities.

'She's started "making love" again and it is really "tender, better than ever".' The words still taunt me. 'She said, I'm not joking, that it's like being "a freshly deflowered virgin". That it means more now, now she realises that sex has a proper meaning: babies.' Sue had spoken in a low, breathy whisper that smelled of parmesan.

'Ugh! Let smug Sue keep her fertilisation sex. You, my girl . . .' Alice strokes my hand, trailing a sugar-pink fingernail along my wrist. It makes my eyes water. I don't want anyone to be nice to me. It will set me off. It's the hormones. 'You need a good *fuck*.'

I sip my champagne, trying not to look shocked. You get a bit bourgeois when you're at home with a baby all day. 'What about you?' I say, emboldened by the saltiness of the conversation.

'Me?' She smiles coyly. 'Well, I do get my rocks off.'

18

'What's um . . .' I realise I don't know her partner's name. 'What's the name of Alfie's dad?'

'John.'

'On the tip of my tongue. John. What's he like?' Stupid question, I adjust it. 'What does he do?'

'John's a darling. A total darling,' purrs Alice, pushing a wayward curl behind her hooped earring. 'Dot commer, own business. Twentieth-century design imported cut-price from Europe. Doing very well, if you please.' She sighs, mentally weighing him up. 'He's blond, good height and very hand-some, of course. Wouldn't have mated with anything but the best genetic material.' I chuckle. 'And he's an amazing father.'

'He sounds great,' I say rather blandly. Alice's exuberance makes me fade to grey a bit.

'And as you are wondering, we haven't had sex for, oh, let me see . . . almost a year.'

A year! Alice is one of those women who looks like she's having knee-trembling sex, 24/7.

'Like me!' I sound rather too exuberant.

'Well, not quite. We're no longer together.'

'Oh God, I'm so sorry.' Done it again.

'No problem.' She blows out a trumpet of cigarette smoke. 'I wasn't that into it.'

I'm unsure how to respond to such glibness. Joe would dis-like her. 'Oh dear. Didn't you want to stay with him?'

'In the beginning, of course.' Alice speaks softly. 'But it wasn't to be. I *was* in love with John, well, as much as you can be in love with anyone after four weeks. We met in Ibiza, real summer of love stuff. I still worry about the fact that Alfie was conceived while I was on E. But, touch wood,' she taps the table, 'he's totally fine.'

'John didn't want the baby?'

'No, John loved the idea! We talked about getting married,

19

on Cala Salada beach, me in a white Allegra Hicks kaftan, orchid in the hair, *fruits de mer* for dinner.'

I can see her so clearly. She'd have made a beautiful bride.

'We decided to stay on for a while in Ibiza, John flying back and forth to London. And then . . . I realised, we both did, that we didn't know each other, not really. I mean I knew he was a nice man who loved calamari with a twist of lemon and could dance sexily *sans* drugs which is always a bonus, but that was about it.'

'Did you stay in Ibiza?'

'No, as I got bigger I couldn't stand wallowing about in the heat like a fat tourist. We came back to London and I rented out my flat in Ladbroke Grove, where Alfie and I live now, and moved into his loft space in Clerkenwell.'

'Gosh. How was that?'

Alice blows up her fringe. 'Ugh. Couldn't stand the East End. No good parks, just lots of people with silly haircuts and neon hoof trainers talking about bad video art. Not my scene.'

How glamorous to care about 'a scene' when pregnant. I just cared about my proximity to the local bakery.

'Got the hell out after the birth.' She shrugs off her cardigan.

'And how was that? The birth.'

'OK. They all come out one way or another don't they?'

Does Alice not want to elaborate? Birth stories, told in exhaustive, gruesome detail, are a staple of the NCT meetings and usually require much distraction – a choking baby, a nearby smoker – for closure.

'But it must have been great living in a loft. I've always wanted to.'

'A loft! Oh my god it was a *nightmare*! Imagine a baby screaming in an echoey aircraft hangar.' She falls back in the chair, spent by the trauma of recollection. 'There were *no* internal walls at all! I had to have a bath in some futuristic pod in the centre of the living room when I really wanted to be tucked away in my antique claw-foot with Diptyque candles. No garden, just a stainless-steel balcony with a view of factories and traffic. No escape. We drove each other mad.' Alice shudders. 'It was awful. Awful.'

'Couldn't you have moved?' Lack of internal walls and ironic mullets seem pretty poor reasons to give up on a relationship.

'We did, back into my place in Ladbroke Grove. Things improved, in the sense that we could be in two separate rooms and close the doors on each other. But the relationship wasn't going anywhere. I don't know . . .' Her voice trails off. 'We were trying to get to know each other while bringing up a baby. Forget candle-lit dinners, romantic holidays . . . the things most couples have to ease themselves into monogamy. We had three a.m. wake-up calls and a baby with colic. You know how it is. Bloody hard. But I think if we were right for each other it would have worked.'

'What was so wrong?'

'Well you just *know*, don't you? It hardly required marriage guidance.'

Even now, I still don't 'just know'. Life gets complex when there are children involved. It seems kind of pointless pondering whether the father of your child is your soulmate. The deed is done. And there are bigger things to worry about.

Alice takes a gulp of drink. I watch the gulp travel, like a broad bean, down her long, slender throat.

'The "soulmate" connections we made on a beach in Ibiza under the influence of high-grade MDMA powder turned out – surprise – to be made of little more than the sand we danced on,' Alice muses, eyes fixed dreamily on the smoky

21

mid-distance. 'Our expectations were very different. He wanted me to stay at home and be this mother earth type, stop doing my jewellery . . . or just keep it to a real hobby level, to be on the safe side.' She sighs. 'Despite all the cool trappings he is a terrible suburbanite at heart. Which is great. Suburbanites make great dads.' There is something rehearsed about this answer.

'You sound fond of him.'

'I am. Alfie gets the best of both worlds.' Alice stretches and the S of her waist rises out of her shorts. 'Now, enough of me. How long were you and Joe together before Evie came along?'

'Only a year.'

'And?'

'The result of post-row, one quick poke roulette sex I'm afraid.'

'So many babies are. The risk of pregnancy makes sex more exciting, no?'

I nod, trying to remember.

'Were you living together when it happened?'

I'm uncomfortable with this line of questioning. I'd rather hear about Alice. 'Joe moved in when I was pregnant.' Alice stares at me quizzically. 'We made the best of it,' I say with some finality, shifting on the leather banquette. I can feel my mouth rebelling against this forced jovial casualness and turning downwards.

Alice studies me for a moment. She knows the subject is closed. 'Another cocktail?'

'Sadly can't. Breastfeeding . . .'

'Oh come on! One more won't hurt. Milk is an excellent mixer. Only a tiny amount gets through. It'll make her sleep. Don't listen to the breastfeeding Nazis.'

'No really, better not.'

'Look, I'll order a water too and I'll drink the cocktail if you find you don't want it.'

I put my hands up, surrender. Talk of Joe has made me glum. A drink could shift it.

'I'm off to the loo.' Again. Need to do more pencil-squeezing pelvic floor exercises but still unsure which muscle is which. When I squeeze I feel a contraction in my left buttock, which doesn't seem right somehow. Outside in the corridor, by the cigarette machine, I turn on my phone. There are four text messages from Joe.

Poo spectacular.
When u hm?
Gt blk cab.
Cn u call me?

No, I can't call him. Can't face it. Don't want to let that world into this one: the crying, the powdery baby fug, the cloying microuniverse of our Kilburn house. In this club I'm cocooned temporarily in an artificial environment, like an airplane. Pressing the green button would be like bashing open a window, the air sucking me out into freefall. So I hide behind a text.

Wll be late. Gv E bttle. Dnt wt up.

In the Ladies I gloss my mouth. My lips are dehydrated and there is a tiny bloody nick on the lower one which I've been biting absent-mindedly. My breasts – without a baby to drain them – are hard and knotty and beginning to throb. I rearrange my feeding bra, hoping to make them look smaller. God! What am I wearing? My 'fat' jeans, waistline stretched from squeezing into them while pregnant, and a silk floral

23

'feminine' blouse, which gives me the sex appeal of a geography teacher dressing up for a school social. Flat, very flat, pink sandals. Quickly painted toenails . . . and toes. The varnish was so old it had congealed into a thick paste, impossible to apply accurately.

In contrast, the other girls in front of the mirror look surreal as billboard girls, all white teeth and shining eyes. They touch up their make-up, pull lipstick faces, angle their heads for the most flattering reflection. It is only now, seeing us lined up like some weird reality TV show filmed through a two-way mirror, that I realise that we are from different worlds, me and these preening creatures. With their peachy flesh hugged tight in denim or sequiny slithers of chiffon, they are dressed for a stroll along a Hamptons beach, heels in hand, heading towards a hot guestlist. I could be dressed for a bracing march around out of season Hastings. I used to love clothes. What happened?

12.20 a.m. Alice is dancing like her body is liquid, a woman from a Bond film score. It's mesmerising to watch. Her boobs pulse gently under her top. Her hips sway. Men stare. For the first time in months, I am dancing too. But I am dancing like my mother. Just when I think I've found my rhythm it changes and each bit of my body moves to a different beat, feet in glued-to-the-floor raver mode, hips gyrating like a pregnant woman doing mobility exercises. Was I always such a bad dancer? I don't think so. I used to feel it instinctively, used to forget myself.

I look down at my feet, hoping to guide them. When I look up again Alice has gone, dissolved into the fizzing crowd. What do I do now? Dance on my own like some sad fuck with no friends? Why am I here? Where the hell is she? I stay dancing awkwardly on the spot for an eternity, edging nearer a group of girls so that I could plausibly look like I am with them, just dancing on the outside a bit. I get more and more pissed off, more self-conscious. Then Alice sashays into view, beer bottle in each hand. Shining ultra-violet, men's eyeballs track her passage like *Scooby-Doo* monsters.

'Ice cold!' Alice juts her hips forward, throws her curls back.

I forgive her immediately. A few old tunes come on. I remember these. Kylie! 'Can't Get You Out of My Head'! Alice is plaiting her arms in front of me, a pretend striptease. There is a dark-haired man sashaying into our invisible dance circle, encroaching on our space. He is not unattractive. But he is a terrible dancer, skipping from one leg to another like he needs the loo. We giggle. I wait for him to hit on Alice. He doesn't. He puts his back to Alice and grins at me.

'Wahey! You've pulled!' Alice lip-syncs behind me.

Despite his odd pee-hop, I am flattered. Nobody has hit on me for an eternity. (I had kind of resigned myself to that part of my life being over and have done the grieving.) Basking in his glances, I let the music under my skin and feel myself loosening up. And for the first time in months I feel like myself, my old self. And my body belongs to me again, not Evie. I want to be trapped in this moment for ever, dancing in amber. I suspect I'm drunk.

The man is drooling, hopping closer, his eyes focused on my swollen cleavage. I feel myself ripen with the attention. Then, suddenly, he stops. Getting bumped by bottoms in low-rise jeans, he bends down and picks something up off the floor, a white disc. Not looking at it, he passes it to me smiling.

'You've dropped something . . .'

Oh my God! Squatting on his hand, domed, sodden, is my breast pad. Seeing my expression he glances down at his

25

hand and inspects this thing, initially puzzled, then obviously horrified. Behind him I see Alice. She's gesturing, pointing at my chest. I glance down. A circle of wet is blooming on my right breast, my nipple a pencil stub under the wet silk. Oh. Shit.

'I'm . . . I'm . . . sorry,' I say, looking up. But the man has gone.

2.30 a.m., Charing Cross Road. We fall into a cab. I feel high, weirdly weightless, not drunk, even though I've drunk more than I have done since I knew I was pregnant. And not sleepy at all. In fact it's the first time I've not felt bone-shatteringly knackered in months. But I do feel guilty. I am a bad mother, dirty with the smell of other people's cigarette smoke and the grime of late-night London. I've probably picked something up from a loo seat, from fetid air filtered through the lungs of strangers, and I'm going to breathe it into the underdeveloped immune system of my baby.

Lights blur. I haven't seen London at night for so long, it gives me a touristy thrill. Alice is framed in near-silhouette, her head at a three-quarters angle to the window, the car lights bouncing off the curve of her cheekbone, the poised ballerina's jaw. Her curls are still smooth, no frizz halo. She is so beautiful. In my drunkenness, I want to reach out and touch her. For a second, I want to kiss her. Then, I want to be her. Rain starts to grease the streets.

'You all right, Amy?'

'Fine, just a bit woozy. I shouldn't have drunk so much, I feel bad.'

'My fault, sorry. But honestly, once in a while is fine. It's not going to kill Evie.'

Almost home. It's been great, but I am relieved that it is just one night, a parcel of experience, sealed as vacuum tight as a jar of baby food. It's not my life. And there is something reassuring about my mundane routine. I'm not sure that if I lived like Alice, with her brio and confidence, I could tolerate being me. Resignation is half the battle. I could wile away hours why-o-why-ing in therapy. Yes, my daddy left for another woman when I was little. It screwed me up. Yes, I have a horrible fear, no a belief, that history will repeat itself. No, I don't want to risk bringing the subject up and forcing Joe to choose between me and someone else. I'll do anything to avoid the inevitable.

What would happen? I'd come off that couch with a lighter purse and with a baby still waiting to be fed and paid for and fathered. Like my dear mum says, once you have a baby you can't fight things, you have to make the best of them. Alice obviously doesn't come from this angle. But Alice is different from me. She's got more money. She's more attractive. She's hardly going to spend the rest of her life on the shelf, is she?

Alice studies my face thoughtfully. 'It's not the only way you know,' she says suddenly.

'What do you mean?' My words slur.

'Your way. "Making the best of things." Pretending it's the Waltons.' Alice's head cocks to one side, curls clumped like a bouquet on her left shoulder.

'Don't know what you mean.' I shift uncomfortably, cross my arms and legs.

'You *do*. I've seen it before, lived it, Amy. Hanging in there with a man because he is the father of your child when you know in your heart it's not right.'

'That's a bit presumptuous!' How dare she?

'Sorry. Just . . . don't feel trapped.'

'You're wrong!' I swivel around on my seat, so that she can't see me blinking back tears. 'It's been tricky. But it's just a

27

patch.' I'm gabbling. I don't want Alice poking around inside my feelings. They're private. 'Babies test things, don't they?'

'First drop-off Ladbroke Grove, love?' rasps the taxi driver.

We sit in silence as the cab swerves into Oxford Gardens, shuddering to a stop outside a big stucco house. The house is very white in the car lights, like it's been newly painted. There's a small sporty vintage Mercedes outside. Alice gets out of the taxi, gives the driver twenty quid, tells him to keep the change and leans into my open window.

'Sorry, didn't mean to upset you. Me and my big mouth! I've had such a cool time.' She cups my face with two hands, planting a sloppy kiss on my cheek. 'You could do with some cheering up.' I nod, rather pathetically. 'Why don't we do a bit of shopping, get you sorted out?'

Shopping? I'm not sure a trip down Bond Street will fix anything. 'I'm fine.'

'But you seem a bit down on yourself and I always find the best antidote for the baby blues is a bit of self-love. You know, new clothes, new hair, that sort of thing.'

'I'm not sure what you're getting at, Alice.'

'A make-over!' Alice's head bobs with enthusiasm. It bashes against the window frame. 'Ouch! Honestly, you'd feel so much better!' The taxi driver drums his wheel impatiently. I shake my head. 'Amy, I'm being selfish,' she whispers. 'I love any excuse to shop. And I'd love to give you a new look. I'm one of those people. I give strangers extreme make-overs in my head.' I look at her blankly. 'It'd be a great project. Project, er, project Amy!'

Fuzzily drunk, I'm not entirely sure what Alice is talking about. But it sounds exhausting and expensive and vaguely insulting. I am tired and want to get home. 'Um, thanks for the offer. But it doesn't sound like my sort of thing.'

Alice's face falls. 'Oh well. Drinks next week, all the girls. You must come and meet everyone. I'm going to phone you.'

The idea of meeting *everyone*, whoever they are, makes me anxious. I haven't felt sociable since having Evie. Indeed, I've been grateful for a decent excuse not to go out. Like a strange inversion of my pre-pregnancy self, I've turned down so many invitations, from the girls at work and single childless friends, that they've stopped asking. The rare times I have acquiesced, I've made sure the social date will take place weeks after the concession. Then I seem to hurtle towards it at breakneck speed, the date getting bigger and more ominous the closer I get, like a fallen rock in the middle of a road. So I swerve, and cancel.

Alice's tall ectomorph strides down the gravel. It crunches like knuckles under her heels. A security light comes on. There is a light on behind the white blinds in the big bay window. Babysitter or John?

The taxi whizzes north, up tatty Great Western Road, past drunks and junkies and boarded-up shop fronts. My body, still soft from pregnancy, swollen with milk, shouldn't be on these dirty wet streets. I want to be at home, desperately. We are speeding, taking corners too fast. Yes, we are definitely going to crash. A tiny baby will be left motherless. And it will be my fault.

Home. The lights are off. I trip up the stairs into our bedroom. Joe is asleep, snoring lightly. I am noisier than I want to be on the floor-boards in Evie's bedroom. My feet are heavy. I peer into Evie's cot. She is perfectly still. I can't hear her breathe. Evie? I put my finger under her nose. No reassuring rush of warm air. I poke her cheek, too hard.

'Owwah!'

I have not been punished.

Three

My darling daughter is alive, pink and snuffling in her cot. Everything is fine. This is my first thought on waking. My second thought, a rather more unsettling one, is that perhaps Alice is right and making the best of things isn't the only way. And maybe I could do with a wax.

Ouch, bright light. Joe yanks the curtains back too hard. A vein throbs on his forehead. Joe is cross. Joe doesn't look great when he's cross. There's an impotence about his anger. It doesn't do much for my penitence.

'Evie must be hungry,' he growls, disappearing into Evie's bedroom.

Tiny legs pumping like pistons, face full of ancient anger, Evie swoops towards me in Joe's hands. As she gets nearer and realises that she is going to be fed, her mouth opens, her fists unfurl. She grabs for my boob, captures my sore nipple in the O of her mouth and sucks violently. I try hard not to think about the Orgasm On A Beach I drank five hours earlier.

'It's just irresponsible,' Joe says, big windshield back to me.

Hairs have grown on the back of his neck in the last few months, below his hairline, where you're not meant to have

them. Parenting has strange side effects: while I lose my hair –
seaweedy clumps of it collect in the bath plug – Joe gets more
hirsute.

'I'm always trying to get you to go out and have a good
time, shopping with Kate or visiting . . . I don't know . . . or,
er, getting out a new video.'

'Wild.'

'Amy, we tried doing the dinner party thing. Twice. Both
times you fell asleep on the sofa before pudding was served.
And when we went to Leo's party we were the first people to
arrive, the first to leave. We were home at nine p.m.! But it's
different with Alice isn't it? Alice phones and you behave like
a naughty teenager. Thing is, Amy, you're not. You're a
mother of a little baby.'

'Funny, I forgot.'

'Amy . . .' He rears up with a great inhalation, puffs his
chest out.

'Don't be ridiculous. I went out and had a laugh. Once.
The only time in, let's see, almost a year.'

'How much did you drink?'

'One glass of champagne.'

Mastering his adrenaline rush, Joe slumps down on the
side of the bed, his hefty frame slipping on the plum satin
throw that was once so sumptuous but now looks like it's
starred in a mammary splatter movie. He strokes Evie's head
as she feeds. This is the closest his hand gets to my breasts
these days. He used to love my nipples, before they became
distended in pregnancy. He would lick and suck them. He
doesn't do that now. That would be weird.

'Have you ever seen such a beautiful baby?' he says, soft-
ening.

Evie smiles on cue, a pure smile springing from that unpol-
luted pool of joy that's hidden just below the surface of

31

babies, like buds of teeth. She looks a bit like my mum, big wide face, paddle-pool blue eyes. My yellowy olive skin. Yes, beautiful. I think I can almost say this objectively, having examined other babies in the park. So many of them look like old Tory MPs. This said, Evie wasn't always gorgeous. When she was born I called her The Purpling.

'I'm sorry,' I say, trying hard to sound like I mean it.

It works. Joe's shoulders drop and he releases the tension with a little cough, relieved he doesn't have to exert authority that he doesn't feel, that I've made it easy for him. My unreachable cantankerousness neuters him, I think. He pushes back hair from my face tenderly, releasing a whiff of stale cigarette smoke.

'Yes, I know, I need a bath.'

Joe turns on the taps in the en suite before stomping downstairs and clattering and crashing about the kitchen. (The sound of Joe is unique as a fingerprint: I could identify him in an acoustic line-up.) I dig deeper under the duvet and admire the perfect whorl of Evie's ear, tracing it with my fingers. The bath rumbles and a cloud of lavender-scented steam billows out of the bathroom door.

Evie dribbles to a finish and grins. I have delivered, fulfilled my function. Her eyes search around the room, her house, her universe. I feel like she's been here for ever sometimes. Soft, pink, and pretty, she fits in. Unlike Joe. He is just too big somehow, his frame too heavy, his breath too meaty for this room, with its tinkle of rose fairy lights and white painted floorboards (scuffed now by his heaviness of foot) and my odd little Portobello finds – the Victorian potty, the chipped pink polka dot jug – that he neither likes nor understands. It's a girl's room, where I used to lounge in pyjamas with a pore strip on my nose and a glass of Chablis in my hand, singing along to Norah Jones. The house has not been adapted to

32

coupledom, let alone family life. Not like those houses with his 'n' her dressing gowns, double-end baths and loos with no doors because the couple are that close they no longer require privacy to pee.

No, Joe and I row about storage. Things have got that bad. True, his knicker drawer is still a cardboard box. What with my maternity clothes as well as my old clothes and Evie's outgrown Babygros, there is no spare drawer space. Joe keeps saying I've got to snap out of denial, pretending I'm a single girl who buys bric-a-brac from Portobello market on a whim. No, we are a family now. I must give in and go to Ikea.

Sometimes, in my blackest, most sleep-deprived moments, I see Joe as a trespasser. When I got pregnant he lived in a one-bedroom flat in Hackney – off the street known as 'murder mile' – with a damp problem and a perilous unofficial roof terrace with no fencing, having troughed all his inheritance into his design company and two Eames chairs. I owned a nice two-bedroom maisonette in Kilburn – not exactly Chelsea, but better than Hackney – with a newly fitted kitchen (a present to myself after a pay-rise in the days when I was rewarded for hard work) and a newly decked large balcony, which my mother sweetly civilised with potted palms. I suggested he move in, had to. Joe is proud. He nodded quickly, wanting the conversation to finish as soon as possible. He wanted to be the one doing the providing. He hadn't won the jackpot, I laughed, trying to joke away any emasculating niggles. I'd made some canny moves, sold property at the right time, inherited just enough when my dad died to make a mortgage manageable. (I should have had enough for a proper house but Dad had fluttered most of it on Las Vegas mini-breaks.)

In my twentieth week of pregnancy Joe moved in, trailing

33

his possessions – a fungus-crusted microwave, a stereo, a PlayStation, an iPod, the Eames chairs – and his clothes in a ratty old backpack he took travelling around Africa in his year off. To my surprise, I discovered that I rather enjoyed having a man living in my house. As my bump had grown so had my sense of vulnerability and my need to be – whisper it – *protected*. Just a little bit. And with Joe in the house I slept better. And I enjoyed the ritual of sit-down mealtimes rather than snatching at hummous and pitta bread. Comfortable. Yes, I felt comfortable.

Aborting Evie was never an option. I'd done that before in a not entirely dissimilar situation, different man. 23rd September, a ghoulish secret anniversary. I can't erase that memory: lying still on the slab, legs up in stirrups, the sweet nurse who couldn't speak English wiping away my tears with a scratchy tissue, the surgeon's hands, cold as equipment. I didn't expect it to hit me so hard. I believed it would just be an unpleasant rite of passage, all my friends had had them. I hadn't expected to feel so empty afterwards. Like waking up from a drugging and finding a scar where a kidney had been. I cried for five days, pretended I had an eye infection. And yet, I don't regret it, not exactly. There will always be a question mark – how old? Dark or fair? – but I don't wish 'it' was here, tugging at my breast. It was a lesson. And if I hadn't had one abortion, perhaps Evie would have been the lesson instead.

So I knew what to do next time. Precisely nothing. Momentous calculated inaction. (I'm good at that.) It was the most significant non-thing I've ever done in my life. Joe held the stick up to the light, as if checking the authenticity of a bank note. 'We are pregnant!' he said, eyes bright and teary. The collusive plural made me slightly uneasy. Still, I didn't realise then that the little blue line would sever our lives in two: single girl/parent; I/we; passion/practicality. No, I thought life was going to get simpler. No more searching for 'the one'. No more wondering when to window a baby into my career. And, I suppose, the eradication of the possibility that I wouldn't find a suitable father for my child until it was too late and my eggs had shrivelled like old peas and I'd turned into one of those 'I forgot to have children' women featured in the *Daily Mail*. Or, worse, that I'd be like my friend Kate who's young enough but just can't get pregnant and no one knows why.

'Breakfast!'

Thud, thud, thud. Joe walks heavily, on his heels. The door swings open, he perches a tray perilously on the bed. The tray, covered in a rose-bud print, is a present – 'something useful now that you'll finally have to be domestic' – from my mother. Joe's breakfast, as always, is a medicinal assortment of vital nutrients: a handful of almonds, great protein, great source of vitamin E; handful of blueberries, anti-oxidants; glass of orange juice swimming with the sediment of a Postnatal Essential Vitamin powder that tastes foul; wholemeal toast with jam (my favourite, peanut butter, is strictly embargoed because of the risk of passing on a nut allergy in breast milk); a poached egg, no runny bits – salmonella, you can't be too careful; two fish-oil capsules, sourced from non-toxic deep Arctic waters, great for DHA, improving baby's cognition. There is an order, a symmetry to the tray's contents, like one of those remember-everything-on-the-tray games played at children's parties. He never used to be this anal.

'Joe, I can't eat all this. Really. It's sweet of you, but I'm just not that hungry.' My stomach is churning.

'Make yourself. You're breastfeeding. Think of Evie. She needs this stuff.'

Joe makes me feel like a force-fed *foie gras* goose.

'Actually, I've been wanting to talk to you,' I say. Deep

35

breath. 'I think . . . the time has come for me to stop breast-feeding.' I stroke Evie's head, pilled with soft down like well-loved cashmere.

Joe's face slams shut. 'You're not serious? She's only five-and-a-half months! I was really hoping you would do it until she was at least one. The baby book says . . .'

'Fuck the baby book! I want my boobs back.' Joe rakes his hair with his hands, brows knitting. 'Alice is very funny,' I add more jovially, realising this needs defter delivery. 'She says breastfeeding is like liposuction. Fantastic in the right amounts, but you've got to know when to stop.'

'Alice says what?'

'Brilliant for losing weight, although I'm not sure it worked like that for me. Point is, if you carry on doing it . . .' I push my boobs flat. 'Hello walnuts in socks!'

Joe clears his throat. 'Some Things Are More Important,' he says, enunciating each syllable for polemical import. 'Besides, you've got great boobs.'

'Boosted to a C cup by a pint of full-cream milk,' I hiss so as not to wake Evie, who has slumbered off to the reassuringly familiar sound of her parents rowing.

'Don't be silly. You look great.' He looks at me disapprovingly. 'Although not today, but that's your own fault.' A particularly low shot.

'Not today? Not fucking ever!' Suddenly I'm angry, boiling angry. This happens sometimes. Everything's bumbling along fine and then feelings spurt out sideways. 'I'm falling apart, Joe. I'm the kind of woman that people with clipboards stop in the street and say "Can I ask you about your hair?" or hand out "Lose 10 pounds in 10 days" leaflets to. I'm fat, Joe! I'm the same weight I was when I was five months pregnant, except that I'm not pregnant any more.'

'You're not fat. You're curvy.'

'Oh please.' He strokes my hair. I flick him off. 'Careful! My hair is falling out! Have you not seen it in the plughole? The tufts that are left have gone curly. Straight, shiny hair for thirty years then, baby! Bingo! Frizz! I look like a lost member of Hawkwind. And . . . and . . . my right arm is more developed than my left on account of picking up Evie all the time. My bum has dropped five inches since I stopped going to my classes. I've got a fold of flab that won't shift on my belly. I've aged about five years in as many months. My breasts are way beyond the help of a push-up bra . . . not that I would ever have cause to wear one now anyhow.' I refuel with a gulp of air. 'My feet have spread like a barefoot African runner's because I've worn nothing more constricting that flip-flops or trainers for a year. I'm still wearing my Hennes maternity T-shirts because they only get covered in sick so what's the point of not. I'm wearing big pants because they're comfortable. I dance like my *mother* . . .'

'Whoa! Amy, calm down.' His hands brake my shoulders. 'What do you mean you dance like your mother? You don't go dancing.'

'Funnily enough I rarely rumba around the nappy mat.'

'You can if you like. I'd still fancy you.'

Fancy me? Sure. 'Then . . . then . . . why — ?' The words catch. I can't actually say it, too humiliating.

Joe sits next to me. The bed dips. He traces a big finger across the uncertainty of my jaw line. '*Listen.*' His hand, large as a dinner plate, is on the small of my back, warm where it aches. 'We need to inject a bit of romance back into our relationship. Part of the problem is sleep. We're both so tired. I know I am, and it becomes harder to find time or the . . .' He stops short.

'Inclination?'

'That's not what I was going to say. I was going to say

energy. It's hard to find the energy. And it's hard to feel romantic when surrounded by nappy bags.'

'But even when I was pregnant, it . . .' I search his face for a flicker of something, like the eye-fall or nose stroke of guilt. Nothing.

'OK, I found it a bit weird.' He raises his hand in glib resignation. 'Like my dick was tapping the baby's cranium.' Well I have breasts! I have lips! 'I did buy you that underwear,' he says, as if that should keep me going for months. 'And it's not an uncommon situation, you know. I was talking to Kate and she said that—'

'It's none of her business.' Mention of Kate at this juncture grates disproportionately, like a strand of hair trapped in a toothbrush. What the hell would Kate know about post-partum passion?

'Come on, it's Kate I was talking to and *not* about all the intimate details, don't worry. She's on your side anyway . . .' he trails off, on slightly shaky ground.

'I wasn't aware that we needed Kofi Annan to negotiate this one.'

'Amy, don't go into one, please.'

Kate is an old friend, partly responsible for this mess because she introduced me and Joe years ago, my final week at Bristol University. Joe was her ex-fling actually, which wasn't much of a recommendation. I don't rate her taste in men. When we first met, Joe was a graphics student wearing complicated glasses and an exhilarated caught-out look, like you'd walked in on him masturbating. He asked me out but I declined, being totally stuck on a handsome drama post-grad with commitment issues and an obsession with Diane Keaton. Nothing happened until years later (by which time he'd lost the glasses and that look) at one of Kate's soirees held at the Notting Hill mews house she shared with Pete, an overbearing merchant banker who she eventually marched down the aisle.

We all had a good time together, in what seemed like an endless youth. Many weekends, after a big night out, Joe and I would stay in Kate and Pete's spare room with the white waffle linen making love, giggling, trying to stifle our rude orgasmic grunts, slightly smug that we were obviously having the best sex in the house. Kate and I would swap bags and heels and gossip. We'd abuse our livers in the local bars, playing at being Notting Hill hipsters. But in truth we were outsiders who didn't quite have the style – I couldn't understand why the locals with so much money wanted to look so scruffy – or the connections. Kate was a suburban girl at heart who'd lucked out with a rich husband, while Pete had seen the film *Notting Hill*, found the property prices reassuringly expensive and got a little rush from saying where he lived when someone asked at work. Sadly, after the Berkshire wedding – held at Pete's parents' vast damask pelmet of a house – Kate and Pete moved to the country. Kate wasn't keen, but Pete decided that he wanted his children to grow up somewhere 'real', away from the fashionable urbanity that had attracted him to Notting Hill in the first place. Two years later the children still haven't arrived. The nurseries have been redecorated twice.

Joe leans back on to the bed, arms crossed beneath his head, staring at the ceiling. 'Shall we take Evie round to your mum's and spend the afternoon in bed scoffing crumpets?'

I can't help but smile. This is the kind of thing we used to do. Crumbs stuck to sweaty flesh. Fingers slick with butter. 'Mum's not there. She's visiting Aunt Lou.'

'Oh well.' Is that relief in his voice? He doesn't come up with an alternative, leaves the bedroom. 'I'm off to the gym then.'

I'm about to ask why it never occurs to him that I can't just drop everything and go to the gym when I hear the front door bang. The afternoon begins to yawn ahead. There is a limit to the number of times I can trot around a park on my own, pointing out Mr Pigeon to a sleeping baby. Sometimes my days are just about the journeys, the getting from A to B, the rhythmical roll of the pram. That kills time nicely, breaks up the formlessness of my day. Take more than two journeys and then, oddly, despite how little I seem to achieve, I'm busy.

OK, Primark. Being a fifteen-minute weave through the back streets of Kilburn, past the tightly packed Victorian houses filled with families who can't afford adjacent Queen's Park, it's a journey. Evie sleeps. I people-watch pedestrian traffic as the white wannabe Queen's Park thirtysomethings give way to the multicultural crush of the Kilburn High Road and its endless belch of pound shops and traffic. I used to prefer Bond Street or Brompton Cross, with their posh intimate boutiques and attentive shop assistants, but I now find them a bit intimidating, too intense. I never know when Evie is going to go into atomic meltdown mode. And I'm not really dressed for it these days, I get followed by security guards.

No, oddly, the brutal neon cut-price bustle of Primark appeals. Evie likes the lights. And everything is astonishingly cheap. I can buy new tracksuit bottoms – my need for anything more formal these days is limited – for under a fiver. Hard to believe I am the same woman who once spent £367 on a pair of Jimmy Choos for the wedding of a friend I was once in love with.

It's mostly women in here. Many are Muslim, moving slowly in their great black tents, flashing trainer-clad feet, eyes averted. Then there are the council mothers; pale, trailing children in gold jewellery. And, increasingly, there are the fashion-savvy twentysomethings, foraging for a must-have at a boastfully low price because they once read 'Primark is the new Prada' in a newspaper and don't know any better. And then, of course, there are those like me, stripped of signatures of class by the raw shock of motherhood. We look similar: hair with three-inch roots rubbered back into scruffy ponytails, no make-up, not slim, with badly mismatched clothes because the baby was crying when we were getting ready and we're only going to Primark after all.

Fifty per cent off. Buy two get one free. G-strings. Beach towels. Vest tops. Flip-flops. High summer gear in the fresh slap of spring. I fish arbitrary things I don't need out of bargain bins: a new pair of slippers, a cheap canvas bag that I persuade myself resembles a Chloé one (from three seasons ago of course, last reference point) and a new wash bag.

The checkout queue snakes towards a line of tills like an airport check-in. An operation Desert Storm of prams, poised to battle their way to the first available till. By this stage, the thrill of the cheapness has palled and everyone wants to get the hell out. The queue takes forever (you pay with your time at these places). My turn. The shop assistant, an overweight lady in her forties with a tidal mark of orange foundation around her jaw, is brisk, surly. Well, I suppose you would be. She studies my signature scrawl, unsure if it matches up with my card. My signature varies according to my sleep quota and last night I got five hours, interrupted twice. It's dodgy, orange jaw is thinking. But she can't be bothered with the hassle of querying it. She passes me the bag.

'Next!'

Something sparkles at the corner of my vision. Glinting buckles, a creamy tan leather handbag saddled to the shoulder of a woman so out of place I can't believe I didn't notice her before. Blonde spaghetti-straight hair. A caramel trench coat, tied around a neat waist. She looks to the side. Little upturned nose. Tanned. Even in this cadaver lighting her skin glows. I pan down from highlights to . . . heels. She is wearing heels!

The woman puts an armful of white T-shirts down by the till. Her hand stretches back and clasps her pram. French manicured fingernails on the handle. I can't see inside. The surly shopkeeper shoves the T-shirts into a plastic bag. Her eyes warily flick from the bag to the lady, lady to bag. The battalions in the queue study her too, suspicion and disapproval twitching at the corners of their lips. Who is this glossy interloper making them feel worse about themselves?

'Thank you,' she says.

Irish? The lady taps a number into the credit-card machine, takes her bag, bends down and slides it into the basket of her shiny pram. No roots. Click click click, go the heels. Whisper of perfume, and she is gone.

Something niggles, a constricting and irritating niggle, like a too-tight waistband. *She* is the mother I thought I would be but am not. If things had been different I'd be coping better, more like her. Or would Joe rather I was invisible, grateful? Because that's what I've become. When I saw him in the park with that woman, self-esteem rushed out of me like air from an untied balloon at a toddler's party. I've been circling to the ground ever since.

Four

Reality check: reasons I am not woman in Primark. Or Alice.

1. Comedy moustache eyebrows.
2. Skin of forty-year-old. Dehydrated. Sucked dry by Evie.
3. Whites of eyes, pink. No make-up, no point.
4. Head, multi-split-ends like forks of lightning. 'Honey blonde' now green. Roots.
5. On legs, new wiry pube-like things growing on back of thighs. Measured: 1.7 cm.
6. Bingo wings. Need to wave goodbye to.
7. Belly. Stretch marks. Curdled custard texture. Crooked smile scar. Etc., etc.
8. Clothes. Maternity. Last fashionable thing bought one-and-a-half years ago and now too small.
9. Pubic hair. Still not recovered from nail-scissor attack two weeks ago.
10. Breasts. Pencil test: failed.

Five

'Mum? What are you doing here?'

'That's not a very nice welcome.'

Mum sits proprietorially on my sofa. She's rearranged the cushions to suit today's ailments, 'a twinge in the lower vertebrae', and rests her rubber-soled 'casual' shoes on my coffee table. She buys these neat, elasticised shoes in bulk from the back page of newspaper magazines, the ones advertised by a woman of a certain age, golfing.

'Sorry, I didn't mean that, just wasn't expecting you. I thought you were at Lou's today.'

'No. She got an emergency appointment at the chiropractor. Bunions playing up again. Anyway, do I need to book an appointment to see my daughter?'

Hardly. Since Evie was born Mum has forsaken knocking. Why bother when she has a spare key and a sweet little granddaughter waiting inside? Any notion of privacy has become redundant. There's nothing Mum hasn't seen. She had a good look at my cervical dilation and shoved my bruised nipple indignantly into Evie's newborn mouth for the first suck. Life has come full circle. After years of me going out and not phoning enough and missing family get-togethers in favour of trysts with unsuitable young men, she is now back on firm ground. She's needed.

'What's that in your hand?' Mum asks, an octave above casual enquiry. 'Writing shopping lists now? There I was thinking you were a lost cause.'

'Very funny.' I quickly shove the list into my jeans pocket.

'Where have you been?'

'Oh, a bit of shopping, a walk.'

Mum sweeps me up and down, eyes like dusters. 'Well that can only be a good thing.' She peers into the pram and tickles Evie under the chin. Evie looks up adoringly, blue eyes unblinking.

Thud, thud. Joe, looking harassed. 'Did you meet the girls? Too early for Alice to get you drunk I suppose?'

'Hilarious,' I say.

Mum scans our conversation for a window. Finding none she dissolves over Evie. 'Can I?'

'Of course.' It's only because Joe is in the room that she asks for permission to pick Evie up. Mum hugs her granddaughter over her shoulder, sinks her nose into the folds of her fat damp neck and inhales deeply. Evie's womb-fresh skin makes my mother look ancient, the tendons in her neck like cello strings, hands meat-red and rough. Old person's hands. They remind me of the unimaginable, Mum dying, lying totally still. I try and shake the image from my mind. But it sticks.

'You all right love?'

'A bit tired.'

'And what about Evie? *Coocchi!*' She tickles Evie under her chin. 'My little sugarplum, are you tired yet? Being so little in this big, wide world?'

I roll my eyes at Joe, who daren't roll them back in case Mum catches him. He still has that polite new boyfriend

45

thing going on even though we've been together almost two years. He makes Mum tea. He drives her home. He listens to her talk about garden centres and the problems of growing foxgloves in clay soil. He commiserates with her that her two sons hardly ever phone and they live in Australia and it's very difficult to get the timing right on the phone calls because they surf such a lot and that the weather is better and the flights are expensive but she still wishes they'd make more journeys over and what a shame it is that flying doesn't agree with her. Or surfing. She tried it once but found it terrifying, convinced she'd end up in the jaws of a great white and doesn't understand the hold it has over her baby boys. She suspects marijuana might have something to do with it.

Joe goes into the kitchen to make tea. Reassuring domestic clatter: taps running, the click of a kettle lid, the thud of Joe's feet. I check the answerphone – any contact from the parallel universe? – when Mum's distinctive odour (Estée Lauder's Pleasures, Persil) announces her presence behind me.

'Amy,' she whispers sharply. 'Your hair.'

'What about my hair?'

'It looks like it hasn't encountered a hairbrush for five years.'

Five days actually. 'Rushed off my feet.'

'That's what it's like with a baby,' she sermonises slowly. 'That's what it's going to be like for the rest of your *life*.' Christ. 'I know you found her birth hard, love.' Thanks for that gentle reminder. 'Admittedly, all the hormones can make a woman a bit loopy for a while, nothing to be ashamed of. But Evie is . . . how old is she? Yes, six months now. So it's time for you to start pulling yourself together.' She pats me on the hand and delivers me a solemn look. 'Think about Joe.'

'Joe? Mum, what *are* you talking about?'

'Men expect certain . . . standards.' She looks at Evie – ally in waiting – for approval. 'They need reassurance.'

'Reassurance? What has this got to do with my hair?'

'They need to know that the mother of their child isn't turning into a . . .' here it comes, '. . . what's the word?' I steel myself. 'A frump.'

A frump!

'We don't live in Greece where it's acceptable for girls to start out so pretty and then get married and eat all that feta and before you know it they're walking around in all that black, size eighteens.'

'The women in black are widows, Mum.'

'Comfort eating, obviously.'

'Oh Mum . . .' Sometimes I find it astonishing that we share genetic material.

'Just make yourself a bit more presentable, that's all I'm saying. A bit of red lipstick, a good dab of blusher . . .'

'So unless I make up like Zsa Zsa Gabor he's off is he?'

'Don't be smart. And don't take Joe for granted, because even the good ones go off the boil a bit if they're not looked after.'

He's already boiled over, I want to scream! It's happened, the worst has already happened! So there is no point in trying. Not for him anyway. I compose myself and play the well-rehearsed bickering daughter role. 'This is like some awful Victorian good wives handbook, will you please get off my case?'

'Case? What case? That's such a silly expression.'

'*Mum!*' I shout, exasperated.

Silenced, wondering whether she's gone too far, Mum plumps heavily down on the sofa, releasing a puff of cushion-trapped air. She dangles Evie on her knee for solace. For the first time this year she's not wearing stockings. Varicose veins

47

root up her legs into the two dark tunnels of her wide-legged, neat, pressed beige slacks, the kind that sit too high on the waist. It's a shame. She always had such fabulous legs.

One of my favourite things is a black-and-white photograph of Mum taken in 1962, Ilfracombe, Devon. Her normally neat brown waves are being blown all round her face by the wind. She's trying to smooth them with her hands and is laughing at my dad, who is behind the camera, because she's losing the battle. Her floral dress is pressed against her body by the wind so that you can see her pointy bra, her tummy, her pubis bone, the gap between her thighs. She's never liked the picture, thinks she looks too messy. But Dad always loved it. He once told me, when I was about eight, that 'This is the Jean that I love the most.' Hearing him call her Jean, not 'your mother', felt almost rudely intimate and rather puzzling. Were there many Jeans hidden inside Mummy like Russian dolls? For me there was always just one Mummy, sometimes short-tempered, often too intense, but always loving and who, when I hid under her skirt and grabbed her legs or curled into her lap, smelt unlike anyone else, yeasty and salty, like Marmite.

'Euch!' Evie's body ricochets with the force of her burp.

Mum looks at her in rapture and strokes the curve of her cheek. Is that how she stroked me? Hard to imagine now. It seems we love our children with the most ferocity when they are most vulnerable. Over the years that intense love must dilute like an over-dunked teabag.

'Wheee!' She bounces Evie up and down on her knee, freezing me out now.

I am about to say something conciliatory when whooom! I get one of those disturbing thoughts that flap into my head like dirty low-flying pigeons. Me, travelling down the red tunnel of Mum's vagina, my head crowning, my nose, ears,

48

screwed-up eyes, sliding into the forty-watt light of my parent's bedroom. Ugh. Hard to believe in the stork now.

Mum looks up and stares at me, eyes pinkish and watery. She looks like she might be about to cry. 'I don't mean to make you angry.'

It's worse when she apologises. I am crucified with guilt. 'It's fine.'

'I worry. You know why, don't you?'

'That was different.'

'Perhaps. But he did leave.'

Silently. I saw him before I went to bed. 'Goodnight, doll,' Dad said and kissed me on my forehead, between the eyes. I imagined there would be a kiss imprint there for ever afterwards, like one of those spots the Indian lady who ran the corner shop had. The next morning he was gone. Not just gone to work, but gone, gone. The hardware of Daddy's existence – his four good suits, cracked brown brogues and drill kit – went too. I was nine. Mum served up our breakfast the next morning without saying much. It looked like she'd lined her eyes with red crayon. Later, while I was at school, she had all her long brown hair butchered off by Julie at A Cut Above. I'd never seen her with short hair before. Soon, the weight began to drop off too. She started wearing red rose lipstick. She looked like someone else, thinner, smarter, not my mummy. And for some time she acted like someone else, quieter and more distant. Another Jean.

We didn't see Dad again for three months. A wet Tuesday in March. Mum took us to the swings, unable to take her eyes away from the familiar figure in the long grey coat who strode towards us, always so sure of himself. He hugged me into the damp scratchiness of the coat's flannel. Then he looked at Mum and said, 'Jean?' Like he was asking a secret question only adults could understand. Mum shook her head and walked quickly away, leaving us careering giddily round and round the perilous seventies playground. We didn't know then, but that 'Dad time' had to keep us going for a while.

'He did leave. But you cannot blame yourself, Mum. He was sleeping with that woman in the ukulele group . . .'

'She couldn't even play properly.' This still gives her a sly kick of triumph.

'And she had terrible hair. Like a Brillo pad.'

Mum laughs, crow's feet folding like a fan. 'One thing I never slacked on. My mother, bless her, taught me to brush it a hundred strokes before bed. It's a miracle I didn't brush it all out, looking back. But still . . .' Long pause. 'It's easy to get complacent.'

'Yes, let's not forget those nighties.' Huge voluminous floral winceyette marquees with lacy Jane Austen necklines. She wears washable 'satin' now.

'Ooo Amy! My nighties were lovely!' She laughs, slaps me playfully on the knee. 'One day *you* will discover the joys of wearing a nice loose nightie.'

'Then Joe really will have good reason to leave.'

Joe appears with tea and chocolate biscuits. 'And what will be good reason to leave?' he asks, smiling.

Six

I like telephones because the person on the other end can't see what you look like. 'Alice, it's me.'

'Who's me?'

'Sorry, Amy.'

'Amy! Hi! How's it going?' Alice sounds a bit distracted, like she might be watching telly or painting her nails.

'Not that great actually. Alice,' I take a deep breath and unintentionally blow it out loudly into the telephone receiver. 'Alice, I was wondering. Do you remember what you said about um . . . you called it Project Amy or something?' This is embarrassing.

'Project what?'

'Er, Amy. We chatted about it after the night-of-the-breast-pad.'

Silence for a few painful moments. Then rustling. It sounds like she's shooing someone away. 'Ah! Project Amy! Of course. I knew you'd come round.'

'My mother's just accused me of being a frump.' There is a shocked silence. Perhaps not everyone has dysfunctional relationships with their mothers.

Alice, rather more hesitant than I'd hoped, says, 'Er, you're not a frump.' I breathe a sigh of relief and feel myself sinking back into the comfort zone of drawstring waists. 'But, well, put it like this.' Alice pauses, choosing her words carefully. 'You don't exactly make the best of yourself.'

'No?'

'No,' she says firmly. 'You really don't, Amy.'

'But I have no time, Alice. When am I meant to beautify myself? Between feeds? At four a.m. when she's roaring in the dawn chorus? It's hard enough to take a shower, for God's sake.'

'It's a question of priorities.'

'Exactly. Which is why, well, I've let things slide. I always imagined feeding Evie took priority.'

'Oh rubbish!' laughs Alice. 'What could be more important than liking what you see in the mirror?'

I laugh nervously and hope she's joking. 'Er, Alice, at the risk of appearing like a complete twit, I've written a list.'

'A list? What sort of list?'

'A list of everything that's wrong with me. Well, not everything. The main bits – hair, belly . . . God, I sound like a neurotic freak.'

Alice snorts with laughter. 'Only you would write a list!'

'Unfortunately, it's not a short list.'

'No?'

I can hear her voice shaking with suppressed laughter. I'm sure there's someone else there. 'No, Alice, I suspect I need a whole body transplant but I'm unsure where to start.'

'This phone call is a good place.'

'Because you know what? I've had enough of being invisible.'

'Invisible? Silly. Of course I'll help. I'd love to. Project Amy! We'll turn you from downtrodden mother into a glamazon. Promise!' She bites into something loud and crunchy. It sounds like a locust eating crops on a wildlife documentary.

'I don't care about being a glamazon, I just want to look a bit less crap, a little more like how I used to, a bit less budget-retailer-discount-bin, if you know what I mean.'

A pause. More distracted crunching. 'Hey, you know what? There's no point doing this half-heartedly. We're going to turn you into a sexpot! We'll need some money though.'

'We haven't got much spare cash at the moment,' I say. Alice sighs, disappointed. I want to appease her. And after all, my thigh is stretching the orange stitching on my jeans. 'But I'm sure I can dig into a few savings.'

'New jeans, new hair,' chirps Alice. 'Oh, we're going to have such fun.'

'It's more than that.'

'Gosh, you do sound serious.'

'I need to sort myself out.'

'O-K.' Alice knows I mean much more than a haircut. She's already guessed I'm unhappy.

'I need a plan, to get my confidence back.' No, I won't let the past crush me down into frumpdom. If Joe wants a safe dowdy *hausfrau* he's not going to get it. And if he did ever leave, which he probably will, like Dad, like most men, then at least if I'm a bit less of a fright I'd have a minute chance of finding someone else, one day, perhaps.

'Great, Amy. We're moving forward. You around next week?' she asks slightly impatiently, like she needs to clear the phone.

'I think so.' I'm always around. Alice dictates where and when our meetings take place. They invariably mean me coming to her. This would irritate me more if she weren't quite so beautiful. She's somehow exempt from normal social rules.

'We'll draw up an action plan!' She munches again. 'Bye, honey.'

I put down the phone and skim through the Bs – banks, builders, breastfeeding helplines – in my ancient Filofax for a beauty salon number. The future starts here! Time to harvest the legs. Ah, Klass Beauty. I dial but just as I'm about to book, Evie explodes, the scream tunnelling into my ears, then screeching through my entire body like a braking train on a track. I tell the receptionist I'll phone back. Evie has needs that must be met. Like right now. Legs, life must wait. My life is ruled by someone weighing twenty pounds with no teeth.

Seven

Eleven a.m. Teaz Time. West Hampstead. Five mother-and-baby units. Two bald babies. One ginger. One brown. One blonde and beautiful (my Evie). Farmyard stink of baby poo. Four breasts on show, nipples dark as tea cakes. One embarrassed waiter.

'My mother was a ten-pound, eight-week-early premature baby apparently!' Sue's double chin trembles when she laughs. I am turning into the kind of person who notices these things. Do I seek reassurance in the failings of others? 'And of course she had a *very* voluminous wedding dress, fitted the week before the wedding, empire line,' she continues.

'Ahhhh, how things have changed,' is muttered under collective breaths.

I hate that cringy collective ahhh. Conversational mayonnaise. You don't hear it in groups of dynamic interesting people with dynamic interesting lives. There is a reflective pause, tea cups are stirred, fingers stab at cake crumbs. A baby grunts into a nipple. The pause goes on a little too long, straddling awkwardness.

'I've been so lucky with Alan.' Sue swallows hard and

waits for a bubble of gas to subside. 'Must be awful not to be married to the father of your child. They never stick around. Statistics bear it out.' Sue quickly puts her hand to her mouth, tries to shove the words back. 'Oh gosh. I am *so* sorry, Amy! Nicola! I just wasn't thinking. How completely insensitive of me.' Everyone registers something that would have slipped by in the conversation had Sue not drawn attention to it.

'Aha, but, unlike you lot, we're almost fancy-free!' I joke.

There is a murmur of 'Good for you' and 'Absolutely', but their sighs of married relief almost mist up the windows. We all know that the halcyon days of being fancy-free are over.

'A ring on the finger would not make a jot of difference. The nappies smell the same.' Nicola flashes fiercely blue eyes – a gift from her Irish-Portuguese heritage – set off by the palest skin, freckled like an egg. She's the reason I come to these meetings. 'And the baby would still use Guantanamo Bay sleep deprivation techniques.'

Sue drums sausage fingers on her cup. 'I'm sure they'll make honest women of you yet. Hang in there. '

There are more murmurs of agreement, a flurry of un-necessary activity with muslin cloths.

'We won't lose sleep over it,' says Nicola.

'Waaaaaaaaaaahhhh.' Beatrice is off again. She's a particu-larly piercing baby, with a round red face like a whoopee cushion. Her mother, Michelle, who is in her early forties and still looks nine months pregnant, scoops what can only be described as an udder out of the *neckline* of her burgundy ethnic blouse and starts feeding, looking around proudly, daring you, the repressed, to look away. Michelle wants to breastfeed until Beatrice can *say* 'Enough milk, Mummy'. Michelle wants to be an extreme lactivist. She read about them in the *Guardian*. (Not necessarily connected, but I should point out – Michelle would want me to – that she uses reusable terry nappies and only buys Fair Trade toys from sustainable sources. This makes her a Good Parent, unlike me with all my planet-gobbling plasticky dummies and landfill Wet Wipes that won't have decomposed in ten generations' time.)

'So you've stopped breastfeeding, we hear,' Sue says tightly, her fine nose for petty conflict twitching.

'Yeah, this week.' My breasts have been throbbing for days. I fantasise about being screwed into a farmhouse milking machine.

'Oh Amy,' Sue exhales, as if I've just announced Evie has a congenital disease.

'What?'

'Such a shame. Evie was doing so well.'

'Still is,' interrupts Nicola, stroking Evie's cheek, tacky with milk. 'Does it hurt?' Nicola is deadpan as always. Smiles twitch at the corners of her mouth. But she's restrained, Nicola. I like her a lot.

'The closest a woman can get to being kicked in the balls.'

'Of course,' Sue says, assuming her Reassuring Bedside Manner voice (other voices in the repertoire range from Officious Secretary – 'So I'll see you at five p.m. at the sand pit then' – to Needling Lawyer – 'Can you describe exactly the colour and shape of Evie's poo?'). 'This is the price we pay if we stop suddenly.'

'Come on, Amy, you can't deny Evie. It's delicious stuff,' says Michelle. 'Have you not tasted it?'

'I prefer cow's milk on my cereal, thanks.'

'You're missing out.'

Nicola and I exchange alarmed glances. Is Michelle serious? God, she probably is. Michelle fried up her placenta with basil and Maldon sea salt and served it up for supper the day after her home delivery.

57

'I'm going to do it until Amelia's two, if I can,' pipes up Hermione, sitting to my left. Pale and tiny, she doesn't look like she could suckle a guinea pig. 'Build up those antioxidants.'

'Anti*bodies*,' corrects Sue loudly.

Sweet, unchallenging and pretty, Hermione is reluctantly admired in the group. Hermione did two hundred pelvic floor exercises every day before the birth which was, of course, a drug-free water birth at Queen Charlotte's. The baby slipped out like a fish. 'All about the breath,' she informed us helpfully. The resulting baby, Amelia, is a delicate, organically reared pedigree, pretty, with eyes shaped like leaves. And, as Hermione regularly drops into the conversation with the accuracy of a smart bomb, Amelia slept through the night at four weeks.

'Waaaaah!' Evie's whimpering is beginning to crescendo. Then she starts to cough. All the other mothers, bar Nicola, pull back, manoeuvring their babies out of Evie's bubonic sneeze line, pretending to smell their nappies, or adjust their clothes. It is a great faux pas to participate in socials with an under-par baby, endangering others.

'Oh, is Evie *ill*?' Sue asks warily.

Just a little cough, I explain. Then Evie coughs again, this time with the ferocity of a forty-a-day Rothmans smoker.

Amelia is quickly strapped back into her pram. 'We've got to go, running late for The Routine,' Hermione says.

Not wanting to destroy the entire social, I give Evie my mobile phone, the only thing that ever truly distracts her. Sue slits her eyes and glares at the phone as if it were a lump of plutonium. But it works: Evie forgets she should be coughing.

'Can I get you anything else, ladies?' The waiter, early twenties, spotty, has been wiping down clean surfaces for the last ten minutes, waiting for Michelle's boob to retreat back to its lair of burgundy linen.

'Another scone, please,' Nicola says. 'Starving.' Nicola reckons, if she could be bothered – which she can't – she would have about a stone to lose. Nicola is tall and rangy but with a tummy that she tucks into her jeans. 'I'm back on the pill. That increases your appetite apparently. Well, that's all the excuse I need.'

'I wouldn't worry. Breast feeding uses up five hundred calories a day. That's a Mars bar, or, perhaps, a large scone,' cuts in Michelle authoritatively. On account of her age (it took her ten years and two changes of husband to conceive) and the number of birth manuals she's devoured, Michelle has appointed herself pregnancy guru, a role contested by Sue.

My phone vibrates in Evie's hands, shocking her silent. A text from Alice.

Mting grls for lunch and film. 12 at Electrc, Prtobello. Do cme.

Oh, it's rather sophisticated being invited to something the day it is happening, the assumption that I am free and mobile and follow my social whims. Such a contrast to these meetings that are organised with military precision, usually days in advance as if we had the diaries of busy diplomats.

'Beckham is it?' Sue says. My eyes must have lit up.

'No, no, just a friend.'

'You're blushing!'

Now all the mothers are staring. Weirdly, I do feel caught out. 'It's Alice, remember I told you about her. Really nice, we went swimming . . .'

'Oh, yes, the glamorous one. The one who puts us to shame,' laughs Nicola. 'The . . . what do you call them? The yummy mummy.'

'Euh! What an awful expression, cooked up by some bored magazine editor I should imagine.' Sue sniffs. 'I don't think

59

such a woman exists.' As if to prove the point, she walks off to the loo, square bovine bottom shuddering with every step, too-tight knickers cheese-wiring her cheeks.

A style faux pas perhaps, but not considered one in the milk and tummy land of new-mummy. In fact it's a badge of camaraderie, a symbol of changed priorities. Michelle's ugly burgundy blouse, Sue's baggy-arsed tracksuit, Hermione's obviously big, obviously once-white knickers grinning from the top of her jeans . . . it all says we now put someone else's needs before our vanity. The scary thing is how quickly these sartorial standards become the norm. When I first ventured out of the house with sick-stained trousers and no make-up and suitcases under my eyes I worried about bumping into someone I knew. I scampered to the newsagent like a worker doing a sickie. Second time I thought, Oh hell, it's only the newsagent. Now it feels weird, almost inappropriate to make an effort. I wear make-up and feel like I should be squealing *I'm a laydee*!

'What does she want?' Nicola is intrigued by Alice. The rest of the group have safely journeyed into a far more interesting conversation about ginger baby's hernia.

'Wants to meet in Portobello, the Electric.'

'How thrilling,' says Nicola, arching a briar of an eyebrow. She doesn't do the maintenance thing any more either: hair in a straight, mousy bob, unmade-up face, a penchant for men's roomy trousers and her partner Sam's shirts. Nicola once adopted a sweater she found in a Queen's Park hedge. But her artless dishevelment still looks vaguely cool in an androgynous arty kind of a way. She's just one of those people.

'Not sure I'm up to it. She's with her mates, and the thought of meeting loads of new people . . .' More to the point, my hair is greasy and I'm wearing old comfy trainers,

60

pink and white, those really naff 'ladies" ones. I can't even do the baby-as-accessory thing due to an acne-like rash under Evie's chin.

'Go.' Nicola curls forward and, using Thomas as a shield, whispers, 'Seriously, that sounds so much more fun. Go, go.'

'Nah.'

'Sue's about to discuss her birth again . . .'

I laugh into the fuzz of Evie's head. It smells of rice pudding and fragranced nappy bags.

'Should she go back to work at ten months or ten-and-a-half months? Let's mull over the latest report regarding the impact of separation from mother on child's development . . .'

'Don't.' I'm getting the giggles. 'They'll hear you. Seriously, I'm knackered.'

'. . . not forgetting the joys of breastfeeding until the child is thirteen. Now, another cup of nettle tea?'

Sue swivels around. Is she missing anything? She needs to regain control of this rebellious conversational tributary. 'Where will Evie go to primary, Amy?'

'Oh, I'm not sure.' Haven't the faintest. Last time I passed the local state primary a boy no older than ten pinched my bum and called me a fat bitch. Besides, the thought of standing at the school gates makes me feel horribly middle-aged and mumsy.

'Hermione has put Amelia down for five schools already!' Sue exclaims. 'Five! It's a world gone mad. The problem with the private . . .'

Nicola studies her tea cup, taking noisy deep breaths, trying not to laugh.

'Sorry, but I've got to go.' I stand up.

'Oh. What's the more exciting prospect?' Sue pretends she's joking.

I shrug my shoulders and smile. Nicola helps me pack up.

61

No small task. Evie travels with an entourage of luggage like a rap star.

'I was going to say earlier,' Sue says cheerily, offering a teaser of gossip in a last-ditch attempt to keep me at the table. 'I saw your Joe at lunch yesterday. Gosh, hasn't he changed? He looks so different from last time I saw him, yonks ago at the antenatal classes. Has he grown a beard?'

'Sort of.' It's called stubble. 'So where were you?'

'Livecatch? Livewait? You know, that fish restaurant in Covent Garden. Alan took me for a special treat. We had grilled trout drizzled with—'

'Who was he with?' I interrupt.

'Sister or someone, I guess.'

'He hasn't got a sister.'

'*Really?*'

I aggressively shove Evie's bottle into my ratty old nappy bag. Nicola taps me on the shoulder.

'Smile, Amy.'

'What?'

'A bit of scone, front tooth. On the left. Yup, gone. Off you go, report back.'

Eight

Antique shops. Picture framer. Tattooist. The Portobello Road is longer than I remember. Joe's 'sister'? Is this worthy of worry? I've so many anxieties it's hard to discriminate. Instead I concentrate on looking for the neon 'Electric' cinema sign. I haven't been to the Electric since it was given a make-over and turned into a private members' club by Soho House. (I read about such things in the *Evening Standard*, yet to regain the attention span for the *Guardian*.) As I walk I pull my tummy in so that the waistline of my jeans sits below my post-natal bulge, thereby lengthening the trousers and reducing the chance of any flash of forest. I never did get my legs waxed.

'Amy! Over here!'

What? I look around.

'No, over here!'

Someone waving a few metres back. A group of four women sat around a Parisian-style table in the mosaic-tiled forecourt, blue neon sign blinking above them. Squinting, I can see they look like any other group of young attractive west Londoners. Only their prams identify them. I walk back slowly. The sun is in my eyes. They are all staring, watching my arrival through the blacked-out limo windows of enormous sunglasses. I feel self-conscious, can't remember how to move elegantly.

'You walked right past us,' says Alice.

'Oh sorry, sorry.'

'No need to apologise. Everyone, this is Amy Crane, mother of the delectable Evie.'

Three heads re-angle themselves. They are all different shades of blonde, like a paint range swatch.

'I'll introduce you, Amy. Jasmine . . .'

Jasmine offers a slim hand, tanned against her day-glo charity wristbands, which I shake too hard, drawing undue attention to the hairy scrunchie around my wrist. Jasmine flicks her hand away as if bitten, embeds it in her thick wavy hair (the least blonde, latte with highlights) and smiles lazily, cheekbones round as plums. 'A new recruit.' She slugs her wine. 'Alice has a habit of finding them in the least likely places.'

'Ignore her,' says Alice. 'Jasmine's had rather too much too drink.'

'*Again*,' slurs Jasmine. She has a huge mouth. Lips like swimming aids. 'Go on, say it.' Alice shakes her head. 'Hair of the dog,' explains Jasmine.

'Cocaine hangover,' whispers Alice. 'She DJ'd last night. Suffering, aren't you darling?'

Jasmine nods slowly, as if nodding hurts her head. Her sunglasses slip down her tiny nose. She thumbs them back up.

'And this is Annabel, with child.'

'You can't really miss it.' Annabel smiles broadly from behind her bump. Her voice is head girl confident. 'You don't mind if I don't get up?' Annabel is wearing a wrap dress covered in black and white geometric patterns. She has long hair worn in a seventies centre parting, like the pages of an open

64

book. Because the rest of her is so slim, so unwaterlogged, her bump looks prosthetic.

'And *this* is the infamous Blythe!'

A crescent of dazzling dentistry. Fake, I'm thinking. Fake teeth. Tan. Corn blonde. Boobs, round as bagels, beneath a tight caramel cashmere V-neck. Fake boobs? Blythe is the only person here without a glass of white wine in her hand. She is drinking something that looks like cranberry juice in a tall glass. 'Hi Amy,' she drawls. Ah, Blythe is American.

'Hullo.' She looks so familiar. 'Er, um, I think we may have met before,' I say apologetically.

'Oh really?' She gives me the once over. 'No, I don't think so.'

'Hmmm . . .' Where the hell would I meet someone like Blythe? Work? Joe's friends? Oh God. Yes! Dare I? 'Primark!'

Everyone starts. Alice's curls vibrate with laughter.

'You must be mistaken,' Jasmine says. 'Of all the people in the northern hemisphere Blythe is the least likely person to be found in Primark.'

'Not her habitat,' confirms Annabel.

The accent. The hair. It's definitely her. 'Last Saturday. You were buying loads of white T-shirts.'

A thought troubles her smooth complexion. Alice looks at her quizzically. 'OK I confess.' Blythe puts up a twiggy tanned arm. 'My name is Blythe and I am a Primark shopper.'

'What were you doing *there*?' Annabel asks. 'It's so cheap. What on earth is there to buy?'

'Oh, I was driving back from Hampstead from yet *another* school open day. Thought I'd stock up on T-shirts for a certain function coming up in the distant future.' Blythe smiles conspiratorially.

'Aha!' Alice colludes and whispers the words 'Baby shower' to me. 'Terribly organised of you Blythe.'

'You know me, I like to be on schedule. And I wasn't about to go to Calvin Klein for things we'll wear once and throw away.' She sips her drink and the lime wedge nudges against her nose leaving a wet dot on its snub. 'I don't know why you have such a problem with it, Annabel. You're missing out. Pile it high, sell it cheap,' Blythe continues, rather too loudly as if she were speaking into a mobile. 'Free market in action.'

Alice nods. 'Amy's on the money. Primark's so cheap it's cool,' she declares, not wholly convincingly. 'Didn't they do a cute military jacket for a fiver or something?'

'Exactly! Of course, you have to remember to wash your hands after touching the money that's touched the sticky paws of the checkout girl,' adds Blythe. I can't tell if she's joking. 'But hey, no issues.'

Everyone laughs, light confident laughter like you might hear in a movie. Jasmine catches her silver flip-flop on my pram and curses.

'Why don't you shove it in here, Amy?' Alice says quickly. 'Get it out of the way.' She helps me nudge my battered old Britex (second-hand, an annoying unturndownable gift from a cousin) in between the gleaming contraptions of chrome and denim with huge wheels and so many First Class Flyer accessories (drink holders, reclining padded seat, meshed air vents) that a retractable DVD screen wouldn't seem extravagant.

'Careful of the Bugaboo,' Blythe says.

'Sorry, the . . . ?'

'Bugaboo.' Alice winks. 'The Frog. As used by Gwyneth et al. Murder to get into the car boot.'

'Unless it's an SUV,' mutters Blythe.

'Now, meet the little darlings.' Alice points down at four toddlers, Lilliputian in their enormous chariots, asleep or zoned out, fiddling with toys. They are beautifully dressed:

mini Converse trainers, cashmere ponchos, Petit Bateau nautical blue and white stripes. Evie is in a two-for-one, grubby white Poundland Babygro, accessorised by two tusks of snot streaming from her nostrils. A pang for the flabby comfort of the NCT group.

'Right. Alfie, my boy, you've met,' Alice says, pointing to a ringletted blond toddler. He looks twice the size out of his swimming trunks. 'Asleep, just how I like him. And that little princess next to him is Blythe's Allegra. Jasmine's Marlon. That's Annabel's Finn. The youngest of her three.'

'Three?' And she's pregnant with her fourth? Christ. Superwoman.

'Absolutely. Annie's single-handedly raising the birth rate of NW6.' Annabel bats Alice playfully with her elbow. 'We're drinking to her health. Now, another glass . . .'

'I suppose Amy should have mine,' Annabel says reluctantly. 'Ms Marhajessh would kill me if she knew.' She swirls the glass gently, sluicing the sides. 'Still, it is only *one* teeny tiny glass, my first glass of wine all week.'

'It's Monday!' Blythe blows out crossly.

'If you got pregnant for the fourth time you'd need a drink too.' Annabel huffs, filling half of her glass with fizzy mineral water. 'Look, a spritzer! Happy?' Annabel turns to me and grins. 'Blythe thinks we're a nation of alcoholics.'

'Now, where's that waiter?' tuts Alice, waving at a model-type who looks like he resents waiting tables. 'Er, where were we before Amy arrived?'

'*Divorce* Envy,' Blythe says, slamming her hand on the table. She has a diamond the size of one of Evie's pram beads on her engagement finger.

'Come on, you've got lovely, sexy, and rich, very rich husbands. Me and Jasmine struggle away at the single-mum-coal-face act,' Alice says archly.

'Hardly, Miss Footloose,' declares Annabel. 'I would love, LOVE, to hand my kids to their father for the weekend and get them delivered back on Monday morning. Like the Ocado shopping service. Gosh, how fabulous.' Her bump judders beneath her dress. 'Imagine . . . lovers and a permanent babysitter in the form of their father to dispel any abandonment guilt.'

I snigger self-consciously and curl my naff trainered feet around the chair legs in the hope that no one will see them. There is a pause. Blythe nods to me.

'And you?' she asks.

'Er . . .' I'm not entirely sure how to answer this. Is Joe my 'partner'? That sounds so gay. We haven't established our new labels yet. 'On maternity leave. Joe . . . my boyfriend—'

Blythe looks interested for the first time and interrupts. 'Oh, what do you do?'

I try and reclaim a bit of my old identity, a bit of status. 'I work, worked, in PR, Nest PR. Er, homes stuff mainly. I work with companies that make watering cans, linen, scented candles, that sort of thing.' Work seems like another life. Am I the same person? Can I still care about a raffia cushion?

'Really?' Blythe brightens. I'm more interesting company now. 'I worked in PR in New York City a couple of years back, beauty products. Great freebies. Never had to pay for any treatments. I'll be mighty tempted to return when we go home. Will you go back to work?'

'Um, not sure. They keep the job open for a year. I've got a bit of time.'

Blythe's mouth slacks. 'A year! Jesus! If pregnant New York girls knew that you'd have planeloads smuggling themselves across the Atlantic in Louis Vuitton trunks claiming asylum. But, then again . . .' Blythe shudders. 'They wouldn't want to risk your hospitals.'

'You get three years' maternity leave in Estonia,' I add, unnecessarily.

Blythe looks at me as if I've just recited a train timetable backwards.

'Not going back five days a week are you, Amy?' asks Annabel, rubbing her belly in a circular motion like a window-cleaner. The question feels loaded.

'Not sure.'

'Do you want my opinion?'

'She's going to give it anyway,' Alice says, face down, texting a message on her mobile phone. 'Annabel doesn't approve of work.'

'You'll find it bloody hard. No picnic. And it's tough, really tough on little babies. God, Alice, do you remember Tess's Zach? That poor little boy.' She pauses, swirls her spritzer. 'Tess went back to her job as a fashion journalist, Sunday newspaper. Left at eight in the morning, didn't get back until eight at night, on a good day. And that's when she wasn't off comparing front row shoes in Milan or Paris. That poor little boy . . .'

'What happened to him?'

'Got the most terrible separation anxiety. Took far longer to walk than my Finn and Cosmo. Couldn't be potty trained until he was four! Shat under the kitchen table like a scared kitten.' She takes her glass to her lips, weighs her thoughts. 'I don't regret giving up work because, and you can shoot me down for being politically incorrect here, babies and careers do not mix.'

'*Annabel!*' shrieks Alice, giving her a play-whack on the wrist. 'Not fair. Tess had to work.'

'Had to? They could have cut back on a few inessentials.'

'Like you do? Come on.'

'Shush, ladies,' Blythe says with an arch wave of the wrist. 'You're forgetting. The thing is, Tess is a bit old school.'

'What do you mean?' I ask, bewildered.

'Well, we've got wise to it now. That old 'having it all' bollocks. Well you can. But you won't enjoy it all. I've seen too many women feeling guilty and frazzled with miserable kids and a pissed-off husband who knocks off his twenty-three-year-old secretary, the one whose breasts haven't been sucked dry by his little darlings.' Will this be Joe in five years? One year? Now? 'Er . . . sounds brutal.' Oh, for an opinion.

'Absolutely! Besides, by the time you've paid the nanny full time and gone up a tax bracket it's hardly worth working more hours,' Blythe declares.

'Because *you* only employ nannies who have worked with European royals and Elle Macpherson,' says Alice dryly. 'If you'd just make do with a nice Eastern European girl . . .'

'Who can't speak proper English and happens to be illegal?' says Blythe.

'My Hana is probably better qualified than you!' interjects Annabel. 'She's a fully trained doctor but, fortunately for me, can't earn more than a pittance back home. Besides, there are always the Australians. Wholesome, reliable, slightly more expensive of course.'

So there's a caste system for nannies too? I strain my ears and apply what's left of my ability to concentrate. Since having Evie I've stopped skipping over the women-at-work debates in the newspaper to get to the lifestyle pages. Nothing shakes one out of a shoe-centred, singleton, apolitical existence quite like a baby. Although this lot may prove the exception to that rule.

Annabel sighs, leans back, hand on bump. 'But you're right, Blythe. Nannies are bloody expensive, without adding the cost of work clothes and travel.' She thoughtfully smooths her curtains of hair. 'My nanny bills will go through the roof when I take maternity leave.'

'But . . .' Can you take maternity leave from *motherhood*?

Alice nudges me under the table. 'I'm loving your wifestyle Annabel.' She leans back in the sunshine, rearranging her top to avoid tan lines.

'Can you imagine full-time motherhood without any help? Who'd organise the parties? The playdates? I swear my little Cosmo's diary is busier than mine. His playdates are booked three months in advance,' continues Annabel. 'Motherhood with no help would be almost as bad as full-time work, you'd just never have a spare moment.'

Right. Motherhood's no exception: the rich are different.

Blythe raises her glass. 'Yes, my dear, life would be quite impossible if one had to look after one's own children,' she says in a comical Queen's English accent. 'Weird English middle-class ideal anyhow. Whoever's left of your upper classes have it sussed. Big, fat, unattractive nanny in the early years. Then pack them off to boarding school to net-work!'

'Speaking of which . . . where are they?' Jasmine cranes her neck and squints into the restaurant at a quiet table of women in their early twenties drinking coffee. 'Plotting a tabloid exposé or comparing pay cheques.'

'Your nannies?' I ask. Jasmine nods. 'How come they're here?'

'Oh, you know, they'll take the older ones – not allowed in – and collect the babies after the film so we can hit Westbourne Grove unimpeded,' she explains matter-of-factly, glancing at her watch. 'Hey, time's up, the hordes are arriving.'

I stop uncouthly drawing faces in the canvas of condensa-tion on my wine glass and look up. From all directions off

71

Portobello Road women and prams migrate towards the Electric with the collective consciousness of wild salmon. How do they all know to come here at the same time? How do they know that the Electric does mother and baby showings on a Monday? No one told me. I've suspected for some time that I am remarkably unplugged into the cool mothers' network. NCT coffee meetings every couple of weeks does not a social life make.

'Unless you've booked it's really unlikely you'll get in. Let me go and check.' Alice springs up from her chair.

'Ahh.' I am making that embarrassed 'ahh' noise. I try to think of something intelligent to say and can't. Fortunately, Blythe and Annabel are transfixed by the approaching competition: SUV motherships disgorge more alien creatures onto the pavement. And more. All around us now, jabbering and laughing and air kissing, twenty, thirty of them. Sunglasses. And not your two-for-one Spec Savers jobs either. Birkenstocks in bubblegum pink or silver. UGG boots, despite the sunshine. Sequins. Apple green bra straps. Frayed denim minis. Tanned lean legs.

Do these women not work? Evidently not. There is no sign of any tailored office clothes. No, these women are either full-time yummies or, like me, on maternity leave, a sabbatical from normal life. If the latter is the case, why aren't *they* frumpy and disorientated and unable to engage in witty adult repartee? Was there some ante-natal class in post-partum glamour that I skipped? And how come they all look like they know what they're doing? Perhaps I am the only mother who feels like she's pretending.

'No joy, I'm afraid,' says Alice, hovering into view. 'It's my fault, should have thought and booked ahead. But I just texted you on a whim, didn't really think.' I love Alice's bright spontaneity. 'Next week.'

'Thanks, I'd really like that.' No I wouldn't. Not at all. I don't want to be hanging out with women who make me feel defensive and inadequate in equally cruel measures. But I'm like a Tourette's sufferer, the way 'yes' spits out of my mouth. Yes, yes, yes.

'And you'll come to Pilates next week? Check out Jasmine's washboard. Josh got her back in front of the camera within two months.'

'Modelling,' explains Jasmine quickly, shoving a baby bottle and a packet of cigarettes into her pale pink tote.

When we kiss goodbye, something rather embarrassing happens. With my friends it wouldn't matter, you'd make a joke about it. Not Blythe. I go to kiss her but miss the socially acceptable facial orbit for kissing. Hurried out of awkwardness, I land on her mouth like a dribbly old relative.

'God, sorry.'

Blythe wipes her mouth with the back of her hand. 'At least no tongues,' she says tartly and joins the mothers foaming around the Electric cinema doors.

Five minutes later, mothers gone, Portobello Road reverts from crèche back to street, half the tables empty. The nannies order a bottle of wine.

Beep! Nicola texts me.

How ws it?
Been smugged

I reply.

I trot home slightly tipsy, energised by new faces. I open the front door to a ringing phone. Scraping the paintwork with the pram, I run to catch it, miss it and wait for the answerphone message. Mum, I bet. But it's not. It's a woman from The Bridge Hotel in Battle checking to see if Mr

73

Costello's reservation for the weekend of the 17th of August still stands. She hasn't been able to get through to his mobile. What hotel? My heart sinks and a new worry line digs its way across my forehead.

Nine

Flashbacks happen when I'm zoning out. It's like staring at the 3D dot poster that Joe still, embarrassingly, keeps Blu-Tacked up in the poky makeshift home office beneath the stairs. A load of old dots. Only when you stop *trying* to understand it does a coral and fish seascape emerge. Focus and the image disassembles. So here I am, lying in the bath looking out over next door's garden, the dance of their sycamore, thinking about the hotel in Battle and who Joe might be taking there, and the Amy project and whether it could possibly succeed and what success means anyhow now I have a baby, and how the thinner you are the better jeans hang, and feeling bad that I haven't phoned Mum for ages and smelling my fingers for that delicious trace of Evie, sad to wash it off. Then, suddenly, with no drum roll, it's there. I close my eyes and the movie's playing on the blood black of my eyelids. Her hair, blowing about and covering her face. Her squeal, a hybrid of screech and laugh. The way he flicked something off her arm. Was it an insect? A bee maybe? The cruel intimacy of the flick. The way he bent down to kiss her arm, in the tender elbow pit. The way he lingered. That said more than any pornographic money shot.

Whooshh! I plunge my head under water. It rushes, warm, into my ears, up my nose. I hold my breath. Ten seconds, fifteen, twenty . . .

'Waah, waaah, waaaaaaaah!'

Evie's cry pierces through the bath enamel, distorted and ghostly. It's supposedly her after-lunch sleep, the golden window in which I'll read or bathe. This said, most of the time the view from the golden window is merely of chores, and I find myself unloading the dishwasher, loading the washing machine or preparing food, resentfully slipping into a gender stereotype.

I leap out of the bath, puddling the floor with water. Evie calms as soon as I pick her up: she wasn't really ill or upset, just fancied a bit of attention. 'Oh Evie,' I say, a little exasperated. And then she smiles. It's the uncomplicated smile of a besotted fan and the annoyance disperses and I love her totally and want to eat her up and keep her as my tiny baby for ever. This is when I miss breastfeeding, that transaction of love and dependence and milk. But she's on the bottle now, doesn't even acknowledge my boobs as old friends, despite the fact she savaged them.

I lie Evie down on the changing mat and remove her sodden nappy, heavy as a bag of frozen peas. I don't mind the smell, find it oddly reassuring. She is so perfect naked, creamy and hairless, the slash of her belly button the only reminder she was once part of me. From certain angles, she is all Joe. That brings it home. The irreversibility of it all. Forever three, branched through genes, through generations. Amy Crane. Joe Costello. Evie Costello. We gave her Joe's surname because it's obviously a much better name. Crane fly. Lame Crane. My mother always said it was a great impediment, the exception being that it came near the top of the alphabet so her files were easily found at the GP's surgery. I wanted

76

Crane-Costello. Joe said it sounded aspiring. It's odd that despite growing in my womb she hasn't got my name, so I avoid speaking it out aloud, whereas Joe enunciates 'Miss Costello' a lot, savouring each consonant, claiming ownership.

Ding dong! Ding dong!

Damn. Who's that? I wedge Evie on to my hip and take the stairs carefully. Do not drop baby!

'It's me!' A voice shouts shrill through the letterbox.

'Kate!'

I open the door to a punch of Jo Malone and damp dog. Kate looks taller and slimmer than last time I saw her.

'I needed a dose of fresh London air. Too much country, I had to break free!'

'Come in, come in. Evie say hello to aunty Kate.'

Kate brushes Evie's cheek and strides through to the kitchen. I follow, Evie star-fished over my shoulder. Kate fills the kettle and puts it on. She never asks, treats this place like her urban pad.

'I'm famished,' she says, delving into the bread bin.

'There's some organic posh bread in there somewhere, with crunchy bits.' I dunk green tea bags into chipped mugs. 'What's been going on?'

'Nothing, Amy. Fuck all. And that's the problem.' Kate sits down at the table and, sighing with the enormity of nothing, sweeps her lush brown hair over one shoulder. She's got new highlights and a new top, silk and expensive with a dark purple and pink flower print trailing like a cottage trellis across her cleavage. 'Toast?' she asks.

I look at her thigh. It hardly squishes on the chair at all. This gives me the will power to resist. 'No thanks. Hey, you've lost weight.' Kate was always the plumper one. She isn't any more. It's like we've swapped our old dress sizes.

'Oooh thank you.' She barely skims her toast with butter. 'I've been trying to do this no-carbs-after-six rule. I noticed everything was doing a thirty-five-year-old slide south.'

Thirty-five? I always forget that Kate is merely four years older than me. I see her as older, as the big sister I never had. In truth she looks a little older than that too, not in a craggy or unpleasant way, it's just her features are more lived in, cross-hatched by too many Tuscan holidays. She may not be nubile, but there is something that catches about her face. Her eyes are the soft brown of demerara sugar, her lips plump with a slight overbite. She's always had what would once have been called a homely face and figure, in more tactful times, curvaceous. But in the last few months, as she's lost weight, she's developed new angles and an unexpected vampiness. I thought she'd move to the country and start wearing tea dresses with flowery Boden wellies, embrace the pastoral. The opposite has happened.

'So what brings you here?'

'I was hoping to meet Joe for lunch but he had a meeting or something, so I thought I'd chance it and see if you were in. Off for some retail therapy later.'

'Yes, you'll have to make do with me. Joe's manic at work, new business.'

'So I gather.' Kate twists her wedding ring round and round like a broken screw.

'Yeah, he's always so bloody busy. He came back at ten last night.' And as I say the words I'm aware of how cuckolding they sound. Where the hell *was* Joe last night?

'Really? And he's busy for the rest of the week, according to yesterday's email. I don't know when I'm ever going to get slated in for lunch.'

I shake my head. Joe and Kate have been having lunch together for as long as I can remember. His friendship with

Kate predates mine. While Kate's a civilising influence on Joe, he calms her neuroses down. It's always been like that. Fortunately, today, Joe's absence is my gain. I run through things that I can do now that I have an extra pair of hands: phone back the Council Tax office, hang the washing out . . . leg waxing!

'Kate, do me a big favour?' Kate doesn't say anything. She's not one to commit blindly. 'Will you accompany me to the local beauty salon so I can get waxed? It's so difficult with Evie and it's a nice day for a walk.'

'Sure.' She's at home in salons.

Kate pushing the pram, we set off down the street. In the daylight, Kate looks drawn. She has things on her mind.

'Everything OK?' I ask.

'Not really, no.' The words shoot fast, ready formed. Evidently I should have asked her earlier. 'Pete, bloody darling husband. We're just not getting on at all. He comes in late, if he comes in at all. He's spending more and more weekdays at the flat in Pimlico. We argue about the silliest things . . .'

'Hmmm. Arguments aren't always bad. Better out than in.' And better than emotional muteness. The great unsaid.

'I wouldn't object if the rows were about the big issues, the things that need expressing. Hell knows what they *are* about, dirty shoes in the hall, the filter on the swimming pool. Never get a swimming pool. Marriage wreckers.'

'But at least you're not battling it out in London.' I'd love a pool. Rather than the litter, the slab of sky, the tall leering zone-two houses split meanly into flats like fractured faces.

'We'd get on better with the stress of London, with something to divert us, something to blame.' She speeds up her walk and I have to trot breathlessly beside her. 'I'm bored,

Amy. Bored of decorating and painting watercolours and pretending I don't mind not having a proper London job. Oh, I don't know. I love the peace. I do. And of course the house is beautiful.' She takes one hand off the pram to gesticulate, which is worrying since we're waiting to cross a busy road. 'But I'm a bit tired of all that having to drive to buy a pint of milk, the locals, their hunting blood-lust, their defensive paranoid politics.'

I tense, poised to grab the pram in case it rolls forward. 'You've always said they're nice enough,' I say. Kate can't make out that they're just a load of bumpkins. Her village is full of families who've downshifted from Fulham. Most of them are too squeamish to kill a harvest spider let alone a fox.

'It's the way they keep asking me how I am. You know, with those coy smiles on their faces.'

A lorry roars past, lifting Evie's cap of hair. I look at Kate blankly.

'Babies, Amy! They are thinking about babies!'

I never bring the baby subject up. Kate must do it. An unspoken rule of our friendship. As is the fact that Kate talks about her problems and I listen. She assumes I don't have any problems because I've got a baby.

'I feel like a useless Friesian cow. The chicken that can't lay an egg. It offends the rural natural order.'

I laugh. 'Don't be silly. Maybe they're not talking about babies. Maybe they're just enquiring about how you are.'

Kate rolls her eyes. Nothing is straightforward in Kate's world. There are hidden meanings behind everything – the way her next-door neighbour eyed her bag of groceries in the checkout queue, or the way her husband greets the pretty farmer's wife. Kate has far too much time on her hands. She needs either a baby or a job.

'You're too hard on yourself. On average it takes many couples—'

'Over a year to conceive,' snaps Kate. 'Don't. It's been two.' Her fingers A-frame up, about to lift from the pram handle. I immediately grab it. She glares at me and puts her gesticulating hand back on the pram. I take mine off. A silent bicker. We cross the road safely.

'But you've been to the doctor. You know there isn't a problem,' I shout over the roar of traffic.

'Not with my workings. But Pete still refuses to get checked out. The idea that he may be unable to produce a son to inherit his father's wheelie bin empire is inconceivable.' Kate flicks off a toast crumb embedded in her lip gloss. 'Amy, I'm over waiting. It's going to take some kind of witch doctor to get me pregnant.'

'You *are* having sex?' Candid. Is Alice rubbing off on me? Kate looks at me surprised – she knows me well enough to hear a new voice – and, thankfully, laughs. I can never guess with total accuracy how she'll react. 'You're not sleeping with anyone else? Romping in the hay with the young farmer boy?' I have to ask. Kate's the kind of person who says, two months after the event, 'I didn't tell you then, but . . .' She releases information as and when it suits.

'The farmer boys! Suicidal middle-aged men on Prozac more like.' Kate suddenly stops, serious. 'Look, although we aren't exactly a hot young couple in love, we *do* have sex occasionally, and at just the right time of the month. Believe me, I've made sure of it.' Kate uses charts and thermometers and the wily arts of her 'fertility pants', navy gym knickers that Pete has a thing for. 'My therapist suggested it could be an emotional thing. That somehow the egg and the sperm are choosing not to fuse because we're not, like, fused emotionally. Our instability undermines their survival.'

81

'Hmmm. Dunno, Kate. That would preclude half the babies in the world being born. I certainly wouldn't be here if reproduction was that emotionally intelligent.' Would Evie? I point up the road. 'Look, we're almost there. That's the salon.'

Kate ignores me. I realise she is talking things through with herself. I could be anyone. A wall, a plant, Joe. 'Pete even asked *me* if I was having an affair. Can you believe it?'

More likely Pete is. Kate could extricate herself pretty easily and meet someone else. But she'll never understand that there's a freedom in childlessness. 'If you're really unhappy you can leave you know, Kate. You've got options. Hey, this is it.'

We stand in front of Klass Beauty's dirty pane of glass. I'm looking at the menu, checking prices, when I become conscious of Kate glaring at me, eyes hardening. This changes all the features on her face at once.

'Options? I'm thirty-five years old. Please don't take this the wrong way, but it's hard for someone who's got a baby to understand what it's like.'

Check mate. 'Of course, I'm sorry.'

'It's very hard. No one seems to understand,' Kate says. 'He may not be the love of my life but . . .'

'He's not?'

Kate straightens up, reins herself in. 'Oh God, what am I saying? Yes, of course Pete is the love of my life. Well, he was.' She jiggles the pram. 'And let's be practical here, Amy. Even if he wasn't, what the hell would I do about it? I am too old to be misty eyed about meeting someone new. It's too tricky, too uncertain a science to risk it. All my friends are in couples. The free-man pool is just pitiful. I don't want to date. I couldn't bear all that waiting for the phone to ring nonsense.' She tucks a wedge of brown hair behind her ear and looks at me intently. 'I'm going to play with the cards I've got.'

I want to scream at her, 'this is how I feel too sometimes! I understand!' But I can't. Kate is not just my friend, she is *our* friend, perhaps Joe's more than mine. She's almost family. I can't say one thing without explaining everything and unravelling the whole sorry tale. So I don't mention the hotel booking.

She sniffs indignantly. 'There's no point feeling sorry for myself all the time, it doesn't get me anywhere.'

Kate does feel sorry for herself a lot of the time these days. But I can't imagine what baby-ache must be like. I never had it and then I had a baby. And, unlike me, Kate is used to getting what she wants, when she wants. She's generally been rather successful. Husband, house, vast decorating budget and an opportunity to paint watercolour landscapes while everyone else has to do shitty jobs to pay the mortgage. And nobody resents Kate her success because she is nice and friendly and not threateningly beautiful. They feel the underdog has lucked out. As if! Kate leaves nothing to chance. When she was single she shamelessly demanded that friends set her up on blind dates, frequented bars patronised by rich single men and threw fabulous parties in which she got all her single girlfriends to bring their most eligible single male friends (no gay men). It worked. Well, she got Pete.

'Let's go in and get you sorted,' says Kate. 'A leg wax, isn't it?'

'Yes, I've cultured an ecosystem above my ankle.'

As we open the door two tiny Pekinese dogs with pink gingham bows tied around their collars yelp and spring up at our ankles. If they so much as sniff Evie I'll boot them.

'Moussy and Henna! Stop it. Stop it now!' screeches a frosted blonde muppet mop behind the desk. The dogs continue. Evie starts to cry. 'Right.' The woman beneath the mop, a craggy fifties, picks them up and tosses them into a dog basket, growling. 'Little rascals. What can I do for you?'

'Er, a leg wax please. I'm afraid I haven't booked though.'

'You haven't booked? Oh, we're very busy,' she croaks, as if she'd just gargled with peroxide. Bar a young oriental woman sweeping up and an old lady in rollers under a space-helmet heater, I can't see anyone else in the salon. 'Sit down in the waiting area and I'll see if I can possibly fit you in.'

The waiting area is two plastic padded chairs the colour of black pudding, opposite her desk.

'Not exactly Bliss Spa, is it?' whispers Kate.

'It's fine, I used it once a couple of years ago. Now what were you saying before we got devoured by the Pekinese?'

'Oh, whinging on.' Kate studies her nails. 'Ignore me. What's been going on with you?'

I take a deep breath. 'Oh, er, things have picked up. I was getting to a bit of a loose end, you know, just me and the baby . . .' I have to be careful here. I can't complain about motherhood. I did once before. I said that I felt a bit lonely and Kate got angry – 'How can you be lonely with Joe and Evie in your life?' I didn't mean to be insensitive. 'And I've met some new mothers to hang out with. Alice . . . you must meet her. She's great, really funny, very glamorous. She's kind of taken me under her wing. God knows why.' Kate laughs, doesn't contradict my self-deprecation. 'She has loads of highly entertaining friends. They look like supermodels, have pots of money and armies of nannies. They've got mother-hood down to a fine art, like shopping.'

'They sound awful.' Kate imagines that when she gets the children she deserves she'll be an earth-mother type who'll want to be with her little darlings 24/7. That will be enough for her. I once told her that Evie was more than I'd ever hoped for but not enough. She looked shocked and didn't get it.

'I don't know that many other women with babies.'

The woman behind the desk stands up. She is wearing a white overall splattered with pink, like a butcher's. A letter has fallen off her white plastic name tag so it reads _rish. 'Five minutes.' An umbilical cord of smoke twists from her mouth.

Kate rocks Evie's pram with her loafer. 'What about your old friends?'

'Oh, we chat on the phone of course. But they're at work. I can't really do evenings that easily and when I do I'm knackered . . .' Excuses. Why don't I see other people? Because I've got nothing to say. My brain feels likes it's been Hoovered. Easier just to grunt at Joe and coo over the baby. Primitive, self-limiting communication is a lot easier than a conversation with someone who has got a life.

'You see me.'

'You're different.'

'Don't your other friends want babies?'

'Not enough to have them right now.' The single ones are still going to drug-fuelled parties and on yoga holidays. The more desperate ones are internet dating. The ones in relationships are agonising about where the relationship is going and still trying really hard to give killer blow jobs so that the man might consider them settle-down material.

'Silly things. If only they knew. Ovaries wait for no one.' Kate picks up a stained *House & Garden* magazine from the coffee table. June 1999, exactly six years old. She flicks through absentmindedly. 'And what about work?'

'Work?' Baffling idea. 'Dunno. Got a few months before I have to make a decision so, well, you know me, I'm sitting on it. Obviously I need to halve my body weight before I start dealing with clients again. Alice, the mother I mentioned, Alice is going to help.'

'You look fine.'

'Fine' never sells to me. Kate doesn't like new people, especially new friends of mine. She made all her friends years ago, mostly at school and university. Anyone she met after the age of twenty-five isn't easily trusted.

'Well I wouldn't change too much. Joe likes you as you are.' Kate and I sit in easy silence for a few moments. The dogs grizzle in the basket. 'When's he back?' She looks at her watch.

'About seven, eight.'

'Oh shit. That late, really? I'm not sure I can hang around until then.'

Kate sounds disappointed and I wonder if it's me she ever wants to see. She's not a woman's woman, not in the way Alice is. At university Kate was the girl who had her mafia of men-friends; gay, straight, bookish. She had one for every occasion. She needed their reassurance. A compliment from a woman didn't count.

'Everything OK with Joe?' Kate asks suddenly.

Actually, he is booking hotel rooms without telling me and I have good reason to suspect he's having an affair. But I can't say anything. I'm not entirely convinced that, with misguided well meaning, Kate would be able to resist interfering. 'Fine.'

Kate's face drops, a flash of disappointment. In a blink I get it. She wants other people to be having difficulties too. There's nothing worse than being the only one who's sinking.

'Things could be better,' I clarify. 'We're both very tired.'

'Sorry to hear that,' she says, looking slightly relieved. 'Things could be better with me and Pete too.'

'Nip in and take your trousers off,' shouts _rish.

'See you in a sec, Kate. And thanks.'

The door of Beauty Room No. 1 – I can't see any others – is painted a pale peppermint green, the colour of a maternity ward toilet. There are no windows. The walls are grubby, sprayed in parts with wax and other unidentifiable substances. There are scummy bits of equipment on trolleys: a beige electrolysis machine that looks like it hasn't been cleaned since the seventies; scary steel instruments languishing in cups of purple liquid; lotions in big industrial bottles, labelled by beauty companies I've never heard of. The stretcher-like bed is covered in white kitchen roll; underneath it is a dog bowl. I kick off my trousers, clamber on to the bed and lie there shivering under the strip lighting. It feels like I have to wait for an eternity. I've forgotten the etiquette. Do I say, 'Ready'?

_rish flings open the door. The old woman under the hairdryer looks straight into the room, straight between my legs. I close them and give her an embarrassed smile. 'Right. Let's have a look then. Been here before?' She leaves the door slightly ajar.

'Ages ago.'

'Hmmm, can see that.' She runs nicotine-tipped fingers down my hairy shins, gloops the wax on to her plastic spatula and spreads it on my legs as if they were toast. Argh, searing pain!

'It'll cool,' she says, violently ripping the wax off my legs with bandage strips.

'Ugh!' She pulls at my rogue thigh pubes with tweezers.

'Done! That's a bit better no?' She squints at her work, then shamelessly stares at my crotch. 'That's not going to get his pulse racing.' Yes, there are pubes curling over the knicker elastic. 'Bikini line?'

For a moment I am tempted, but can't face the thought of

87

_rish's yellow fingers rooting around down there. Besides, it's not really necessary. No one will see it. 'Not today, thanks.'

'Suit yourself.' _rish walks away. A fluff of dog hair wakes behind her shoe.

I jump off the bed. My legs are covered in livid red pimples and a sticky residue of wax. But they are hairless. First bit of Project Amy done! I get dressed.

'*Sans* hair!' I throw open the door but Kate and Evie are not there. The dogs growl at me as I walk over to the window.

'Oi, missy, that's fourteen pounds please.'

'Sorry, just trying to locate my baby.'

_rish drums the counter impatiently. I pour change out of my purse and give her a pound tip because I daren't not. Where the fuck is Kate? The dogs frenziedly start barking: Kate backs into the salon with the pram, pushing the door open with her bottom.

'Where have you been?' I say, relieved and cross.

'Evie started crying so we went for a little walk.'

'Oh right.' But I know Evie didn't cry. The beauty-room door was ajar and I can distinguish her cry in a room full of babies. But I let it go. Because that's just Kate. And sometimes she likes to pretend that Evie is hers.

Ten

Joe gets back from work early. A client cancelled.

'You've just missed Kate,' I say. 'She's been trying to get hold of you.'

'Kate? She gone?' I nod. 'Oh good. I'm *so* not in the mood for a Kate and Pete marriage analysis right now.'

'Not very nice.' Joe helicopters a squealing Evie above his head. I take a deep breath. 'Joe. There's a message from a hotel receptionist on the answerphone.' He looks blank. 'Said you had a reservation.'

Joe levers himself up from the sofa and saunters over – deliberately casually? – to make coffee. Standing at the island unit, Evie on his hip, he positions his back to me so I can't see his face. He puts his left hand in his back jeans pocket, like he needs to put it somewhere or it might start tapping.

'I thought it could be a nice night away for some of the new design team. A thank you for all those late nights last month and the Cucumber Project. But anyhow it's . . .'

Joe's thrown these thank you sessions before. They went to Cornwall last year. They spent the weekend surfing and drinking and smoking dope. I spent the weekend sleeping and practising breathing exercises and wishing I could go out and get properly drunk.

'But why Saturday, bang in the middle of our weekend?' My voice is high-pitched, needy. It's not my voice. I hate him for making me sound like this. And I'm not convinced by his explanation: he won't meet my eye.

'Thought you might like a night free of me. You could get Alice or someone round for a . . . Chardonnay playdate. But as I was saying . . .'

OK, he's struggling. Only yesterday he declared Alice 'a bit shallow'. He thinks it despicable that she left the father of her child. Now he's encouraging me to see her? 'But you don't—'

'Amy!' Joe snaps. 'If you'll let me get a word in edgeways, I'm trying to explain that it's been cancelled. Loads of them can't go that weekend. Let's do something nice together instead.' He rattles the biscuit tin. It's empty. I finished them off last night when I couldn't sleep. 'Never any bloody food in this house.'

'You do the shopping then.'

'You're at home all day . . .'

'Just sitting on my arse!' I snap. 'You try hoofing round Sainsbury's with Evie having a meltdown and everyone staring at you like they're going to report you to the social services, while weighing up the comparative merits of Digestives or Hobnobs.'

'OK, OK.' Joe picks up his coffee and buries his head in *Design Week*. 'I get the point. Sorry.' He stabs at the crumpling paper, shakes it out. 'Oh, yes. Forgot to say, Alice phoned. Says she's booked you in for some beauty appointment or something in town. Bumped you up the waiting list. I've written down the details on a Post-It.' Ah, eyebrows. 'Amy?'

'Hmmm?'

'Don't burn money. Tweezers in the bathroom cabinet.'

Eleven

At the pelican crossing Evie lets rip, emitting a noise totally disproportionate to the size of her lungs. An old woman tut-tuts into the pram. 'She's hungry,' the woman says tersely, as if it were any of her business. I stamp on, from Kilburn to Queen's Park. The high-rise council blocks disappear from view. In their place, rows of pretty Victorian houses, clouded by magnolia trees. While the perimeters of the two areas blur a little, Queen's Park has distinguished itself from its less salubrious neighbour in the last few years. With neat avenues radiating from its eponymous lush green park, it is what estate agents call a bijou 'urban village', populated by wealthy, trendy Londoners – media, music industry, the odd actor – who downshifted from Notting Hill when they had families. They recycle. They drive gas-guzzling SUVs. Their children do yoga. They also get extra tuition to give them the edge on their classmates. Oh yes, and the local boutique sells out of UGG boots within days of their arrival on the shop floor.

In the park café I collapse like a pushchair, folded arms clicked tight to my ribs, knees crossed, shyly constricted. Nicola is late, always. Normally I time myself to be about twelve minutes late, then we coincide. Slurping a cappuccino on my own, I watch the hubbub elsewhere. At other tables women breastfeed beneath peacock blue kaftan tops and fork salad. Toddlers squabble over trikes and skateboards. Everyone laughs loudly and chatters intently like they're having a boozy lunch in the south of France. Everyone seems to know each other. Why didn't anyone invite me to the party?

The other mothers look too thin to ever have been fertile. That they are thinner than I was at my prime (aged twenty-four?) is demoralising. That they all look like they have been dressed from the pages of *Vogue*, even more so. Do they not have impossible spring wardrobes full of drab, stretched vest tops and mismatched separates in different sizes bought to fit their expanding and contracting figures? It seems not. The park is paintballed with colour – floral dresses, sparkly little halter-necks and teeny skirts that show if you've got cellulite or not. (They haven't.) Some of the mothers co-ordinate. Some of the mothers accessorise. I really can't remember the last time I had the occasion or motivation to put on a pair of earrings, let alone an extravagant fall of cleavage-bouncing Bloomsbury beads.

Some of these women I recognise from the sandpit. Some of them I may once have misguidedly attempted to talk to, in the early days when desperate for adult daytime company. That was before I'd sussed the sandpit etiquette. Rule number one: Don't attempt to use your child as an entrée into a clique of mothers who already know each other. It won't work. The children *may* play with each other but embarrassing disinterest or, worse, violence is just as likely. (If your child hits one of theirs, apologise profusely and quickly remove yourself and your offending child. If their child hits yours never *ever* tell their child off. Smile sweetly and say it doesn't matter even if your child is bleeding and their child is about as cute as a rabid pit bull.) Rule number two: Don't expect a friendly aside about spades or sandy nappies to result in a friendship with another mother. In my experience, such asides meet with a slightly embarrassed smile and brush-off, as if you were a gawky guy trying to hit on them in a public place. Rule number three: Look like you have lots of other mum-friends or, alternatively, are happy in your own company. Playground politics apply: No one likes a needy loser.

Evie asleep, I seize the moment to flick through my celebrity weekly, something I'd once have been a little embarrassed to be seen reading in public. But I'm too tired to care, about most things actually. And – luck's in – there's an article about Pilates, most of it taken up with pictures of celebrities, pre- and post-partum. The caption above their lollipop heads tells how many months (or weeks in many cases) it took for them to regain their figures. Two months . . . with a diet of oatcakes and watercress soup. Three months . . . on the Zone. Four-and-a-half months . . . on Atkins. Me? Six-and-a-half months and counting, on the toast and anything-in-the-fridge diet. No wonder nothing's shifting. Must try harder. Must try and be more like Victoria Beckham. But the photos make me feel worse about myself so I seek solace in a gooey flapjack, scoffing quickly, without pleasure, as if that would nuke half its calories.

'Nic!'

Nicola pushes her pram like an aged gardener might push a wheelbarrow. 'God, I was miles away. Sorry I'm late.'

'You all right?'

Nicola's eyes are orbited by Saturnine shadows. 'Hmfsk! Thomas was up all night wailing. Sam snored through. Me, up and fucking down trying to appease his lordship.'

'Oh dear. What's the matter dear Tom-tom?' I bend down

to her pram. Thomas grins back. Unlike his mother he looks thoroughly well rested.

Nicola collapses on a bench, grabs my magazine and flicks through harumphing. 'I can't believe you buy this crap.'

'Just light reading.'

'You'll give yourself all sorts of new insecurities if you're not careful.'

'I'm inspiring myself to lose weight.'

'Why the hell would you want to do that?' Nicola pulls Thomas out of his pram and bounces him on her knee. When he starts to cry she spoons him some froth from my cappuccino.

'For me.'

'That's the worst, pat, women's magazine answer I've ever heard. If we were left to our own devices we'd all eat doughnuts all day and never exercise. And I hate the notion that we're meant to look like this,' she pokes the magazine, 'like a prepubescent girl and just weeks after having a baby.'

'It's not about that.'

'Hmmm. Do what you want.' Girlie foibles wind her up. 'Just don't expect me to join in. What's wrong with a bit of extra upholstery?'

'You won't be joining me at my Pilates class then?' I tease. 'Alice has invited me. Does wonders for baby belly apparently.'

Nicola snorts. 'If there's a babysitter around, I'd rather sleep.'

'We're embarking on Project Amy! I'm going for an overhaul. Body, clothes, eyebrows . . .'

'Project what? Seems a bit of a drastic course of action. You'll be having a bikini wax next.'

We giggle because we both know that we haven't had a bikini wax in months. Not that Sam, her partner, would

94

notice. A shambolic fiftysomething academic (once mistaken for Thomas's grandfather) studying public policy at UCL, he worships Nicola like a goddess and would be unlikely to object if she grew a full yogi beard.

'Project Amy!' mutters Nicola incredulously as she stretches her arms above her head with a yawn. 'Hilarious.' She rummages in her nappy bag. 'Do you think I'll get lynched if I have a cigarette?'

'Probably.'

'I promise not to breastfeed at the same time.'

Nicola lights up and we sit easily for a few moments watching the carousel of children and outfits and trikes on the path circling the grass. I try to find the courage. Words don't flow easily. My mouth feels dry. Nicola starts reading the magazine.

'Nicola.' She doesn't look up from the page. 'Nicola, I think Joe's having an affair.' My voice is very quiet.

She starts. 'WHAT?'

'An affair. I'm pretty sure of it. He's been acting funny. There's this hotel . . . Oh maybe I'm being paranoid. But remember what Sue said about that lunch. And Nic, he comes back so late from work and his mobile is often switched off and I can't help but wonder . . .' I can feel my eyes watering up.

'Whoa! Amy love, you're gabbling.' Nicola puts Thomas back in his pram and places her hand momentarily on mine, pressing it down for a second, a tiny but poignant movement. She doesn't do superfluous body contact. 'Now speak slowly and start at the beginning.'

So that's what I do. I tell her about the text that Joe sent that was meant for someone else, and how I went to the park, unbeknownst to Joe, and saw him with that someone else. And that she was a woman with long hair. And how I could

95

only see her from behind and not clearly because of the wind blowing hair over her face and me being bloody short-sighted, but not short-sighted enough because I could still see how close they were with their cosy interlinked arms, and how Joe kissed this woman's arm – why her arm? – and how I thought I was going to throw up the five croissants I'd had for breakfast and how I ran and I have been running ever since.

Nicola is quiet for a moment. She isn't the hysterical type. 'What did he say when you confronted him?'

'I didn't confront him.'

'Why not?'

'Because . . . because . . . I was eight months pregnant. And, it's humiliating admitting to it, it sounds so wet, but I didn't want him to leave. I didn't want to corner him. I didn't want him to have to choose between us.'

'But there may have been an innocent explanation.'

'Yeah right! I couldn't risk it. I just couldn't. I was pregnant, freaked out. I needed him.' I flick away a tear. A woman from an adjacent table is staring.

'Oh dear. I'm really sorry, Amy.' Nicola sighs. 'I would have thought you'd have asked him though. You're no Stepford wife.'

'Hope not.' I giggle through my tears, like a draining plughole.

'The worst-case scenario would be awful, I'm not saying it wouldn't. But you'd survive it. Isn't it always better to know the truth?'

'Hmmm. I'm not sure I'd ever find out anyhow.' My nose is beginning to snot up like Evie's. 'I've never been the kind of woman who looks good crying. 'Problem is, it's about more than just what's gone on. It's about me. It's almost like . . .' Light shafts into the muddle. '. . . I have a terror of history repeating itself. It's kind of irrational.'

'I'm not with you.'

'It's my big fear, always has been, ever since Dad left. I saw what happened to Mum. The weird Christmases, no man to carve the turkey, or unblock the U-bend. The way Mum stopped getting invited to dinner parties because she wasn't in a couple. The way she cluttered her bed with pillows to make the empty space shrink. She's never learned to sleep in the middle, you know.'

'God, that's awful, and a bit seventies if you don't mind me saying. Things have changed.'

'Suppose. In some ways.' I think of Alice. 'But that's not the point.'

'Sorry.' Nicola squeezes my shoulders in a brief hug.

'I'll ask him when I'm ready.'

'And that'll be?'

'When I can afford to lose him. Look at me. Nicola, I'm a mess. I've been depressed for months.'

'The baby blues?'

I ignore her. 'I look like shit. I'm not sorted out about work. I'd be at sea on my own right now. You know why? Because I'm no longer sure who I am. Who am I Nic? Where's the old Amy? I need her back. I'm not going to confront him until *I'm* ready to face the possible consequences.'

Nicola picks up my coffee and drains it in one neat whisky gulp. 'What do Kate and Alice think?'

'You're the first person I've told.'

'Jesus! No wonder you feel crap. Why? Why keep this to yourself all these months?'

'Well, Kate's too close to Joe. It's awkward, she'd start interfering. And Alice . . . I'm just getting to know her and she's a bit funny about Joe anyway. I can't deal with pressure from her right now.'

'Understood.'

'And . . . this sounds really silly. I didn't want to tell anyone because it feels disloyal to Joe.' I laugh weakly. 'Yes, I know. Ironic considering.'

'Honestly, I understand.' Nicola moves slightly closer to me on the seat. I can feel her warmth down my left side. 'It's hard when you've got a baby. You feel you have to present a united front.'

'You won't say anything?'

'Of course not. But Amy, he's probably completely innocent. And if he's not, well, maybe you should ask yourself, hand on heart, whether you and Joe are well suited.'

I shrug. Perhaps the question should be: If circumstances were different, if we didn't have a baby, would Joe and I still be together? But that's impossible to know, like whether the light in the fridge stays on after you shut its door.

Twelve

I stand in front of Alice's full-length French mirror, almost naked bar an old vest and mismatching knickers. She points at parts of my body with a long make-up brush, like a school teacher with a chalk. Five minutes ago I was laughing at the absurdity of it. Now I am chilly and rather self-conscious.

'Pilates can get rid of this,' she says, stabbing at my belly fold with the brush.

'How long?'

'Ten sessions I'd say. But I can see evidence of the demon baker! You need to stop eating so many carbs, watch your GI.'

'How about I stop eating altogether?'

'Overrated. It slows the metabolism. Some kind of GI diet is your best bet. Now do this.' Alice breathes in and stands like a ballerina. 'Suck in and stand tall. Posture!'

I do as she says, too naked not to be compliant and almost enjoying the submissive role-play.

She pulls my shoulders back firmly. 'There! What a difference! You have a fab waist you know. It's hidden under a bit of baby blub but it's there all right, very defined. I wish I had your curves.'

Yeah right. As Alice stalks around me, I'm hushed by her physical prowess. She's somehow more impressive in her downtime home clothes – chocolate brown Juicy Couture tracksuit bottoms, white vest, UGG boots – than in all her heels and clattering jewellery. She looks like one of those celebrities snapped darting from their Santa Monica home to a yoga class. When I put on a tracksuit I look like I'm darting out of a council flat to buy cigarettes.

'Now sit down, let's see what we can conjure up with a bit of war paint.' She puts a cool hand on my shoulder and presses me down on to a stool upholstered in cow-skin. It itches my buttocks.

'Can I have a dressing gown or something?' I demand, tiring of the game.

She tosses over a delicate pale grey and lilac silk number which collapses around my shoulders like a parachute. Then she opens a huge black box, with interior trays that fold out like beetle wings. More make-up than I have ever seen in my life.

'Don't be alarmed,' Alice laughs. 'I am not an obsessive. I've got generous friends who work at glossy mags. I never use it all. Most of it goes off.'

'Goes off? What, like milk?'

'Yes, sort of. Make-up does have a shelf life, especially the good stuff.'

'But I've had mine for centuries,' I say, thinking of my battered lipsticks. Improbable how I once considered their application in the morning to be as essential as brushing my teeth.

'Don't!' she laughs.

Alice loses herself in her box of tricks, smudging colours on the back of her hand like bruises, crackling into smart packaging. I study her bedroom: creamy rugs so thick the foot sinks into them like snow, an enormous chandelier dripping candy-coloured tear drops, walls covered in a shimmer of silvery green wallpaper. Five mirrors bounce back Alice's beauty as she walks across the room. Along her white marble fireplace march glass potted candles, incense cones and framed photographs of Alice and Alfie: in a Moroccan market; on a beach, buried in the sand, laughing. One whole wall is a wardrobe. When she opens the dark wood doors spotlights burn like stars. There are hundreds of Perspex boxes filled with shoes. More shoes than I've ever seen. There are shelves of folded sweaters, folded with tissue paper. I've never met anyone who folds clothes in tissue paper before. Her bed is even bigger than mine, with a soft grey cashmere blanket folded across it in the manner of a hip hotel. On the floor next to the bed, squatting on a copy of Italian *Vogue*, is a pink glass ashtray with what looks like a half-smoked spliff stalk. Not very childproof, notes my inner Sue.

'Too pink. Too red. Here, this could be the one!'

Suddenly, Alice is upon me wielding make-up brushes and powders and lipsticks. She daubs my lips and eyes. Tells me when to look up, when to look down. Gets me to look to the left, to the right. She talks to me only through the reflection in the mirror like a hairdresser. I find this rather unnerving. I also find it hard to look at my reflection. When I pull my silly mirror face, all scrunched eyes and jaw tilting, Alice chastises me. Anyone else and I'd tell them to bugger off, but I let Alice get away with it. She's one of those people. And it's such an odd situation that the only way to deal with it is to go with it.

'Oh dear, when did you last go to the hairdresser?'

She's not interested in an answer, which is just as well. Instead, she pulls and tugs and moans about the condition, the bad highlights, the roots. It's as if she's stopped seeing me as entirely human, more a kind of broken doll. She asks questions, answers them herself. Blasts me with hairspray like a crop duster. Blow-torches me with a hairdryer. By the time she has finished I feel drained, like I've been sucked into a peculiar girlie vortex, pummelled by blusher brushes and spat out the other side.

'Now, Amy! Look! Look at what you can be, honey!'

Oh! 'I don't look like me.'

'You look like a better, more polished Amy.'

Once I get over the shock of seeing someone else's face staring back at me, I have to concede, she's right. There's a brightness to my eyes that I haven't seen since first dating Joe. (I used to love the way I looked then, enormous light-absorbent druggy pupils.) My skin glows like I've been digitally enhanced, the sleepless nights wiped from my complexion. And my hairstyle is softer, kinder to my round cheeks.

'Funnily enough, I do. Thanks, Alice.' I am impressed. 'It's a bit odd though. I do look like someone else. Me younger perhaps. Or me with a different life.'

'Well go get one, girl.' She hands me a tube of Chanel cleanser. 'But then again, if you want to cleanse it off . . .'

'Are you mad? No way. I'll never be able to replicate this myself.' I spring up and get dressed into my clothes – jeans, a scraggy T-shirt. They feel old suddenly. Like Oxfam clothes that smell of someone else. Alice shoves a bundle of make-up – 'Everything that's on your face' – into a large envelope and insists I have it. I slide the envelope into my handbag and laughingly point out that I already have a lipstick, an exploded one in the purse pocket. Alice tells me that it must go and that I must invest in a proper make-up bag, and when are we going shopping? Soon, I say. Call me. I push Evie back home for a late bedtime.

*

'Where have you been? Euh! What *have* you done to your face?' Joe says crossly when I come in. 'Your mouth looks all . . . all dribbly.' I lift my hand to wipe the lip gloss off. But something stops me. Instead, I root around in the envelope Alice gave me, find the lip gloss tube and slick another layer on.

Thirteen

It's three forty-five a.m. and bedtime breath whistles out of Joe's slack mouth. We argued before we went to bed. He said that Alice made me look ludicrous. I said, did he want me to look like a drudge? He said he liked me as I was, not pretending to be someone else. I said that is rich, and stormed upstairs to bed. I pretended I was asleep when he came to bed. Four hours later I'm still here, fiercely awake, thoughts rattling my head: Mum, haven't phoned; Grandma, haven't written; Evie, needs a teether. Why is it that I have a brain like a cocaine-fuelled city boy yet I supposedly don't even 'work'?

I slide out from under the duvet and plant my feet on the warm floorboards. Pad, pad, pad over to the window. I pull up the blind some, as quietly as I can, so that the room is half lit by the dirty London moon. I check Joe again. No signs of waking. Then I pick up a stool, put it by the wardrobe and clamber up. At the top of the wardrobe sit three boxes stuffed full of clothes I haven't worn for a year-and-a-half, maybe two. They are the other Amy's clothes. They are too small. Pretty little slips of things. My sexy jeans. That long silk dress that I got in the Selfridges sale for a song. These are the clothes that Alice and I are going to edit. But I can't wait until morning. Restless, awake, I want them now.

'Eeee orrrrrrrr!'

Christ that's loud! Joe gulps down a parcel of air and rolls on to his left side. I freeze and watch him. He pushes the rest of the duvet off. It twists around his calves. Half lit by the filtered night fuzz, he is sculptural, a sleeping Pan. His willy, wide and symmetrical, sleeps on his thigh. Do I desire him? I like the aesthetics. But I don't want to jump him. There was a time when I'd wake in the middle of the night and slip my palm around him and massage him into hard consciousness. Then we'd have sleepy sex. Often neither of us came. Instead, we'd fall back into a contented sleep, bodies still locked together. Then he'd soften and slip out.

That was before Evie. Now my most passionate physical relationship is with her. I spend my days lost in her flesh, cuddling, kissing, inhaling. And by the end of the day I'm spent. I don't crave skin on skin. I put her to bed and my body is once again mine. And I withdraw back within my boundaries, not wanting another human being pawing at me, wanting something. There's nothing left to give.

I reach back up for the boxes.

'Eeeee arrrrrrrrrrr . . .' Joe rolls over and faces me, his eyes half-open but looking dead as a fish on ice.

Nope, I definitely don't want to jump him. We've been there. And there's nothing more depressing than bad sex. It creates this awful emptiness deep in the solar plexus. And you have to pretend that it's not bad, depressing sex. If you don't it's worse, and creates issues. And sex with issues is the worst of the lot. Joe grunts and turns over, his back facing me. I'm sure it was this box to the left. I lift the box over my head. It's heavy. My left foot slips. Shit. I clatter to the floor.

'Amy? Are you awake?' he mumbles sleepily.

'No.'

Then silence. I wait for a few long moments until I'm sure he's asleep again. Then I break into the old crunchy cardboard and delve in. My old life! Wispy chiffon tops that clung prettily to my pert 34Bs. A mini-skirt! God, how things have changed. Jeans. My old jeans. I slide my leg into them. It's difficult as I'm sitting on the floor and I don't want to wake him up and make too much noise. I tug and tug and then I get to the point of no return, the zip. I breathe in like Alice says and tug again. No joy. Pubic hair gets caught in the zipper because I'm not wearing knickers and I can only unzip it with a sharp, painful depilatory action. I try not to cry out. Despairing, I toss the jeans aside and forage for the dress. And here it is! Blue and green silk, full-skirted and halter-necked. This is the dress I fell in love with Joe in. I pull it on over my head, carefully threading my arms through so as not to rip the seams. Old seams. Sixties seams. This was my mother's dress once. She dated my dad in it. But it hasn't dated.

Still, the dress is very much tighter than it was two summers ago. I wore it in Oxford, punting on the river Cherwell, our third 'date'. There is something rather lovely about going on a date with someone you already know. Suddenly there's more mystery, not less: you can't believe that what you are feeling you didn't feel before. Perhaps it's all just about timing then. In fact I pondered this as we tugged along the river, the weeping willow caterpillars catching in my hair, trailing a hand in the ice-bucket-cold water. Joe laughed and joked and the sunlight caught in his eyelashes like flecks of gold leaf. He steered the punt so well and refilled my wine glass with champagne and fed me honey-roasted cashews and tried to make sure I didn't get splashed. Despite his gentlemanly intentions, I did get drenched by a splash of the pole. Then the silk of the dress clung to me, tracing the shape of my bust, hardening my nipples. I remember being secretly pleased that it had happened. I kept catching Joe staring at me when he thought I wasn't looking.

I bury my nose into the dress's folds of fabric and sniff deeply in the darkness. It doesn't smell like it's been washed, which it probably hasn't, being a hand wash only garment. I'm lazy like that. For a moment I can smell the green river. I can smell that wonderful day, the sandwiches we couldn't eat because we were full with erotic anticipation, the way Joe picked bits of tree out of my hair, our first proper tongue-kiss, the way I loved the smell of his armpits when he pulled me close and wanted to curl up in them like an animal. I'm pushing my face deeper and deeper into the fabric, inhaling the past. Then I become aware that it is wet. The silk is sodden with a flash flood of tears. Suddenly they're pouring out in gulps and sobs, big monsoon tears, deliriously sad.

'What's the matter, sweetheart?' Joe's voice slurs with sleep. A big bulge slowly travels from one side of the duvet to the other. Joe tumbles out of bed, stubbing his toe. I hear him curse. Then he's behind me, enveloping me in his arms, half asleep.

'There, there. It's all going to be fine. I promise it's all going to be fine. Shushhhh . . .'

I gulp and swallow and try to stem the flow of tears. I can't speak.

'Hey, hey, hey. Sweetheart, it's OK. It's just a dream. Just a bad dream. Let's go back to bed. Here . . .'

Joe lifts me up. I'm still wearing my dress. I put my arms around his neck like a newlywed. We drop on to the bed together and he is asleep within seconds. I know this because I'm still awake.

Fourteen

'Off you go to your palwartez then,' says Mum, standing in the doorway, Evie gurgling happily on her hip and pulling at her neat beige skirt.

Mum confronts the sartorial obstacles of summer head on with swathes of linen or 'easy separates' from Country Casuals, which reveal as little of her swinging underarms and creased neckline as possible. She always looks immaculate.

'Pil-at-es,' I say, pointlessly.

'Pill-whatever-it-is. I'm so pleased you're taking my advice, although I'd have thought a run round the block would do just as much good and it's free. Don't worry about Evie. We'll have a knees-up, won't we?' Mum bends down and dead-heads a flower from a neglected potted plant. On her crown, concrete-grey roots are just visible, pushing up into the dyed silvery blonde. 'These plants! What would you do without me? I may have a bit of a tidy up if that's OK.'

This is not a question but a statement of intent. I don't want Mum poking around. But I can't argue because I'm late and I'm nervous.

'Now you go and get in shape. Byeeeeeeeeeeeee!' Mum slams the door. I can hear her talking to Evie as she walks down the corridor. 'Now blossom, let's get you some proper food, none of this organic silliness.'

I'm outside The Studio on Chamberlayne Road. A note, flapping in the wind, says the bell is broken. Knock. So I knock. No one comes. I knock again. I peer through the letterbox, straining to see through the wire letter holder. Stripped pine floors. Converse trainers lined up along the hallway. Steep wooden stairs. Footsteps. A man! I start away from the letterbox, hoping he hasn't seen me.

'How's the peep show?' The voice is smiling. I'm mortified. The door opens.

'Oh sorry . . . er . . . I was knocking and no one came.'

'No worries. I'm Josh.' A handsome blond man, late twenties, extends a hard-grip hand. His eyes, an intense cloudless blue, are almost on my eye level, making it hard to look away. His arms are tense with muscle that sinews up to the armholes of his cut-off T-shirt. He is wearing old tracksuit bottoms. Tanned bare feet. He smiles and wipes a tangle of soft blond curls off his forehead, beaded with sweat. He looks vaguely familiar. 'You're Amy? My new recruit,' he says, in a mockney accent.

'Er, yeah. Is Alice here?'

'Yep, upstairs. Hey, don't look so freaked. It's really not hard, we'll take it one step at a time. I'm very gentle with beginners.'

I blush, too aware of Josh's physicality in this narrow hallway. I can almost taste his perspiration. He puts a hand on the small of my back and gently pushes me down the corridor.

'Loo in there,' he says, pointing to a corridor off to the left.

And that's when I see it. A bike, leaning against the wall. A bike painted in rainbow stripes. In a flash I know why Josh is familiar. I blush again. *Please* don't remember me as the girl with loo paper on her shoe.

'Up here,' he says.

We walk up the stairs to the studio. It's a big room in the attic of the building, lit by skylights, rectangular cut-outs of sky. The walls are painted white. The floors are stripped here too. Strange bits of equipment – benches dangling with leather straps and springs – hang from walls and make it look like the set of a porn movie.

'Amy! You made it!' Alice lies flat on her back on a rubbery blue mat. Her legs are splayed apart in a diamond shape, feet touching. Lying next to her, looking equally pornographic, are Jasmine and Blythe. Propped up by lots of pillows, Annabel relaxes on her side. An incense stick dangles precariously from a beam above her head.

'You can change in there,' says Josh, pointing to a cosy side room filled with Moroccan cushions.

'Er, I'm actually wearing my gear.' Baggy old pink tracksuit bottoms, a long T-shirt that covers my bottom. I thought I looked OK when I put them on, but I should have known that Alice and friends would have upped the stakes. Alice is wearing white Thai fishing trousers tied around her waist and a tiny towelling vest top. Ditto Jasmine. Blythe is wearing a low-slung chocolate velour tracksuit. Annabel looks huge and celestial in a billowing white muslin kaftan.

'Great.' Josh doesn't seem to mind. 'Just pop your shoes and socks off then.'

I notice Josh has two pointy canines like David Bowie's (before they were done). Next to Alice and the comfort of a wall, I lie on my blue mat. Our feet say everything: Alice's perfectly pedicured darling toes – glossy pink – and then my neglected yellowing hobbits. Blythe stares at them, horribly fascinated.

110

'Right. I'm not going to give you a long and boring explanation about what we do here,' says Josh, singling me out, making me blush. 'It's Pilates, customised with a bit of yoga. My own special recipe. As the class has heard it all before, far too many times I suspect, I won't bore them. Don't want to send you all into sleep nirvana before we start.' Everyone laughs. 'Amy, you'd be better off staying behind one evening and having a one-to-one. I'll take you through it then. Right now I'm going to throw you in bare feet first and see how you get on. How does that sound?'

Appalling. 'Fine.'

He walks up to me, bends down and whispers, 'Just holler if you want me.' Standing up, he takes command again. 'Right ladies, let's start with a good stretch. Spine stretch forward! Bend over your feet. Amy, watch Alice. Follow her and I'll come and adjust you. Now, first breathe deep into your stomach . . .'

There is a low orgasmic exhalation coming from Annabel's direction. Not to be outdone, Blythe joins in, blowing the air out so loudly and distinctly that you can almost detect her American accent. I feel far too shy to make a noise breathing.

'Now fold over further, wilt like flowers . . .'

I fold, painfully and stiffly. Everyone can touch their toes. I can just about reach my ankles. Then we're doing a thing called 'rolling like a ball', which means curling up like a comma and rocking back and forth. It's harder than it looks. Everyone else rolls backwards neatly. I career off the side of my mat and land on Alice.

Josh walks over. I look up. He hasn't got hairs in his nostrils like Joe. 'You're stronger on one side than the other,' he observes. 'It's very common. You probably pick heavy things up with your right arm.' Evie? 'Or there may be an imbalance in your life.' He looks at me for silent collusion. I don't give him any. 'We need to learn how to balance. Breathe the energy from one side to the other.'

I try to redistribute my energy but still end up rolling off the right-hand side of the mat.

'That's better. You're doing very well.' I appreciate the lie. 'On your tummies. Feet lift. One! Two! Three! Bang those heels together like Dorothy returning to Kansas!' Josh swings his legs off the Pilates Cadillac bench and strides towards me. 'Now ladies, on your backs. Legs above your hips. Open in a glorious V.'

Oh my God. There is a hole in the gusset of my tracksuit bottoms.

'Open, Amy.' Josh is standing in front of me, holding my ankles and pulling my legs gently apart like a compass. 'Open.'

It feels horribly gynaecological. I can feel my legs trying to shut out of embarrassment. The hole. The hole . . .

'Relax, Amy. Now breathe, deep.'

I give in. My legs open. It pulls my inner thighs.

'Beautiful. Feel that stretch all down here.' Josh's finger strokes firmly along my inner thigh, from shockingly close to my crotch to just above my knee. His touch tingles. Josh smiles knowingly, like we've shared a secret, before moving on to Alice who laughs and flirts as he pulls and pushes her into different positions. They spend a lot of time whispering to each other, faces inches apart, curls tangled. Similar physical pedigrees, they could be brother and sister.

Blythe fidgets, impatient. 'It hurts just here,' she whines, transformed from chic New Yorker to needy toddler under Josh's gaze. Josh sits down and puts his knees on either side of her hips and rubs her back. 'That's lovely . . . that's it.'

I'm beginning to understand why Josh is so popular. There are more weird exercises. Most hurt in an assortment of ways. Others threaten to make me break wind and I spend the whole exercise gripping my sphincter muscle. I'm ready to go home when we embark on the agony that is the stomach exercises.

'Elbow to opposite knee. Come on Amy! Breathe in. Pull in that tummy. Squeeze that pencil!'

'Pencil?'

'Your pelvic floor.'

'Oh, OK.' I never was a great one for pelvic floor exercises.

'Squeeze, squeeze . . .'

I'm squeezing. And I'm looking at Josh to ease the pain of the tummy contractions. His curls are gilded by the light in the corner. Behind him is a weeping fig plant. A Greek god.

'Are you feeling it Amy?'

'Umm. Not really.' This only makes Josh more determined. He crouches over my mat, sticks a fist into my lower tummy.

'Right. Hold tight below my fist. Fight against it. Imagine that you are sucking into the earth as you move up towards the sky. Good girl. Squeeeeeeeeeezzze! Do you feel it? Again. And again.'

I squeeze and pull up, panting. Josh is there, encouraging. It's peculiar being so physically close to a near-stranger. I can smell nuttiness on his breath. It's not unpleasant. I pull and I squeeze. Pull and squeeze. And then I feel it. Not the painful crunch of unused tummy muscles, but heat, not unpleasant, glowing between my legs. Is this really a special Pilates recipe?

'Do you feel it?' He studies me intensely.

'Yes, I think I do,' I manage breathlessly.

'Now everyone lie back, shut your eyes and relax.'

Head swimming, I'm relieved to be horizontal. I half open one eye and squint through my lashes to check if everyone else has got their eyes shut. They have. Josh catches my sneaky eye and smiles.

'Breathe.'

A satisfied grunt comes from Annabel's direction. Jasmine's breath vibrates like an asthmatic's snore, while Alice sighs, steady and soft beside me. Suddenly Josh's palm is over my eyes. His hand heat buzzes.

'Relax, sleep for a few moments if that's what your body is telling you to do,' hushes Josh. 'Feel yourself sinking into the floor. Listen to your body. Be mindful of how different it feels compared to an hour ago.' He removes his hand. 'You are feeling sleepy,' he whispers.

But I'm not feeling sleepy. Every time Josh murmurs something soothing, in a quieter and quieter voice, warmth thrills through my lower abdomen. So no, I don't feel sleepy. For the first time in ages, I feel very much awake.

Fifteen

'Coooeeeeeeeeee!' jolts me out of a rather delicious reconstruction of my Pilates class in my head. I was just getting to the good bit.

'Who the hell's that?' mutters Joe. 'Shit! She's let herself in again. I don't believe this.' Joe tugs the duvet up above his head and burrows into the pillow, hung-over after a night sinking pints with Leo.

'Anyone up? Didn't want to wake you so I let myself in,' shouts Mum from downstairs. 'Hope I didn't disturb.'

'Waaaaaaaaaaahhhh!' Evie's rudely awoken too. (She's been up all night so is sleeping in like a teenager.)

Josh scrambles from my head and I'm howled back into the brutal normality of my domestic life. 'Coming Mum, coming. I'll get Evie.' I stumble towards the epicentre of noise. 'Shusssh! There, there.' Unzipped from her sleeping bag, Evie is warm and sweet with the bake of sleep. Gasping at the injustice of being a baby, a woken baby, she nuzzles pathetically into my neck, face wet with tears and snot as I stagger downstairs. My mother stands in the hallway eating an apple vigorously.

'Oh. What are you doing here?'

115

'Some welcome!' My mother is affronted. 'You asked me to come.'

I look at her blankly. There's apple fragment stuck in her lipstick. Something about it, so early in the morning, repels me.

'Eyebrows, remember? Alice booked you something in town and you made a big deal about wanting to go so I've trudged all the way up here, quite happily mind. I'll do anything to help you, especially if that means you smartening up a bit.'

Like you? Pass me the not-too-high court shoes. Buttoned up M & S cashmere cardigan. The white shirts done up to the collar. The tiny row of Grandma's pearls. The look that screams mid-market, mid-England divorcee of a certain age, don't touch! Oh, what am I thinking? I'm so not good first thing in the morning. I bite down hard on the rogue uncharitable thoughts. 'Yes, you have, sorry Mum.'

I try and hustle the baby routine along. Milk powder. Porridge. Spoon thrown on floor. Bowl on floor. Evie screams. Evie snatches at my blueberries. Evie giggles. Mum worships at the altar of the Ikea high chair.

'You've been blessed with such a beauty,' Mum says, swiping my blueberries and halving them with the edge of a tea spoon before popping them into Evie's ready mouth.

'Hmmmm.'

'I said, you've been blessed with such a beauty in Evie,' she repeats loudly.

'I know, thanks.'

'Not in the mood for talking?' This is an accusation. This is the same conversation we've had for years. Mum trying to demand my attention, me retreating. Sometimes the same pattern appears with Joe, despite the fact he's far less pushy, far more self-contained. But familial blue-prints are hard to shake.

'Sorry, I'm just trying to get out of the house.' I must make the appointment. Eyebrows, 'a cheap face lift', Alice calls them, must be one of the easier routes to self-improvement.

'Oh. I won't keep you then. Just one thing though. Remember that nice new neighbour who moved in? When was it? Eleven days ago.'

I shake my head.

'You don't listen, Amy. Well, Norman is his name. Nice man. Tall, all his own hair. He moved in, with a few bits of furniture. And not bachelor furniture either. Looked more like divorce furniture in fact. A Victorian dining table, too big for one, a family coat stand . . .'

'You've been spying!'

'And nice curtains. You can always tell the decent ones by their curtains.' She looks thoughtful. 'I suppose he could be a widower. Yes, that would make sense.'

'Mum!'

'You never know who you might end up with as a neighbour. And I don't mind telling you now – I didn't want you concerned – that I *did* wonder. The funny ones, the ones in the news, are always the quiet types who live on their own, aren't they?' She sighs, discards the teaspoon and starts lazily breaking open blueberries with her teeth before regurgitating them and feeding them to Evie.

I try really hard not to bristle. I'm not one of those mothers, like Hermione, who obsess about hygiene. Hermione sterilizes a dummy if it falls on the floor. I lick it and pop it back in Evie's mouth. (Hermione is astonished Evie has survived thus far.) But I do draw the line at other people's spittle, related or not. Evie is my baby, made from my womb. I don't want her to share bodily fluids with anyone but me. But I'm late, I let it go. 'Really must be off.'

Mum ignores me. 'Luckily I've met him and he isn't funny

at all. Not odd funny I mean. In fact I'm pleased. I think he might be rather helpful. Such a sweet-natured man, he's already offered to come and have a look at my washing machine, damn thing. I was carrying a big basket of dirty stuff – knickers, how embarrassing! – to the launderette when I met him. Had to explain why I was looking like a gypsy! And he offered then. He's an optician, you know. Understands technical things.'

'Like eyes and washing machines.' I sling on an old denim jacket, the one with too-long sleeves that I always intended to get turned up but never got round to.

'You enjoy yourself. Oh, very quickly, I won't keep you . . .' This invariably means she will. 'Where do I find things for Joe's breakfast?'

I look at her blankly, imagining my eyebrows growing longer and bushier by the second like a speeded-up wildlife film.

'Um, don't know. Bread in the freezer? I don't think Joe expects a breakfast from you, Mum. Seriously, just relax and enjoy Evie.'

'Rubbish. Every man needs a decent start. I'm kind of sur-prised you don't have more in the house for him really. You are at home all day.'

'Mum!'

'If you go back to work it'll be different. Then you can call on the "new man", if such a being exists, which I doubt very much. But at the moment—'

'Byeee.' I kiss Evie and run out the door. 9.32 a.m. Shit. I'm never going to make it to Brompton Cross in time. But I can't let Alice down, nor the potential for life upliftment. The choice is stark. Stay with moustache eyebrows or dare step back into Klass Beauty.

*

118

Seeing I've returned, _rish manages a look of triumph, despite the fact that much of her face is shadowed by a vast stye that bulges and weeps over her left eye like a subtropical larva. I am horrified.

'Don't fret, I'll wash my hands,' she says curtly.

Then I notice _rish's eyebrows, how they flick up at the ends and fall towards her nose like skinny men jumping off diving boards. I want to leave, run out of the door. But it would be so rude. Even though _rish repulses me, I don't want to offend her. (Very English.) So I take a deep breath and resign myself to the stained beauty bed, listening out for the squirt sound of the liquid soap dispenser behind me.

'Now, bear with me. It's going to take a little bit longer than normal because I can't see that well today,' _rish croaks. I squeeze my eyes shut and try to mentally practise Pilates exercises. But all I can think of is Josh's brown feet.

No sound of the soap dispenser.

Sixteen

July. Maternity leave nine months in. Evie, eight months and still not sleeping through. Joe in a strop. Run out of nappies. What do I not need? I do not need work to call.

It's not an official call. HR aren't legally allowed to at this stage. Instead I get toxic Pippa, big boss, who sits in a glass office partly obscured by a vast white orchid, 'another gift from a satisfied client', and a huge rolodex that spins and gleams like a piece of industrial machinery. Walking into her office is like stepping off a cool airplane into a suffocating new climate. It has a different atmosphere to the rest of the building: the viscous miasma of Pippa's ego reaches into all of its corners, behind the whiteboard, the Perspex PR awards and the spare pairs of Manolos propped like books on shelves. It catches in your throat like an inhalation of overpowering perfume and remains there long after you've left.

'Hiya! It's Pippa!'

Stunned silence.

'Pippa Price. Work. Remember work?'

'Oh, Pippa! Hi! Hi.' I don't know what to say. 'This is a surprise. Lovely to hear from you.' Obviously it's not.

'Just phoned to see how you are. How's the little 'un?'

'Oh, fantastic.'

'An easy baby?'

'Oh yes. She's no bother,' I lie. And, on cue, Evie shrieks away her good PR. I pick her up and place her on the padded play mat, telephone wedged between ear and shoulder.

'Sorry. That time of day. Um, er . . .' This is her cue. She initiated the call. But Pippa doesn't help me. 'How's work? How's Anastasia doing?' Anastasia is my apparently very beautiful and, I'm fast realising, fiercely ambitious maternity cover.

'She's doing great. Just great. She's won four new accounts since you left. Sits at the desk past eight every night. You couldn't have found a better replacement.'

My heart sinks. 'That's good.'

Evie's foot is caught in a hoop hanging from her play mat and she starts to wail.

'Excuse me, one sec. Sorry. Baby.' I unhook her. 'Yes, sorry about that. Pippa?'

'Still here! Now, I wanted to run something past you quickly,' says Pippa, her voice quickening. She hates the sound of crying babies. 'There are a few accounts I'm not entirely sure what to do with right now. A fabulous new pottery company, make ceramic cutlery. Another doing divine garden tools for the *Desperate Housewives* generation. Well, they're kind of gestating with Anastasia and I'm wondering whether I should let them grow with her . . .' She lets the thought hang in the wire. 'Or prepare the clients for the fact they may soon be moving.'

Help. I need a translator, a code-breaker. I've forgotten the secret language of offices. The silences, the omissions.

'And I was wondering . . . when you might be thinking of coming back, unofficially, just to give me an idea.'

121

'Gosh, Pippa. Um, I really don't know. Can you give me some time to think about it?'

'Nine months not enough? I'd have thought you'd be gagging to get back into the civilisation of an office after all those nappies and nipples. Never saw you as the mother earth type.'

'I need to think things through.'

'Amy . . .' Pippa pauses for just too long to be comfortable. 'Anastasia is very good. That's all I'm saying. Think about it.'

'I'll think about it.'

'Now, I insist you bring Evie into the office so we can all get a look at this tiny new client of yours who's getting all the preferential treatment.'

I laugh weakly. 'Sure. Yes, should do. Thanks Pippa.'

'Look forward to hearing from you very soon, yes?'

'Yes. Bye. Thanks.'

I slam the phone down. Shit, shit, shit. Don't want to think about work. Can't even imagine it.

'What the fuck do I do, Nic?'

Nicola squishes a blunt knife down on to soggy carrot cake. 'Eat this. I'm afraid it's a Nicola Smith creation. Hope you survive it.' She dumps a lump of cake on my plate. It is the ugliest bit of cake I've ever seen, baked ineptly by the worst cook in north west London, but somehow, served up in Nicola's warm yellow West Hampstead kitchen during a blood sugar slump, it's appetising.

'Why pay those ridiculous bijou bakery prices?' she jokes.

'You'll be joining the WI next.'

'Just watch me.' Nicola shovels cake into her mouth. 'Now, that annoying itch that won't go away.'

'Work?' I lean forward in the wicker kitchen chair and stab my elbows on Nicola's old pine table. They stick.

122

Nicola's also the world's worst cleaner. 'You know at times I yearn for it, but part of me, well, I recognise that that life has gone, Nic. Going to work ain't gonna bring it back.'

'What do you mean?'

'A life. And that person. The one who strode off to work, got paid and spent her money on clothes and holidays and bars. That's over isn't it? My income will go towards a new nappy bag or something.'

'Tragic.'

'And part of the fun of my job was not knowing what was going to happen next. You know, being sent off on foreign assignments, meeting new clients . . . the possibility of getting poached. Funny, those once sexy uncertainties now terrify me. What if toxic Pippa tries to send me abroad or something? Nightmare. Who'd look after Evie?'

Nicola laughs. 'Whoa! Amy, no one is about to send you abroad. And if they do, I'll be scrunching myself into your suitcase. Gosh, you're just buzzing with anxieties.'

'No sleep again.'

Nicola nods. She understands completely. This is why it's so much easier hanging out with fellow mums. 'OK, let's work through it. Cons first then.'

'Easy. Evie. Miss her already just thinking about it. Then there's the commute down there. Hideous. Tube journeys with constant fear of being blown up by a terrorist or the morning breath of fellow passengers.' Nicola nods. 'Then, I get to work. I don't want to spend forty hours of my life, Evie's precious life, every week, in a skyscraper.'

'Hmmm.' Nicola's unconvinced. 'But the freedom. Imagine, no more sandpits in the rain, no more—'

'The lifts. I hate those lifts. They have sensors that instruct them to miss a floor if I'm standing on it. They're crammed full of office people with waxy air-con complexions and bad shoes talking inanely about sandwich fillings and their flu symptoms.' Then it hits me. The truth. 'Working in an office, well, it's a bit crap isn't it?'

Nicola smiles dryly. 'It's work, that's why you get paid. You're not stacking shelves.'

'No, but choosing Evie's booties in the morning brings on an existential crisis. How can I PR ceramic cutlery? I'll end up impaling myself on a designer watering can.'

There is a loud scuffle, the sound of nails on wood. 'Miaaoow.'

'Here, Hasselhoff! My beauty.'

Hasselhoff, Nicola's fat old Tom, slobs into the kitchen. Evie and Thomas squeal with delight. Evie's chubby little fingers paw at the air for a whoosh of tail. Nicola fills a cereal bowl with carrot cake and gives it to the cat. He gobbles it noisily.

'Try and ignore Hassie. He eats with his mouth open. Now, back to the nine-to-five dilemma. What are the pros?'

'Money. I've worked harder than I've ever worked in my life looking after Evie and haven't earned a penny. And she never says thank you. And I did love my job, at times. And I was bloody good at it. It would be good to be good at something again.' I sigh and think of my grandma who so wanted to work but granddad wouldn't allow it. 'And I know this sounds a bit silly, but I think I'd feel a bit of a traitor if I gave it all up to bake cakes. After Dad left, Mum worked in crappy jobs, boring clerical jobs, to pay for us all, help us through college, so that I could get a better life and a decent career. She did it without complaining, worked her way up, harder than any man, she always said.'

'Aha! She was a bra-burner?'

I laugh. 'God no. She would never leave the house without peach satin scaffolding. No, Mum just got on with it.'

'So it's about the sisterhood?' says Nicola a little archly.

I laugh. 'Hmmm. Or maybe it's more that I fancy a holiday from the grind. Expenses. Discounts. The chance to spend the day emailing my friends.'

'Sounds like you could go back to work seven days a week now.'

'No way. Having time off has brought home to me that I never felt wholly fulfilled by it.'

'Don't worry, only the tragic ones are. Perhaps subconsciously you were waiting to have a baby.'

'Hmmm, don't think so.' I chew tentatively on Nicola's cake, concerned about my fillings. 'Thing is, I'm not wholly fulfilled by motherhood either. So I suspect I fail rather spectacularly both as a career woman and as a mother. I'd feel less of a freak if I did want to "have it all".'

'No, no, you have mixed feelings. There's your answer,' declares Nicola. 'You must return part time. Work will sort your head out. Sounds to me like you're just in a housewife tizz. You need some structure to your life. Christ, I know I do.'

'Part time? There hasn't been a good precedent for that at Nest. Poor old Abby got fired soon after that "experiment" as Pippa called it. They said she couldn't fit five days' work into three and demanded she work four, and when she refused, off with her head! It's like an Elizabethan Court.'

Nicola laughs and picks a hair out of her mouth. It came from the cake. 'Oh rubbish. You'll be fine. You're brilliant. And besides, the law has changed. They're watching their arses, paranoid they'll dirty their name and be forced to give you a whacking great payout. More cake?'

'No thanks.'

Nicola goes to the loo. I glare at Hasselhoff who is slitting his eyes at Evie, periscoping his tail.

'Hasselhoff, she's a *baby*. She didn't mean to pull your

ear,' I chide, sounding uncannily like my mother. The cat sulkily drags its belly along the floor and leaps on to a chair, spitting dribble on impact. The chair creaks. The fan in the window rattles. The fridge hums. It's a noisy kitchen. Busy on the eye too, a kind of archaeological dig of a house, piles of matter stratified by books, papers, nappies. Chewed photographs flap on the fridge: a flushed Nicola and Sam holding a newborn Thomas; Nicola and Sam kissing on a rainy pebbly beach. Joe and I have no pictures of us up in the house. They sit in boxes, always ready to be framed but somehow never making the framers. Maybe we don't want reminding.

Rat a tat tat!

'Who can that be? This is London, no one just drops round,' shouts Nicola from the loo. 'Can you get that, Amy? I'm mid-pee.'

'Too much information.'

The stained glass of the door tessellates a large figure. The postman? I fiddle with the locks ineptly. I hear someone tutting. A throaty smell of rain hitting dust.

Sue glowers from the step, baby Oliver slung across her body like a third bosom. 'Amy, what are you doing here?'

'Oh, just popped round.'

'You're not coming mother and baby swimming too?' she asks anxiously. 'I didn't book for you as I wasn't informed. If I'd been informed I'd . . .' Sue doesn't enjoy spontaneity. She's one of those women who compensates for the swirling vortex of baby chaos by scheduling and neatly Tupperwaring up the rest of her life.

Nicola rushes into the hall, still buttoning up her trousers. 'Shit, shit. I completely forgot. Head of scrambled egg. Sorry, Sue.'

'You forgot? Oh. Well we'll have to wait a few minutes

anyhow. For Hermione. Her routine doesn't allow her to come out just yet.'

'She's not still doing the dreaded Gina Ford to the letter?' Nicola asks somewhat incredulously. We both gave up on the rigid Ford routine weeks ago because we couldn't bear to wake our happily sleeping babies up for that military schedule. No, we stumbled into a more free-wheeling bohemian approach and have the bags under our eyes to prove it.

We walk through to the kitchen, Sue clocking each scuffed plank of wood, every fur-balled tile and dirty light switch on the way.

'It's very, er, homely,' she notes. 'You have animals?'

'A cat,' says Nicola.

'Oh. With a baby. That's brave,' Sue says, as if Nicola admitted to breeding Rottweilers. She glances at Evie and Thomas, contentedly sitting side by side in their car seats, great viewing platforms for the big game. 'Well, it seems they're surviving it,' she adds quickly. 'I wouldn't leave them too long in those seats though. New research says that it can compress their spines and cause all manner of damage.'

Nicola bristles. 'Thomas is happier in a car seat than anything else. As long as it's not in the car of course. Yes, I know, he's eccentric. He hates Baby Bjorns with a passion, car motion, baby bouncers.'

'Still, I've read—'

'If it works . . .'

Sue sits at the table and carefully swipes away the crumbs in front of her with the side of her palm and snow-banks them beside the teapot. She leans back – the chair groans – and fixes me with a watery eye. 'Your eyebrows! Have you had an accident?'

'Yes, a couple of weeks ago at the hands of a beautician with a vision-impairing stye. But I thought they'd grown back.'

'A stye!' Sue recoils back into her chair, rolls of flesh rising between the chair spindles like unbaked baguettes. 'Isn't that contagious?' She pulls Oliver deeper into the valley of her lap. When she picks up the cup of tea that I've made her, she swivels the cup round and doesn't touch the handle. 'Interesting cake, Nicola. Right girls, what's news?'

'We were just discussing work. What Amy should do. Came to the conclusion she should go back part time.'

'Hmmm,' says Sue, fat pink fingers busy with Oliver's cradle cap. 'Tough one. I'll go back to teaching eventually, but only when I'm ready. Alan's very good like that. He's been saving. Not everyone has Alan's foresight mind you. I'm sure Joe would have done the same had it occurred to him.' Any money Joe and I had was frittered on holidays and meals out and good wine. 'What about you, Nicola?'

Nicola's eyes are drilling into her cup of tea. It's a dangerous moment. We must not look at each other or we'll start giggling. And the guilt we feel for giggling makes the giggles worse. No, Sue doesn't really deserve it. She may be tactless, interfering and idly competitive, but she means well. While we certainly wouldn't have hung out in any other circumstances, only thrown together because our labour dates coincided after all, we've learned to rub along. The days are very long otherwise.

'Back to work. Full time. Probably in the not-too-distant future,' says Nicola, guardedly.

Sue puts down her cup loudly. 'Really, Nicola? *You*? I would never have guessed,' she says, as if Nicola had just come out as a suburban swinger. 'And a newspaper too? That *must* mean long hours. Having to write all those upsetting stories about murdered children and door-stepping grieving parents?'

'Sue, I'm a sub. I sit at a desk and edit copy.'

'That poor little boy. He'll miss you so much, Nicola,' says

Sue, an expert at the disturbing backhanded maternal compliment.

'He'll be fine.' Nicola is putting a brave face on things because she has to.

'But Nic—'

'We've got a two-income mortgage here,' points out Nicola, exasperated. 'And I actually happen to like my job. Full-time motherhood will never be for me. I'd be miserable.'

The crackle of social static is broken by a knock on the door. It is Hermione. Tiny, pretty in a floral Boden jacket, she shakes the rain off her hair and removes her doll-baby from a Baby Bjorn papoose.

'Sorry I'm a bit late. Amelia was in doze time.'

'Carrot cake?'

'Is it organic?'

Nicola shakes her head. Hermione declines. Sue fills her in on the disastrous revelation and locks Hermione into a conspiratorial we-must-save-her gaze.

'Oh, Nic,' whines Hermione. 'I'm sorry.'

'What about you, Hermione?' I say in an attempt to save Nicola from further goading. 'Aren't you going back to your accountancy job?'

'My priorities have changed,' Hermione says solemnly. 'Numbers, too dry. Hours, too long. I just don't care as much as I used to. So no, I'm not returning to accountancy . . .' She clears her throat and announces solemnly, 'I am going to open a cashmere baby sock mail-order catalogue.'

Oh God. Death by boredom. What am I doing in this conversation? With these people? Am I one of them? Nicola looks similarly aghast: she pummels Hermione with invisible booties fired from between her eyes.

'What a wonderful idea, Hermione,' says Sue, waving a just-picked crust of cradle cap between finger and thumb.

129

But Hermione doesn't answer. Hermione has gone pale, upper lip curling in disgust, eyes fixed on the chair adjacent to her where Hasselhoff dribbles and purrs at the enchanted Amelia.

'A cat! The bloody cat! It just *licked* Amelia,' she gasps. 'Amelia is *allergic* to house pets.' Hermione scrabbles her things into her multi-pocket pink nappy bag, scoops up Amelia and backs towards the door. Amelia stretches out for her feline tormentor.

'And such a wormy looking creature too,' Sue adds unnecessarily.

Office life just got more appealing.

Seventeen

Joe slumps on a wooden chair on the balcony, long legs stretched out, feet blue-white and bare. His eyes are shut, just crescents of black lashes. The late afternoon sun breaks over him, Crayola orange. As a wasp vibrates noisily past his ear his face suddenly tightens, black clouds blow behind his eyes. Trapped in an uncomfortable dream, the dozy carefree man has gone. Eyes still shut, Joe twists his hands, locks his knuckles.

Joe's anxieties are revealed in detailed minutiae – a leg twitch, a word that comes out too fast, too hard – and they're manifesting themselves more frequently. Perhaps infidelity exerts its own revenge. I stare at him intensely, this troubled, beautiful man cast gold, as if I can bring him into wakefulness by will. He jolts.

'Amy? Evie? Where's Evie?' He is panicked.

'Zedding away.'

'God, I was having the most awful dream. That you'd got lost by the sea and I couldn't find you and something was chasing me, me and Evie . . . Waves. Ugh. Horrible. You don't want to know.'

The hair on my arms prickles. Because Joe has funny

dreams. He once dreamed about a plane's emergency landing on a flight back from Paris, two nights before it happened, to us. He dreamed about Kate's mum dying in a car crash, a year before her Golf drove into the back of a horse truck. He dreamed about us getting together. Little coincidences, he says. Freaky, I say.

My bad dreams are usually about Evie, about my fears; fears that cling to my legs like a scared child. Pit bull attack. Terrorist biological attack. Meningitis. These are the fears you can't voice as that would be neurotic and you can't ignore them because that would somehow tempt them into being. You have to warily keep them at a respectful distance, like an odd-looking man walking in front of you on a dark street.

'She's fine. I've just checked her. Blowing bubbles in her sleep. Chuntering away.'

'Come here.' Joe pulls me on to the bench of his knee. 'It was a horrid dream,' he says softly, voice clotted with sleep. 'So nice to wake up and there you are.' He buries his face in my hair. 'Don't ever go.'

I should perhaps say, 'I won't ever go,' like a mother to a child. But I can't. So I stroke his head, wondering if this is how our relationship is going to be played out. Sideways, half asleep.

'But you are leaving me, aren't you?' he says, squinting. 'Very soon.' What? 'Aren't I looking after Evie while you go to Pilates?'

'I thought you were talking about work.'

'Work?'

'My job, remember? My past life.' Joe rubs his eyes. 'They phoned yesterday. Wanted to know when I'm coming back.'

'Isn't that illegal?'

'Do I look like I'm going to press charges? It was Pippa.'

'And?' Joe is one of those men who doesn't want to be seen to be influencing a woman's key decisions, a kind of inverse sexism, well intentioned but slightly irritating.

'Sometimes I think I just want to stay home with Evie all the time, live like Annabel and Blythe, get some extra help and do my courses, go to the gym . . .'

Joe's face drops. 'Isn't there a middle ground? With just one salary, I'm not sure we can—'

My mobile beeps: Alice.

'I'm late. Sorry, Joe. Let's talk later. You OK looking after Evie for a bit?'

'Of course. I love looking after Miss Costello. Besides, if it stops your mother coming round it's worth it. And you need some time out. Really, take as long as you need.' He staggers up from the chair and brushes down his cords. He has a crease on his cheek where his head's lolled against the hard wood, like a baby's pillow mark. 'Come on, I'll put Evie in the back of the car and drive you down there.'

Joe's sweetness pinches. I am not the self-sacrificing mother he thinks I am. My whole day has been a mere box-ticking countdown – walk, lunch, nap, tea – to get to this point. Then I remind myself I have nothing to feel guilty about. Not where Joe's concerned.

'Right, how are we feeling?' asks Josh, nimbly picking his way between the blue mats like towels on a crowded beach.

'Wonderful,' says Alice. 'You're a magician, Josh.'

Her toes curl with pleasure. They are Glastonbury toes, still sporting a backstage tan and a Green Field henna tattoo that twists over the tendons. I feel a shudder of nostalgia for my old life, my leaking tent, Radiohead live, the glorious mud-pie of '98. Looking back, it seems that all happened to someone else. I fear that if I returned to the festival I'd be one of those slightly embarrassing thirtysomethings who bring smoke-free firelighters, camp in the family field because it is stewarded and complain about the noise from the dance tent.

'*Fab-u-lous*,' mutters Blythe stretching her body violently as if in spasm.

Whoomp! A foot in my shin, a hand in my face. 'Sorry,' I say, automatically.

Blythe, eyes closed – possibly glued shut with mascara – doesn't apologise but inches her limbs out of the collision path. She has no spatial awareness. Anyone with the misfortune of being on an adjacent mat to Blythe finds themselves assaulted by her during the class. Her hair in your mouth. Foot on your foot. Blythe is the kind of woman who always stands within your personal space even if there's hundreds of square footage.

'How's this, Alice?' Josh massages Alice's shoulders, the usual routine.

'That hits the spot, Josh. Great.'

It's amazing how relaxed Alice is with Josh. I can't imagine ever unwinding that much with a man with whom I wasn't intimate.

Josh tuts. 'You've got to take more care picking up Alf.'

'I know, I know.'

'Get that nanny of yours workin' girl,' mutters Blythe sleepily. We all laugh.

'Right, you can all get up now. Slowly. Roll on to your right side – Annabel you stay on the left – and push yourself up gently. Breathing . . . that's it. Amy, don't forget to breathe. You'll die if you don't.'

I take a lungful of air. Too close to the floor, it tastes of dust.

'Now give yourself a clap and a hug.'

A hug?

He demonstrates by wrapping himself in his muscle-knotted

134

arms. So we clap and then we self-hug. Josh seems to sense my cringe, walks over and presses down on my shoulders.

'Relax, Amy. I know it's a bit weird but it works. Don't worry, you don't look as silly as me.' I smile appreciatively. 'You are dismissed!' He laughs. 'Go get changed. Amy, I think we should have that quick chat now and run through a few of the basics.'

'Er, no, sorry, I've got to go . . .'

Alice looks up sharply. 'Amy! What did I say? Spend some time on yourself. Stay and have a chat with Josh, it'll be interesting.' Is that a wink?

I follow her into the stuffy changing room. She poufs up my lank hair.

'Oh dear.' Alice pulls a finger along my disfigured brows. 'Not good. But it could be worse,' she adds, with forced jaunt. She was really pissed off when I told her I visited _rish. 'Eyebrow pencil will fix this temporarily. Then you'll have to go and see my eyebrow fairy in Brompton Cross.'

Right now, it seems highly unlikely that I will ever become the kind of woman who has an eyebrow fairy in Brompton Cross.

Blythe appears and zooms in for a close-up. 'Can you sue?'

'At least Luigi won't make a folly of your follicles,' says Alice.

'Luigi?' A delicatessen?

'Hair, Amy. Hair. Get with the program. Next week isn't it? It'll make the biggest difference. It'll take five years off you.'

Oh. I'm only 31.

Everyone starts stripping, shaking off their tracksuit bottoms, tugging at little white vests, down to their underwear. What underwear! Even Annabel's knickers are a froth of lace and polka dots, while Jasmine looks positively burlesque.

135

Me? Big off-white knickers, fraying elastic. Old pink bra. How could I have been so stupid? Again.

'No-sex-please . . .' Alice whispers into my ear, pointing at my knickers.

I manage a laugh. 'Must try harder.'

Blythe is the last one out, slamming the door behind her, making the palm plant quiver. Josh squats down on a Pilates bench. His drawstring trousers – picked up on some Goan beach probably – ride up. His lower legs are hairy and tanned. Without the others, the room shrinks rather than grows because there are no obstacles between me and Josh, not even a blue mat, let alone the giant swell of Annabel. I am directly in his sight line, wondering whether to sit down casually or carry on standing, weight falling from foot to foot.

'Do sit down,' says Josh. 'Here, for starters . . . on that ball.' He points to something that looks like a large beach ball. 'It's really good for the spine. Straddle it and bounce up and down, very gently.'

I roll the ball towards me and aim my bum as if mounting a space hopper.

'Steady!'

'Whoa! Got it, got it,' I gasp, restraining the ball between my inner thighs.

'And bounce.'

So I bounce, gently, trying to close myself off to the innate pornography of the movement. Got to stop thinking like this. A Pilates class. Not a date.

'Okey dokey. That's great. Whoa! Steady, steady. Good. Before we go through the basic physical stuff – I've got a printed sheet for you – I need to work out where you're coming from. My personal theory is,' Josh clears his throat, 'that so much of our physicality comes from our emotions. It's about the bright lights that whirr around your head, the chakras. Everyone has different coloured auras. Like the northern lights.'

'Sure.' I try and concentrate on what he's saying, but my eye is sucked towards his tanned bare feet. It's so unusual to see a man with good, edible feet.

'I think yours is a rich hemp brown.'

'Oh.'

'Hey, don't look so put out! Brown like the earth. That's a good thing.'

'Lilac or pink sounds prettier.'

Josh laughs. 'Well, let's work on it.' His head drops to the side, suddenly serious. 'It'd be good if you felt a bit lighter.'

'Yes, there is this size ten dress I've been dying to get back into.'

He winks playfully. 'Don't mean that. I mean lighter, more colourful.'

'I'm not with you.'

'It must be hard. You know, motherhood, being a parent. Such a big responsibility.' His laugh ruffles the air like a fan. 'I still forget to feed my cat.'

'Well, you learn.' I stop bouncing, gather my breath and thoughts. 'I was never the nurturing type before I had Evie, you know.'

'I find that hard to believe.'

'No, really. I thought other people's babies were really cute, like puppies are cute. But I didn't crave one at my breast like some women do. I didn't ache for something to look after.'

'It just kind of happened, huh?' He looks at me intensely, like he's trying to work me out. No one's looked at me like that for a very long time. 'It was obviously meant to be. You must be harbouring great genetic material.'

'It seems that way. Evie's the best.'

He raises an eyebrow. 'And you don't forget to feed her?'

'Something kicks in,' I laugh. 'Don't worry, you'd make a fine mum.'

Grinning widely, he pushes one leg under the other, into the lotus position. 'Tough for the relationship too?' he asks casually.

I look up sharply. This isn't Josh's terrain.

'Sorry. If . . . if you don't mind me asking.'

'At times,' I say quietly, aware that confession is a betrayal of confidence. But Josh is surprisingly easy to talk to.

'One minute you're lovers, the next grown-ups thinking about inoculations and child trust funds. I'd find it, well,' he pans the ceiling for a word, 'discombobulating.'

'*Discombobulating*?' I smile.

'You love that word too?'

I do. It's one of my favourite words. He must be the only man I've ever met who's used it.

Josh unfolds his legs, fluid when he moves, oiled joints. Flipping off the Pilates bench, he walks towards me, cutting the distance between us in quick, long paces so that I have to stop myself from gasping because he's so close I can almost reach out to him. The air seeps with his smell – laundered cotton and fresh perspiration – and I wonder if I'm entirely sane, and wish that I'd just snap out of this silly crush-like thing that's developing.

'Keep bouncing.' Josh is behind me, hands on my shoulders. I bounce on the ball manically, feeling increasingly uncomfortable because suddenly he's all too present. I can feel the pulse in his palm.

'You know what I think?' says Josh softly.

An image of him bending me over the ball flashes through my head.

'I think,' he presses his palms down firmly, breath dampening my earlobe. 'I think you want to feel *visible* again.'

138

I stop bouncing. What? I am astonished to hear my words fall from his pink mouth.

'Am I right?'

'Er, yes, kind of.' Am I that obvious? Or is Josh incredibly intuitive? It's like he knows me already.

'We'll make you the most visible girl in the room,' he declares, walking back to the bench. Suddenly I feel his absence, want that firm touch back. 'It's mostly about posture and breathing and this muscle that runs behind your spine, the source of the back's strength and your power as a woman . . .' And so Josh goes on.

I continue bouncing and nod my head but I'm not really taking anything in, just entranced by the cadence of his voice, the flash of brown ankle, his biceps, round and hard, like potatoes under the skin.

After the class I walk home, feeling somehow denser, more significant. There is an unfamiliar hum between my legs, white noise. Could my libido finally be waking from its long afternoon nap?

Eighteen

A sticky hot July day. I stir gravy, mind elsewhere. Since my last class, my body has become what Josh might call 'present'. But not spiritually present. No, if anything life's gone a bit Carry On. I keep catching the swell of my breasts in mirrors. Parsnips make me smile. And I look at the banisters and imagine myself sliding down them, naked.

'Oh it's just not fair.' Kate wipes a tear from her eye with a napkin that I used earlier to wipe Evie's nose and I'm jolted back to normal life.

Kate has invited herself over for Sunday lunch. She's not happy. She has had an argument with Pete. *Kate* wants to fill in the swimming pool and create a landscaped Japanese garden. *Pete* wants to keep the pool. Not that bad? Oh, it is. You see, it's not about the pool at all. No. There's a subtext: babies. Pete doesn't want to do any more work on the house because he doesn't want to have any more on-going commitments to Kate because she has not produced an heir to his father's wheelie bin empire. He won't admit this, of course. It's a big mess.

'Joe, what do you think?'

'I think,' says Joe, exasperated, 'you need to take a deep breath and pull yourself together.'

'Oh Joe!' Kate dissolves into the snotty napkin again, shoulders shaking.

I look at Joe sharply. 'Bit harsh,' I mouth over Kate's head. 'There, there Kate. It's going to be fine. Wine? A lump of garlic bread?'

'Atkins,' she sobs, shaking her head. Then with a guttural gasp she sucks the sobs back in, fans herself with her hand. 'I'm being silly. This is ludicrous. God, sorry for causing such a scene on such a lovely sunny Sunday.' She shoots Joe a long apologetic look. 'I know you don't want to hear about me and Pete.'

Joe smiles weakly. 'Don't be silly.' He slices into the honey-roast chicken carefully, smiling at its perfect honeyed crackle. Joe's a good cook. That was one of the things I first liked about him. He'd fry me pancakes in the morning, big gloopy American ones stained with berries and syrup. He didn't really like them – he's more of a savoury man – but he knew I did. Previous boyfriends always stopped cooking food – and exhausted their recipes – by about date five. Then they'd expect me to do the cooking.

Joe mashes Evie's roast potato with a fork. She thumps her fist on her high-chair table, sending bits of it flying on to Kate's fawn cashmere jumper. Joe flicks it off, apologising. Kate tells us about the Nook, how she's wallpapered the annexe off the main guest bedroom for Evie. (Osborne and Little.)

'Amy? Hello?' Kate waves a fork in my face.

'Sorry, miles away.'

'I was saying that you and Joe must come and stay. August? The 17th would be good for us. We're pretty booked up this summer. It should be really great weather by then.'

'Lovely, don't you think, Joe?'

Joe frowns. 'Um, I think I've got a work thing,' he says. 'I'll have to check.'

Right. My heart sinks. Please not another one. Then I suddenly remember. 'No. That's the weekend you *were* going to go away.' I dagger Joe across the table. He studies the slick of gravy embracing the carrots. 'The thing you cancelled.'

Kate catches the slice in my voice and looks at me quizzically. Joe looks moody.

'Oh come on!' exclaims Kate, with the exuberance of the just-stopped-crying. 'The 17th it is.'

'Let's speak nearer the time,' says Joe. 'It'll probably be just the Friday.'

Why can't he just commit to arrangements? What's the better option he might miss out on?

Now Kate daggers Joe. She doesn't like her hospitality refused. It's not unconditional.

Luckily we have Evie as a distraction and peacekeeper. I fuss, pick up the plastic cutlery that Evie jettisons from her high chair, mash her banana, mix her milk, pretending I'm on planet infant while actually, perversely, living on planet Josh. The lunch drifts on for another couple of hours in a brothy cloud of chicken and babies and private dangerous thoughts.

'Amy? You're really not all here today.' Kate snaps the lid on to her lipstick. 'Joe has kindly offered to drive me to the station. The Range Rover is being serviced after the collision with my neighbour's bloody free-range goat.'

'Hmmm. No, you don't look quite yourself,' says Joe concerned. 'A bit wild-eyed and pale.'

'Thanks.'

Joe helps Kate into her light cashmere Joseph coat, the kind I've always wanted but costs more money than I could ever justify now. (Joseph coat = ninety packets of nappies.)

'Why not have a sleep?' Kate says.

'Would love to. But, in case you haven't noticed, I have a baby to look after.' Shit! Wrong thing to say. Kate winces.

Joe puts a *shush* hand on my arm. 'I'm going to pop into town after the station if that's OK.'

'Really?' Another little absence.

'Selfridges. Ashak at the shoe menders says these old boys are beyond repair.'

The door slams. Kate's perfume hovers over the kitchen table. I wave it away with my hand, move the tulips back to the sideboard and Joe's black media TV glasses off the table. I mentally reclaim my house. Mine, all mine. How I miss living alone.

I change Evie into a fresh nappy, ready for her sleep. Her skin is so soft it feels damp. Her eyes are locked into mine, following me around the room. Sometimes this dependency makes me dizzy with love. Other times, like today, it brings on a strange, cloying claustrophobia. I have to push down the clawing desire to break free, to run, to dance, into the pit of my stomach. And there it stays, a silent creature spitting up disorienting vapours, tastes of freedom.

Josh slips straight into my mind as I surface into consciousness; curls trembling around his face, breath hot, arms outstretched as he falls towards me against a block of Yves Klein blue sky.

The radio alarm flickers 4.05 p.m. Does the screening of a Pilates instructor rom-com (in privacy of own head) make me a bad mother? Does motherhood really require a complete sublimation of the self, or just the bits that are public? Hmmm. I swing myself off the bed, in that wobbly sleep-in-the-afternoon way, feet slapping the waxy white floorboards. Check Evie. Asleep, good. Food. Mum filled the house with 'men's rations' – bacon, eggs, sausages – last time she was here. Armoury for me to keep my man. I pick at some salami, chewing the flecks of white fat like gum. I turn on the baby monitor. Evie, purring. On the sofa, sinking into a fake fur cushion – dreadlocked by regurgitated breast milk – I conjure back the warm sugar rush of my dream. And for the first time in months, naughty thoughts streak, trip and cartwheel through my head, the head of no-sex-please Amy Crane! How ridiculous.

Then I get an idea. It's a silly idea. But it's a harmless idea. And it's a challenge. Astonished at my audacity, I go upstairs, face my chest of drawers, take a deep breath and plunge my hand into the deepest recess of the top left drawer, a lair of bras that no longer fit and odd socks. No, not it. No. No. Oh? My fingertips stick to something rubbery and vegetal. I pull it out. No batteries? I scamper into the kitchen and dis-embowel the cappuccino frother. Back in the privacy of the bedroom I slide the batteries into my dusty, much-unloved Rabbit. Despite its age and lack of use it leaps into alarming life, purring and pulsing like a Magimix. I can't. I must. I need to know if I still can. So mother and machine meet, somewhat awkwardly, with more than a little performance anxiety. I wait for my Meg Ryan moment. Nothing. Nothing. I think about Evie sleeping next door – such a sordid mother – and check the time on the radio alarm. Three min-utes already. Takes its time. A twitch? Yes, yes. Definitely something. Yes, this thing is persuasive. Focus. Succumb to the drum. Close my eyes. Concentrate.

Oh! I can.

Spent, exhilarated and as thrilled as I was when I had my first orgasm age seventeen, I lean back on the pillows with a satisfied sigh. A milestone. I close my eyes and feel like Sophie Dahl in that Opium ad.

Then a shout. 'Amy? Are you OK?'

Joe! Back already? Christ. 'Er, fine. Down in a sec.'

I yank on my knickers and jeans, throw the offending object to the back of the drawer and hurtle downstairs, red faced.

'Hi love. You OK? Haven't hurt yourself?'

'No, why?'

'Baby monitor.' He points to the loudspeaker. 'I have ways of hearing what you do . . .'

Nineteen

Last night Evie went off like a smoke alarm. I did the 'controlled crying' thing, as recommended by Hermione, but gave in after the second five-minute stint because Evie sounded like she was dying. Cue me rocking her like a madwoman, tunelessly wailing 'Old Macdonald had a farm' while Evie chewed her pink teething gums on my little finger. Both of us collapsed in a bundle of exhaustion on the spare bed at about five. I feel truly dreadful. Some kind of punishment for my selfish encounter with the Rabbit?

I squint out of the fume-misted bus window. Could that be it? My eyesight is worse than ever. Squint again. Big plates of sparkling glass. Women shaking out shiny hair as the doors swing behind them, hailing cabs. 'Luigi's' picked out in black serif-free letters against a sage-green background. I'm not feeling up to this. I haven't been to a decent hairdresser in an age.

I leap off the bus into the path of a cursing cyclist, who narrowly misses amputating my toes. Luigi's doors are so heavy I must lean all of my bulk against them. Then, unexpectedly, at about a forty-degree angle they fling open easily, flipping me across the hall to the reception desk like a skittle. I brake with my elbows, sending leaflets flying.

'And how can I help you?' snaps a lipsticked mouth, curtained behind conker-brown hair. Her long thin fingers scrabble together the leaflets, sideways like crabs.

'Highlights. Trim,' I say. 'With Luigi, I think. Then I'm seeing Mia for a cut.'

'Your name please.'

'Amy Crane.'

She suspiciously double-checks her notes, lightening somewhat when she sees confirmation. 'Please get an overall from Judith and take a seat.'

Judith, the middle-aged posh lady in the coat cupboard, holds my three-year-old Kookai coat at arm's length and hands me a complicated-looking grey overall, trailing ribbons. I plunge my arms into what are possibly armholes.

'No, the other way, Madam,' she corrects. 'It ties at the back.'

Sinking into a leather chair – too low for elegant entry or exit – I eye my fellow customers. A model type giggles into her mobile phone, cupping a mini-me dog in the other hand. Two Chelsea middle-youth types – the clothes and hair of thirty-year-olds, faces ten years older – study magazines intently, searching for that husband-keeping beauty tip. No one looks at me; off radar. I flick through a price menu. What? It costs how much? *OhMyGod*. Ridiculous! Surely it never used to cost so much. I'm out of here.

I'm almost done untying the Houdini-thwarting overall when the doors blast open. A gust of fumey warm air. A clatter of colliding studded belt, bag and bangles.

'And where are you going?' says Alice.

Getaway foiled.

'Um, nowhere.' I'm humbled by the sight of Alice's legs,

147

tanned with strappy Roman sandals coiling up them like snakes. She is by far the most glamorous woman here and everyone else knows it. They study her discreetly over the tops of their magazines and double-take when Alice hugs me.

'I was just round the corner and after browgate thought I'd better check in. How are you getting along?'

'Oh, just realised my entire life has been a bad hair day.'

'Tracy!' Alice calls over to a sulky, overly tanned teenager fingering a hairbrush aimlessly near the reception desk. 'Two cappuccinos please. Thanks, sweetie.'

'You look so well, Alice. Radiant.'

'Thanks. Shouldn't do, had about two hours' sleep . . .'

'Really? So have I.'

'. . . After a night of shagging,' she giggles. I notice her lips are all puffy, almost bruised. 'You?'

'My insomniac daughter.'

'That won't be the reason for long. Luigi is going to turn you into a sex goddess. Joe won't be able to keep his hands off you.'

'Who with?' I'm not letting this one go.

'What?'

'Who's the fellow shagger?'

Alice blushes. She must like him. 'No one you know. Now where are those coffees?'

It irritates me that Alice is so private about her private life while being so invasive when it comes to mine.

'We thought Annabel had started the big push last night.' Alice peers over her cappuccino, which is served in a cup the size of a breakfast bowl when it arrives.

'It's coming? Early?'

'No. Only pretending apparently. Fake contractions. But it does suggest she may not stay pregnant for ever, as we were all beginning to suspect. So, after some serious procrastination, the baby shower has been scheduled at last. You're invited. A week Friday. We should just about be able to throw it before the baby crowns.'

'I am?' This is the invitation I was dreading. What the hell do you buy the mother who has everything?

'I'm worried about her actually,' says Alice, suddenly serious.

'Oh?' I wouldn't put Annabel on any kind of At Risk register.

She groans. 'That bloody doula, Ms Marhajessh of Belsize Park. Annabel is disregarding most of the expert, and hugely expensive, medical staff at St John and St Elizabeth's and instead following Ms M.'s bizarre pregnancy diet and fanny-stretching practices.'

I'm lost.

Alice laughs. 'I'll dilate on the subject. Annabel is not allowed to eat sugar . . .'

'My pregnancy would have been inconceivable without it.'

'. . . Or bread or anything with a white grain in it, which is fine for the rest of us – including you, Miss Crane – but even I draw the line at the pregnant woman denying herself. And then she spends most of her evenings stretching her fanny. I'm not joking. While the rest of us are considering fanny tucks, Annabel's lying flat on her back, pulling down on her perineum to make it wider! She's lost it.'

'*LADIES*!' shrieks a high-pitched voice over my left shoulder. '*Oh, ladies.*'

'Luigi! Baby!' Alice wraps herself around Luigi like a bendy roller. They smother each other in kisses.

Luigi is a fiftysomething in cowboy boots, leather trousers and an open suit jacket, flashing a fuchsia silk lining and lipo belly. His black (dyed) hair pouffs above his forehead like a wave about to break, trickling into a pony-tail at the back.

'This is my friend Amy. The one I wanted you to meet.'

'Oh, niceshhhh to meet you, Amy,' says Luigi, looking vaguely disappointed. 'You gonna stay, Alice?'

'Can't I'm afraid. Got to pick up Alfie from his celebrity play date.'

'Networking already?'

'Ah, get away!' laughs Alice.

I wish desperately that Alice would stay. The thought of having to make small talk with Luigi for hours is excruciating.

Another cappuccino and three glossies later (I'm kept waiting – as soon as Alice left my stock fell), I'm finally ensconced in a swivelling leather chair, Luigi BacoFoiling up my hair. The small talk I feared hasn't materialised – Luigi is saving his voice for more important customers – and I am desperate for the loo, made worse by my view of the salon's centrepiece, a sheet of shimmering water tumbling on to a pile of white stones. But it seems the master cannot be inter-rupted mid-flow, because when I mention the loo he ignores me as if I've mentioned something unspeakable like vaginal dryness.

'How do ya know Alice?' he asks eventually, breaking his metallic crunch and fold rhythm.

I swivel my head round to face him, but he continues to address my reflection in the teak-framed mirror. I forgot about the hairdresser–client refractive relationship. Dis-combobulating, I think suddenly. Josh's smile, his Bowie teeth flashing again. 'Babies. Similar ages, hers a bit older.'

'Okaaay. Divine girl. If I were the marrying kind, she'd be mine by now. Just wish she'd pick a nice man though. Every time I see her there's another d-r-a-m-a,' Luigi whines. 'Alice comes in here and she's like, "Luigi honey, Tom's so sweet". Ten weeks later, it's like "Tom's an arse. Andreas is just a darling . . . I think he might be the one." And so on. If she could just find a man that outlasted her roots I'd be happy.'

This smarts. Why doesn't Alice talk about men with me? There are whole compartments of Alice I never knew existed, which are walk-in to everyone else.

'Who's the latest?' I sleuth.

'Sheeete, what was his name?' Luigi rubs his belly. 'John? No. Jeff? No. God, I don't know. But you should. Sounds like you ladies talk about everything. Enough to make a man blush. Now, sweetie, you're done.'

My head looks like a scrap yard.

'Tortoiseshell gold. Divine.' He pats the crunchy folds of his work. 'Tracy!' he shrieks. 'Where *is* Tracy?'

The doleful Tracy appears and attempts to install me under a helmet heater. No. I leap up. I *have* to go to the loo.

'Just down there on the left,' monotones Tracy, nail-bitten finger pointing vaguely.

I finally find the loo in the maze of mirrors and basins and swivelling chairs. And it is the most beautiful loo I have ever seen; gleaming white marble, rows of orchids, individual soft towels. I'm moved, almost to tears, by its beauty. It's been so long, a different life, since I stepped into this candle-scented world of 'me time'.

I fight through my overall, squat and pee. Check myself in the mirror. I look washed out against the silver of my highlight wraps. Pale lilac butterflies have settled under my eyes. I pull my overall ribbons to tie the waist. Wet. They are wet. I sniff them: pee. Oh god! I have peed on my overall ribbons! The shame! I try to run them under the tap but the stainless steel proboscis is so minimalist I can't figure out how it works. I push and pull it in different directions and no

151

water seems to come out. Then finally, like the door, it gives in suddenly and easily, water spurting loudly, splashing my overall. I could have spilt a glass of water I tell myself, walking out, fast and flustered, into the halogen sparkle of the salon.

'Ooops,' says Tracy, eyeing my overall and pushing me under the heater with the briskness of a negligent care worker. She clicks some switches and wanders off.

I sit there for forty-five minutes, head hot with highlights and images of Josh's feet and thinking how wonderful it is not to be dealing with the poos and possets of a small baby, and trying not to think of the cost, which looks like it might amount, shamefully, to the same figure as Evie's recently received government baby bond.

Foil removed, Luigi appears. 'Gor-geous,' he drawls, clinking his cowboy boot toe against the chrome chair leg. 'You love it?'

If I didn't I wouldn't dare say so. But I do. For the first time in years my hair doesn't look like it needs a wash. I am a different colour. I am a blonde. Not mousy. Not green-tinged. I am a real life honey-blonde! It does make a difference. Alice was right. Project Amy is working! I am getting there. My reflected self breaks into a sunshine smile.

'You look happy,' says a woman's voice behind me without introduction. 'I'm Mia.' A tiny woman with red corkscrew curls tugs at my hair with marmoset hands. 'You're a bit wet.'

'Spilt water.'

'Funny smell. Must be the peroxide.'

Unexpectedly, I am not crucified by this observation. My new blonde hair has emboldened a little of a new self, the kind of self that would think, never confess, never apologise. 'Must be,' I say.

Mia lifts up a shaft of hair with a comb, different lengths and feathery split ends haloed by the light. 'Dear me. Who last cut it?'

Oh what the hell. Deep breath. 'My mother.'

Twenty

Josh loves my hair. He bent over my blue mat yesterday evening and, breath fragrant with roasted pumpkin seeds, whispered, 'Your hair is stunning. I adore your new hair.' I blushed from my ears to my toes and my rolling-like-a-ball went skew-whiff.

Joe doesn't love it. 'Not really, Amy, no,' he says, leaning against the white penguin enclosure wall at Regent's Park Zoo.

Evie fell asleep within ten minutes of arriving at the zoo. Real animals don't match up to any of her Baby Einstein DVDs. But Joe and I are persevering in order to justify the extortionate ticket price.

'Everyone else likes it.'

'OK, it's fine. There's nothing wrong with it, other than that now, presumably, you have enrolled in the hairdresser-every-month club. It'll be like a second mortgage.'

'You're a misery,' I spit, looking anywhere but at him.

'Amy, your hair was fine *before*. Especially when brushed. Why do you have to change everything?'

'Brushed! You sound like my mother. And what do you mean by "everything"?'

He ignores me and points at Evie. 'Shall I wake her up? She'll enjoy this lot.' The penguins shuffle and huddle like toddlers.

'What am I changing, Joe?' I pick at this one, not because I particularly want it to go anywhere, but because it's a shitty cloudy day and he's pissing me off and I had a terrible night's sleep and we're obviously standing downwind of an elephant turd and I've never had a rapport with creatures that live on ice floes. Besides, the bench, the ponds, the boating lake, the kiss, the betrayal, the hurt, lie just north west from where we're standing, on the other side of the park. Too close for comfort.

'Little things. I just get the sense that you feel you aren't good enough, that we aren't good enough and that the solutions lie in changing your hair and getting skinny again, which is kind of shallow.'

'So I am fat now. Is that what you're saying?'

'Argh.' Joe puts his hands to his face. 'There you go again. It's this fucking Alice, isn't it? Putting these ridiculous ideas into your head.'

'What has Alice got to do with it?'

We both instinctively stamp away from the penguin enclosure, fuelled by adrenaline, needing to exert ourselves in some direction other than inwards. We follow a painted green arrow trail along a tarmac path and it strikes me that I'm just as trapped as these animals, but trapped by responsibilities rather than sheets of glass.

A camel sits just the other side of the fence, legs bent beneath him at odd broken angles, callused knees. He chews a mouthful of grain with an air of captive disappointment, like a diner at an overrated restaurant.

'Fucking miserable creatures aren't they?' says Joe.

'He's trapped in a zoo. You'd be miserable.'

'Depends if he was born here. If he was he won't be fantasising about sand dunes.'

'Bet he is.' Even a camel must suspect there is more to life.

'If all you've known is a zoo then you'd be happy in your zoo. You wouldn't know any different. You'd accept the boundaries without questioning them. It's only when we throw ourselves against them that they hurt.' He shoots me a poignant I'm-not-talking-about-camels look. 'And if the camel escapes, what's he going to find? Another zoo if he's lucky. The lion's cage if he's not.'

We leave the grumpy camel dreaming of sand dunes and continue along the trail, peering behind fences and glass walls for signs of life. Happier, noisier families bustle past. I can see other mothers looking at us thinking, They've just had a row. You can always tell.

'Typical. We come to the zoo and all the animals decide it's time to go on Trappist retreat.'

Joe grabs my arm excitedly. 'Look! Tigers!' Less than five metres away is a tiger who looks through us as if she were surveying a horizon rather than a group of people huddled behind a curved Perspex riot shield of wall. 'Look at that regal reserve, that coat, the eyeliner. She's the Joan Collins of Regent's Park,' grins Joe.

'But she shouldn't be here. She should be free.' And suddenly I'm hit by the tiger's incarceration and her dignity and I feel my eyes filling with tears.

'Do you remember the one we saw in India?' Joe says softly.

'Of course.' How could I forget? Two years ago, our first holiday. Precariously perched atop an elephant, the tiger snarled at us from a rock no more than a metre away, so close I could see saliva foaming around her mouth. It blew me away. India was Joe's idea. I was rather hoping for a dose of

Delhi Belly to lose some weight. (As it happened, I suffered acute constipation.) And I had no idea that India would rattle my world. That I wouldn't care about flushing loos. That Joe's navy eyes would flash sari-bright in the fierce Indian sun. That I'd have orgasms that would sweep through my body like a raging Ganges. That I'd fall dizzy in love. That I'd see a tiger from the back of an elephant. What happened to that intensity? 'I can't bear to watch. It's just so sad.'

'Protecting the species,' he mumbles.

'Please, let's go.'

'You look pretty today,' he says suddenly.

'You can't patch it all up that easily.'

Joe rolls his eyes.

'Where were you last night?' I demand.

'Not this again. I told you, working late, a quick drink with Leo.'

'With your mobile turned off? What if I needed you? What if something had happened to Evie?'

'I turned it off in a meeting and forgot to turn it on again. I'm sorry.'

'OK, OK.' I shrug, feeling myself distance from him, from the potential for hurt. 'Evie's stirring. Let's go.'

We walk the green trail in silence, following it uphill past the vultures, the parrots, the baboons, before stopping opposite a gorilla cage, as good a spot for her to wake up as any. There is only one gorilla out of his shack, his breath misting up the glass, muscles pulsing beneath his dark brown coat.

'Why is what I say never enough?' Joe demands suddenly. The gorilla fixes him with intelligent eyes. 'If I say you're pretty you brush it off. If I say your hair is great it doesn't count. But if Alice says it would look better dyed blue you'd do it. You don't listen to me, everything you do is for other people.'

The gorilla gulps down a banana in much the same manner as Evie. But we're dulled to its wonder by our own fight for survival.

'It's not for other people, Joe. It's for me. I didn't think my hair was great before. I didn't think anything about it and that's the point. I've become numb to myself since having Evie. I want some . . . some vanity back.'

Joe exhales a huge sigh and leans against the thick pane of glass that protects gorilla and man from each other. Our relationship could use the same thing.

'Jesus, sometimes I wish I still smoked.'

'Look at the gorilla, he's just behind you, sizing you up.'

Joe turns round and, startled by his proximity, steps back. Man and beast eyeball each other for a few moments, then the gorilla scratches his armpits and bounds forward confrontationally, fist-foot-fist, towards the glass. Joe bows his head and instinctively pulls the pram away. 'Nope, I'm no silver back.'

Twenty-one

I think my diet has more in common with that of The Very Hungry Caterpillar than the GI. I munch on fruit all week but by Saturday I've given in, snacking on cake and salami and sweets. By Monday I've disciplined myself back to eating a nice green leaf. It's working, I'm losing weight. I know this because my fat jeans are now baggy around the waist. A full night's sleep couldn't give me more pleasure.

I'm not there quite yet. I still require low wattage when I'm undressing, but seen by the Vaseline glow of my side light (cunningly draped with a pink silk scarf), I'm passable, improved. Of course there are bits that will be for ever wrecked by my darling daughter: the lattice of stretch marks along my lower back, the flop of my bust, thickening where a waist used to be. I think these bits are permanent, like reckless tattoos. (I spent years going to the gym, honing and toning, and it was pretty much all destroyed in nine months.) And I'd have to sleep for years to lighten the dark shadows beneath my eyes. Even on those days when she's only woken up once or twice I look knackered. But I'm trying not to dwell on the tiredness any more. Instead I'm learning to just get on with it, sometimes with limbs so heavy I could be wading through baby rice. Life can't stop. Nor can Project Amy.

Where is that damn box? I have various boxes and dusty things on wheels below the bed, full of old clothes. I check Evie's room.

'Waaaaaaaaa!' Evie's going through a clingy phase. Today I'm flattered rather than suffocated by it. (Mothers go through phases too.)

'Evie honey, Mama is just next door, back in a sec.'

'Amy! Alice,' roars Joe.

A canter down the wooden stairs.

'Hiya! Nice place,' says Alice politely. We kiss. 'What's eating Joe?'

'Male inability to mix sleeplessness with civility.'

'Good-looking isn't he?' Arch of eyebrow. Alice assesses me with slanted eyes. Sizing up our relationship.

'Yes, we're a bit of an oddly-matched couple!'

'I wasn't saying . . .'

I shoo the comment away and lead her upstairs. Alice sinks down on my huge bed and tugs her olive green jewelled kaftan over her knees. She is one of those women whose beauty is enhanced every time you see her in a new setting. The leafy green of Queen's Park brings out the colour of her eyes, the sandpit, the gold of her skin, and the plum satin of my quilt makes her look opulent, a model in a velvety baroque fashion story.

'Big bed,' she purrs, lying back until she's stretched out, head on the pillow.

Argh! Flashback of the Rabbit encounter! It happened there, where she is sitting. Rude ghosts, too weird. I blush and turn away, busy myself with opening boxes.

Alice props herself up on an elbow. 'Right, let's get on with the task in hand. First outfit please.'

Out of my under-bed storage box I pull a jersey dress – size twelve – M&S, strappy and pale blue. Joe's always loved it. I step into it. My flesh creates no seam-strain. I'm delighted.

'Awful,' says Alice, shaking her head.

'Oh, really?'

'Really. It makes you look about forty. It's a mum dress.'

Next. My fat jeans with peach silk camisole, circa 1998. 'The jeans don't fit. The cut actually *gives* you saddle bags, no mean feat. Have you got a hand mirror?' I grab one off the dresser. 'Now examine the top from behind. See? It's stretching along the back. The bra is redistributing flesh so it's bulging under the strap. Nasty. You really need some new underwear.'

I nod. Next, crepey khaki dress. Bias cut. Hem below the knee.

'Hmmm.' She twiddles a curl thoughtfully. 'Keep. Wear with high heels or flat flats, nothing in-between. Definitely change the buttons. That would make a massive difference.'

Pink cheesecloth trousers that I bought in Bombay.

'Cheap backpacker gear. Very, very wrong.'

The door bangs open. Joe's huge frame shadows us, blocking the light from the hallway, crackling bad humour. 'You can't throw them out,' he growls.

Alice sits up on the bed, arches her waist and tugs her kaftan. A flash of cleavage. 'Joe, hi!' She smiles brightly. 'A distinguished male eye could be just what we need.'

'Really?' He gives me a once-over. 'Well I think they look great.'

'Joe!' Alice recoils back in mock shock. 'They add inches to Amy's hips.'

'Alice, if you don't mind,' Joe is bristling. I look down. If I close my eyes maybe what could happen won't and he'll go away. '*I'm* Amy's boyfriend and *I* love her hips—'

161

'But they're *not* her hips, it's fabric. She's lost loads of weight. Or haven't you noticed?' Alice says this with the most calorific of smiles and half-shut sleepy eyes. It's a look that sends men gooey. Joe doesn't react but I notice that his left hand, buried in his back jeans pocket, is writhing.

'I have noticed, yes.'

'Don't you think she looks wonderful?'

'Yes, but not because she's been dieting.'

'It's probably the Pilates.'

Hello! Over here! I am not a plastic mannequin. Annoyed with them both I walk over to change and untie the waistband.

'Oh, don't change. I love those trousers,' says Joe, not smiling and not sounding like he loves them at all.

My hands freeze.

'But Joe they *have* to go.' Alice rises up from the bed. 'C'mon Amy, whip them off.'

I look from Joe's imploring eyes to Alice's half-amused insistence. I pull apart the tie.

'Don't!' Joe hisses, super-quiet, really angry.

I start. Alice glances at him, eyes wide. I don't think she's used to men disagreeing with her. He shoots her a dark look. I feel hugely embarrassed. How dare Joe show me up like this?

'This is getting out of hand,' he says, the vein in his neck throbbing. 'It's not up to Alice what you wear.'

'And nor is it up to you,' I seethe. 'Listen Joe, we're playing with clothes here, not our life savings. I want a second opinion. And you know what?' Joe looks a bit sheepish. 'I agree with Alice. These are horrible.' I let the trousers fall to the ground. 'They are a relic.' The swathes of pink cheesecloth puddle around my ankles leaving me in black M&S minis. 'And they are going.' I pick them up and throw them on the 'no' pile.

'Fine.' The door slams behind him. The air shivers.

Alice perches on the side of the bed, not so louche now. But not embarrassed either. Her eyes shine. I think she's enjoying the drama. 'I'm sorry, Amy. I didn't mean to—'

'Don't be silly. It's his stupid fault. I'm just so sorry you have to be caught up in this.'

Alice looks at me, eyes pooled with pity. 'Is there anything I can do?'

I shake my head.

'Well, another time. Probably best if I go.'

Outrage bucks inside. 'You know what, Alice? I'm throwing the whole lot out and we are going shopping.'

'That's my gal.'

Twenty-two

I stab the buttons of my phone. 'Nic? It's me, Amy. What? Yes. Sorry, loud music. In a shop, hang on while I go outside. Better? I was just wondering if you're around. I'm in Westbourne Grove. With Alice. Yes, shopping. We're meeting Alice's friends at the Westbourne for a drink, five-ish, and I thought you should come and meet Alice. I know, I know, it's not your kind of thing, but . . . What? I can't hear you. You will? Excellent, see you at five.'

Alice stands opposite me. She's on the phone too, but I can't hear her conversation. She is giggling and talking breathily. Seeing I've finished my call, she hangs up, sharp. 'Follow me,' she says.

The posh boxy bags bang against my knees as I walk. The handle strings cut into my palms. My heel is on fire because my invisible trainer sock has slipped off it, and my eyes are itchy from the dry glare of shop target-lighting. But I feel fantastic. 'Major. You've got to get it,' has been the refrain of the last three hours. So I have. A pair of Seven jeans that make my legs look twice the length; a Diane Von Furstenberg wrap dress in green and white geometric patterns; three white Gap T-shirts; one black Brora cashmere wrap cardigan; pink

164

Converse trainers; a silk Issa top; a Heidi Klein bikini; ugly trainers with four-inch soles called MBTs, that look like hovercraft but apparently change the way you walk, make you use up extra calories and detonate cellulite.

Yes, Alice can make me buy almost anything. Alice was born to shop. It's as if a big band plays every time she walks through the shop door. She expects attention and she gets it. Assistants swarm around her. She knows many of their names. They give her discounts. Why? 'Because I'm Alice,' she laughs. In her company I am a little fêted too, rather than treated like a potential shoplifter. My bank account is over a thousand pounds lighter.

'Right, Miss Crane. I've just spotted the shoes *de résistance*. Back to Matches!'

'I can't. I've spent too much.' But Alice tugs me back to the shop.

'Oh what the hell! One extra thing isn't going to break the bank . . .'

'Not when it's already broken.'

'Back so soon,' quips the doorman. I grin.

'Here, try this. They'll look AMAZING on you, I promise.' Alice hands me a pair of blue satin open-toed heels. They have a diamanté butterfly near the toe cleavage. 'Marc Jacobs.'

The shoes are laughably not me. Not now. They seem far higher, more delicate than the knackered old heels that languish unloved at the back of my shoe drawer. And I have nowhere to wear them. 'Perfect for the park, Alice.'

'What about work? You'll need them for work.'

'But they're too high, I'd be crippled.'

'Rubbish. You could jog in these. You've lost your judgement, Amy. You've forgotten the power of a good pair of heels.'

'Hmmm, maybe. But they're too expensive. I can't spend this much money on shoes.'

'Well, you could buy four pairs of shitty shoes that will scuff and look shit, that you'll never really *love*, only tolerate. I'm telling you, Amy, when it comes to shoes, buy cheap, buy twice.' A hovering shoe assistant nods her glossy black bob vigorously.

I examine the shoe. They are the same blue as my Pilates mat. I peel off my trainer and stinky invisible sock and slide my foot into the soft satin skeleton. Oh! I had forgotten what a good shoe can do. My foot is no longer a carrot-toed object to be masked at all costs. It is an erotic *objet*, balletic and gently arched.

'You need to wear them with something cool. Let's go and try on some stuff. That OK, Emma?'

The assistant nods and leads us through a swish of curtains to the conjuring box changing rooms. I climb out of my skirt and vest-top and prepare to be transformed by designer denim and a draped jersey top.

'You look incredible.' Alice examines my new outfit approvingly then pats my bum. 'I'd shag yer.'

'Really, Alice, I *love*. But . . . no . . . can't justify them.'

'You can. They're for the new Amy!' says Alice, who despite the great style chasm between us still has an uncanny ability to read me like a price tag. 'Not the one who slaps around the park all day in old Nikes feeling miserable.'

'Hmmm.' I feel an unexpected pang for the post-partum Amy. In my head I can see her pelting down the corridors away from me, past gleaming stainless steel racks of clothes rails, dropping leggings and old trainers and bras that don't fit as she runs, hair bleaching as she gains on the vanishing point between the racks. What will happen when she gets there? I twist around, cricking my neck to get a look at my bum in the jeans from behind. It's the best bum I've had in years. Heart-shaped and swelling the dark denim pockets in more or less the right places. This, it suddenly dawns, is a bum worthy of Josh.

'Amy?'

'Sorry, miles away.'

'Did you hear what I just said?'

'Er, sorry. No. What?'

'I said, sweetheart, I will buy the shoes for you. A present from master to student.'

'You're joking?'

'It's no joking matter. I want to treat you.'

'Why?'

'Because someone has to,' she says pointedly.

Alice makes me promise to wear them now, so I gratefully totter out of the shop, legs buckling at unexpected rises in the paving. Without asking, she tosses my old trainers into a Kensington and Chelsea bin, on top of greasy fast-food wrappers. Is that really where the old Amy belongs? I resist the urge to squirrel them out, slap them on and run back home to watch daytime TV, safe and dowdy.

Twenty-three

A tap on my back. 'Amy? Is that you?'

I swivel around on the fulcrum of my blue heel.

'No way!' Nicola crushes her hands to her mouth with astonishment.

'Oh God, have I turned into a footballer's wife?' I should have prepared myself for this reaction.

'Yes. No . . . I think. It just gave me a shock, that's all. From what I've heard of her, you've been Aliceified.' She examines me carefully, head to heel. 'They look comfortable.'

I look down at my blue shoes. I particularly like the view from this angle, the toe cleavage, the butterflies' full wing spans, the soft oval of framed flesh. 'Well, to tell the truth they are beginning to pinch a bit.'

'A bit?' she laughs.

'OK, they're agony.'

'But you look fabulous, that's the main thing,' says Nicola, grinning. 'Look at me . . . and remind yourself what you're missing out on.' Nicola's wearing a grey linen dress and cheap sparkly flip-flops, surviving sequins trailing on the pavement. 'Thomas was sick on my nice dress. Sorry to let the side down.'

'Don't be silly. I'm just so pleased you're here, didn't think you'd want to come.'

'Well it was this style safari or Richard and Judy. Where are they anyhow?'

Nicola scans the forecourt of the Westbourne pub. It is crammed with people who gleam with wealth and good diets since birth. Girls flick back shiny hair and laugh loudly into their huge glasses of wine. Handsome scruffy men smoke lazily, eyes playing between tanned cleavages, licking up legs in heels.

'Here.'

Alice's glass of wine is shaking as she laughs furiously about something with Jasmine, who's just turned up wearing a lime green tiny tennis dress that appears to be covered in dandelion fluff. 'No!' Alice is saying, disbelieving, snorting with laughter. 'No way!'

I touch her elbow. 'Let me introduce you to my friend Nicola.' Alice carries on laughing. I've never had perfect social timing. 'Er, Alice, can I introduce my mate Nicola.'

'What? Oh.' Alice turns round. 'Nikki? Sorry, Nicola. Hi. Alice.' She dazzles Nicola with her dentistry and re-angles her body back to Jasmine.

'So will you pick up the chiropractor bill?' Nicola asks.

Alice's hair flicks back round. 'I'm sorry?'

'The shoes. The toe-crunchers.'

Alice smiles. 'Much cheaper than a therapist.'

Nicola laughs, lights a cigarette and offers one to Alice.

'Thank God I'm not the only smoker around here,' says Alice, plucking a cigarette out of the packet with slender advert fingers. Alice likes people who answer back. She warms to Nicola instantly and the two fall into playful banter about the merits of smoking.

Jasmine and I stand on the sidelines, surplus to requirements. I expected Nicola to loathe Alice and, in truth, was quite enjoying the prospect of defending Alice while, perhaps, fuelling the critique. There's something nice about having life compartmentalised. My friends in boxes, all friends with different parts of me. Deeply immature, I know.

'So, er, how's it going?' I say to Jasmine, who is glazing over, surveying the pub for other social opportunities.

'I've broken it off with Janet,' she says starkly.

Janet? Janet is a girl's name.

'My girlfriend,' she spells out. 'I'm a little concerned she may turn up here. If you see a crazed six-foot red-head stalking me, do tell.'

Gosh, you never do know, do you? I always assumed Jasmine was straight. She does have a baby. 'I'm sorry.' I can't think of anything else to say.

'Nah, don't be sorry.' Jasmine exhales Pinot Grigio. 'I couldn't give her what she wanted.'

'Oh?' All these secret lives, possibilities.

'Commitment. Settling down with another woman who wants to borrow my shoes and discuss issues the whole time is not my idea of fun. I'm too busy. And call me old fashioned, but I don't want Marlon growing up with two mummies.'

It strikes me that I'm likely to die without experiencing a curves-on-curves experience, which is perhaps rather old fashioned, the twenty-first-century equivalent of dying a spinster. Admittedly, it was not something I ever particularly wanted to do when I had the chance (the university hall of residence lesbian, Mary White, had halitosis), but now that the future that lies ahead seems as flat, solid and predictable as a Dutch landscape, I rather wish I had.

'Anyhow,' Jasmine continues, eyes lighting up. 'I've met someone else.'

Alice suddenly breaks back into the conversation. 'Your

knees. Go on, show her your knees,' she whispers to Jasmine, who dissolves into giggles. Both Nicola and I immediately seek out her knees. They are raw, pink as steak. 'Fuck wounds,' explains Alice solemnly. 'Jasmine is having better sex than any of us. She's shamelessly come straight from the long grass in Kensington Gardens.'

'Cool,' says Nicola dryly. 'I find that scooping up toys on the floor on all fours achieves the same look.'

Jasmine tries to pull her mini-dress down, knowing that it misses the mark by about four inches. 'New lover,' she confides to the entire pub.

'Married!' titters Alice indiscreetly.

A wife? How modern. Jasmine blushes. Nicola frowns.

'Not intentionally. He didn't tell me at first.'

Oh, a he.

'But now I wouldn't have him any other way. I can walk away whenever I like,' whispers Jasmine, obviously enjoying the rapt audience. 'It's great.' Suddenly she grabs Alice's sleeve, face paling. 'Alice, we've got to go. There's Janet! Fuck, fuck, fuck.'

Alice mouths sorry as she is tugged through the crowds by a panicking Jasmine, her wine glass sloshing on to legs and handbags.

Nicola pulls deeply on her cigarette. 'Beats NCT meetings.'

'Yup. Drink?'

I dive into the squirming mass of people – it's getting busier and busier by the minute – and edge towards the bar, worming past tanned fragrant flesh to the beer-splashed bar top. I rest my feet on the brass foot rest, ready for a wait. I'm always the last person to get served. But not this time. The barman ignores both man and woman either side of me and zooms straight in for my order. The man standing next to me, good-looking, dark, messy hair, shrugs and smiles, his elbow a patch of warm against mine. Then the crowd surges and I'm sandwiched, arms pushed flat by my sides, cleavage squeezed together, bursting out of my neckline. Another man, glimpsed between pint glasses and gesticulating hands, grins too. His eyes are glued to my chest. Then he's gone, swallowed by the crowd. I cross my arms self-consciously. And it is then that I realise. Something has changed, a slight raise in temperature. Gulp. Could it be that I am no longer invisible?

Twenty-four

I take off my toe-pinchers as soon as I get into the house, pairing them neatly at the bottom of the stairs, and put the bags discreetly beside the sofa armrest. The door opens and Joe pushes a big bunch of pink waxy tulips into my arms.

'For you.'

'What? Wow. Thank you!' Joe rarely buys me flowers. It's one of those things I've come to accept. 'What a lovely surprise.'

Joe takes a deep breath. 'I'm sorry. I acted like a jerk. I fucked up with Alice. I just saw you in those trousers . . .' He sits down heavily, the weight of our relationship cleaving the sofa.

'Hey, it's OK.' The argument seems like decades ago already. Retail therapy has worked wonders.

'I felt she was pissing on our past. But I overreacted. Amy?' Joe clears his throat nervously. 'This . . . it's not really me, you know that. It's not really us. What's happening?'

'Let's just forget it.' I swipe the subject away like a nasty outfit on a shop's clothes rail.

'Don't you want to talk it through?'

'No, honestly, it's OK. I probably overreacted too.'

'Tea?' He stands up and steps on to a corner of crunchy shopping bag. And that's when he sees them. The big fat

173

mountain of dizzy consumption. '*What*,' he thunders, 'are *they*?'

Suddenly there does seem to be an absurdly large number of absurdly expensive-looking bags. It seems rather unlikely that I bought them. I will them to disappear. They don't.

'Bags.'

'Amy . . .'

'OK, clothes.'

'New clothes?' His face drains of contrite. 'Have you gone stark raving bonkers?'

'Oh come on, Joe. I haven't been shopping in months. You suggested I buy myself something new.' My argument is weak. Without Alice it's hard to keep the conviction afloat.

'Something. *One* thing. Not a Paris Hilton trawl. Amy, in case you haven't noticed, we're skint. You haven't received any money for over a month. Your maternity allowance has finished. Nada.'

'But . . .'

'How much have you spent?

'About five hundred pounds,' I say, knocking off fifty per cent.

'Five hundred pounds! Jesus, Amy!'

Oh dear. If only I'd put the bags upstairs first, then I could have siphoned the clothes out gradually. 'Joe, wait until I show you. I've got these cellulite-burning trainers . . .'

'What? Why don't you just buy spells and be done with it? What are—'

'. . . and beautiful clothes. You'll love them.'

'Like your hair,' he hisses.

'Like my hair.' Of course he's not going to be pleased for me. Joe wants to keep me frumpy and fat, in the kitchen, while he dazzles off to work and God knows where else with his Prada briefcase full of important non-domestic things and

174

sexy little secrets. No, flowers aren't enough. 'You may as well say there's no point in it. Go on, say it.'

'You've said it, and you know what? You're right. I look forward to seeing you at the farm zoo in that designer haul.'

'Joe, you are not the only one who needs nice clothes. You may remember that I did once have a social life. And you know what? I am determined to reclaim it.'

'Oh.' Joe looks a little floored, as if the idea that I could pick up my old life again where I left off is incomprehensible.

He's got used to seeing me at home, in tracksuit bottoms. He's got used to milk in the fridge and dinners rustled up and laundry put on. Until recently, he never knew he wanted a housewife, mistakenly believing he liked the ambitious, un-domesticated modern woman. But now he knows otherwise. He can have a fun, freestyle woman outside of these walls, but in the house? This arrangement suits him rather well. Of course, I am no domestic goddess – my main culinary trick involves pureeing carrot – but I am at home, at the family's service, awkwardly forced into the role of housewife. And Joe perhaps revealed more than he intended when he wistfully mentioned last week how wonderful it was that time (it was only once) he came home to find all his freshly laundered socks paired up.

'Oh come on, Joe. Don't be such a killjoy!' I try and pick up all the bags at once in order to dramatically stomp upstairs with them but in the fluster of the moment and with a handful of tulips I can't. Bags fall to the ground. A top flops out. I shove it back in roughly. This rather undermines the theatre of my exit. And then the doorbell goes. We both wait for the other to get it. But there is no need. There is the rattle of a key in the lock.

'Your mother,' groans Joe. 'Timing spot on as usual.'

I hear Mum's footstep, a kind of fast two-step shuffle. As

175

a child I'd recognise her footsteps instantly. She never surprised me with her entrance. Peter Pan's ticking crocodile, I told Dad.

'Coooeeeeeeeeeee! Anyone home?' she calls unnecessarily loudly in the hallway before blasting into the sitting room. 'Amy! Joe! You're both here, how lovely.' Mum takes off her cream linen jacket, folds it neatly in half and places it on the sofa. Joe completes this ritual by picking it up, shaking it down and hanging it on a coat hook. 'Where's the lady of the house?'

'Asleep?' I ask Joe, who nods.

'Gosh, you two don't half look peaky. Coming down with something?'

Joe is mute. I'm left to join the conversational dots. 'A bit tired probably. Everything OK? What can we do for you?'

Mum notices the catch in my voice and looks a bit wary. She pauses and in this pause I can see her brain whirring. No, she decides, the tension will pass and she should persevere with the purpose of her visit, not that one needs a purpose to visit one's daughter. 'Well, you remember I mentioned my new neighbour, Norman, you know the one who moved into number forty-three? I told you all about him when I was last here, didn't I Joe?'

Joe twists out a smile.

'Well, the strangest thing happened. Yesterday morning I'd just finished hanging out the washing and was wondering whether it was an OK time to phone your brothers in Australia, and thinking how I'd like to go on holiday but it's so hard when you're single and older and I couldn't bear to go on an organised group holiday, but just a change of scene would be nice . . .' She sits down on the sofa and smooths down her floral dress. '. . . and the doorbell went.' She looks at me and Joe for a reaction. 'It was *Norman*! My new

176

neighbour. He said, "I would like very much to invite you on a picnic." I was floored, Joe, floored. I didn't know what to say, it's been so long since anyone's asked me out . . .'

'That's great, Mum. When are you going?'

Mum winces slightly. 'I said no.'

'That's a shame. Why? Is he spooky?'

'No, Amy, he's a nice man, A Very Nice Man. But you know my thoughts on all that. I'm too old. I don't want to get involved again, not when everything runs pretty smoothly on my own, except for holidays perhaps.'

'Mum, he didn't ask you to marry him. He asked you for a picnic.'

Evie starts to whimper upstairs. Relieved, Joe excuses himself.

'I kind of realise that now,' she sighs. 'It's all very awkward. And to make matters worse, my washing machine is playing up and I feel I can't ask him to have a look at it now.' Mum twiddles the worn-down gold wedding ring on her finger. She never took it off after Dad left. It's been quite an effective dating deterrent over the years. 'So I was trying to think of a way in which to open up relations again but make it clear to him it is just as *friends*. You follow? And I thought, perhaps you could do me a favour here.' She smiles her fakest, breeziest smile, the one she turns on when she's stressed. 'Perhaps you could lend me Evie?'

'Evie? She's not a pair of shoes.'

'I thought I could ask him for a walk. I won't wear my best or anything. And I'll take Evie. That spells out very clearly that it's not a date. That it's a friendly neighbourly walk.' Mum's throat flushes.

'Suppose so.'

'And then I can ask him about my washing machine.'

Suddenly there is a loud rumble, a thud and a 'fucking,

fucking hell' coming from the hallway. Shit. Joe. I run into the hall and find Joe lying on the ground at the bottom of the stairs, eyes shut. Oh fuck.

'Joe? Are you all right.'

Nothing.

'Has Joe had a little accident?' enquires Mum, emerging from the sitting room. 'Dear me.'

Then Joe's hand moves. Slowly, creakily, he pulls a blue Marc Jacobs shoe from beneath his lower back. 'Things can only get better,' he mutters, lifting a leg, an arm, then staggering his huge frame up slowly as if erecting a badly designed tent.

Twenty-five

Josh is so damn physical. Not one for polite boundaries, he'll arch his whole body – 'a communal tool' – over mine if it increases my back stretch. There's no ceremony about it, no 'do you mind if . . . ?' And his touch, rather inappropriately given the circumstances, still thrills me. I try my best to hide any reaction, usually with a very technical question or self-deprecating comment, but I've noticed Josh often has a smile playing around the shallow curve of his lips like he knows anyway. And I probably thank him more than is necessary. But he is giving me back my figure. Day by day it emerges from the baby blub, like a statue from a block of stone.

'Have you time for a coffee, babe?' Josh stops tying his trainer laces.

'What?' But I heard him the first time. Blythe and Alice have gone. (Annabel's so big now she's sofa-bound, Jasmine's got a mid-morning rendez-vous with her married lover.) And I'm shocked. We've never taken this teacher-student relationship out of the studio. Is this part of the practice?

'Coffee. Beer if you'd prefer.'

'Um, think I have to go and . . . er . . .'

'Please. I could really do with a break,' he implores. 'I

won't make you roll like a ball along the coffee counter, I promise.'

Curiosity and the eyes clinch it. 'Oh, OK.'

We trip down the stairs to the hallway. It is narrow but rather than walking single file something compels us to walk side by side, each with one arm dragging along the corridor wall, shoulders bumping. Then we head into the grubby urban cool of west London, up litter-strewn streets, past the tilers, the Spanish food wholesalers, the ancient tailors and the 'new antiques' shop that sells extraordinarily horrible velveteen sofas. We stop at a caffe that spins bacon and white toast smells out of whirring fans embedded in its greasy window. It's the kind of caffe that fashion photographers like to use as an ironic London set. There's a fat old woman behind the till, dark, perhaps Greek. (Too much Feta, Mum would say.) Her eyes – black, the whites pinked by hot stoves – light up when she sees Josh.

'Hello mister. Come back for more?' she laughs, wipes her hands on her apron and winks. '*Another* new friend today, heh?'

Josh studies the pot of teaspoons. I don't ask.

We sit down at a small square table covered in a tired gingham oil cloth. Our knees just touch.

'I love this place,' he says. 'Hope it's not too greasy spoon for you.'

'No, it's great. No-frills, how I like caffes.'

Josh grins. 'That's what I love about it too. Can't stand the corporate coffee shops.' His hand shoots across the table and grabs the sugar pourer which is about two inches from my right elbow. My instinct is to pull back in my chair, increase the distance between us. But I don't, because that would draw attention to my awareness of his hand on the sugar pourer and that would be embarrassing.

180

'Sorry, I'm such a twitcher. All this yogic energy rattling around my veins,' he says wryly. Terribly cute.

I am about to say, 'Don't worry, my other half twitches all the time too,' but something stops me. Joe has no place at this table. So I say, 'It uses up a huge amount of calories.' And I feel like a total fool, because I really don't care about how many calories twitching uses up and I sound like a stupid girlie. Luckily Josh cracks into a smile.

'*You*,' he says. 'You make me laugh.' His hand leaves the sugar pourer – I relax – and he leans back in his chair, tugging his shirt sleeves up. Those sinewy forearms again. 'It's been really nice having you in the class, Amy. Sometimes it gets a bit serious. A bit earnest. You lighten things up.'

'Even with my soil-brown aura?'

'Very funny.'

'Or because I'm about as well suited to Pilates as an elephant seal?'

'Rubbish. You're getting better. Really you are.' His eyes dance. 'It's just that the others treat it more like . . . oh I don't know. Less playfully perhaps. '

I'm secretly thrilled that my ineptitude has been mistaken for comedic tendencies and do nothing to contradict him.

'I've really needed a bit of playfulness recently,' he adds quietly with a slow exhalation.

'Oh? Everything's OK I hope,' I add stiffly, unsure how to respond to this invitation to intimacy. The caffe table suddenly seems very small.

'Amy, have you ever felt like you might be living the wrong life?' He's staring at me direct now. 'That by twists of fate and misunderstanding you've come off the motorway at the wrong junction and you know that to get going in the right direction may mean driving miles in the wrong one before you find a slip road?'

181

'I think so,' I underplay. Yes, I fucking well do could be too strong. 'But you look so at ease standing on your head.'

'I love what I do, don't get me wrong,' says Josh, fingers majorette-twiddling a teaspoon. 'It's just other things in my life . . . I don't know. It's hard finding the right person isn't it?'

That Josh is asking me this question at all is, well, discombobulating. I don't chat with men other than Joe any more. I certainly don't discuss relationships with them. New motherhood is a female landscape, like stepping back into the nineteenth century or a strict Islamic country. Apart from the odd househusband (and they usually claim to be 'freelancers' anyway) men mostly disappear – to work, to the pub – and women are left to create days together with a baby, a park and cups of tea. Most of my male friends lost interest when I got pregnant, as if that was proof I was finally off the market and couldn't be kept as a reserve girlfriend for a rainy day.

'It's hard to know if the one you're with is the right person I suppose, if that's what you mean. People change,' I say, disappointed to be spouting clichés already.

'Has Jonathan?'

'You mean Joe.'

'Sorry, sorry. Has Joe changed?'

'Well . . .' I stumble, uncomfortable at incriminating Joe, wanting to present a united front out of pride more than anything else.

Josh spots the hesitation. 'It's OK, Amy. I'm a safe place. It's going no further than this table. Talk to me, babe.'

My eyes water. I hold so much in that with a little prod I pucker like a balloon. 'Maybe he's changed a bit. Well, *we* have. Inevitable, I suppose.'

Josh frowns. 'Is it? I'd like to think I'll be as in love with the mother of my child the day she gives birth as the day we met.'

'You speak with the certainty of the childless.'

Josh looks down at the table a little bashfully, fingers a salt packet. 'You're right. As always. Wise old bird.'

'Less of the old.'

Josh laughs, rakes his curls. 'Joe's lucky to have you.'

I stare into my cup and wonder why Joe doesn't feel lucky enough not to risk losing me.

'Hey, don't look like that, babe! What's the matter? You carry your sadness over your shoulders like a coat.'

I brush him off with a wave of my hand. 'A nice one I hope.'

'An old fur. A soft and inviting sadness.' Josh smiles, reaches for my hand. It's like being plugged into an electric socket.

'Listen, Josh. I'm fine, really.' I pull my hand away. 'This conversation seems to have done one of your back flips. You were the one who felt down. Don't project.'

Josh raises an eyebrow. 'Having troubles in a relationship doesn't make you a bad person. You should let it all out. I may be able to help.'

'I very much doubt it.'

Josh looks hurt. 'Try me.'

I pause, resist, cave in. 'It's just tough. You see, Joe, well . . .' I stumble. Josh looks at me expectantly. 'He hasn't been, I don't think . . . hasn't been faithful. Not always.' I pressure the bridge of my nose with arrowed fingers. 'I don't know why I'm telling you this.'

'That's shit, man.' He grabs my hand again and squeezes it. 'Jona . . . sorry, Joe, must be mad. You're a fine catch.'

I laugh weakly into my cup trying not to betray how insanely grateful I am for this comment. Or how insanely flattered. To think that Josh, sexy, hard-bodied blond Josh thinks I, wobbly, tired new mum a catch!

'The problem is, couples get too used to each other. Familiarity breeds contempt and all that,' he says, looking up for a nod. I nod. 'And you stop seeing the other person, don't you? Joe may have forgotten there's this beautiful sensual woman inside the mother.'

'I think she's on sabbatical.'

'Nonsense. I'm looking at her.'

'Very funny. What about you?'

Josh flashes his Bowie teeth. I imagine them biting into my shoulder. 'Me? I'm just looking for The One. All men are really. But I think I've been looking in the wrong places.' He slumps forward a little sadly. 'I don't want some supermodel now you know. I'm over that. I want someone with soul.'

'But preferably a size ten.'

'No, no. You've got it wrong. Women always get it wrong. Give me a J-Lo bottom any day. It's not about that anyway. I think I'm coming to a new stage in this life. A family, that's what I'd like. A little boy who I could take fishing and teach T'ai Chi.'

'A girl might be able to learn too.'

Josh rocks back on his chair, grinning impishly. 'Yeah, yeah. But hey, I can't go planning my brood until I've got the woman, can I?'

'Not really. But don't worry, you'll meet someone, everyone does eventually.'

'But then you get close and they take off their masks, and you're meant to be grateful for this removal of the mask because that's what relationships are all about, aren't they? But what if they reveal themselves and you're not sure you like what you see? Do you understand?' He takes my silence as a yes. 'What if they show you their pain, their vulnerability and you find it repellent? Sorry, I'm rambling.' Josh's head is tilted downwards, towards his coffee. He lifts his eyes. I

184

wonder if he knows he looks devastating from this angle. 'I just feel so comfortable with you, babe. I feel I can say anything.'

I smile helplessly. Please don't say such things.

'You know when we first met . . .'

I blush furiously.

'Outside the Salusbury. That was me. You remember. I *know* you do.'

I nod.

'I just thought you were the sweetest thing. Scruffy, child-like, unmade-up.'

'Brilliantly accessorised by loo paper.'

Josh laughs. 'That was the finishing touch. A woman in her raw, unpainted state is a rare find these days. But you're a natural. And you look better and better every time I see you.'

That might have something to do with the dyed hair, the plucked eyebrows and The Very Hungry Caterpillar diet. I sit tight on my secrets.

'Didn't I tell you that Pilates would work wonders? It's a free way to change your body and your life.'

'A tenner a go, actually,' I correct, gulping the last dregs of coffee.

Josh laughs. 'Oh Amy,' he sighs. 'We're similar, you and I. It's like we've known one another for years.'

My body throbs beneath the gingham tablecloth. 'I've got to go, got to pick up Evie.'

'Whoa! No rush.'

'No really, I've stayed too long already. I must go.' I stand up and pull my handbag over my shoulder. 'It's been lovely. Thanks so much for the coffee. See you next week at class.'

I feel Josh's blue eyes burn into my back as I turn left out of the cafe's peeling door. I try my best to walk normally, but my body is a coil of energy, wanting to skip, to power jump down the normally grey streets, now golden in the sunlight. I can't face going straight home – where will I tell Joe I've been? – so I trot towards Queen's Park, a thick green rug between the smart Victorian houses. Through the horse chestnuts, the oaks, I instinctively follow the toot, beat and anticlimax of jazz coming from the Victorian bandstand. Orbiting it are groups of families and friends, lying on the grass, tearing at sourdough bread and sipping beer, their daughters in fairy costumes, Superman sons. I find a springy patch of grass for myself, adjacent to the mini-golf, away from the hubbub but in earshot of the grey-haired musicians. And, adrenaline sapping, I lie back and study the sky, baby-boy blue and cotton wool. Tiny ink-drip flies circle above my head. Josh, Josh, Josh go the drums.

Twenty-six

'Gosh, have you been unwell?' demands Sue, shortbread crumbling on her tea-wet lips.

'No. Why?'

'You've lost so much weight.' An airborne shortcake crumb shoots over her tracksuit bottoms and glues itself to the side of my mug.

'Why thank you.'

The other mothers smile weakly: weight loss doesn't do much for group morale.

'And what's happened to your feet?'

Eyes fall to my MBT trainers. 'Oh these! A bit like walking on a tyre, but I'm assured by my friend Alice that they burn up loads of calories.'

Nicola starts giggling. She thinks I'm bonkers.

'They're kind of orthopaedic-looking. Why not just go barefoot?' asks Michelle, who once met us in the park in a loosely tied sarong that threatened to swish open like curtains in the breeze, but no bra or shoes.

'My feet are still awaiting a pedicure.'

'Pedicure?' Sue conquers her irritation by masticating more shortbread. 'Gosh, Amy.'

Silence. Everyone shifts politely on the blue canvas sofa, rearranging their lower backs, rolling back their aching shoulders. It is the world's most uncomfortable sofa, 'sofabed actually,' qualifies Sue. 'If anyone ever wants to come and stay . . .'

Sue's house is on a recently gentrified terraced Kilburn street off Willesden Lane. The outside looks normal enough, red brick and to-be-replaced PVC windows. But inside, despite Sue and Alan having lived here for four years, there is scarcely any evidence of the house being inhabited by any person above the age of two. Coloured plastic toys carpet the living-room floor. The coffee table is a blue plastic toy basin. The cushions are embroidered with farm animals. The alphabetically organised DVD collection consists solely of baby-flicks. Although Oliver can neither walk nor crawl, every inch of the room anticipates his first step: baby-proof video locks, socket covers and rubber corners. Photos of a bald, grumpy Oliver glower from every horizontal surface with the repressive repetition of a dictator's portrait.

'So what does Joe think about this . . . this wasting away?' demands Sue.

'Oh, don't think he's really noticed.'

'No?' Sue thoughtfully strokes her hand under her chin which has the unfortunate effect of scooping and dragging all the loose flesh. 'Well I may be two stone heavier since conceiving Olly, but Alan says he likes my figure better post-partum, real womanly curves, he says. Men like something to grab hold of, don't they, Hermione?'

'And new clothes too I see,' chirps Hermione, changing the subject, uncertain she's able to back Sue up on that one. (Piers likes his wife as slim as his ex-catalogue-model mother.) Bar these NCT carb-fests – a little of what you

188

fancy . . . – Hermione is as mindfully strict with her own diet as she is with her daughter's, and usually carries a Tupperware box of sprouting seeds and Tofu chunks in her handbag for those every-three-hour snack windows. Pregnancy gave Hermione a whole nine months to obsess about food groups and vitamins and trace elements, without being labelled neurotic or eating disordered. And after such knowledge? Well, there can be no forgiveness of sour cream potato crisps or the Kit-Kat. Oh no. Inspired by Gwyneth Paltrow – icon of post-natal nutrition – Hermione has recently slain a mild head-cold with large ingestions of raw purple sprouting broccoli and a Chinese herb called *Bai Gou*.

'Had enough, munchkin?' Michelle asks her fed-on-demand (i.e. twenty-four-hours-a-day) daughter Beatrice, who is smacking her lips like an old man over a pint of Guinness. Beatrice strains away, milk dribbling down her chin. But Michelle makes no effort to put her breast back. It protrudes from her gaping cheesecloth shirt like a large root vegetable.

Nicola averts her eyes. 'And how's your cashmere baby sock company going, Hermione? Are the mills spinning?'

'Ooh, nothing concrete as yet. Just investigating Scottish mills on the internet, when I have the time, which . . .'

'. . . As we all know,' adds Sue, drowning out Hermione, 'we just don't get. There just aren't enough hours in the day, are there Oliver?' Sue's son eyes her with displeasure. Oliver's not a rewarding child, prone to unsightly rashes and bad humour.

'I think there are rather too many,' says Nicola.

'You won't think that when you go back to work,' observes Sue.

'That's the idea.'

'Well, some people around here will have even less time very soon too.' Sue beams, displaying sore red gums. 'Hermione? Can I tell them? *Please*.'

Hermione resignedly nods her head, knowing resistance to be futile. Heads swivel to Sue, who puffs out her mono-breast.

'Hermione is *pregnant*!'

There is a hushed silence as we absorb this mind-warping information.

'Isn't that the most wonderful news?' she adds, trying to jolly things along.

Nicola pales. 'Oh dear, there's a lesson to us all.'

Hermione looks hurt. 'Nicola, it wasn't *un*planned.'

'But you're still breastfeeding. How can your body do two things at once?'

Sue plants a slippered foot on the blue plastic toy table. Cornered by nipples and toys, not knowing where else to look, we all stare at the slipper. It is checked, lined with fake sheepskin and has a frayed hole near the big toe. All I can think is, Hermione is having sex. Everyone is having sex apart from me.

'Well, I'm jealous,' says Michelle suddenly. 'It'll probably take me a decade to conceive another one, by which time I'll get mistaken for a grandmother.'

Nicola shakes her head. 'If I never have to look into the bowels of the toilet bowl again I'll be happy. God, how I hated being pregnant. The nausea, the fatigue . . .' She groans at the memory.

Michelle sighs. 'I found it so sensual. I felt like an ancient goddess.'

'You are joking? It's bloody awful and I don't believe any woman who says she enjoys it. I really don't know what I'd do if I got pregnant right now . . .'

Oh. Silence. Eyes knife into Nicola, who by saying she doesn't know what she'd do implies she might consider a termination, and a termination after having had a child is inconceivable to the likes of Sue, liberal or not. Because they know what happens when the cluster of cells grows and divides and the frog's spawn becomes a little Oliver or a little Amelia. Nicola sips her tea nonchalantly.

'Well, Alan wants another one quite soon,' mutters Sue, deciding that moral confrontation must take second place to the rescue of her tea party. 'But obviously not until everything's back to normal . . .' she points to where her cords camel-hoof between her legs, '. . . down there.'

Euw!

'Oh please have one at the same time as me,' implores Hermione. 'It would be so much more fun. We could go to NCT classes together.'

'Again? Wasn't once enough?' Nicola looks pained.

'Well, I do have a few queries.' Hermione sighs musically. 'I'm concerned that my body may be depleted. I haven't been taking my pre-pregnancy vitamins, I've been taking the breastfeeding ones, so it's all rather confusing.'

Nicola looks over and rolls her eyes at me quickly, like lottery balls.

Sue stands up. God, she is big. 'Now, anyone for more tea? More shortbread?' There is a hum of vague assent and Sue crashes towards the door through the minefield of plastic toys, each tread detonating recorded nursery rhymes.

Nicola breaks the protocol. 'Actually, Sue, I'm not feeling great,' she says, looking rude with health. 'I think I'm going to call it a day if you don't mind.'

'Oh dear! Poor thing.' Sue's cheeks wobble with empathy. 'You're not dieting like Amy are you? Here, have a shortbread.'

'No really, thanks.'

'Sit down, lie down. You can lie down in the spare room. Here, follow me.'

Nicola shields herself behind her pram. You can almost see her feet scrabbling towards the front door, cartoon-like, while her head holds its position.

'No, Sue. I'm going to go.'

I leap up. 'And I will come too. We'll walk back together.'

Hermione rearranges Amelia on her lap briskly. 'I'm afraid it's time for us to go too, isn't it, Amelia?' Sue lifts a heavy eyebrow. 'I don't want to, Sue,' protests Hermione. 'But we're running close to the wind. It's almost doze time. I've got to race back and get her in the cot.'

'Cots are cages,' mutters Michelle under her breath. (She practises co-sleeping.)

'But Amelia doesn't look tired.'

'It's The Routine, Sue, sorry. I can't break it. And it has to be her cot. The rules say so.'

Sue looks crestfallen. The tea that she had planned and baked for so rigorously, the best Habitat china . . . What a waste.

'OK, another ten minutes. I imagine Amelia will survive it,' says Hermione reluctantly, checking her watch. 'I'll finish my cup of tea. OK, it's 4.15 . . .'

Sue watches me and Nicola walk down her shingle path, her large square face framed by the red canvas curtains and geranium window boxes. She waves at us, all fingers flopping down on the palm at once, an infant wave. Her eyes are sad as a cow's.

Nicola plants Thomas in the baby swing and starts to push. Thomas starts to cry.

'Please tell me why I have a baby who is allergic to anything babyish. Did I eat something funny during pregnancy? Read the wrong book?' Nicola mutters to herself, persevering with the swing until Thomas's screams start to attract concerned looks from the other mothers.

'He's happiest when I'm sitting in the garden smoking a cigarette, blowing smoke rings.'

She scoops Thomas out. A wide-eyed Evie takes his place.

If I squint, I can almost make out, in an impressionistic blur, the bandstand. Back with Evie, in my role as mother, that moment – Josh and jazz – is like a yellowing postcard from a distant relative. I push Evie back. Whoosh! Whoosh! Up and away! Her fine baby hair blows flat. Her toes curl with pleasure. Evie and I laugh, each delighting in the reaction of the other.

'You look happier,' says Nicola. 'Is everything better at home?'

'Nothing's changed, Nic. Not really.' Am I really happier? Perhaps I am. Pilates has certainly put a spring in my step. (Unlike my MBTs).

'You haven't said anything to Joe?'

'Nope. I'm concentrating on myself at the moment. I've got other things going on. Somehow it's less important.'

'I can't believe that. What's so important?'

I stop pushing Evie. She waggles her feet impatiently. 'Well, maybe important is the wrong word.' I'm not entirely sure what I'm saying here. 'I've lost a bit of weight . . .'

'You didn't need to.'

'Far better being in a bad relationship weighing in at nine-and-a-half-stone than ten stone plus.'

Nicola smiles. 'Well, I am presuming you're getting near the point of asking him what the hell went on? That Amy make-over thingymajig must be achieved now?'

'Achieved? Oh no! Not yet. I'm getting there.'

'Yes, there's the boob job, the buttock lift.'

I laugh.

Nicola shifts Thomas to the non-aching hip. 'And Joe. What does he think of this self-improvement?'

I stare back at Nicola's pretty blue eyes blankly, thoughts forming as the words fall from my mouth. 'Er, the truth is . . . I don't really know. Sometimes he seems to appreciate it. He kind of likes my new shoes, now that he's forgiven them for assaulting him. And I think secretly he likes my hair. But he has a problem with Alice.'

'Alice? Why? She's harmless enough. I thought she was quite funny actually.'

'Sees her as a bad influence. Possibly she's too attractive and that disturbs him. Maybe he's just an awkward sod. God, I don't know.'

Nicola puts Thomas – 'my dear fat lump' – on the ground where he fillets and sucks fallen leaves. 'I think,' she says solemnly, 'that he is threatened by *you*, not Alice.'

'By me? Don't be silly. I'm Amy Crane, masquerading as someone else in more expensive clothes, but Amy Crane all the same.'

'You're not. I discovered what you are when I was on the internet yesterday, when I should have been giving Thomas his dinner.' She clears her throat. 'You are a MILF!'

'What the hell's that?'

'A Mother I'd Like to Fuck!' Nicola says, unable to hide her delight. Nicola likes to abbreviate things. 'An American expression. There are millions of sites on the internet devoted to your species.'

'Only a sub-editor . . .'

Walking back from the park, I roll MILF around my tongue, let it dissolve sweetly. Could I ever really be a MILF?

Twenty-seven

Mum's kidnapped Evie for her non-date date, leaving me and Joe without our prop. We wander around the house not knowing what to do with ourselves, straining to relax. We turn Franz Ferdinand up really loud, just to reassure ourselves that we haven't turned into our parents. (Secretly we'd both prefer a bit of peace and quiet.) I apply a face mask, a gift from Alice, and scrape the dirt crescent out from under my thumbnail with a yellow stick. Joe sits down on my old pink upholstered bedroom stool, observing grumpily, splayed knees jutting out. What is it with men and personal space? Why can't they ever sit with their knees together like women do?

'We've ceased to notice that this room smells of poo,' he mutters, pointing to the stinking huddle of nappy bags. 'We've ceased to notice a lot of things.'

My face is tight. Any movement cracks the mask. I raise an eyebrow. Something squeaks.

'You're not talking to me?'

'Trying to. A bit difficult.'

'I don't know why you put crap like that on your face, buy into that whole beauty company propaganda.'

'Who are you? Naomi Wolfe?'

Joe blows out noisily, lifting his fringe, revealing the creep of his hairline. 'I can't quite get a handle on what's going on, Amy.' He moves his legs further apart, elbows on knees. 'I'm so pleased to see you happier. You seem lighter somehow . . .'

I crack a smile. 'By about eight-and-a-half pounds.'

'With people, I mean. With everyone. And you're pulling your life together. Thinking about work.' He looks doubtful and crosses his legs. 'Although you haven't told me your decision yet. It would be nice if you communicated.'

'Sorry. It's just that I haven't made a decision yet.'

'Well, you've been thinking about it I'm sure. Anyway, that's by the by. My point is that you seem happier around everyone . . . everyone but me.' Joe shoots a moody unfathomable look. I used to find these looks really seductive, in the earliest days. They suggested he was brooding, deep and thoughtful. That's endorphins for you. Now I'm not entirely sure what's going on beneath those glass paper-weight eyes. 'It's like I'm just the person you have to eat dinner with. All we ever talk about is Evie, or domestics – the washing, the laundry – and who will be looking after her and when. It's not a proper relationship.'

'It's . . . it's . . .'

'Careful, you are developing a fissure around your nose to mouth lines.'

'Very funny.'

But Joe isn't laughing. Joe looks miserable. And Joe looks tired, his handsome features crumpled. 'It's what, Amy? *What*?'

The sun sheets through the windows, catching the dust disturbed by Joe's tapping foot. Boom, boom, boom! The bass gets louder, more insistent. Just tell him, I hear Nicola say. Risk it. Face the truth.

'The park,' I say, mumbling through the ever-hardening face mask.

'Ark? What are you talking about?'

'Regent's Park. That day. I was pregnant . . .' Joe looks puzzled but an anxious muscle twitches in his jaw. '. . . I came down . . .'

Slam!

The door goes. Evie's primordial wail snakes up the stairs. 'Cooeeee!'

And that is that. My soundtrack drowned out by Evie, by Mum. The film that could have played doesn't. And five minutes later I'm still here in the same domestic space, my life dramatically unchanged. Part of me is actually rather relieved that I haven't forced an issue. What was I thinking? Where would I go? Far better this, for the moment. The conversation will soon be lost in our busy day-to-day airspace. I wipe the mask off in milky circles, revealing skin as pink as the sole of Evie's foot.

'Let's talk another time,' says Joe. 'Now, have you seen my clean blue socks?'

Twenty-eight

A reaction to the face mask: my face is fluorescent pink, as if I've spent the morning sunbathing. (Joe thinks this highly amusing.) With weird symmetry, Evie does actually have a mild case of sunburn. (Joe is furious.) My mother, evidently distracted, 'forgot' to put on Evie's sunscreen while using her as a romantic chaperone. As a tan, let alone sunburn, on a baby is tantamount to child abuse, I fruitlessly try and smear the heat away with baby lotion. This inflames my mother's guilty hysteria further, which, coming unhelpfully after the event, irritates Joe. The house crackles with tension. And I am late.

With Evie sheltered like a maharaja under a broderie anglaise parasol (the roses on her cheeks taken down by a canny dusting of baby powder), we set off for Annabel's baby shower. We pound past the tight terraces of Kilburn, the delis and bakeries of the Salusbury Road, towards the streets framing Queen's Park where vast million-pound houses sit, bloated with rising equity, like smugly pregnant women.

Annabel's house, one of the largest, gazes directly on to the park from its northern border, Chevening Road. (How pleasant it must be not to live within sight of a Poundland.) Her door is sage green with finely etched glass panels. The gleaming door furniture invites a sharp chic knock. There is a scuttling sound, a low shadow behind the glass. A beautiful blond boy opens the door. He stares at me solemnly. 'I'm Cosmo,' he says in a pipey BBC voice. 'Are you invited to the party?'

I try not to scuff the dove grey hallway with my pram. Up the staircase, eye directed by twirly Victorian banisters and a run of black-and-white photographs, is a huge well of light cut into the ceiling, a rectangle of sunshine. Further down the hall, a hall as wide as Evie's bedroom, comes the sound of music and laughter and squealing children.

'Amy! Through here,' yells Alice. 'In the kitchen.'

Alice, Blythe and Jasmine are perched around a huge oak table piled high with pink glittery cup cakes, creamed meringues, white-chocolate-dipped strawberries and vegetable crudités. Polite women with thick foreign accents, presumably staff, pour flutes of pink champagne. Scampering around their feet are children who look like they've walked off the set of a period drama. They're dressed early nineteenth century: the girls in twee little pinafores and T-bar patent shoes and the boys, little Lord Fauntleroys, in sailor boy suit-like things. Evie, once again, rather misses the mark in her Velcro sandals and Britney Spears-style Hennes jersey dress.

'Here, here.' Alice pats the tan leather-padded chair next to her. 'Champagne?'

'Oh Amy!' shrieks Jasmine. 'Have you had a peel? Dermabrasion?'

'No, funny reaction to a face mask.' Amy Crane does it again.

Blythe stares at Evie. 'Oh Lord, is that the sun?' she says in horror, as though Evie had first degree burns. (Admittedly,

Evie has rubbed away the baby powder and blooms with free-radicals.)

Pretending I haven't heard, I scan the kitchen. The handleless cupboards, the phone-box big American fridge, the gleaming granite worktops and rows and rows of happy family photographs – beaming, lovely children – suspended on a tiny steel wire above the table.

'That's my husband Charlie.' A pink-nailed finger points at a handsomely chiselled man in a good suit, his arm protectively circling around his wife.

'Annabel!' I swivel round and kiss her. I've kind of missed Annabel since she's been at home resting, missed watching the reassuring weekly growth of her bump in class. (So much nicer when it isn't yours.) Her belly is almost surreally big now, resting on her knees. But, bar the remarkable bust, the rest of her hasn't changed. She looks like an ancient fertility symbol.

'Welcome to my pen,' she laughs. 'Sorry it's such a tip, cleaner called off sick.'

'Don't be silly. It's lovely, like a magazine shoot,' I reply, failing in my attempt not to sound awestruck. But it's tidier than my house ever is. And she's got three children. Where is their mess?

'Sadly, I'm now too huge to wear my shower T-shirt.'

'But *you're* not, Amy,' says Blythe. 'Here.' She chucks over a white T-shirt with 'oh baby' scrawled across the front in pink glittery letters. Alice and Jasmine are wearing them too. 'From your favourite haunt.'

These are the T-shirts I spotted Blythe buying all those weeks ago in Primark. How bizarre that our co-ordinates went on to criss-cross, such an unlikely Venn diagram. Funny how life works.

I nip into the downstairs bathroom to change, eyeing the

minimalist taps warily. After a quick struggle I manage to squeeze into the size ten T-shirt and wonder what etiquette would be put into play had I not been able to. The door opens with a soft click and I walk back to the dining area.

'. . . so, yes, I'd have a fanny tuck but not in England. I'd have one back home,' drawls Blythe as I re-enter the room. 'I've tried the exercises but they are just so damn tedious. And while dear David is happy to pay for it . . .'

'A fanny tuck!' Annabel swallows her cupcake whole. (She is noticeably the only person eating them. The others pick on carrot sticks.) 'Blythe, that is extreme! I'll give you the name of my birth guru in Belsize Park. She's got some great exercises.'

'Not the fanny stretcher in a sari!' shrieks Alice, slapping the table, trembling the David Mellor cutlery.

Annabel tuts. 'This one will just drop out, you'll see.'

'It is your fourth after all,' remarks Blythe dryly. 'I give it twelve months before you ask for my surgeon's number.'

Annabel rubs the hard orb of her belly. 'I so won't. But I will be asking for your nutritionist.' She picks up another cupcake then slaps it back down on the plate. 'God, you've got to stop me eating all these cupcakes. I'm meant to be on a no-sugar diet. Hopeless.'

'Your guru would be very disappointed.'

'I know, I know. But I'm sure it's the baby making me do it. Where are the kids? Let's feed them so I'm not tempted. Here Cosmo! Constantine! Lulu! Food to make you hyper-active!'

'Allegra doesn't eat sugar or anything made with white flour,' Blythe tuts, just as I pop a lump of icing into Evie's mouth.

There is a clattering stampede as the other children flood the kitchen, followed in hot pursuit by nannies, babies on their hips. The room is a jostling bob of heads and sticky grasping fingers and licking and sucking. We coo at them for a few minutes. Then the nannies are given a nod and all are removed to a chorus of entertainers and a ball pool in a distant playroom, their dropped bright paper plates, streamers and echoing cackles the only evidence they were here, like the morning after a funfair.

We pick up where we left off. 'As soon as this one's out I'll be back to my dirty little secret,' says Annabel. 'I do so miss the magic needles of Doctor Sopak, your best tip, Blythe. My husband keeps saying to me, "Darling you look so tired," and I want to tell him it's only because I can't have Botox while I'm pregnant.' Annabel giggles. 'But one must retain some kind of mystery.'

The others nod their heads casually. So that's why! I examine their foreheads. Smooth as skating rinks. No wonder none of them ever look stressed.

Alice looks at me. 'You should try it, Amy. Fantastic. Wipes away the sleepless nights better than any cream.'

I laugh. Me? Joe would die.

'You don't?' Blythe looks amazed. 'Frown . . . Gosh, you really don't. Right.' She scrambles into a vast brown handbag, more buckles than bag, and pulls out a pink leather address book, licks her finger and flicks through scrawled lists of names and numbers. 'Here it is. You owe me.' She pens a number on to a pink napkin, pushes it across the table. I reluctantly fold the napkin up and throw it into my handbag, where it's immediately lost in the swim of Tampax, receipts and old bus tickets.

'Right, *presents*,' says Alice clapping her hands.

Presents? Oh shit. I realise that in the rush to get here I've left the white Gap Babygro at home. However, it transpires that this is a blessing. As the present-giving begins, it becomes clear that the Gap Babygro so would not do. Annabel receives cashmere cardigans, pink baby Dior slippers, Tiffany baby rattles and an acre of protected rainforest. Worse, she's incredibly gracious about my social uncouthness.

'More bubbly, Amy,' says Jasmine refilling her own again, then mine. She turns back to Alice. '. . . And so I said to him, Don't you dare leave your wife for me!' She waves her champagne flute around tipsily, ignoring her son Marlon who is tugging on her T-shirt for attention. 'Married men. They're as needy as lesbians.'

'Well, you should count yourself unlucky,' says Alice. 'Most of them would rather leave their dick than their wife.'

Annabel giggles, jabs me with her elbow and whispers, 'Terrible. Single mothers.'

'I know you don't wholly approve, Annabel.' Jasmine fends herself against the tug of her son. 'No, Marlon, later. Mummy will play later. Because you are happily married. But I was happily married once too. Gosh, I thought Judd was just the sexiest music producer alive.'

'Quite a catch,' Alice murmurs.

'Then the rot set in. Wanted me to be the perfect fucking Notting Hill housewife while he fucked the studio assistant.' Her words are thick with sadness and Dom Perignon. 'Believe me, it can change.'

Blythe arches away from Jasmine, her thin back pressing into her chair, as if Jasmine's drunk bitterness could be catching.

'But don't be disheartened.' Jasmine stares directly at me, bloodshot eyes. What have I got to do with this? 'We have our fun.'

I shift uncomfortably.

'I've heard all about you,' she continues. Jasmine is a bad drunk, a liability. Alice glares at her. 'All about that dreadful

203

boyfriend of yours. He's unworthy! Listen to Alice, chuck that man and come and play!'

Alice whispers 'Sorry' to me under her breath and puts her hand on Jasmine's arm, just as she raises it to top up her glass. I want the limestone floor to swallow me up.

'That's *not* what I said, Jasmine.'

'Oh come on, Alice. Let's not whitewash over this, she'd be better off without him, wouldn't she?' Jasmine goes hammily serious. 'You said so.' The kitchen is suddenly silent. Heads swivel from me, to Alice and back again.

'Well?' I say to Alice, my voice a bit squeaky, undermining my attempt to brush it off casually. 'Did you say that?'

Alice squirms in her Seven jeans. 'Kind of.'

Before I have a chance to tell them that no, they're wrong, Joe is a good, decent man and to mind their own business, Jasmine raises her glass.

'I'd like to propose a toastshhhh,' she slurs. 'To Amy Crane, the new single yummy mummy! Lock up your husbands!'

Twenty-nine

My nose to mouth lines are like brackets. I wrinkle my forehead again and study the betrayal in the mirror. It's not so much the lines that are the worst bit, but the way the skin sits slightly loose on the bone, laid over like a rumpled blanket that might just slip off completely if confronted with a particularly powerful centrifugal force. It strikes me that it is undoubtedly better to have the babies earlier, in one's mid-twenties, because at least then the stretch marks and aging process wouldn't coincide so mockingly.

Shit, what the hell does one do when really old? Avoid mirrors altogether? Strive to look 'presentable' and not offend anyone with inappropriate flashes of turkey neck or sagging knees, and wear Harrods green, glad that your husband no longer hassles for sex? Shit, what happens when the unspeakable horror of a grey pubic hair sprouts?

I really don't think Mum's there yet. But there is a certain forgetfulness, and a C curve to her back as she hugs a cup of milky tea, and pale brown stains on her hands, prescient hints of that process that turns the old back into infants. In my darker moments, I can't help but wonder if that's what is in store for me. Years of looking after Evie followed by years of looking after Mum. Or, perhaps, even more alarmingly, I will become Evie's burden, the dribbling incontinent mother, phoning every day, demanding payback.

I adjust the mirror to get a three-quarter view, holding my chin up to avoid my worst angle. Yes, I have managed to shed a good few pounds and my cheekbones are more pronounced, two distinct planes if seen at certain artful angles. At least I no longer look like I've squirrelled away a winter's supply of marshmallows in my cheeks. I'm almost there. But not quite. Those wrinkles . . .

I roll the little rip of pink napkin between my fingers like a Rizla. The telephone number is written in clear, well-schooled handwriting. Could I? Should I? Or does a daughter's neurosis start here, with her mother's disappointment in the mirror? Some legacy. I bend down to stroke Evie's cheek. She flumps sweetly on her stomach, so happy in her skin. No, I'm not going to pass age-phobia and eating disorders on to my daughter. That would be a narcissistic Mommie-Dearest thing to do. I flick the napkin into the bin. And there it stays. For about ten minutes. Then the telephone beckons. Just a call. An introductory call to work out how much it would cost. It's not going to do any harm, just curiosity. As with my attraction to Josh, I'll section the possibility of Botox to the crèche in my head where young unformed thoughts play, safe, penned in.

Thirty

The door is huge and panelled, painted a shameless red. There's a strong smell of metal polish. The brass name list gleams. Dr Sopak's name is second from the top. Sopak? What kind of name is that? Sounds like a noodle. I take a step down the white steps, tight grip on the ornate handrail, ready to backtrack down Harley Street, away from the terrifying proposition of turning into a footballer's wife. But something stops me. I take a deep breath, think about my perma-tired face and press the button. This is the last step.

'Er, I'm here for, um, Dr Sopak,' I whisper, huddled close to the bell, not wanting to be identified by passers-by as someone who goes to Harley Street cosmetic clinics.

'The Skinsense Clinic,' says a posh voice loudly over the intercom. Buzzzzz.

Am I in? I'm in.

The building's reception area looks like a tired country house. There's a big fireplace full of ornamental logs, springy velvet sofas, paintings on the walls of chinless ancestor types and stacks of *Country Life* magazines on the side tables. A dowdy sixtysomething, irretrievably wrinkled, glowers behind the dark wood reception desk.

'Skinsense? Third floor,' she says, eyeing me with undisguised distaste. 'I'm not certain you'll be able to fit the pram in the lift. No one has ever brought their baby *here* before.'

Evie smiles up at me from her buggy. My mother was going to babysit but asked if I could excuse her at the last moment as Norman had offered to fix her shelving just before he went away to Asia or somewhere exotic, and the shelves were in such a state, threatening to collapse and cause severe head injury or worse.

We squeeze into the old wrought iron lift and rattle up to the third floor. A door: 'Skinsense Clinic, wiping the years'. Ah, this is more like it. The clinic is white and clean, an orchid on the desk, fashion magazines. The woman behind this reception desk is reassuringly glamorous.

'Amy Crane! Welcome. I'm Amber. Dr Sopak will receive you in one minute. Do take a seat. *Cute baby*!' Amber smiles. Nice name. But there's something odd about her. It takes a moment to spot, like good dubbing: her mouth moves when she speaks, but nothing else. Amber caught in amber.

Dr Sopak appears. White overall over a suit, clean shaven, hooded eyes, too sleepy for a doctor. Aged about forty? Hard to tell. His skin is waxy and smooth like the leaves on the yucca palm in the corner. Like his secretary, no smile lines.

Oh God. I'm only thirty-one. Please don't freeze my face. 'I haven't done this before,' I blurt. 'I really only want a little bit, if you think I need any, which perhaps . . .'

Dr Sopak laughs, a shallow, easy laugh. His eyes don't crease. 'Please do not worry, Miss Crane. Everyone feels like that on their first time, believe me. You'll soon realise it's about as eventful as having your eyebrows plucked.' He wouldn't say that if he knew. 'Come this way, Miss Crane.'

He ushers me into the examining room and tells me to hop on to the chair and make myself comfortable, which I can't. 'Hmmm. I can see we've got a bit of work to do here,' he says, inspecting my face. 'Don't look so worried. It'll be so subtle. No wind-tunnel effect, promise.' Then he gets out what looks like a black marker pen. 'Frown,' he says. 'Grimace. Smile . . . there's a good girl.' There have only been two other people who have called me a 'good girl' in adulthood. My abortionist and my caesarean surgeon. Not a good precedent.

Sopak draws on my face, following the contours of my lines like a relief map. He pens my nose–mouth lines. I smell instant coffee on the tips of his fingers. To ground myself I concentrate on studying Evie, who rather than falling asleep as hoped, is sitting bolt upright in her pram, straining at the straps.

'See, it's just a 'ittle needle,' Sopak says, unwrapping not such a little needle from its cellophane. 'And I just put a teeny weeny bit of this Botox in here . . .'

I'm not sure whether the baby talk is for my benefit or Evie's. He's giving me the creeps. Sopak sucks up the botulism and flicks the needle with his wrist. I sit up from the bed.

'No, no, lie still, honey, totally still. It's just a little prick, won't hurt a bit.'

The needle stings into my skin. There is a crunching sound, a stepped-on-cockroach sound.

'What's that weird noise?'

'Just the muscle. Lie back, there's a good girl.'

I feel something warm drip down my face. The needle comes at me, again and again, like a furious wasp. Please stop, please stop. Breathe. *Breathe*. It's only Botox, for god's sake, people have parties with the stuff. But it's no good, I can't see parties, I can only picture *Daily Mail*-style Botox – 'my face-droop horror' – front-page stories. Biting my lip, like

209

a brave child, I focus on my new Nicole Kidman complexion, Josh's admiration, the bad nights wiped away. More stings. More crunches.

Suddenly there is the most terrible howl from Evie. I jolt.

'Do not move!' commands Sopak, needle raised like a sword.

This inflames Evie further. I feel utterly helpless, being unable to pick her up. More warm trickles. More screams.

'I'll get a tissue,' he says quickly.

I sit up and catch my reflection in the mirror and gasp. Blood is streaming from my forehead down my face, rivulets feeding into my mouth, trickling under my jaw, Catholic red. Then I turn and look at Evie. Mistake. She stares at me in silent horror for a few moments. Then her face turns burgundy and she sucks in a huge backdraught of air, fills her lungs, swells her chest . . .

'Waaaaaaaaaaaaaaaaa!' Evie is beside herself.

'Tissue, tissue,' chatters Sopak nervously, smoothness lost. 'There, all gone.'

I jump off the bed and pick Evie up out of her pram and cuddle her to my chest. She writhes and kicks in my arms like something possessed, purple in the face now, gasping for breath.

Heels click clack urgently on the tiled floor. 'Is everything OK?' Amber swings open the door. A frown has even managed to worm its way between her frozen lakes of Botox. 'Poor baby, what happened?'

'Just got a bit of a shock seeing Mummy with a bloody face I think,' says Sopak, looking desperate. 'Let's get Miss Crane's transaction done as soon as possible.'

'WAAAAAAAAAAAA!'

What have I done to my child? Have I scarred her for life? I rummage in my bag trying to find a bribe biscuit. She throws it across the floor. Dummy. Across the floor. I bend down and bundle Evie into her pram.

'Miss Crane!' shouts Sopak above the racket. 'Please avoid bending down. Try to stay upright for the rest of the day. No alcohol. Keep frowning for the next few hours.'

I frown into car window mirrors all the way home, just to check. Only a few red dots on my forehead. It'll take a while to set. Evie, calm now she's lost her audience, munches bread-sticks and gurgles happily. As we trip through Marylebone, euphoria tickles beneath my skin. I did it! The mother of all make-overs! Done.

Thirty-one

Joe sits on the sofa, feet scuffing at the scuffed patch on the floorboards, moulding the house to fit his shape like a shoe. Beer in one hand, he turns the stiff pages of a photo album, licking his finger, flicking. These albums are usually hidden away at the back of the airing cupboard, he's never shown the slightest interest in them before.

'So, how does the present measure up?' I grin, still pleased with myself.

'Ah, getting all sentimental on you,' Joe sighs, smiling gently, absorbed. 'Just got a real urge to see these. Wasn't she the cutest?' He points to a picture of a just-born Evie, tiny in the bowl of his huge hands. A nurse took that picture. I was in too much pain to move, the caesarean scar felt like a shark bite. 'And you . . . sweet.'

So not sweet. It must have been a couple of weeks after the birth. I am collapsed on the sofa, eyes glittering with exhaustion, shell shocked and pasty.

Joe pats the sofa next to him. I yank off my jacket and sidle up, inhaling his yeasty smell of beer, relieved to be momentarily freed from my schoolgirl pangs and the jubilant vanity that led me to Harley Street. Closed in on one side by the wall of his solid, warm body, I can contain myself, the thorny garden of desires and doubts. His hands work the pages over quickly.

'Nice hair.' I point to a picture of Joe taken a few years ago, hair battling his collar like Michael Bolton's.

'It's rocking out. I may grow it again,' he teases.

'You will not. It's lost in translation. What is OK in Goa is not OK in NW6.'

He nuzzles into my hair and sniffs. 'I have to confess, I do rather like yours now,' he says unexpectedly, stroking it gently. 'If I can forget about how much money you spent and the fact it's bleached, it's almost like it was in India, lightened by the sun.' He lifts bits of my hair and lets it drop again. 'Smell that sandalwood.'

'Remember the lice?' We got the most terrible lice in India, ferocious tropical things. The underbelly of our sunset romance.

'You really do know how to kill a moment, don't you?' Joe goes back to the album, fingers trailing the pages from one photo to another. 'That was a boiling summer, do you remember? I got embarrassingly sunburnt.'

He points to a photograph of me, Joe and Kate in Kate's garden, late August. Joe is standing between me and Kate, arms cradling both of us. I was about five months pregnant, had just come out of my sick phase and looked overweight rather than pregnant. Kate's been caught at an unfortunate angle. While Joe and I smile into Pete's lens, Kate's gaze hits just below the camera lens, so she's there but not involved somehow. She was having a rough time with Pete. She did her best to mask it but my pregnancy hit her hard. She'd been trying for a baby for months by that point.

'Don't forget we're going to Kate's this weekend,' I say, suddenly remembering myself. Without the regime of work or a diary (little point in one without the other) days slip into

213

weeks, months. The park's change in season is the nearest I get to a clock.

'If we must,' he says grumpily.

'We promised. You know Kate will have cleared Waitrose and redecorated the entire house in a new shade of Farrow and Ball for the event. We can't not.' Part of me is dying to know if she notices anything different. Will the wrinkles have gone by then?

'OK, just the Friday.' He tucks a wedge of hair behind my ear and kisses me on the nose.

'What's that for?' A guilty conscience?

'I don't kiss you enough.' Joe stares at me, a little tenderly at first. Then his expression changes into puzzled concern. He peers closely into my face, eyes fixed on my hairline. 'Amy, what are those?' His finger taps the sore spots on my forehead. 'You have little bruises all over your face.'

'What?' I stand up and look in the sitting-room mirror. Christ. All the little white needle dots have ripened into pink circular bruises. They track along my forehead, between my eyes, like a red ant's footsteps.

'Not sure.' Despite my attempts not to, I can't stop myself shifting guiltily. I'm the world's worst liar.

Joe knows this. He frowns. 'Amy? Please tell me what these are? I can tell you're hiding something. These are not normal bruises. What have you done?'

'I've had . . .' I take a deep breath. Why should I be ashamed? I am merely making the best of myself. Besides, few women in west London can frown any more. '. . . Botox.'

'BOTOX!' Joe thunders, face puce. I don't have to wonder where Evie gets it from. 'Botox! You are fucking joking! You're completely insane. That poison . . .'

'Calm down, Joe, please.' But I have no effect. Joe's chest bellows with fury.

214

'What the fuck is going on, Amy? Who are you becoming?'

'I thought it would just be one little prick.'

'One little prick! I'm going to phone Alice.' Joe's nostrils flare into two black tunnels.

'Calm down, it isn't Alice's fault.'

'Yeah right. I bet she made you go. She did, didn't she?' He strides towards the phone. Shit, he really is going to phone her.

'Stop! Joe, it's got nothing to do with Alice.' My pleading works. He stops, hands shaky. 'What's wrong with making the best of myself? Tell me? I'm looking so fucking rough, haven't slept properly for months.'

'You are not the only fucking mother in the world who has a baby who doesn't sleep through. I don't see them nipping from the baby clinic to the Botox doctor. I'm not even going to ask how much it cost. It'll make me too angry.'

'Please, Joe, try and understand.'

He looks at me bewildered. His mouth opens to speak but he seems to think better of it. 'I'm going out,' he whispers and closes the door softly behind him, rather than slamming it, just to show his restraint.

My mistake: I should never ever have told Joe. And I shouldn't have to apologise for a choice I make about *my* body. It's fine for me to be sawn in two like a magician's assistant by a scalpel-happy caesarean surgeon, but not for me to choose to have a few small injections.

I cover my forehead in the thickest foundation I can find, reach for the solace of the biscuit tin and slump on a kitchen chair, running my fingertips lightly over the lumpy tracks beneath my skin. Hmm, Sopak didn't mention how long they might last. In fact he didn't mention them at all. A heat, he'd said, just a heat that would go away in a couple of hours. And yes, a rather expensive heat.

215

I suppose Joe's right though. Funny, without the hours put in behind the desk, money's value is lost and something of an heiress's casual sense of entitlement sets in. The idea that the money may completely dry up becomes harder to grasp. I haven't looked at a bank statement for over four months. It's about time.

In the office under the stairs is a scratched silver filing cabinet, filled with old mortgage repayment reminders and two-year-old telephone bills. I scrabble through its dusty files and pull out the bank statements. Oh. Did I really spend that much at the hairdressers? On Westbourne Grove with Alice? The joint account is in a similarly bad state. Notably, our food bills have doubled since Evie moved on to solids, as the fridge is now entirely stocked with locally sourced organics, such is our fear of pumping our darling daughter full of sex hormones, antibiotics and radioactive ingredients. However, Joe's account – I can't resist looking – isn't doing too badly. He doesn't spend all his income every month, as I always have done. His expenditures are neither excessive nor glamorous: Amazon, The London Underground, Sainsbury's, Boots and Bloom's Hatton Garden Jewellery. £2575. What?

Thirty-two

Golden afternoon sun shafts through the Velux windows. Spacious, calm and warm, it contrasts with the space I've just fled with its question marks hanging in the alcoves, doubts and suspicions huddled like moths in the corners. At first the studio seems empty. But then I see Josh, sitting quietly, legs crossed, alone, monk-like on a mat. Beneath a tousled mop of curls his sienna skin glows, plumped and tightened by a new tan. His back is infant-straight. From this angle I can see his eyes are shut, the lids shadowed by the sharp cliff-cut of his eyebrows. It feels rude to wake him from this quiet meditation. I consider leaving again to face the music, pretending I never came.

'Don't go,' he says suddenly. 'Sit down, on the mat next to me.'

He doesn't open his eyes. It strikes me that it takes real confidence to address someone with your eyes shut. 'Where is everyone?'

'Oh, er, flu I think. Lovers. Annabel's gone into labour.'

'Gosh, really? Wow.'

'Sit down opposite me. On my mat.'

I do. It feels OK, not too embarrassing because his eyes are shut.

'I knew you'd come.' His blue eyes spring open, pupils spreading and shrinking to focus. 'Have you ever played this game?' The corners of his mouth curl. 'Group therapists love it.'

Game? I look at him puzzled, remembering how unpredictable he can be.

'Look at me.' He edges forward on his mat so he's about a foot away and just stares at me, unflinching, like Joe stares at Sky News. 'You hold eye contact with the other person for as long as possible. It's an incredibly intimate thing to do, always makes me go gooey.'

I laugh nervously.

'Hey, don't look down! Not allowed.'

I lock my eyes with his and stare. It is hard, very hard. I just want to blink him away, glance at the floor, ceiling, anywhere to escape the drilling honesty of Josh's eyes. It feels like we've been sitting here for an eternity. Call time, call time. He doesn't.

'You OK?' he says.

'It's difficult.'

'Yes, it's about opening yourself up. Makes you feel vulnerable, doesn't it?'

How long has it been? Five, ten minutes? He is still staring. I'm blinking now and my right nostril itches. I imagine two pipes running from my eyes to his. Emotions begin to trickle along it, like chatter on a telephone wire. Back and forth. Mostly sadness pouring out. I think about the hotel and the jewellery bill and Joe's secretive, jumpy behaviour of late. How could he?

'You're crying,' Josh says, voice conveying neither sympathy nor judgement.

Shit, I am. I wipe my eyes, brimming with hot tears, and laugh. I can no longer hold his gaze. 'You win.'

218

'No one wins. It's not a competitive game.'

'Sorry, I don't know what happened there. My eyes just got all sort of watery, as if I'd been staring into the sun or something.' This suddenly strikes me as very funny. I try and choke back my giggles. Josh doesn't laugh. But, interestingly, this doesn't bother me. I feel incredibly comfortable with him, like all the awkwardness of our social encounter had been burned away by the brutal intimacy of the staring.

'Bleuhhh!' Josh shakes his hands and his head, lips wobbling. 'Need to wake up. I'm very Zen today for some reason. It's going to be a very relaxed class.' He yawns, stretching his arms back. They arch like bows. 'I'm so pleased it's you who came,' he adds quietly, almost purring.

'Well, if you wanted an easy class, I'm your woman.'

'No, really.' He lays a hand on my forearm. 'I would rather it was you than anyone else. It makes sense.'

I cannot help but soften weakly under this blatant flattery.

'Let's do some stretches.'

They are powerful stretches, creating space between my knees and hips. I'm flexible today. My body feels intelligent, obedient. No longer a lump of playdough.

'Cobra,' he commands, squatting by my side, his palm pushing down on the small of my back.

So I lie on my front and push myself up, spine arching improbably upwards.

'More, more. Towards the sky.'

'I can't go further.' It hurts. I might snap.

'You can. Let me hold you up.' He slides a hand under each of my shoulders and supports the whole weight of my upper body on his arms, veins swelling.

'There, you see!'

A rush of pride. Josh breaks all my old limits. That's why he's such a good teacher. Flushed and exhilarated I flop down on to the mat, my cheek resting on the sticky rubbery surface. Then I remember. Botox. '*Do not bend down for the rest of the day.*' I spring up. Shit, shit, shit. Swamped by the deliciousness of having Josh to myself in the sunny studio, I'd totally forgotten the doctor's advice.

'You OK?' Josh looks concerned. 'Don't leap up. Take it easy.'

Will my eyelids droop? Christ. 'I've got to go.'

'What? We've got another twenty minutes.'

'Really, I've got to.'

'Amy, you do not *have* to do anything. The world won't collapse without you . . .'

Excuse? I can't tell him about the botulism worming its way under my forehead.

'. . . And you were just beginning to let go.' He looks a bit crushed. I feel bad.

We stay frozen in this odd tableau for a few moments, me crouched on the mat, like a runner at the start of a race, him squatting next to me. Each waiting for the next move. Both not wanting me to leave. He sighs heavily, eyes darkening as his lids lower.

'God, Amy . . .' his voice tails off. '. . . I think you are *so* beautiful.'

Each word hits with the force of a punch. Me? Josh thinks I am *beautiful*? No one calls *me* beautiful. Breath catches in my throat. My heart thumps and a confused heat spreads inside like a blood stain. *I didn't imagine it. I didn't imagine it.*

'I've spent so long wanting you. Wishing . . .' He looks at me for some kind of response. I can't give it. '. . . That I could get you on your own.'

I never thought I'd ever hear a man say that to me ever again. It's like tasting a delicious soft cheese after the embargo

220

of pregnancy. He raises his hand, my eyes follow it, wondering where it will end up. My face. His fingers trace the curve of my cheek. They feel hot and damp.

'There's something between us. I'm not sure what, something . . .'

I still cannot speak. Why would such a man desire someone like me? His fingers tremble down my neck, across my breast bone, over one breast. As it journeys over my nipple I shiver. Perhaps I am desirable.

'Do you feel it too?'

'We . . . we . . . shouldn't,' I gasp, breath unlocked now, coming faster.

'Probably not.'

His fingers walk each bump of my spine. I'm frozen, unable to knock his hand away, to stand up and do the right thing and leave. He pushes me against a piece of Pilates equipment that jabs into my leg, as if trying to prick my conscience.

'Here.' Josh grabs my hand and puts it on his chest. His heart thumps through his rib cage into my palm.

He pushes my hand down so it skids on his honey skin, towards the sweat-damp V of hair around his belly button. I want to pull away but the message is lost somewhere in the journey between brain and hand. He leans forward, cups my face and kisses me, the pillows of his lips caving my mouth into his, our tongues, first tentative and tasting, then folding together like spatulas of cake dough. I haven't French kissed for months and its intimacy is shocking.

'You taste nice,' he whispers, pushing my hand down further, over the erection tenting his trousers.

First I think, that's pretty big. Second I think, that's not Joe's. The unfamiliarity is shocking. No, whatever Joe's done, I won't do it back, lower myself to his level. This is not the way forward. I pull away. 'Josh . . . I . . . I can't do this.'

221

But Josh ignores me, nuzzling his mouth into my neck and pulling me towards him, trapping me in an embrace. I don't fight it too hard: a shameful part of me wants to be trapped, to absolve myself of responsibility. Then his hand tugs at my tracksuit bottoms, my big white mum knickers. He pushes them towards my ankles, his bare brown foot on the gusset, until I am harnessed by them, immobilised, partly naked, sincerely wishing I'd got round to that bikini wax.

'Josh, I really don't think I can—'

'Shhhush . . .' Gasping loudly, like a diver before submerging, Josh bows his head and buries it between my legs.

I freeze. *Go on*, I hear Alice cry, *go on girl*. I resist and resist and then I think about Joe's betrayal and something in my brain snaps like elastic. I give in, legs scissoring in pleasure. Josh tugs up my top, exposing wild red nipples. Involuntarily, I buck towards him, astonished at the appetite of this body which no longer has anything to do with babies or breastfeeding or stretch marks and has become just a vessel of pleasure. I dissolve into a space that I'd forgotten existed.

Oh? I freeze again. What's this? Advanced sexual technique? There is a peculiar vibrating sensation beneath my naked bottom. A quick twitch. Then a ring, an extremely loud ring.

'What the fuck's that?' pants Josh.

I arch myself up and scoop my mobile phone from beneath me with a trembling hand.

'Man,' Josh sighs, glaring at the intruder.

The green caller interface flashes insistently. Joe, it reads.

Thirty-three

It's 10.45 a.m. and we are driving down the M23. But I'm a few hours behind, ground-hogged in the studio. I can still smell Josh's scent on me from yesterday, feel the after-shocks of his tongue in my mouth like an exploding sherbet sweet. Christ, what would have happened if Joe hadn't called?

I am horrified by what I've done, but unable to stop relishing the memory. My body feels different, alive at last. Surely I must look different in some way, indelibly branded? But Joe doesn't notice anything. He stares at the road ahead, aloof, preoccupied. We don't talk much, which is a relief. I'm terrified I'll incriminate myself with an answer to the simplest of questions. He doesn't even seem pissed off with me any more: the 'B' word hasn't been mentioned, like a dirty liaison ignored for the sake of stability (the bruises have gone). And I haven't mentioned the jewellery. Not yet, not now. How could I? Where can I find the appropriate outrage? It's gone. Josh was the price Joe paid for his dalliance. Joe and I are quits.

Time passes slowly. Joe coughs, massaging his shoulders into the back of his seat-rest. I sit primly, legs crossed at the ankles, skirt tugged politely over my knees, occasionally swivelling around to check on Evie, who sleeps in her car seat behind me, peaceful as a Botticelli *puttio*. We sit quietly like this, not uncomfortably, for over two hours. We stop to grab coffee, change Evie's nappy, the capsule family scene appallingly incongruous. Road markings zigzag past; signs, junctions. And I notice that with every mile on the clock, yesterday begins to drop away from me, the fade of a vivid dream. Have I just been unfaithful? Was that really me?

'This is the turning isn't it?' asks Joe, pulling off the motorway and on to an A road clouded with trees and cow parsley. Flies dash to their deaths on the windscreen. He relaxes as the traffic subsides and turns to look at me. 'You look exceptionally well today,' he says. 'That blue top really suits you.' He doesn't see me blush because his eyes return to the road, admiring the vintage green Bentley ahead.

'Thanks, Joe.' My voice is girlish, softly submissive, a natural reaction to my infidelity, the insistent gnaw of guilt. Not only for yesterday. The guilt for the fantasies. The guilt for the coffee in the greasy caffe. I never did tell Joe where I'd been.

'Here we are. Brace yourself.'

He turns off the road. A lane. A stone tablet reads 'The Nook'. Joe turns the car into it, leaves brushing the window, before crunching up the gravel of Kate and Pete's drive. The Nook is a large square house, Georgian with an arched trellis of honeysuckle over the door. To the left of the house you can glimpse an orchard, the nubbly twists of pear and apple trees, fruit shiny, still hard. To the left, framed by the gap in the open wooden gate, is a slice of pea-green lawn.

'Oh, I prefer the traffic jams of the Harrow Road,' quips Joe dryly. He's always viewed Kate and Pete's growing wealth with wry detachment rather than envy, bemused at how their personal problems seem to keep pace with their share options. Joe fully expects that he'll have all this himself one day, when he's older. Not a doubter. He used to say that all his grand plans for the design company were just a means to an end, the end being a glass-fronted eco-house, by the sea in Cornwall. He hasn't mentioned these plans for a long time.

Barking dogs. Three Labradors lollop around the back of the house, jump up at us as we get out of the car, flicking saliva on the windows. Kate swings open the front door and runs into the drive.

'You're here! Welcome!' she shrieks with delight, rushing up to Joe and squeezing him tight. She nuzzles Evie and air kisses me on both cheeks, slides an arm over my shoulders. 'You're looking *fab-u-lous*. Have to tell me your secret over lunch.' She laughs. 'I must look like quite the country bumpkin to you now.' Nothing is further from the truth. In her pink Ghost dress, coral-encrusted designer leather flip-flops and large straw hat, Kate looks every inch the city-imported country wife. 'Come this way, this way. Such a lovely day. We can eat in the garden if you don't mind sharing your pudding with the bees.'

We're ushered into the bottle green hall, the dogs hungrily sniffing Evie's dangling pink feet. As we walk, Joe grabs my hand and holds it very tight, showily, like we are new lovers who want to display their coupledom. I squeeze back reassuringly hard and feel like a two-faced wretch.

Installed on teak patio furniture we pick at olives and oily focaccia while Kate buzzes around the kitchen, opened up to the garden by her new architect-designed folding concertina doors. I close my eyes and throw my head back into the sun. Josh. Josh on the back of my eyelids. I open them again and the images vanish, like a magazine flopped shut in a hurry. I notice Joe is staring at me, his eyes soft and affectionate, but slightly puzzled. Am I giving off clues? Does he *know* on some subliminal level?

'Guys! Hi. Welcome to fair Sussex.' Pete's monotone. He shakes Joe's hand stiffly as if greeting a bank client and kisses me like a dog, leaving two wet lip prints that I discreetly wipe off on my napkin. 'Er, so . . . nice day,' he mutters, glancing over at Kate, wanting her to take the conversational responsibility. He readjusts his trousers – thorn slacks, the kind advertised at the back of the *Sunday Telegraph* – as if they were pinching. Since I last saw Pete, business lunches have pumped up his face. And he's lost more hair, the polish of his forehead creeping further up his square skull. How old is he? thirty-eight? forty? Funny, as Kate gets thinner and prettier in her thirties her husband seems to be aging at an exponential rate.

We chat about the weather, the dogs, things that have no relevance to the tumult in my head. I'm a little stunned at how easy it is to operate on two different levels. So this is how people get away with affairs?

Pete has a disconcerting habit of looking at my hairline when he talks. Not so much shyness as a certain arrogance, so rich he need not try. Still, it's easy to spot the strain, the bitten-down nails, the way he and Kate dosi-do around each other rather than risk physical contact. 'Bess! Naughty Max . . .' he says. But it's too late. The dogs have singled me out as the number one attraction, nudging their noses between my legs, sniffing greedily. Christ! The dogs know! I try and kick them back beneath the table, but everyone can see because the table is perforated. Joe thinks it's hilarious.

'Sorry, Amy. Such damn randy creatures.' Pete taps them playfully on the nose and banishes them to the kitchen.

The dog kerfuffle distresses Evie. Pete tenses, involuntarily backing away from the cry. He's much more comfortable with dogs than babies. Kate notices this reaction and glares at him, before cracking a tight white smile. She flicks her eyes up to check that Pete is watching and scoops Evie out of Joe's arms.

'My little sugar plum, whads da matter?' Kate buries her head in Evie's crisp yellow dress, then starts back violently.

'Sorry, she probably needs changing,' says Joe, smile twitching his lips.

'Oh, *I* don't mind,' says Kate rather unconvincingly. 'Pete might though!'

Pete, registering the dig and trying to be polite, shakes his head. Evie responds to being the centre of attention with a howl. Her eyes fix on me, begging me to rescue her, which I can't do without offending Kate and ruining her orchestration of this marital psychodrama.

'Don't take it personally,' I say.

'You're going to have such a lovely holiday,' coos Kate. Evie eyes her warily. 'I've redecorated your nursery . . .'

There's one thing Evie hates more than holidays and that's strange nurseries. Any change to her familiar routine offends her. She is the world's worst house guest.

'. . . I've warmed the swimming pool, bought you some floaters because I bet Mummy forgot to bring them, didn't you, Mummy?'

I nod and lean into the frill of the chair back. Joe rolls his eyes. Pete looks bewildered and excuses himself to get the drinks.

Evie retrieved and slumping her reassuring warm weight on my lap, I whoosh with a maternal-love rush, a relieved pleasure that she is back in my physical orbit once again. Then I notice a nick on the inside of my lower lip. It flavours my mouth with the rust of blood. A passionate love nick?

Was that really me? The same Amy that is sitting here now, baby on her lap, visiting old friends in the Sussex countryside. I am an awful person. I am despicable.

Two large glasses of cold Chablis take the edge off the self-loathing. And, like a perilous cliff edge, my current situation offers a new vantage point. I can see clearly that, next to Pete, Joe shines. Apart from anything else, his body is hard and lithe where Pete's is flaccid and fat-logged. (How can Kate sleep with him?) And Joe is funny. Joe is kind.

Perhaps I am so keenly aware of Joe's attractiveness because I'm the nearest I've ever been to losing him. Joe could leave me for another woman, whoever she may be. My indiscretion could be discovered. In theory, I could even leave Joe for Josh, for sex, for selfish pleasures. Alice's words dance around my head: *Life doesn't have to be like this, you can change it, Amy. Look at me, if I can do it you can . . .*

'Swim?' Kate hands me a fluffy white towel. I obediently follow her, padding across the lawn to the black mosaic swimming pool, a glittering trench of dark water, splendidly out of keeping with its rural surroundings. Newly potted ferns and palms arch over the water: Kate's been busy with the joint account. Rather ruining the effect is Pete, flopped out on a sun lounger in satsuma orange swimming trunks, scratching an overhang of belly. I suspect Pete believes his wealth exempts him from the exertion of physical maintenance.

Splash!

Joe dives into the pool, a V-shaped shadow trailing bubble pearls. For a few seconds, under the water, time suspended as I wait for him to surface, he is simply my big Joe, the man I fell in love with. At the end of each length he comes up for air with a gasp and shakes his head, spraying rainbows in the sunshine. Then he's under again.

228

Relationships are like this, mostly submerged, the action going on beneath the surface.

'Come on Amy.' Kate pulls me away from the poolside. 'You can't stare at Joe for ever. Let's get changed.'

In the tongue-and-groove changing room I step into my costume, bought with Alice from Westbourne Grove's Heidi Klein. It's showier than feels appropriate right now, a mocha-brown confection, held together with big loops of tortoiseshell plastic. Not to be outdone, Kate appears from her room in a scarlet halter-neck bikini, like Teri Hatcher's.

Relaxing slightly, I lean back on the sun lounger and sit Evie – shrouded in white muslin and sun cream – on my belly. Act normal.

'What's *that*?' demands Kate loudly, pointing at my thigh.

I glance down. Shit. There is a pink mark on my left thigh. It looks like a love bite. I don't remember Josh . . . oh, was it the Pilates equipment? I glare at the mark, a brand of infidelity. 'Oh . . . oh. Banged it.'

'Yeah right.' Kate doesn't do the polite thing but continues to inspect it intently. 'God, at least someone's having fun,' she concludes, not sounding too pleased about it.

Joe finishes a length, pulling himself up at the deep end, his great weight bridged on his straining shoulders, water dripping off him like tears. He must not see it.

'I'm too tipsy to swim. And I feel kind of burny,' I say, managing to flick a sarong around my waist, quick as a matador, before Joe appears holding a pink rock rose. He silently puts it behind my ear. I smile and wonder if he's checked it for ants. Sitting on the side of my lounger so it dips, Joe shades me like a cool, wet lump of rock and the temperature around him drops deliciously. He strokes my right leg. I shuffle my bottom into the lounger fabric to prevent sarong slippage. Kate, lying on her back, studies us from the tiny slit of her mostly closed left eye.

The day continues at a slow, sun-drenched, wine-in-the-afternoon pace. Pete and Joe play poker. Kate and I play with Evie who, of course, loathes the swimming pool. A toe dip ignites an ear-cracking wail. Kate furrows her brown brow. (She hasn't had it done then.) Only a mother can love a screaming baby, I say, thoughtlessly.

Kate's smile melts away. 'It's all I want.' She turns away from me. 'My baby could scream all it liked. I wouldn't care.'

'Of course. Sorry.' Kate's desire is so much more complicated, harder to sate than mine. I pat her arm and feel rather useless and guilty for being blessed with a baby. I feel like an undeserving mother. The day shifts slightly, gets denser.

'I've redecorated all my rooms, spent thousands on interior designers and architects. What else to do? It's just a question of waiting.' Her eyes squint amber in the sun. 'But what if what I'm waiting for never comes, Amy? What then?'

I tell Kate to try to live in the moment, enjoy the beauty of her surroundings, her wealth, her health. We both know it's a trite response but Kate humours me, knowing I'm doing my best to understand. We sit silently, watching Joe and Pete sipping beers in the shade, both now slightly pink as they deem high sun factor too girly. Pete has the shadow of a large fern leaf on his chest like a fossil.

'Gosh, I'm starving.' Kate sits up, wiping hair, sweat and sadness off her face, slipping the wife mask on. 'Barbecue time! Come on Joe, give us a hand.' Joe looks irritated at the order. 'Pete, give Amy a break and look after Evie.'

Pete's smile freezes. He rears up a little with fear, like a cornered animal, and then, not wanting to appear intimidated, falls into a fake can-do flippancy. 'Toss the child over.' He holds Evie slightly away from his body and sits down carefully and as far from the pool as possible, just in case Evie suddenly learns to walk and goes for a suicide dive.

Kate smiles at me warmly, a thank you for letting Pete have a go.

An hour later, I lie back on the lounger, wondering about Josh, wondering what would have happened had the phone not rung. I feel bad, but, still, thinking about it makes me a little marshy between the legs, my body and life suddenly incompatible. The sun drops in the sky. Pete waddles over with woman's hips and a cold San Miguel. Finding babies less troublesome than he initially thought, easier than the wife, he holds Evie close now. The sun bleeds rare over the Sussex countryside and our little party – friends, for so long, social survivors of fickleness and house moves – sink too much red wine around the glowing barbecue embers. As I get drunker, drowsier, my infidelity begins to seem like a wisp of dirty gossip about someone else. And for an hour or two everything is beautiful, weirdly perfect, like a cleverly lit TV ad.

That night, under crisp white waffle linen, I snuggle up to Joe and spoon to his contours, my knee inside his, my belly breathing into the fur of his lower back. Enjoying the stick of our flesh, I feel sensual, desirable. On some deep buried level this makes sense, that one man can reignite love for another. I sniff Joe's neck, sleepy, forgetful and inexplicably at peace.

Thirty-four

I'm woken from sleep by a beeping text. Josh! My heart thumps as I open it, eyes flicking nervously between the phone and the sleeping lump of Joe.

Ws so wondrfl. Hp I hvnt ruind thngs. Lts keep as 1 off. Josh xx

My stomach drops like a falling lift. How dare he? How presumptuous! A 'one-off'? Actually I was going to suggest we run away to Rio. 'Wonderful'? Thanks for the charity. 'Ruined things'? Our close friendship! I snap the phone shut, fighting the urge to text him back with a juvenile insult. No, this is no good, no good at all. I shouldn't care. I'm a grown woman, a *mother* for Christ's sake, not a dumped teenager.

Joe wakes and reaches for me but I am already up, scrubbing manically at my teeth, under my fingernails. I am angry that it ever happened. I am angry that I risked my family's stability for a moment of passion. I am angry that my body has leapt back into its sexual skin with a man other than Joe. And yes, I am angry at myself for caring what Josh thinks. I feel confused, guilty, and murderous.

'What's got you?' Joe mumbles sleepily. 'Chill.'

'Nothing, nothing.'

'Someone woke up on the wrong side of the bed.' Joe sits up, ruffles his hair. 'What time is it? Already? Evie's slept in too, must be the country air. We need to think about making a move.'

'Please can we stay? Just one more day?' Anything to avoid going back to London, the scene of the crime.

'I've got plans.' Joe smiles coyly. 'You go have some breakfast. Today is your treat.'

'I don't deserve it.'

'You do.' Joe hugs his knees, creating an Alp in the middle of the bed. A smile plays around his mouth. 'Amy . . .'

'Hmmm.' I work my floss aggressively – a shard of last night's barbecue chicken is caught awkwardly between my incisors.

'I thought it'd be really nice for us to . . . er . . . have a special day together. I've arranged for Evie to stay here with Kate and Pete.' He waits for my joyous reaction.

'Really? Joe, to be honest, I don't feel happy leaving Evie,' I bend down and whisper. 'Kate and Pete for the day – she'll end up as dog food. They don't know—'

'Don't be silly. I've been through everything with them. If anything happens they can phone.'

They could drop her, feed her too much salt, leave her too close to the swimming pool . . .

'We're going for the night.'

'A night! I've never left her for a night. What . . .' Oh God. No. I can't do this, not right now.

There is a loud rat-a-tat on our door. 'Bacon and eggs?' shouts Kate from the other side.

'Please,' hollers Joe, beaming. He's in such a good mood this morning. I have no appetite.

Breakfast dwindles into lunch: delaying tactics. Despite all

233

my cursing of Evie's insomniac night-time habits, the thought of a night apart is awful. I miss her already. And a night *à deux* with Joe right now seems so wrong, so dishonest. But I have to go along with it – Act Normal – as everyone else seems to think it's the best thing ever. They gabble excitedly and ask Joe where we're going and Joe says it's a surprise. Well, kind of. Pete tells me that he never succeeds in springing a surprise on Kate and that I am one lucky woman to have Joe. And he's right. And I feel worse.

'Come on, Amy, kiss Evie goodbye,' urges Joe. 'We won't get there until dark at this rate.'

'She'll be fine. I only like to eat babies on toast now and again,' laughs Pete, with a roar of cooked-breakfast breath. 'I'll try and contain myself.'

'Bye-bye, my darling,' I whisper into the silk of skin behind Evie's ear. 'Mummy loves you so much. Back very soon.'

Evie grimaces at me and stretches her arms out for Pete. Kate's Marni-clad bosom swells with triumph.

Thirty-five

Twee village. An old hotel with Tudor beams and bulging plaster and a dark lobby filled with the piney smell of log fires and old pot pourri. A fat, friendly country receptionist. The Bridge Hotel, Battle it says in gothic olde worlde writing on the beam above her head.

'This is the hotel!' I exclaim. 'The one you booked for work!'

Joe smiles coyly. 'You understand now?' I look blank. Nothing makes sense any more. 'It was always meant as a surprise for *you*, but you rumbled me. I would have changed the hotel after that, but I'd already paid the deposit. I hope you're not disappointed.'

'Of course not.' I think of the wasted hours I've spent worrying about this hotel, imagining it to be a flash, sexy place, with fluffy white towels and discreet room service where businessmen dallied with mistresses. But here it is, about as sexy as my grandmother's living room.

'Do you like it?' Joe looks uncertain. 'Leo recommended it. Perhaps I should have known better.'

'Don't be silly. I love it. I really do.' I kiss Joe's stubbly cheek and he responds by cupping my face and lengthening out the kiss like in a movie. The receptionist coughs, embarrassed. I'm not quite sure how to respond to this unlikely show of affection either. It seems rather out of relationship.

She leads us up creaking narrow wooden stairs to our room: oak-panelled, badly lit by rickety paned windows, full of dark brown furniture with a large four-poster bed.

Joe bounces on to it, a shaft of dust pirouetting beamwards. 'Only the best!'

'I don't understand, Joe. You were so angry with me a couple of days ago. Now . . .'

'Now this?' Joe twists on the damask bed throw. He looks at my puzzled face and sighs wearily, as if I shouldn't have to ask. 'Amy, I love you. And . . . I'm over it. I don't hold grudges.' He laughs. 'No, I want to move things forward. It's been a hard year, hasn't it?'

'Tough, yes,' I understate, slightly floored by this shift in Joe's mood. Here I am, sullied by an encounter with my Pilates teacher, and the father of my child is behaving like a newly courting suitor. Are we on opposing routes? Me on a flight path out of the relationship, Joe trying to land? There could be a God-awful crash somewhere.

'Walk before supper?' He chucks my denim jacket over and crunches the old key in the lock as we leave. 'It's idyllic around here.'

Joe sets off purposefully towards the rural idyll in his head. We stride on to a roaring A road, then back-track up a muddy path only to hit the boundaries of a fenced-off battery chicken farm. 'You come to the fucking countryside and you're not allowed into it,' fumes Joe as we walk back to the hotel, where the receptionist advises us to drive to a beauty spot on the top of a hill, five miles away.

Ten miles. But when we get there it is beautiful. Wild flowers tickle my flip-flopped toes, their water-colour smell catching when the breeze changes direction. Below us is a loosely sewn patchwork of downs, undulating like the rushes of guilt and unexpected contentment that tumble over me in waves.

Joe, eyes flickering quickly from side to side, studies my face. 'Your eyes get bluer in the summer,' he says softly. 'Maybe it's your tan. Or the carbon-monoxide-free light.'

I look away, unable to meet his eye, thinking of Josh's staring 'game'. Was it foreplay? Had he planned it?

'You are quiet this weekend. But that's OK. I want you to relax.'

Joe's niceness complicates things, makes me feel worse.

'Amy?' He looks at me, suddenly terribly sombre, frowning.

'Yes?'

'I want to ask you something . . . it's been bugging me.'

My rib cage contracts. Heart thump thumps. He knows. I know he knows. How can he? Please don't ask about yesterday. Please don't make me tell the truth. Not now. Not here. Not ready. 'Yes, I'd love a cream tea,' I joke weakly, trying to divert the conversation on to less dangerous ground. 'Besides, I'm getting the most horrible blisters and I really need the loo.' I pull him a couple of steps down the hill. 'Let's go.'

Joe looks relieved. He doesn't want to go there either. 'OK, let's go.'

So we follow a white stony path down towards a plait of river. My body feels strong, my steps sure. It's not the same body as it was a few months, weeks, days ago. Somehow Josh has retrieved my body from the mud of motherhood, shuddered it back into life.

'For medicinal use only,' Joe says, reaching into his pocket and pulling out my favourite organic dark chocolate, chipped with ginger. 'To keep us going.'

We break off waxy chunks and continue walking, mostly in silence, lost in our thoughts, connected through interlaced fingers. It's an easy silence, easier than all the antagonistic chatter at home, easier than questions. And the walk helps the stiffness between my thighs, each step flexing me back to normality.

Thirty-six

Dinner time. About the time I'd be bathing Evie. Is the ability to miss your baby so viscerally, even when you're supposed to be enjoying a night off, just another of nature's tricks to make mothers stay at home? It seems to me that if you're not within touching distance of your baby, they worm their way into your head like a catchy pop song that you can't shake, poke their little fat fingers into your brain, pull at your heart, reminding you that child-free freedom is not what you hunger for after all.

I throw on a floral blouse, an old favourite, not something Alice would ever approve of. Not sexy enough, she'd say. Jeans. No heels. I don't want to dress provocatively. Not now, too guilty. Besides, this is the country. No one dresses up.

We clatter down the staircase, talking loudly, and walk into the lobby. Oh, I've misinterpreted the dress code. The floral sofas sag with sixtysomething couples dressed in Weekend Country Wear: forest green, navy ties and brass-buttoned blazers. Coiffed heads turn to stare. Joe and I are the youngest and scruffiest people here.

'Not exactly Babington House,' whispers Joe. 'Sorry.'

239

'I'm so pleased it's not cool. Cool is totally unrelaxing.' Scrutinising, heavily powdered eyes dart above sherry glasses when they think we're not looking. 'But shall we skip the mingling and just go and eat?'

The dining room is oak panelled, hung with sentimental Victorian oils. Spotty local teenagers dressed in black and white uniforms hover shyly. The hushed mutterings of the other diners stop as we sit down. Who do they think we are? Out of towners, obviously, a couple on a romantic mini-break? A mother who almost fucked her Pilates instructor?

'The menu, sir.' The teenage waiter's hand is red-raw, as if he's been doing too much washing up.

Joe flicks over the wine list, too flippant for this place. 'Ugh, swirly font, practically illegible,' he mutters. Such things affront Joe. 'Hmmm. The Côtes du Rhône please. Two glasses of Moët first. Thanks.'

I dig into the hot bread basket. It's impossible to keep to any type of diet away from home, where the calories don't seem to count. From the menu I choose grilled goat's cheese and then, to compensate, honey glazed salmon. Joe wants *foie gras* and steak. He is intent on enjoying himself, holding up his champagne flute for a smart conclusive clink.

'If someone had told me a year ago I'd be sublimely happy in a naff, overpriced country hotel in Sussex I'd have laughed,' he says.

It occurs to me that while I feel too guilty to feel happy, I am enjoying Joe's company more than I have in months.

Joe leans forward. 'It's wonderful to be alone, without the threat of Evie waking up. To be able to *really* talk.' Ah, he's been waiting for this face time. I shift on my padded seat. 'Don't you think?'

'Um . . .' This should be my cue, rather than settling into a pseudo romantic meal. *Ask him, confront him now*, I hear

Nicola saying. *Ask him the truth about that September day. Clean slate and all that.* Instead I say, 'Yes, you're right. It's a real treat.'

'I know it hasn't been easy for you,' Joe says earnestly, negotiating the napkin origami to get to my hand. 'What with Evie and everything. I'm just beginning to understand . . . er, why you felt unattractive. Your hair, why you want to Alice yourself up.'

'It's not about Alice,' I sigh.

'OK. But it's about reclaiming yourself, isn't it? Trying to locate . . . well, the creative, sensual old self, hidden beneath relentless practicalities?'

Starters are slid in front of us. It's too personal a conversation to have in front of a waiter. I hold back tears by staring intently into the dancing candle flame. It's amazing that Joe can still do this to me. I think I'm hardened to him and then he peeps inside, understands so well, and it floors me.

'I suppose the thing is, I always thought that *me* saying you were pretty should be enough,' he continues. 'I was angry that it wasn't. And I kind of felt . . .' He stumbles, finding this hard. '. . . A bit left out.'

'If I'd known you wanted to come to Annabel's baby shower . . .'

Joe laughs, a candle reflected in each iris. 'No, God no. I'd implode. But still, you lot are terrible, like a secret society.'

'Not as secret as you,' I say, tracing my finger tip down the sharp edge of the fish knife.

'It doesn't matter how many nappies I change, maybe I'm physiologically unable to understand. Like you'll never understand how a clutch works, or the genius of New Order.' He frowns, features drooping. 'I don't get why you're so keen to "get back into shape" and all that nonsense. Why not just

241

embrace this period in your life, tummy and all? I mean, who gives a shit?'

'I give a shit.'

'It'll always be unfathomable to me why you care so much.'

'As you said, it's something about reclaiming the old me. Listen,' I huddle forward, stumbling for an explanation. 'Lots of women cope superbly well with having a baby. For some reason I was useless. It sent me into a tailspin, and . . .' I give the sentence up. The fish knife isn't sharp enough to cut my skin.

'You are an excellent mother. That's what matters.'

I shrug, knowing different, knowing I've been unfaithful both to him and also, by proxy, Evie. Because I've threatened the stability of her world. I set out to be the kind of mother who threw everything into motherhood but I'm evidently not that person. I have distracting, rogue desires.

Joe sips his champagne thoughtfully, the glass tiny in his huge hand. 'Why, Amy? What is it? I just feel there is something that I haven't got that you expect me to get and it's really frustrating.'

I concentrate on the goat's cheese melting in my mouth. Silence slips around us like gravy. I can't speak because I fear that if I say anything Josh will find a way of sliding beneath my tongue and dropping on to the table. Joe drops his fork down with a clatter.

'Oh, I'll shut up. No more depressing talk. Or we'll end up like all the other miserable couples in this room who look like they find the floral arrangements more interesting than each other.' He laughs. 'The husbands have probably taken their wives for this "fine dining" mini-break to compensate for the fact they're having affairs with Tracy from accounts during the week.'

242

Affairs? I jump. How can he mention it so lightly? Then, with an almost physical jolt of recognition, I realise this has gone on long enough. We can't pretend any more. Now is the time. We both deserve to know the truth, no more second-guessing, no more risk aversion. I must confront him.

'Joe, you're . . . right.' *Honesty is always better*. Deep breath. 'We must talk. I need to ask you something.'

Joe looks disappointed. He wants to direct this dinner. 'Amy, I wanted to ask *you* something.'

Of course. He suspects. Like Kate's dogs, he just knows on some weird primordial level. 'You go first.'

'No you.'

'Nah . . . go on. Bring it on.' Here it comes. In a millisecond I decide that I can't lie to Joe. He deserves better. If he asks, I will tell him. I'll confess the lot.

Joe leans forward, his long back curving over the candle making an intimate cave of space. 'OK, if that's what you want. Amy. I've been trying to ask you this all day but, well, with one thing and another, the motorway, you needing the loo . . .'

'Sorry.' I smile thinly and steel myself.

'I should have asked ages ago and then we'd understand where we stood a little better.'

I nod. We both should have aired things earlier. At least we wouldn't be living a lie.

'And I know I haven't been the best boyfriend in the world . . .'

Not always, no.

He smiles. 'I'm sorry about being so crap, working so late. I know it's a pain but I've been working on a new project, to save up for something special. Because sometimes I see this, what we have, slipping away, and it terrifies me.' He takes a deep breath, his eyes pooling wide, hand crunching mine tight. 'I'd love it so much if . . .' Joe is sweating now, glistening in his laughter lines. He swallows hard. 'Amy Crane, will you marry me?'

The words hang above the table like hummingbirds. Everything freezes, the waiters, the cutlery clatter. Heads turn and I realise that the restaurant waits with Joe. His eyes are contorted with the stress of the moment, his mouth agape wanting to mouth my words for me. But I cannot speak. He slides a blue jewellery box shyly across the table, clearing its path of forks and fish knives with shaking hands. I pick it up, this unexpected velvet box, click it open. On a cushion of blue silk is a square-cut diamond suspended on a simple platinum band. It's exquisite. I hear a cloud of 'ahhs' coming from other diners. But I can't look up, not knowing where to look, or what to think.

'Do you . . . li . . . like it?' stutters Joe.

I nod, swimmy, mouth soaking with saliva. And I want to smile but can't. My stomach trapezes and the blood rushes from my head.

'Amy? Are you OK?'

And then they come. Not little, sweet feminine tears. Oh no. Globules, dollops, heaving out involuntarily, shudders of guilt and shock. I try to smile and brush them off with a wave of the hand but my body isn't having it, convulsing and sobbing and creating a scene. 'Sorry . . .' I gulp.

Joe, aghast, reaches for my hand across the table. 'Hey, it's OK. Shit . . . sorry.'

Flapping my tear-soaked napkin against my eyes, the restaurant fuzzes at the edges and I feel faint. 'No I'm sorry . . .' A waiter hovers awkwardly into view. Diners stare. And the tears keep coming. I can't get my breath. I'm shaking. 'God do . . . do . . . you . . . mind if I clean myself up?'

'No, absolutely. Do what you have to do.' Joe looks slightly shaken. 'Shall I come too?'

'I think I need to be alone for a minute.' Heads track the exit of the most wretched, unworthy person in the entire world as she makes her way to the Ladies. I stand in front of the mirror and splash cold water on my blotchy red face. Marry me? Who'd marry me? Breathe. Breathe. Christ. I've fucked up. Eventually I lean back against the sprigged pink wallpaper, spent, strangely purged.

In the restaurant, Joe fiddles with the cutlery while the other diners talk about him in funereal whispers. He looks relieved to see me. 'If I'd known I'd have that effect . . .'

'I am so, so sorry. I don't know what happened.' I huddle forward in my chair. 'I don't know what to say. What a mess.'

'Here, drink this.' Joe passes me a glass of water. I want to put him on pause, just to give myself a moment to think. Life couldn't get any more preposterous.

'Feeling a bit better?' Joe strokes my arm, which is gallant, considering.

'God, I'm sorry.'

'Stop apologising. You've got nothing to feel sorry for.'

I gag on the water.

'Do you want to go upstairs?'

'Not sure I can face this audience for much longer. Would you mind?'

Joe signs a bill – the waiter avoids eye contact – and we walk out of the hushed restaurant self-consciously, the little blue box a bomb in my handbag. All politeness lost in the urgency of getting the last look, the diners stare brazenly. We are probably the most dramatic thing to have happened in this restaurant. Ever. Upstairs on our big four-poster bed, Joe and I lie down. Joe can't keep still. There is a question to be answered.

I hold the ring up to the side light's dusty halo. 'I love it, Joe.'

'You do?' he says, disbelieving.

'Yes, yes . . . it's extraordinary.' I put my hand on his shoulder, rather awkwardly. I have no script for this. 'And I am absolutely dumbfounded. I had no idea!' Joe looks up at me shyly. That look. For months I've interpreted it as a guilty look. Perhaps it's not. Perhaps it's a sweet, coy look.

'I wanted a new start, Amy. I love you so much.' More tears. He brushes them away gently. 'You get amazing eyelashes when you cry.'

'There's a beauty tip.'

Joe folds me into his newly washed shirt against the beat of his chest, solid and certain after the reckless abandon of the last week. I try to swipe away the deceit that sways above this romantic moment like a column of midges. Will Joe be faithful? Can he be faithful? Perhaps I am better off cutting off now, making myself strong, single and sexy, protecting myself against more hurt, against the pain of him leaving. Marriage didn't stop Dad leaving Mum, did it?

'Are you feeling better, sweetheart?' he says softly. 'I am so sorry if I upset you.'

'You didn't, it's me.'

Joe strokes my hair away from my forehead tenderly. I breathe deeply, the oxygen slowing the race of my heart and clearing my head. Evie deserves a tighter family unit, a public statement of intent. Where can this relationship go now if I say no? How can I still be angry about that day in the park now that I've done the same? And Josh? Josh dumped me! Josh is nothing! A sordid mistake. Yes, Josh will disappear from my head if I get married. This could be a fresh start.

This *is* my second chance, glittering in the blue box. My chance to atone, a chance to build a proper family. A way of making it all better again. 'Joe?'

'Don't feel you have to give me an answer.' He is staving off a rejection. I can feel his heart thump harder. 'Please, you're upset, let's just leave it.'

'Joe, I don't want to leave it.'

'I understand, Amy. It's too much, too late. I don't want to pressure you into anything.' Joe looks terribly sad. He's made his mind up: I'm turning him down.

'I want you to ask me again.' I sit up, exhilarated by my decision. 'If you haven't changed your mind, which would be perfectly understandable.'

He smiles uncertainly. 'Well, if you're sure.' I nod. 'Sure you're sure?' I nod again. He gets off the bed and kneels. I giggle. 'Amy Crane, dear unfathomable Amy, will you marry me?'

'I think I will, Mr Costello.'

'Really?' Flushed and grinning, Joe stands up and hugs me in a rib-crushing embrace that in different circumstances would be more like an assault. 'Tissues at the ready!' he cries and we fall giggling on to the bed.

Thirty-seven

September. 8.45 a.m. Queen's Park.

Nicola grins at me. 'See, I was right,' she says, leaning back on the child's swing, kicking her feet up. 'You muppet! He was innocent. The hotel, the jewellery bill . . . Doh! Here, let's have a good look at it.'

I hold up my finger, shattering the breakfast sunlight. My first diamond. I'll never be able to wear diamanté again.

'It is truly lovely,' she says. 'Gosh, you're lucky having a boyfriend with good taste. I daren't imagine what Sam would buy.'

'You know what I like best about it?'

'It's started,' mutters Nicola to Thomas. 'What, dear bride-to-be?'

'Imagining Joe buying it, puzzling over all the different styles.'

'Sweet.'

We stare around the park for a few moments: Juicy-clad Joggers, skinny mothers and fat squirrels feasting on the organic rice cakes tossed from Maclaren buggies.

'I presume you confronted him, just to put your mind at rest?'

I bend my head sheepishly. 'Well, not . . . not exactly.' I fucked up too! We're quits! But I don't say this because I can't quite face telling her about Josh in the same breath as announcing my engagement.

Nicola shrugs and gazes out through the horse chestnuts. 'Amy, there's no right way,' she says, somewhat resigned. 'And if you're happy to take on the frankly terrifying prospect of walking down the aisle with everyone you have ever known staring at your backside, well, your decision.'

'Oh, it won't be for ages. A long engagement.'

She laughs and kicks back on the swing. 'No denial. You're going to be preoccupied with napkin colours and confetti shapes for the next few months. You may have to call me when it's over.'

I bite off a split-end. Nicola stares at me, suddenly sombre. 'It's what you really want, isn't it? To be married?' she asks.

A million thoughts tunnel through my brain in the second before I nod my head. Because, it's true, in the cold light of London, something about our engagement niggles. Well, there's the obvious. And there's the worry that we're doing it because of Evie. If it weren't for Evie would we have split up by now? And does that mean that as a couple we're invalid? Or would half the parents in the world split up if they no longer had children to bind them? There is also a nagging awareness that much as I want it all to have a happy ending, I can't quite believe in it. And that anger towards Joe still throbs just beneath my skin like a particularly painful menstrual zit. So I'm going through the motions but holding a little bit back. And if you subtract part of yourself, even a little part, it's not a deal breaker, but you're not committing yourself wholly. I suppose that's it.

'Here, bride, fatten yourself up.' Nicola passes me a brown bag from the bakery. *Pain au chocolat.*

Oh well, diet later. Flakes of pastry snow my jeans.

'Imagine, you'll soon be a bona fide yummy mummy wife! All kaftan tops and Seven jeans accessorised by your handsome media husband.' She laughs and puts on her best fashionista voice, 'You've made it darling!'

'I won't get into these much longer if I carry on like this.'

'Oh, don't develop a west-London-wife eating disorder. You've lost quite enough weight already.' She doesn't understand that thing about keeping it off. 'Here, do you mind holding Thomas while I light a cigarette?'

I study Nicola's face as smoke twists around it like ghost ringlets. There's something different about her. Then I realise. Nicola's briars are now tamed, perfect arches.

'Nicola! Your eyebrows. You've had them plucked! Pots and kettles . . .'

Nicola actually blushes. A first. 'I'm going back to work soon.'

'You never told me!'

'Haven't seen you. Our babymoon must end. The bank manager calls.'

'And?'

'Hmmm. Met my boss and he started talking about my "new responsibilities". Hey, no more lead stories! Minor digital TV pages, things that "would fit in better with my new role". Can you believe it? The mummy track.'

'Bollocks.'

'Sure. Then I caught sight of myself in the staff loos. Have to admit, Amy, I looked kind of mumsy. A Gap label sticking out from my shirt collar because I got dressed while Thomas was screaming because he'd stuck his toast into the DVD player, nappy in the handbag. And while I'm not about to start Project Nicola . . .'

I'm weighted by a heavy lump in the chest as I imagine

Nicola moving up and away, out of her tracksuit bottoms, into her tailoring and the bright busy world of the office. 'What will I do without you?'

'Oh, don't go all sentimental on me. Anyway, aren't you thinking of going back soon?'

'Work? As you know, I'm rather good at the ostrich-like denial thing. I kind of think that if you ignore something it'll go away. That it's only when you think about something you bring it into being.'

'Yeah right.' She laughs. 'Your head's probably full of white tulle anyway.'

'No, seriously. You are right. I must start thinking about work properly now.'

EeeeeEEKKKK!

A sudden screech, burning rubber. The sound of a sports car. Except it isn't. A large Audi pulls up on the other side of the park railings.

'Now there's a man in need of a Ferrari,' mutters Nicola.

We peer over the bushes. A long-legged woman in a leopard-print cape, holding a toddler under her arm, stands on the pavement, one hip jutted forward as if she were at the end of the catwalk pausing for the snappers. Jasmine! I wave, ring sparkling. Jasmine flutters back her free hand then bends down and, despite holding Marlon, manages to get into the passenger seat with the graceful swoop of a movie star. The car accelerates with an unnecessarily loud roar. Nicola looks stunned, open-mouthed.

'Nic? What's the matter?'

'No way,' she mutters under her breath. 'I can't believe it. Did you see who was driving that car?'

Thirty-eight

Joe and I have had sex. It happened at 2.46 p.m. yesterday. Evie was asleep. There was nothing on TV. I didn't have my period. And it was beginning to get weird that we hadn't done it already. We'd only managed a cuddle in the hotel. I felt too guilty to throw myself into anything more conclusive. And I was worried that rather than being the newly engaged pash-fest it was meant to be, the sex would be an anticlimax, that I would think of Josh and would want to stop it and not be able to without hurting Joe's feelings. And Joe hadn't initiated anything because he couldn't face rejection. But yesterday he took a deep breath and pulled me towards him on the sofa and I didn't resist or pretend I needed to go to the toilet or that I was too tired. I surrendered to him, to this relationship. And it didn't hurt. Nor was it boring or awkward or embarrassing. It was nostalgic, like returning to a favourite old walk.

No, I didn't lose myself in him as I lost myself in Josh. I knew the landscape too well: the way his willy bends slightly to the left, tapers to a point like a bulb; the surprising flatness of his nipples; the gulp of his Adam's apple as he comes. And did he come! But not first. There I was considering faking it, just once, just to reassure. But as his fingers traced the paths that Josh's had a few weeks before, they tingled with a curious sensual déjà vu. My skin remembered how to react, how to release. Is it possible that by some strange perverse logic Josh has put my body back in touch with Joe's? Was Josh just the rehearsal?

'Hello, my zenned-out goddess.' Joe peeks his tufty head around the sitting-room door.

I laugh uncomfortably. That is the kind of thing Josh might have said, but without irony. (I'm still not quite able to master total indifference to Josh. But I'm trying.)

'How are you feeling?'

'Sleepy, eaten rather too much Sunday lunch. It was delicious though. Thank you.'

Joe and I have slipped into a state of suspended niceness. Wary of conversations that dig up the past and wanting to behave as we imagine a newly engaged couple should, we're tiptoeing round each other, being really nice. I make him a nice breakfast. He makes a nice lunch, runs me a nice bath. It's very civilised. I'm not sure how long it can be kept up.

'Sweet,' says Joe, pointing at Evie who is flopped on her tummy like a baby seal, fiddling with the remote control. 'She's into hardware now,' he says. 'Not interested in any pink things or dolls. Should we be worried?' Joe absentmindedly pokes Evie's teeny feet with his big toe. 'Your mum phoned. She was wondering if she could borrow some heels, a particular pink . . . is it, er, LK Bennett? Said they were the "only thing, dear, the only shade that will go" with her new dress. Don't shoot me that look! Only the messenger.'

'What's the excuse?' It's a liability having the same size feet as your mother. There's no two-way traffic either. I can live without Mum's court shoes.

'She's going to some do with "all his own hair" Norman.'

253

'Again? We haven't seen her for ages.' I've missed her. Mum thinks that now I'm safely engaged – 'about time too' – I don't need her so much. Sadly, my diamond ring can't babysit. I roll my shoulders. 'God, I'm stiff.'

Ding dong.

'I'll get it,' Joe says, striding to the front door, perkier and more relaxed now he's sure of his status. The marriage thing suits men. 'Alice! This is a surprise. Come in.'

Alice's light eight-stone footsteps on the floorboards. Joe shuffles behind her, still slightly sheepish because of their row and, like all men, probably disarmed by her beauty. She's looking particularly hot. I jump up from the sofa and kiss her. There's a scent of crushed rose petals on her skin.

'Sorry to arrive unannounced,' Alice says, laughing. 'Glad you love birds are decently dressed.' Is that sarcasm in her voice? Since news of my engagement Alice has cooled a little towards me.

Joe works a smile. He's doing his best for my sake. This is our fresh start, after all. 'Tea? Or something stronger?'

'Thanks, Joe. But I'm not stopping. I just thought I'd pop by and see if I could pick up your pretty fiancée . . .' That word. Surely enough to put anyone off getting engaged. '. . . Because I'm on my way to Pilates.' My stomach drops. 'And Amy hasn't been for ages.'

'Great idea. Amy was just complaining of being stiff and . . .' Joe looks at me enthusiastically.

'Er, no, actually. I was thinking of a walk,' I stutter.

'But you said—'

'We could go to the park,' I suggest hopefully to Alice.

Alice brushes me off with a wave of discreetly polished pink nails. 'No way. I've got park-fatigue. Amy, I insist you come to Pilates and work that pencil!'

'Pencil?' Joe looks baffled. 'Oh go on,' he says, giving up

trying to work it out. 'You'll feel so much better.' And this is how I am pulled out of my house – my precarious new stability – back into the danger zone of tanned feet and newly awakened chakras.

Outside, the warm wind carries the smells of the street: Indian takeaways, traffic, uncollected rubbish.

'Set a date yet?' asks Alice tersely as she click-clacks along the hot pavement in insubstantial summer thong sandals.

'No, no date.' I try to explain. 'We'll probably be engaged for ever.'

'Well, at least that way you get a nice ring out of it.' Alice swings her red tote over her shoulder and flicks her curls, flecked ash and gold in the sunshine, striking a group of builders mute with lust. 'Well, you know what I think. But hopefully you'll prove me wrong. Shit, these shoes. I should have driven. Hail a cab if you see one won't you?' She bends down to readjust the thong between her toes. 'Still, perhaps you've been my most successful project yet.'

'What do you mean?'

'Project Amy! Not only do you look fabulous, but you managed to get a marriage proposal! One hot make-over I'd say.'

I laugh. 'Sadly, I think Joe preferred me as I was.'

'Rubbish!' says Alice, slightly offended. 'They all say that and think they mean it. But give them the choice between a size sixteen and a ten and the ten will win every time. Don't you go all complacent on me and start reaching for the brownies and digging out those old clothes. It's an easy psychological slip, Amy. One day you're slouching about, comfortable in roomy "fat jeans", the next you've filled them.'

'But look, Alice, look at this!' I stop Alice's stride and stand up close and frown.

'What?' She looks puzzled.

255

'Look, no lines!'

'You did it!' she squeals, delighted.

'I did it.'

She hugs me, one of those tight schoolgirl exam-result hugs. We turn the corner and suddenly we're on Chamberlayne Road. Alice stops with a click-clack. The door. The out-of-order bell. The scene of the crime. My heart slams in my chest. I'm not sure I can go through with this.

'Alice, I'm not feeling that good, really I . . .'

'What's wrong with you? Amy, you can't blob out just because you've got a ring on your finger! You're not married yet, girl.'

'I know. It's just . . .' Should I tell her? I can't, not here, not opposite the damned door. 'Listen, I'm off.'

'Shush, it's all so fine,' she says in a way that implies that she knows *everything*. The door opens slowly. Please don't let it be Josh. It is.

'Hi Amy, what a nice surprise,' he says with a relaxed smile, slumping against the door frame. Those sky blue eyes. The soft marshmallow of his lower lip. The smell of seeds. I've got to get out of here. 'You look well.'

'Actually, Amy is wavering.'

Alice and Josh exchange glances. Then Alice gives me a push and I'm in. As we walk quickly down the narrow corridor, Josh's white muslin shirt billows out like a sail. Josh turns around.

'How's Annabel?'

'Gosh, yes, of course. How is she?' I ask quickly, feeling bad for being so distracted by the thought of meeting Josh that I didn't enquire earlier.

'She's having trouble settling the baby in,' says Alice. 'She's very tired, not really up for visitors. She looks a bit scary to be honest. Made the mistake of pushing with her eyes open and all her blood vessels burst. There is no white of eye left. Just blood. She's scaring the wits out of her own children and has hired a child psychologist to reassure them.' The corners of Alice's mouth twitch. 'I suspect she will be asking Blythe for that fanny tuck doctor's number after all.'

'Oh dear.'

'Split asunder. *Begged* for drugs like a junkie.'

'Remind her to keep at those pelvic floors,' Josh laughs.

How can he laugh and quip so casually with me here? Did it mean *nothing*, nothing at all? I go into the changing rooms and walk straight into Jasmine's heart-shaped lacy bottom. 'Jasmine . . . that man, driving the car . . .' I ask, on strictest orders from Nicola.

'What? How are you too?' She kicks a leg into her tracksuit bottoms.

'Sorry. But that man, is he your new lover?'

'Not so new. But yes.' Jasmine smiles coyly and pulls the bottoms up to her tanned midriff. 'Cute isn't he?'

'Is he called Alan?'

'How do you know?' She looks puzzled. 'Why?'

'I know his wife.'

Jasmine pales beneath her blusher. 'Oh God, really? Not a friend of yours?'

'Yes.' Unsure of my role, I want to defend Sue but decide the best (and, shamefully, the easiest) course of action is to let Jasmine's guilt be the punishment. I've found it to be quite effective. 'A *really* nice woman called Sue.' Jasmine looks relieved, as if a really-nice-woman-called-Sue is never going to upset her moral universe. 'She's in my NCT group.'

'No! She's got a *baby*?'

'A little boy called Oliver, same age as Evie.' Jasmine purses her lips around an invisible cigarette. 'He obviously removes Oliver's car seat when you're around.'

'The fucker,' she mutters. 'The fucker.' No remorse, no shudder of female solidarity then? No, just anger. 'Why the hell didn't he tell me? That would have changed everything.'

'It would?' I say hopefully, not wanting to dislike her.

'Well, OK, maybe not everything. But I won't be lied to! What other stuff has he lied about?'

Is it so unbelievable that a man who would lie to his wife would also lie to his mistress?

Alice and Blythe trip into the room, Blythe wearing huge sunglasses and just-saloned Jemima Khan hair. 'Have I just walked into a morgue or something?' she drawls, pushing the glasses back like an Alice band. 'What's with you?'

Jasmine shakes her head, muttering at the affront of it.

'Man or woman?' asks Blythe wearily.

'Man.'

'Well, there's a surprise.'

Alice slides her arm over Jasmine's shoulder and all three shuffle into the studio, interlinked, bonded by Jasmine's apparent victim status. *What about the wife? What about poor old Sue?* I want to scream, but don't quite have the guts.

Thirty-nine

Just like old times: the fan swirls air heavy with hormones; the skylight halos the frizz in every blow-dry; and Blythe's sun salute whacks my nose. I search Josh for some kind of recognition. None. Just the same dance in his eyes, the same smile he bestows too generously upon everyone. Despite the ring on my finger, I still feel a little humiliated by Josh's text, unceremoniously cut off before I'd finished. Because I was the involved one. I should have sent that text, or one similar. And I'm annoyed that despite having a baby and a fiancé my ego is still vulnerable to such an unworthy slight.

'Amy, you've really tightened up since I last saw you,' Josh says. 'Here, pull on my hands and lean back.'

I don't want to take Josh's hands, but nor do I want to arouse suspicion of A Situation. His palms are hot and dry. His arms knot as I fall back. My tummy! Only now do I realise my hard-earned shark-fin hip bones are totally submerged beneath a layer of cosy suppers and pastry breakfasts. Only now do I care.

'Relax into it. Breathe.'

Relax? I can almost feel his hand between my legs. His honey skin. That thrum beneath the pubic bone. Damn him!

After lowering me to the ground with a grin, Josh pads on to Alice – 'Me next Joshy!' – then hushes us back to our mats. 'Right, that's about it girls, shut your peepers.'

I can still sense Josh, a kind of erotic sonar. He walks past and I get a rush like when you stick your head out of the window of a moving train, the wind rushing past made more delicious by the slight risk of being decapitated. We 'relax' for five intensely stressful minutes. I need to get out of here.

'Get up in your own time, wake your body up, bit by bit,' says Josh softly. 'Slowly as souls. There's no hurry.'

There is an urgent rustle: Blythe bolts upright. 'Excuse me, but there is a hurry!' she says. 'Completely forgot to say, spoke to Annabel. She said we could go and visit her after class but no later because her doula's visiting. As long as we don't bring cameras.'

'And I'm afraid we've run over by ten minutes,' says Josh. 'So you better go now.'

Jasmine and Alice leap to their feet.

'You coming, Amy?' Alice asks.

'I'd love to see her but I need to collect Evie first . . .'

'Whatever. You can see her another time.' Alice is too quick to excuse me. This is a private moment for old friends. It's a little reminder that I'm still not really in the inner circle, and even if armed with Kate Moss's wardrobe still wouldn't be.

'Send my love,' shouts Josh as the three tumble out of the door, Jasmine still raging about the lying cheek of Sue's husband, untouched by £10 worth of yogic calm.

I throw my clothes on quickly and avoid brushing past Josh as I pick up my bag to leave. 'See ya then,' I say, my voice too high to be as casual as I'd like. A long pause. My hand cups the cool steel door handle.

'You're pissed off with me,' Josh says slowly.

I don't turn round. 'Not pissed off . . . fine.'

'You have every right to be pissed off. I shouldn't have sent a text message like that. Sorry.'

'It doesn't matter, really. I couldn't care—'

'Less?'

I face him. He's smiling, baring Bowie teeth. 'That's about the size of it, yes.'

'You're lying. I always know, you rub the side of your nose.'

I laugh, slightly flattered that he's noticed. And I hate myself for laughing that appeasing girlie laugh.

'Do you want to talk about it?'

'Er, no, not really Josh, thanks.' I resent him trying to turn me into the victim here. 'Do you?'

Josh sits down on the Pilates bench and holds its bars like a monkey in a cage. He casts his eyes down, sadly. 'Actually I do,' he says softly. 'Will you give me five minutes?'

I turn the door knob. 'I don't think so. Don't see the point,' I lie, every cell of my body aching to ask him if he liked me, how it was for him. Just so I can put it to bed, so to speak.

'Please.'

Caught in the shatter of his ice-blue eyes. 'OK.'

'Here, sit down.' He shuffles along the bench and pats it, pulling me towards him with an invisible cord. 'The thing is, my life is kinda complicated . . .'

'Not half as complicated as mine.'

'No, probably not. And that made me feel bad too.'

'There is no need to feel guilt for me, I'm managing perfectly well on my own thanks.'

Josh bends forward. His face is inches from mine. 'Amy, what have I done to you? You're so brittle, not the gentle, funny Amy of old.'

'Please don't flatter yourself. *You* haven't done anything.

261

I'm actually rather happy at the moment. It's just this . . . this is a bit weird, that's all.'

We sit in silence for a few moments, listening to the moth-wing whirr of the fan. I stare at the big studio light above the doorway that beams round and white, unnecessarily, like the moon in the afternoon.

'It was good though, wasn't it?'

I can hear the smile curling around his lips. I can't look at him. Despite myself, I find myself smiling too.

'You are very gorgeous.'

Don't melt. Don't melt. He's lying.

'And I'm so sorry if I hurt you,' Josh says, reaching out for my hand, which is clam-clenched on the side of the bench. His touch is fluttery, insincere.

'Don't.' I move my hand away. 'It's not appropriate.'

He groans, puts his head in his hands. 'I can't bear this, Amy.'

'What? Don't be such a drama queen.'

'It was never meant to happen, not like this. I feel like I've really fucked up something . . . a good friendship.'

Friendship? Me and Nicola are a friendship. Me and Josh are nothing, a passing infatuation. How can he even elevate himself platonically? 'Don't worry, you'll find other Pilates students to be friends with.'

'It was about you, Amy, honestly. We have a genuine con-nection. If we'd met at a different time in different circumstances . . .'

'Like if I didn't have a baby and wasn't engaged to some-one else?'

He starts. 'You're engaged? Since when?' He looks down at my ring finger. The diamond glares back at him.

'A while ago.'

'Oh. Alice didn't tell me. Well, er, congratulations.' Josh

slumps, pulls his knees up and curls his gleaming body into a ball, like a hard shrink-wrapped fruit. Then, suddenly, he slams the bench with his palm: whoomp! My turn to jump. 'God! Why does this always happen to me! I only realise when it's too late.' He doesn't talk to me, rather to the blue mats. He's directing a romantic drama in his head, with himself, of course, in the starring Colin Firth role. 'But are you happy? Do you feel *visible* now?' he implores.

Cheap shot. 'I think so.'

Josh brightens, spotting an opening. 'Amy,' he sighs. 'I think maybe I . . . I . . .'

My heart pumps saliva into my mouth. Please don't complicate things further. Please don't say you love me.

'I . . . I . . . still really fancy you.'

Oh. Josh puts his hand on my thigh. What is he doing? Not again. Then, suddenly, Josh leans towards me, hand in my hair, cupping the back of my head. Before I can stop him, his lips crash into mine, his mouth open and expectant. It takes a second or two before Josh realises that I am actually pushing him off, not engaging in a passionate love tussle. Something catches my eye in the doorway. A movement. A dark figure, big, silhouetted against the round studio light. There for a tiny moment. The next, gone. Retreating footsteps.

'Amy? Are you OK?' Josh pulls back. 'What's the matter? You look like you've seen a ghost.'

Forty

The sun smacks me across the face when I open the studio door. It can't have been, surely. But I know, deep down I know. Rattle the key in the lock. Step in. 'Hello? Joe?'

Nothing. The sitting room is still, dusty, hot. Our palm wilts. A bluebottle throws itself at the window. The kitchen is as I left it, scattered with unwashed tea cups and toast crumbs. Evie's bib is still pasted with regurgitated apple puree. Her nappy ferments in the bin. Where the hell are they? Upstairs, nothing. Nothing.

'Cooeeee! Through here.' Mum! I walk through to the balcony. Mum's bouncing a grumpy hot Evie on her knee. 'Are you OK dear? You look terrible.'

'Just been running. Where's Joe?'

'I thought he was with you.'

'No, he isn't. Why?'

'You must have just missed each other. I popped over to borrow some shoes – did Joe tell you I wanted to borrow some shoes?'

'Yes, yes. And?'

'What's got you?'

'Mum, please. *Where* is Joe?'

264

'Let me finish. As I was saying, I popped around here to borrow some shoes and Joe asked if I'd mind looking after Evie for fifteen minutes or so as he wanted to go down to your Pilates studio and pick you up, as a surprise.' Oh God. 'He said you were quite tired.' Mum looks at me, concerned. 'As I say, you must have missed each other or something.'

I slump down on to the step, hug my knees, fall into them. Shutting my eyes, the world blackens. And, flickering on the inside of my eyelids: Joe's frame silhouetted, the dead slam of his footsteps.

'Amy? Are you OK?'

'Fine. Just tired.'

'Tired?' she says a little disapprovingly, as if it were self-inflicted like a hangover. 'Have a lie down. I'll look after Evie.'

'Thanks.' Feeling strangely out of body, I wander into the kitchen, sink on to a chair and prod the keys of my mobile phone. On answerphone. Do I leave a message? No. He'll be able to see that I have phoned. Now what? Wait, I suppose. Pick at my fingernails. Bite off split-ends. Try his mobile again. Again. And again. I've been sitting here for an hour now. Not moving. No response from Joe. Nothing. My eyes are dry, itchy, as if I slept in cheap mascara. I rub them red. Footsteps. '*Joe?*'

'Only me,' says Mum cheerily, Evie on her hip. 'Not asleep? Well, as you're up, about those shoes . . .'

It's 1.03 a.m. Joe is still not home, which means he must be home soon. He can't stay away for ever, can he? He's not a cat. I won't have to advertise him on lampposts. 'Lost! Large male, responds to the name of Joe . . .' I snap shut our bedroom window, sit on the bed, propped by pillows. My stomach growls, I haven't been able to eat. The light shifts around the room as the night bores on, shadowing different bits of Joe – shoes, dry cleaning, gym kit – like a portraitist capturing new angles.

Evie wakes up. Weakening in my resolve to let her 'cry it out', mostly because I'm glad of the company – bad parenting! – I sit by the cot, stroking her dandelion-fuzz of hair. Evie, delighted to find I've finally come round to her preferred schedule – the hours of a dedicated clubber – doesn't want to be stroked, or soothed. Evie wants to play, screeching excitedly when I whisper 'shush, bedtime' as if it were a call to party.

Eventually dawn bleeds over the city, the sky marbled pink and pale yellow like a cut of fatty meat. Evie, despite a surge of will-power that kept her going until three, has reluctantly dropped into sleep. I toss in bed, eyes so tired now they feel bruised. I finger the hollow within their sockets. Sleep, I must sleep. Only when I finally resign myself to insomnia and the improbability of ever sleeping again do I drop off.

Six a.m. Shussh! A noise! Definitely a noise. Downstairs. Pulling on my dressing gown, I stumble out of bed, shivering slightly. Thump, thump, thump. The stairs seem endless. There he is. Thank God. 'Joe!'

Hair tangled, eyes ringed by black, Joe looks like a burglar financing a drug habit. 'Where is my briefcase?' he asks in a quiet monotone, as if nothing had happened.

'Upstairs, under the chair,' I whisper.

He marches past, trailing a whiff of unwashed-man. A few moments later he comes downstairs gripping his briefcase, and a bag stuffed with clothes. 'I'll collect the rest of my things another time,' he says, not looking at me.

'Joe! It's not what it looked like . . .' I grab his sleeve. If he'll only just listen.

Joe shakes me off. 'Please, spare me those lines. Give me that dignity.'

266

'Hear me out . . .'

He turns on his heel towards the door. It's all happening so fast. I stand in front of the door, blocking his path, feeling slightly silly, melodramatic. 'Joe, you cannot leave like this. Not until we've talked, please Joe.' He pushes me aside roughly with a strength never used before. 'Don't go.'

'Should have thought about that before you . . .' He yanks the door and slams it with a crashing finality. I fall against it, slide down, catching my back painfully on the lip of the letterbox. Evie starts crying upstairs. A long pitiful howl, like she's woken from a nightmare. For the first time since her birth I don't rush to her. I can't move. The howl gets louder. I match it.

Forty-one

Three days. Three improbable days. OK, suffered now! Punished now! Come home! But he hasn't. I can guess what he must be feeling. I've been there. But, crucial difference, I didn't leave. Mothers can't just leave. Fathers can, and they do. That's what Dad did. That's what Dad's Dad did. When things got tough, grandpa Hackney, as he was known, got a job in a cruise ship's kitchen and sent postcards back from the Caribbean and other impossibly exotic places. (The furthest south Granny Hackney ever got was Brighton Pier.) And my aunt Sheila's husband Gerry left, six times, until she said enough was enough and changed the locks. While my aunt Grace's second husband ran off with her next door neighbour's nineteen-year-old babysitter seven months after my cousin Tom was born. Even her dog (castrated, male) left her. So no, I shouldn't be surprised.

I sit on the balcony, watching and waiting. Evie is restless and grumpy after her night-time antics. Or could she already be disturbed by this shift in her galaxy, the unprecedented absence of daddy? How long before the psychological scars set in, disfiguring her trust in life's essential benignity? Grey lumpen clouds slug across the sky. Nippy, the weather's turned. I take off my moth-nibbled cardigan and wrap it around her, relishing the sacrifice, the feeling that I'm protecting her at my expense. I stab Joe's number into my phone, hiding my number. My fingers tremble: too many HobNobs and hardcore espressos. Answerphone. I try his work. The secretary fields my calls.

Next best thing: 'Nicola? It's me, Amy.'

'Hey, how's it going?'

'Sorry to bother you Nic, but he's gone. Joe's gone.'

'What? Gone where?'

'Walked out, left me.'

'Shit, you're joking?' Silence. Shock waves bounce between satellites, across space. 'Obviously not. You'll have to excuse me whispering. I'm at work. Just gone back.'

'Gosh, I wasn't thinking, sorry.'

'First week . . .' Her voice becomes officious. 'So that's line one, second paragraph?' She pauses then whispers, 'Sorry, editor on the prowl again. Wants me to give it "a hundred and ten per cent", surely the most irritating phrase known to man.'

'I'm going a bit bonkers, Nic.'

'Right, what time is it? 12.30. I'll sneak out for my lunch hour. Amy, I'm sorry. I had no idea.'

'Don't worry, nor did I.'

The phone clicks shut. I sob quietly into Evie's downy head. She looks at me puzzled, confused by this un-mummy-ish state and worms a finger into my nostril as an offer of support.

'We'll be OK.'

She pulls my thumb into the soft sea anemone of her mouth and sucks hard. I can feel a little tooth ridging beneath her gum. 'He'll be back, I promise.' Then I remember that rule about not making promises to children you can't keep.

*

Nicola wraps her hands around a cup of badly made tea. 'Oh why didn't you tell me?' she implores.

'I felt so ashamed. And it was a blip, a . . . a malfunctioning.'

'Your conscience crashed.' Nicola smiles. 'Have to say, that Josh guy sounds like a tosser.'

'I'm the tosser here. It's my fault.'

'Well, yes but . . .' Nicola grapples for a justification that will make me feel better. 'You thought Joe had betrayed you and it sounds like there was an element of point scoring.'

'But, ironically, our relationship was getting *better* after the Josh incident,' I interrupt. 'I put it behind me, well, thought I had.'

Nicola leans forward. 'You know what, Amy? Some people have to cock things up before they get them right. They have to choose again.'

'Huh?'

'A pet theory of mine. You fall in love. Then that endorphin frazzle fades and you worry that the love has gone so you go looking for it, kind of off-piste, in the thrill of a new lover's body, only to find out it's there where you left it, dozy and cosy at home. You have to choose your partner all over again, in a different climate, a more real one. Don't you think?'

'Hmmm.' I stare into my tea. Joe's face stares back at me, not drinking, drowning beneath the Assam. 'Christ. What *was* I thinking?'

'Well I guess you weren't thinking at all.' Nicola attempts a smile but the situation is a bit too icky. Infidelity leaves a bad taste in the mouth. It tests camaraderie. She sneaks an anxious glance at her watch.

'I was pushing him off. But Joe was already there, Nic. Too late.' I put my head in my hands, squirming at the memory.

'Oh Nic, Shit. Shit. SHIT! What now?'

'You must talk to him,' she says sternly.

'I've tried! Joe's gone into one. He won't take my calls. I don't know where he's staying.'

'You've phoned around?'

'Who? Kate? His work mates?' I blow hair off my face. 'No, no, I can't face telling anyone, not yet. I'd rather try and sort it out myself first before it hits the airwaves.'

Nicola digs a Kit-Kat out of her handbag, snaps it in half. 'Chocolate helps.'

The chocolate tastes sugar-cube sweet. I can't take another bite. 'I've lost my appetite.'

'Always the redeeming factor in heartbreak,' says Nicola, matter of factly, finishing it off herself. 'Listen, Amy, go to his work. Force him to talk to you, try and explain.'

'Will you come with me?'

Nicola looks at her watch again, torn. 'I'm so sorry but I really can't. I shouldn't even be here now. I've got the boss breathing down my polo neck, checking that I'm not sneaking off to baby yoga during work hours.' She puts on her jacket, the officiousness of the tailoring changing her radically. 'I know,' she says. 'Weird, feels like an eighties power suit.' Nicola hugs me tight. She smells of soap. I watch her from the dirty sitting-room window, a rangy figure walking sharply down the street in new uncomfortable office shoes. What a relief it would be to be her right now. How strange to be me.

Forty-two

Evie's in her cutest cashmere gear, Annabel's hand-me-downs. I'm wearing my designer jeans and a pretty floral silk top, which hopefully gives me a fresh, innocent aura. No heels. Virginal flats. Invisible no-make-up make-up. Don't want to scare the horses. OK, deep breath: the tube. I've never dared take Evie through this aggressive subterranean crowd of shoulders and knees. Although an urgent sense of mission gives me courage, it is, as I suspected, a nightmare. Signs on the escalator announce, 'Fold your pushchair'. As if! Where would Evie go? Where would her gubbins go? How would I carry it? So I mount the escalator, obviously the wrong way, me on the lower step, so that the pram is precariously tilted upwards. People shoot pitiful looks but don't offer to help. There is a baby-gobbling gap between train and platform, a drunken loon breathing cider breath into the pram and a man bearing a striking similarity to Osama Bin Laden sitting opposite. But we get there. It is raining. I haven't got an umbrella.

'London, little lady,' I say to Evie as we surface at Oxford Circus and walk down Argyll Street towards Soho, past stubble-chinned men in architectural spectacles and thin purposeful women in heels: people with exciting jobs and social lives and a clear sense of direction. Music pounds from shops and cafés and the petrol smell of possibility smokes down the street, catches in my throat and fills me with a nostalgic longing for working life. No wonder Joe stays late at the office.

The doors are vast slabs of frosted glass. Six companies work from this building, most involved in design and film production. Joe is on the third floor. There is no lift. Steps and a pram will ruin any elegance of entry, so should I intercom up from down here? What if he doesn't come? He's due out soon. No, I will wait.

Five, ten . . . seventeen minutes. Evie's getting bored, whimpering. I resort to handing her the house keys, her (usually embargoed) favourites. Giggling, she tosses them out of the pram, deftly aiming at puddles. She howls if I don't pick the keys up and hand them back. Twenty-two minutes after arriving, a big hand presses on to the other side of the frosted glass door, an imprint in the snow. The door swings open grandly and Joe strides past on to the narrow pavement.

'Joe! It's me,' I say rather too cheerily. It's difficult to get the tone right.

Joe stops still, as though I'm holding a gun to him. 'What are you doing here?' He has tired watery eyes.

'I've, er, come to talk . . .' I mean apologise but the words gabble out all wrong.

'What about? I saw what I saw, Amy,' Joe says wearily, like he's already repeated this line to other people countless times.

'Where are you staying? With Kate?'

A pulse pounds on his temple. 'No, Leo. Crouch End.' Leo is an old university friend of Joe's. He's single, knows lots of attractive women. 'I was going to contact you today actually.'

'You were?' Thank God.

'Yes, to arrange when I can see Evie.'

'Oh. Whenever you like, obviously. Evie, look it's Daddy.'

Evie grins gummily at Joe. He pulls back the rain-cover, bends into the pram, squeezes his cheek against hers and shuts his eyes. He stays there for a long time. Passers-by smile: dads are always cuter than mothers. 'I love you,' he whispers into her ear. She tenderly pokes a key into his eye.

I can feel myself welling up, not because I'm touched by the intimacy of the moment, but because I am so excluded from it. Joe straightens, expression hardening, rain pancaking his hair. 'Joe, please can I try and explain?'

'What the hell is there to explain?' he says coldly. 'I've already worked it out. And it all makes sense. What a fucking mug.' He crashes through the puddles on Poland Street. I try to follow him but forget I've put the brake on the pram and it doesn't budge and I can't shift the brake lever and he's a few metres ahead before I can catch up with him, soaked, mascara running into my mouth. 'What, Joe? What do you mean?' I gasp.

'So fucking obvious! Screaming in front of me all the fucking time and I didn't see it. No, I thought I'd ask you to marry me instead!' He breathes out a low, bitter laugh and walks faster.

'You've got it wrong.' I realise I will say anything, lie if I have to, just to get us back to where we were.

'All your fucking pissing around with Alice. I bet she knew, didn't she? I bet she was in on it?'

'That's ridiculous!'

He stops still for a second. 'Don't you, of all people, ever call me ridiculous.' He marches on. 'New hair! New clothes . . . weight loss. For who, Amy? For me? I don't think so.'

274

'That's got nothing to do with it.'

'It has everything to do with it.' The truth nips my ankles. 'So how long was it going on for? I suppose I should know,' he says, voice quiet now, almost blocked out by the roar of traffic. I notice that his shirt and trousers clash, not his usual fastidiously well dressed self.

'There was nothing going on.' The lie hurts. But I can't explain the truth, partly because I haven't got a handle on it myself, but mostly because I don't want to lose him.

'So I didn't see you excavating the throat of your Pilates instructor then?'

'Yes . . . no!' My mouth is dry, empty husks of denial rattle around it.

'Look, Amy.' Joe stops sternly. 'This isn't easy for me. Don't make it harder. Go home. We'll sort something out.' His baseball-glove hand cups Evie's cheek. I catch a quick vague scent of him, leathery and male, already a nostalgic smell. 'Go home,' he says again, almost nicely. And the hint of niceness kills me because this is Joe being detached, Joe's full stop.

'If that's what you want.' I swivel the pram around and walk away, ears pricked, waiting to hear him shout 'Come back, Amy', or the squish of his size-twelve feet. Instead, I hear the clatter of keys on a wet pavement and a rattle as they drop down a drain.

Forty-three

One apple and cinnamon crumble, dropped off with a note ('I'm waiting to hear what I can do to help . . .') on my doorstep, Sue. Three phone messages, Alice. Four phone messages, Kate. Two lunchtime visits, Nicola. Disbelief and a set of spare house keys, Mother. The word is out: I have Been Left.

Thing is, no one is entirely sure why. I've curled the truth into a ball and suck on it privately, greedily. Only Nicola knows the full story. My mother got an abridged version. And that was bad enough. She had to sit down.

Yes, I've seen Joe again. He came round to take Evie out yesterday morning. He spoke officiously, face shut like a cupboard. I tried to get him to talk. He wasn't having it. And I realised that the more I pushed, insisted, the further he retreated. Very Mars. So, when he returned, I tried to out-casual him, pretended not to be bothered. A clever dating trick of Kate's. Except it didn't work.

'Got to go to a design conference in Barcelona for a few days,' he said. Then he walked out of the front door – *our* front door – into the cool September evening. I watched him from the bedroom window, his hair lifting in the breeze, the shirt I bought him last Christmas echoing the V shape of his chest. He didn't look back.

'Eeeee!' Evie yelps like a kitten. She is playing peek-a-boo with the adorable creature in the board book's shiny foil mirror. It is nappy-splittingly funny. She grips the beanbag with her fat little hands, balance improving, edging forward on her tummy, poised to crawl, a reminder of the breakneck speed at which babies grow. Already Joe is missing tiny milestones. She looks at me for collusion with her joke, and I cannot help but smile. Darling Evie. The person who kept me up at night now gets me through it.

Ding dong.

I shrink towards Evie, away from the suddenly crippling decision as to whether or not to answer the door. Leave me alone until this bit's over! Joe needs to lick his wounds, punish me. Then he'll be back. Of course he will. And, apart from anything else, I'm too exhausted to socially integrate. Looking after Evie without Joe's help feels like triple the amount of work rather than double.

Pushed from outside, the letterbox flaps open like a mouth. 'Miss Crane! It's Alice, let me in!'

Alice! Oh. That life.

'Hey,' I say, opening the door. A rush of mild air ruffles the hallway. Alice steps back and crosses one brown arm over the other, charm bracelet tinkling.

'Whoa, Amy! Look at you!'

'I'm sure I look ghastly. Give me a break.'

'What are you talking about? You look fabulous! So skinny.'

'Am I?' My waist bands are looser but any sense of satisfaction has been subsumed by the fact I appear to have fucked up my life.

'Didn't I always say you'd make a great single yummy

mummy? Here, this is for you.' A bottle of champagne. 'Get the glasses out.'

We sit cross-legged on the living-room floor. Alice holds her glass up. I reluctantly clink flute. 'Thanks. A better hit than the apple crumble.' I nod to the tea-towel-covered dish on the table in the kitchen. 'A sympathy gift from Sue at NCT.'

'The Sue who shares a husband with Jasmine?'

I nod, relieved to be reminded that others have problems that are worse than mine, then instantly feel a pinch of guilt because I still haven't intervened in any way. I've just uncomfortably straddled the fence.

'Well, that's coming to the end of its shelf life.'

'Really? God, I hope so.'

'Me too. Affairs have to operate within a framework of honesty, between the mistress and husband at any rate,' Alice says coolly. 'Jasmine should say "Enough."'

When did moral outrage make way for this libertine, quasi-French realism?

Alice leans back on a cushion, tanned knee flopping out to one side exposing the white gusset of her knickers. 'Amy, I never thought I'd be asking you this, but have you got anything I can eat? I'm starving and I can't drink bubbly on an empty stomach.'

'Stale pitta, pureed carrot or apple crumble?' There seems very little incentive to shop without Joe around to wolf it all down. Surprisingly, I miss having a man to feed.

'Sue's? God, it seems a bit perverse considering. It'll probably choke me, but, go on. Nothing like a glycemic boost mid-morning.' I serve her a tiny Alice-sized portion. She picks at the apple, avoids the crumble.

'How's everyone? Annabel? Blythe?'

'Blythe has gone!' Alice cries, wiping mock tears away

from her eyes. 'She's left us for New York. Said she couldn't bear the weather and the bad grooming any longer.'

'No!'

'Well, not exactly. Husband's been relocated back to his New York City bank. Blythe is pretty happy about it. She wants to be in a country with long summer camps. And, of course, she's looking forward to being reunited with her old therapist and plastic surgeon.'

Blythe's departure is surprisingly flattening. We were never close – I suspect I was dismissed as a little boring and unfashionable – but I'm sad that we never said goodbye, sad that another little chapter, a footnote in my recent, happier life has been closed. And any kind of ending makes me a little weepy because it reminds me of Joe. 'And Annabel?'

Alice frowns. She coils Evie's hair around her fingers and puts it precisely behind her ear like a stylist. 'Oh, the eyes are much better. But, Milo . . .' she pauses. 'The doctors say he's fine but Annabel isn't convinced. Says she's had enough kids to know. She's quite worried, poor thing. But I'm sure he's fine. Annabel is London's most effective beautiful-baby-making machine, isn't she?'

Yes, Annabel is a perfect mother, a perfect wife. No, someone like Annabel would never risk it all for a romp, would she? I split the skin of my second glass and it feels like two hands pushing against my skull. It's a new kind of drunkenness, almost like flu symptoms, but not wholly unpleasant. 'This is actually rather nice,' I mutter, articulating my surprise that anything could feel nice after the horribleness of the last few days.

Alice gives me an understanding I'm-feeling-it-too look. 'It's like you'll never be able to cope at first,' she says. 'But actually you do. It's a mental adjustment. And if Joe is a good father, well, you've got a babysitter for life.' She raises her glass. 'Here's to your new independence!'

I can't raise mine. I'm not exactly feeling the carnival. 'I just want Joe back.'

Alice arches back in surprise. 'What? You want him *back*? Why? I thought that this is just what you needed, a clean break. I thought you'd be pleased! Your relationship didn't seem that functional, if you don't mind me saying. A few eyebrows were raised when you announced your engagement.' Alice stretches out her long legs, the calf muscles elongating and tensing. 'We're all here for you now. I certainly am.'

'Thanks.'

'It's not like you're going to be alone in a world of happily dysfunctional Sue'n'Alan couples.'

'Suppose not.'

I watch the champagne bubbles fizz up the glass, hiss and pop like the hot, bad relationships I had in my twenties. How I grieved for them after having Evie: the idea that I'd be stuck making love to one man for the rest of my life was appalling. But now the thought of climbing back on to that casual sex carousel is far worse.

'And you'll be back at work, no? You'll be too busy to be lonely.'

'Yeah, maybe. I've got to contact my boss.'

Alice looks at me and sighs. 'Oh dear. You're really not happy, are you?'

I bite my lip, shake my head.

'OK, let's start at the beginning. What happened exactly?'

I thought she'd never ask. 'Um, it's complicated, a bit seedy.' I don't want to tell her, but my tongue, wetted and disorientated by the champagne, longs to let loose its curled-up little secret.

'Seedy? How fabulous, do tell.'

'Josh . . .' I say, the secret unfurling, like a rolled-up rug dropped from a great height.

'Yes?' Alice bends forward encouragingly, as if talking to a small child.

'Joe caught me and Josh kissing.'

'*Whoa!*' Alice's eyes widen. 'You got caught? That was the reason he left? Shit, that's bad.'

'Really fucking bad.'

Alice pauses then waves her hand. 'Hey, what's a kiss? It's not like you've been having a Jasmine-style affair.'

I'm a little stunned, and relieved, by Alice's flippancy. 'If I tell you something, *promise* not to tell anyone else. You see, Joe doesn't know the first bit.'

'The first bit? Oooh, there's more?'

'Well . . . there's no nice way of putting this. There was a bit of a heavy session before the kiss too.'

'You naughty devil!' Alice nudges me hard with her elbow. 'This is exciting. When?'

'A few weeks ago. After a Pilates class. It was mistake, a weird thing. Like all this sexual energy that I thought had gone for good suddenly . . .' And I explain. The morning sunlight thrums moodily through the half-closed blind. A pause. I wait for chastisement, head bent, eyes drilling the floor.

'Go girl!' Alice says, clapping her hands.

I look up. 'Alice! This is serious.'

Finally acknowledging the situation's severity, Alice stares sheepishly into her glass, the champagne reflecting a golden trembling disc of light on her cheek. 'I suppose it is. But he only caught the kiss, nothing else?'

I nod my head.

'No problem, Joe'll be back.'

'You don't know what he's like.'

'Hey, come on. It's not going to do any harm for Joe to realise that you are a sexual woman. That other men fancy the knickers off you.'

Alice does not get it. I put my head in my hands and sigh deeply, head swimmy with sadness and alcohol. Alice puts a silky smooth arm around my shoulder and hugs me into her breasts. They smell like almonds. 'Hey, hey, my baby, Amy,' she says. 'I didn't realise it would hit you like this. I'm sorry.'

'No need for you to apologise, I did all the fucking up.'

Alice stares out of the window. There's a bit of an awkward silence, punctuated by me sniffing. Then her phone beeps. She scrabbles it out of her bag, quickly, as if relieved to have something to do. While other people's crises are a tonic to the likes of Sue, they make Alice ill at ease. She doesn't do downs. Tut-tutting at the screen, Alice stands up, brushing crumble crumbs off her gleaming brown legs. 'Shit, I need to shoot.'

'But we haven't finished the champagne.'

'Alfie, er, he's unwell.' She flings a bag over her shoulder and walks to the door. 'Hey, look after yourself,' Alice says, voice flat now, as if the mood was contagious and had hopped from my head to hers, nimble as a louse in a school playground.

Forty-four

No news from Joe. Restless, I slither about the house wearing a new Marks & Spencer's fondant pink faux-satin nightie. Mum bought it to 'cheer me up', but it makes me feel like I'm about to go to hospital for an overnight stay. (She's also bought me a new hairbrush, which I've deemed inappropriate and ignored.) The blinds are at half mast. I'm eating baked beans out of the can. Evie has registered her disapproval of this subdued atmosphere by refusing to eat her vegetable mash and feigning boredom with her Baby Einstein DVDs, which used to keep me sane by keeping her quiet. (Whereas I used to disapprove of children watching television, I now long for the day Evie gets into the respite that is the all-day programming of CBeebies.) I try to amuse her with hearty renditions of 'Row Your Boat' but, as with toy telephones or toy keys, she won't be duped. She knows a fake when she sees it. Every time I anxiously check my voicemail, she looks at me strangely, demanding attention, answers, explanations.

'What, Evie?' I snap. 'I don't know. Sorry.' Hurt clouds across her eyes. Christ, who am I becoming? I can't expect her to make up for Joe. She's not a big enough human to fill the space he's left. She's about the size of his thigh. 'Sorry.

Sorry. Come on sweetheart, we need to get out.' I kiss Evie's head all over, trying to make up for Joe's absence, doubling the love. 'Baby massage?'

This is a sign I'm getting desperate, because I tried baby massage once before when she was about two months old. There were only five mothers in the group, all so cliquey you'd think they'd suckled each others' babies as a group bonding exercise. The teacher was bossy and New Age, and sported electrified spirals of dark hair, not wholly unlike Carole Caplin. In the kind of hushed intimacy that instantly makes me feel awkward, the mothers massaged their babies into Zen-like states: Evie imploded in inexplicable fury. But she's older now. And I've got to do something. The house is hardly a whirl of social activity. No one's visited for the last couple of days. Perhaps I've had my quota of sympathy. Or there's the fear that Being Left might be catching.

The evangelical church is ugly, concrete, sixties. It could be a Conservative HQ or a scout club. On its flat planed blue double doors is a note in swirly handwriting, 'All God's toddlers welcome here for tea and biscuits between 10–12, 50p little person, £1 grown-ups.' Hope I haven't got the wrong day. Levering bum against the doors, they screech open.

Oh, I have. Rather than sweet kicking babies on mats, the church looks like it's been ransacked by barbarians. Toddlers wielding plastic swords run around in hysterical circles beneath a huge mural of a Chris Martin lookalikey Jesus and a banner inviting us to 'Jump the Hallelujah train!'

Around the edge of the hall, in a horseshoe shape, is a row of padded maroon chairs, like the ones you might find at a cheaper private dentist. Sitting on them are women huddled together talking intently. A lot of the women are fat, possibly because they're all eating chocolate biscuits. The women chat over the remaining empty seats, leaving no option but to intrude on the conversation. I settle on a seat between two benign-looking women in their late twenties.

'Sorry,' I say as I sit down. They ignore me, dunk their biscuits. A pretty little blonde girl, about two, comes up to the knee of the fattest lady on my left. She doesn't look like her. And she is whining. She wants another biscuit.

'Mummy says no more than one biscuit in the morning,' the woman mutters half heartedly. Australian accent. 'Oh well, what she doesn't know won't hurt her.' She gives the girl a biscuit and exchanges glances with the woman to my right, their eyes meeting somewhere near my forehead.

'Are you a nanny?' I ask shyly.

'Oh yes, we're all nannies here,' she smiles, slightly surprised I've addressed her.

'Where are all the mothers?'

'Good question.' She rolls her eyes like I've hit on a topic she could talk about for hours but won't because she's not like that. Then she engages her friend back into loud nanny talk – pay, holidays, the husband's habit of pissing all over the loo seat. I want to ask them if they know anyone who could look after Evie when I go back to work but can't find a window in which to interrupt. Instead, I bend back into the chair, out of the way of their conversational traffic, and feel rather superfluous, considering that Evie is by far the youngest at the playgroup and displays an almost autistic disinterest in all the other children.

A swell of loneliness threatens like an overdue sneeze. I feel – how pathetic is this – like the new girl no one wants to talk to in the playground. Where are all my comrades? I was sold the line that becoming a mother meant immediate membership to some kind of club. But it doesn't, not now. Mum says she spent years popping from neighbourly house to house in the seventies, with sultana rock cakes in her stripy shopper and children hanging from her Laura Ashley skirt: 'Such easy, sociable years.' But it's not the seventies. In London it's not really the done thing to pop round to someone's house unannounced. Chances are only the nanny will be at home anyway.

Suddenly, there is a large cold gust of wind and the door screeches open. The sea of children parts.

'Kate!' A more astonishing sight than the second coming.

Kate smiles her overbite smile and surveys the room curiously. 'Your mum said you might be here, been trying to hunt you down.' A seat is liberated from an impressive bottom two seats down and the nannies budge up reluctantly. Kate puts her hand on my knee. 'How come you haven't got back to me?' she says softly.

'Sorry, been really crap at returning calls. It's been difficult . . .' My fears of Kate being too involved or too Joe-sided suddenly seem unfounded and silly. A pause.

'So Joe's not back then?'

'In Barcelona. A design conference.' Kate looks surprised. 'He didn't tell you?'

'No, Joe's been almost as bad as you, holding everything in, not talking to me.' Kate gazes out at the toddler carnage and looks doleful. 'He always retreats into himself when something goes wrong, doesn't he?'

I nod. It is good to talk to someone who knows Joe almost as well as me. Has the shorthand.

'Or do you think he's pissed off with me?' she asks.

'You? Why?'

'He hasn't confided in me at all.'

'I'm sure he didn't mean it like that.'

'You don't think so?'

'No, really. Joe adores you, Kate.'

Kate smiles and sits straighter on her maroon chair. She

286

looks different. Slightly plumper, but not in a bad way. And radiant. Her skin gleams with health, her eyes and hair shine. 'This is bedlam.'

'Meant to be baby massage. Got the wrong day.'

Kate laughs. 'Oh well, easily done in your state I'm sure. Now, are you going to tell me what the hell went on? One minute you're getting married . . .'

'Joe hasn't told you?'

Kate shakes her head. Joe, loyal to the end. He wouldn't humiliate me, not even when I deserved it.

'Well, er . . . it's complicated . . .'

'Go on.'

'I . . . I . . . Joe caught . . .' I can't do it. She'll take Joe's side. Who wouldn't? And I can't cope with Kate turning against me too. 'Irreconcilable differences.'

'Amy? You can tell *me* you know.' She waits for my response, doesn't get it. 'But I understand if you don't really want to talk, not right now.' Sweet Kate, trying so hard to be accommodating when she's dying for the gory details. 'I'm so sorry. It shouldn't be like this.'

I shake my head and think back to all those happy times, me and Joe lounging around her Notting Hill flat, the lazy brunches, the boozy child-free nights. No, it shouldn't be like this. Kate slips her hand into mine and squeezes it and I feel a strong, very real flow of love from her flesh to mine like a kind of broadband Reiki transfer. Dear Kate, dependable, contrary Kate. I squeeze her back.

'Let's go.'

Back home, she picks a photo off the fire surround: Joe on a Goan beach against a shrieking red sunset, smiling, stoned. I found it in the office, put it up yesterday for company. Solitariness is doing funny things to my head.

'You're still surrounding yourself with him? I'm not sure this is healthy. I don't want you to get more hurt, Amy. And by pretending it's all fine and he's coming home—'

'You don't think he will?' I interrupt. Does she know something I don't? Is this her soft way of letting me down?

'Maybe. But probably best to accept he isn't and move on.'

'Move on? Where the hell to?'

Kate perches neatly on the sofa arm, crossing her legs and cocking her head to the side, warming to the counselling role. 'A life, for starters. Amy, I can see you've been moping around, living in this . . . this pit.'

'It could probably do with a clean.'

'This isn't *you*! Last time we met you looked like the sexiest mother on God's earth, groomed, glamorous. And now, well, look at you.' She pulls something out of my hair. 'Egg! Euw!' She shakes the yellow crust off her finger. Evie, who is sitting on my knee, stretches out to catch it with a delighted shriek.

'But—'

'Moping isn't going to win him back.' She slaps her hand on the mantelpiece, tossing a blanket of dust into the air.

'Suppose you'd know.' I'm not being sarcastic. Kate understands men. She's read hundreds of self-help books about them and has always navigated the harsh Darwinian dating jungle like a native bushman.

'Moping makes a woman less attractive. It gives too much away.' Kate leans forward on the sofa and holds my hands in an evangelical clasp. 'You need some fire back! Don't feel sorry, get angry! Ask yourself, why *hasn't* he phoned from Barcelona? Why isn't he back here with you now? Stop making excuses for him and get on with your life!'

Evie raises an eyebrow. I slump on to the sofa, surprised

and winded by the force of her conviction. 'I was rather hoping he'd come back.'

'Doesn't matter.' Kate's cocked empathetic head is now almost at right angles to the rest of her body. 'You know what I think? I think you should pack up his stuff, show you're no doormat. It will help wash him out of your hair!'

Wash him out of my hair? Do people without children have any idea of the impossibility of doing that to the father of your child? 'This isn't a teenage fling, Kate. It isn't that easy.'

'No, no of course not, I don't mean to trivialise it. I'm just suggesting a fresh start, that's all. I care about you.' I'm touched, and feel bad for doubting her mixed loyalties.

'I suppose it may give him a jolt. Show him this isn't a game.'

'Exactly! Come on, this place needs a tidy at the very least. I'll help you.'

After putting a protesting Evie down to sleep – she hates to miss the action – Kate and I get to work. Kate stacks his books in an old cardboard box, dusty books dancing with yellow mites. I start on his clothes. Socks, with their familiar residue of trainers. Joe's winter jumpers. The cashmere navy one I got him two years ago to match his eyes. There's a little hole in the left sleeve where Evie likes to wiggle her pinky finger. Unworn jumpers from Christmases past. One from my mother that he'd never dare give to Oxfam, certain that she'd find out. I press them down into a holdall, fold tissue paper over the top like a shop assistant and imagine him opening it, touched by the care that had gone into its packing. His bath-room cabinet. Shaving foam. Aftershave, the smell of Joe's chin. Joe's comb. Bits of his hair. Bits of DNA. Bits of Evie.

Kate comes upstairs and puts a hand on my shoulder. 'Are you OK? Is this difficult for you?'

'Nah. Weirdly, I kind of feel like I'm packing to go on

289

holiday.' There is a curious elation to this process, a kind of release, as though I were venting my feelings in a bad amdram.

'That's the spirit!' She sits down on our bed, bounces on it a little, as if testing the springs. 'Afraid I'm going to have to go soon, to feed the dogs.'

'Oh, don't go. It's nice having you here.'

She gives me a hug. 'I can't leave the old hounds starving can I? They'll attack an organic lamb or something and I'll be cattle-prodded from the village.' In the ferocity of the hug Kate's hair gets caught in my mouth. It tastes how shampoo smells. 'I'll get my stuff together. Is there anything else I can do for you before I go? Make Evie's tea, ready for when she wakes up?'

'No, bless you. Thanks.' Trust Kate to offer proper practical help, rather than an inappropriate bottle of Moët like Alice. She pads downstairs. The sound of another human being on the stairs is so reassuring.

I stand on the stool and pull down boxes from the top of the wardrobe. Oh, my old clothes. My first-date dress lies crumpled at the top of a box, dappled from my tears all those weeks ago. I throw it on to the washing pile. Another box? Maternity stuff: bras with cups as big as hats; wrap-over dresses; bump tights. Another box. Joe's stuff: pictures, postcards, bank statements, solar calculators, keys to unknown locks. Some stuff I want to keep, like Evie's hospital identity bracelet, so I empty it on to the floor and start sorting through. I stack the postcards: an unsent one from Nice, written on a train by me, almost illegible; another one featuring a Bournemouth beach scene, 1977, but sent in 2004 from Joe's late grandmother who always believed, rather confusingly, in using up old postcards in her dresser drawer before buying new ones; New York cityscape, blank; Regent's Park . . .

'Amy, I'm off.' Kate stands in the doorway, lush hair coiled over one shoulder, hand on hip.

'I'll see you out. Thanks a million, Kate. I needed a boot up the bum.'

'Oh, sorry, I didn't mean to be too—'

'No, seriously, thank you.'

Kate's bullish Range Rover accelerates loudly. I feel like I should be waving a white handkerchief at an ocean liner. My throat is dry, heart hollowing as Kate, dear Kate, source of much-needed advice and shampoo-smelling hugs, is dehumanised into a noisy green dot on the horizon.

People leaving. Sometimes that's all I can remember.

Forty-five

The postcard: Regent's Park, willows slumped like drunks, framed by Nash's architectural confectionery and a black frill with 'Magical London Views' swirled across the bottom. I flip it over. Sent last September, from Sussex. Oh? Kate's confident round writing.

That special September day. You take the sting out of life, thank you. K.

I sit in shock, jigsaw bits raining down and slotting together neatly. Oh God. Not Kate. Please, not Kate. But it is her handwriting, her name. A new fear somersaults in my stomach, tangible and fluttery as a young foetus. I shiver, pick up my mobile.

'Hiya!' she booms cheerfully.

'I've just found evidence that Joe had an affair.' My voice is slow, doesn't betray the acrobatics inside.

'What? An affair? You are joking!'

'No, I'm deadly serious.'

'What evidence? Who with?' Her voice is high, reedy.

'It's a postcard . . .'

'You sure, sure?'

'Yes.'

'Really? Shit. Christ. I can't believe it. The *bastard*. The absolute bastard!' She sounds almost teary. 'I'm coming back over. Be with you in ten.'

Kate's back in five, screeching to a stop outside. I let her in solemnly, holding back. She follows me into the kitchen begging, 'What? What? Show me. Who is this girl?' She grabs the postcard out of my hand hungrily. Ah, Kate is jealous of herself.

'This. Can you explain it?'

Kate studies the postcard, face egg-pale.

'Bitch,' I say, mouth hardly moving.

Kate flicks back as though I've slapped her. 'What? What did you say?'

I glare.

'It's from me. What the hell has this postcard got to do with an affair? Don't be bonkers.'

'Kate, I was there. I saw you and Joe, except I didn't know it was you. He . . . he . . . kissed your arm . . .'

Kate's eyes open wide, the whites pinking with the pressure in her head. 'You were *there* in Regent's Park?' She grips her Tod's bag tight as if preparing to be mugged.

'Yes, I was fucking there! I saw you!' All control gone, I am shaking and grip the back of a kitchen chair so hard its legs rattle. 'It was you! I don't fucking believe it.' The betrayal by Kate, my friend! My confidante! Joe's mouth on her inner arm. The arm I know so well. That shrugs around my shoulders. That hugs Evie. I feel sick.

'I've got nothing to apologise for, Amy.' The kitchen knives glint seductively on the knife rack. For a millisecond I imagine digging one into her head, splitting it like a coconut. 'You're totally . . . like . . . overreacting.'

I step forward confrontationally. 'Bitch.'

'Listen, *nothing* happened.' Kate backs into the fridge nervously, knocking off pieces of Joe's fridge poetry. The word Suck falls on to my left big toe. 'We were in the park. We used to go to the park together a lot. Don't you remember?' Like it's my fault if I don't. 'You were always too tired . . .'

'Fuck you.'

'And too . . .' Kate's face darkens. Something shifts. A look in her eyes I haven't seen before. '. . . Smugly pregnant.'

I flinch now. Smug? How could she ever have thought that? I hated being pregnant!

'We were getting pretty close, Amy.' Kate steps out into the room again, more confident of her line now.

'What are you trying to say?'

'I got stung by a wasp,' she continues. 'He kissed my arm, to make it better. And he tried to go further but . . .' her voice softens to a whisper and she looks down at the floor. 'Well, I stopped him for *your* sake.'

'*You* stopped *him*?' I am shaking properly now, tight little spasms. 'For *my* sake?'

Kate walks to the other side of the kitchen table, putting its pine bulk between us. She's red in the face and beginning to cry. 'He . . . he . . . loved me. He always did! But . . . but . . . Joe's a good man. He *wanted* to do the right thing by you.'

'You are evil.'

'Joe was my ex, remember?' spits Kate. 'You don't fucking go out with your friends' exes! Not the ones they really loved.'

'He was a fling!'

'You know that, do you? You know nothing! And you've rubbed it in my face all these years.' I don't recognise the woman who is speaking. 'You thought you fucking had it all, didn't you? Poor old Kate stuck with boring Pete, can't even get pregnant. Well, I'll tell you this now, Amy Crane, Joe loves me, not you!'

294

My stomach is curdling again. Breathe. Don't be sick. Don't be sick.

'And if it wasn't for you . . . maybe I would be with Joe. Maybe *I* would be pregnant right now . . .' All the features of Kate's face scrunch up to a central snarling point.

'So that's what it's about.'

'We would have made great parents. Then you . . . You came along!'

I am dumbstruck.

'No, you can't say anything, can you? Because you saw it. With your very eyes. You saw how he loved *me*. I can't pretend any more. No, I can't pretend it's all all right any more. Joe should be with me!'

'Get out! Just fucking get out!' I shout.

Kate lurches towards me and I wonder, for a brief moment, if she's going to attack me. But she grabs my sleeve.

'This is such a mess. Let's talk . . .'

'Don't touch me,' I scream. 'Just leave me alone. Leave.'

'But I *didn't* sleep with him out of . . . out of loyalty to you. I really didn't. I wanted to wait until he left you.'

'Shut up!' I headphone my ears with my hands.

'I can't help who I love. Please, Amy, I'm telling you this for your own good. You must let him go.'

'Out!' I push her to the door, along the hall.

She trips on a baby bouncer and yelps as she falls down the front step, bag and legs and glossy hair flying, whimpering in a heap. 'Listen, please listen to me Amy . . .'

I pick up one of my huge brick-like MBT trainers from the hall floor and toss it at Kate. It hits her thigh. *Whoomp!* I slam the door: life as I know it bangs shut too.

I vomit violently into the baby bouncer.

Forty-six

'Alice.' I open the door bleary eyed, twenty-four hours later. You don't expect someone like Alice to make a cameo appearance in your nightmare.

'Gosh, you look exhausted,' Alice says, crinkling her tiny nose. 'Euh, what's that smell?'

'What smell?'

'Bins? Nappies?'

I'm immune. The mess has become like wallpaper. Surprising how much Joe actually did do around the house. The evidence is accumulating. He always said I didn't appreciate his inner Domestos Goddess. 'Probably the baby bouncer.'

'You need to get a cleaner around, honey, one with an obsessive compulsive disorder.'

'Yes, must.' Ah, there's my shoe. I bend down behind Alice and Alfie's buggy, scoop my MBT trainer from the doorstep and pair it neatly in the hall. 'Er, um, tea?' Surreal how life just marches on. You imagine it might stop, out of sympathy, for a few days, just enough time to get your head together, to replot life to these new coordinates. Or something spectacular might happen. Like a newsworthy storm. A flood.

Something to reflect the implosion inside, like in romantic novels. But no, London presses on with its mild grey weather. Nappies need changing. Alice drops round. I offer her tea, while inside I'm cracking and splintering, like an old chair jumped up and down on by an obese angry child.

'Thanks, herbal if you have some.' Alice is in morning-mother mode: furry knee-high boots over jeans, face scrubbed bare of everything bar her tan. She has an air of hurried mission and throws her beige monogrammed Louis Vuitton bucket bag down abruptly. It falls over, spilling its contents on to the kitchen floor with a clatter. 'Damn, damn,' she says, agitated, scraping up a Blackberry, Tampax, Juicy Tube gloss and an arsenal of Calpol sachets. I try to help her but she bats me away. 'You need to rest.' She closes the bag and hugs it protectively on her knee like a small baby. 'Now, how *are* you, sweetheart?' Alice asks, like she means it more than anyone else might mean it.

'Um . . .' The enormity of the story pulls down heavy on my body like a sleepless night the following afternoon. I don't know where to start. Alice doesn't know Kate. 'I've just found out—'

'He isn't back yet?' Alice interrupts.

I shake my head.

'Oh, I'm sorry.' Alice purses her rose-bud mouth like a geisha's and twitches it from side to side. 'It's hard on your own, at first, but it gets . . .' She tails off, losing conviction in the rest of the sentence.

'It makes a real difference knowing I'm not the only one, you know,' I say softly, meaning it, so grateful to have her single-mum tonic around me at this time. 'That someone understands . . .'

Alice closes her eyes. There's a faint white Chanel sunglasses mark over her temples.

'. . . That I'm not the only single mother around here.' God, there, I've said it! Single mother. Fuck Kate. Fuck Joe. Me and Alice, girls together!

'Amy,' Alice suddenly looks terribly serious and terribly beautiful. 'I need to talk to you.' She studies her tea bag intensely, fingers fiddling its string. 'This is not great.'

'It's a bit Extreme Make-over isn't it?'

'I've been thinking hard about . . .' She looks up, eyes flat and green as lawns. 'If there's anything I can do.'

'Thanks.'

Alice bites her cuticles. 'But I wanted to tell you. Well, there's something I've been thinking about for a while and in a funny way your situation has been a wake-up call, it's put everything into perspective.'

'Oh?'

'I'm getting back together with John.'

'John?'

'Alfie's dad.' She smiles brightly, obviously unburdened by telling me. 'We're moving to the country. Devon. Starting again . . .'

Whoomp! The air vacuumed out of my lungs. 'But . . . but Alice.' I feel dizzy. Tears, ready tears well up, already so close to the surface. Alice in Devon! My gateway to a life outside Joe. 'But you are so happy, such a yummy mummy. So sorted. You said it'd never work.'

'Me, a yummy mummy! Sorted?' Alice smiles. 'Well that's very sweet of you to say but I'd beg to differ. The reality is a bit more complicated. And I'm so over crappy non-committal men, I can't tell you. Actually, it hasn't been all that easy. I just don't want to do it on my own any more.'

'That's . . . that's great, Alice,' I say, trying to mean it. Part of me feels like she encouraged me to relocate to the other side of the world and then left when I got there.

'You look like you're about to cry.'

'Sorry.'

'You can come and stay . . .' Alice shifts uncomfortably.

'Of course. Just being wet. I'll miss you . . .' I can't tell her that every time someone leaves, it's like a little bit of Dad, a little bit of Joe leaving all over again, the rejection, that hollow feeling in the chest.

'Come on, things aren't all bad.'

'They're not?'

She looks at me brightly. 'Well, you've lost tons of weight. You pulled off Project Amy.'

'Project fucking Amy?' Rage whooshes open like an umbrella. 'Look where it got me!'

Alice starts back, defences immediately rising. 'That's not my fault. It's not my fault.' She stands up from the table, flushed, reaching for Alfie. 'Don't blame me. I only ever tried to do what I thought best.'

'You told me to leave Joe!'

'Come on Amy, I know you're upset. But when did I ever use those words?'

And I try to think. I can't remember the exact moment she said them although I'm certain she did. If she didn't actually say them, then the insinuation had the same effect.

'Those words never came out of my mouth. You hear what you want to hear!' says Alice. A tremble starts in my knee, moves up my thigh. I clamp my legs shut tight to control them. 'It's in your head, Amy. You live in your head!' Alice, shaking her curls crossly, packs Alfie into his pushchair and wheels him towards the door. 'I'm not your life coach!'

'God, I'm sorry Alice, I didn't mean . . .'

Alice looks down at the floor and swallows hard. 'I wanted to help you reinvent yourself. That was all I ever tried to do.'

Forty-seven

7.07 a.m. A noise downstairs. Since Joe's left I hear a lot of noises: burglars, rapists and baby-killers scuttling around the house like rats. Or perhaps it's Kate coming to pour sour milk across my face as I sleep. Heart slamming, eyes crusty, I drop out of bed and take up my hairdryer – with extra-large diffuser nozzle – as a weapon (where are the MBT trainers when you need them?) and creep softly down the stairs, cringing every time they creak. Peering through the banisters, I squat down, whiffy with sleep smells. A crash. A scuffle. I tighten my grip on the hairdryer. Then . . . a head. A scruff of hair.

Joe! Nut brown, muscular in a T-shirt. He crashes quietly around the sitting room, like a loud whisper, picking up his spare mobile phone charger, a notebook, an old *New Yorker* and shoving them into a big black sports bag. I crouch on the stairs, hug my knees tight. How could he? How could he have kissed Kate? I hate him completely.

Joe picks a photo of Evie off the bookshelf, studies it and smiles before putting it back, carefully adjusting its angle to the room. Then he stoops down and picks up the pink nightdress that Mum bought, dumped after my bath yesterday morning, sniffs it and bunches it to his face like a hankie. He flumps down on the sofa, head bent to his knees, face covered by the nightie, making strange snorting noises like he might be crying or foraging for truffles. He stays there for what feels like for ever. And I love him completely.

'Joe?' He looks up, doesn't see me at first. 'It's me.' I unfold myself and stand tall, proud, hand on the banisters. Then I realise I'm wearing my midriff-exposing LA Hottie T-shirt (which should come with a 'Not to be worn over the age of twenty-five' warning) and immeasurably unsexy navy knickers, so hands-off they're usually worn only during my period. No, not the grand staircase entrance I had envisioned.

'Hi,' he says, startled, dropping the nightdress on to the sofa.

We stare at each other awkwardly, greenish morning light bouncing off the mirrors, the whites of his eyes china against his tan. I pull my teeny T-shirt down but it still doesn't cover the knickers. I want him back so much and yet cannot bear to look at him, his mouth, his lips. Did they use tongues?

'How's Evie?' he asks.

'Asleep.'

'Can I see her?'

'She's your daughter.'

While Joe is in Evie's bedroom I check my reflection, for the first time in days. I'm relieved that there seems to be little evidence of a drooping Botox eyebrow, which I feared would be my Dorian Gray-style punishment for Josh. But I do look a state. Perhaps that hairbrush wouldn't be such a bad idea after all.

It's funny how the men you make the biggest effort for in the early days – push-up bra, Hollywood wax, Atkins – are

301

the ones who leave you looking the most raddled by the end of the relationship. Emotional toxins, they should come with a warning: This one's Tom. He'll come along when you're twenty-six and encourage you to fall in love with him then say he doesn't want commitment and leave you with a nice dose of chlamydia as a parting gift. How about Jesse? Good-looking with a small but skilful dick, he'll explain that he only likes black women because they don't have that wobbly bit under their upper arms, but it's been an interesting experience nevertheless. This one, Joe? Joe will say he loves you, get you pregnant and then . . .

Joe reappears. 'I've missed you both horribly,' he says, voice barely a whisper.

Missed?

'I should have let you explain, not run away.' He digs his hands in his pockets and looks at the floor. 'Maybe I jumped to conclusions . . .' He shakes his head and asks warily, 'Did you miss me?'

How I long to say yes. 'I found a postcard.'

'A postcard?' Joe looks puzzled. 'What about a postcard?'

'It's there.' I point with a trembling finger to the offending object on top of the TV.

He twizzles it in his hand, reads the back. 'This!'

'I was there, Joe. I went to meet you that day in the park when I was pregnant and I . . . I . . . saw you. I saw you kiss her arm . . .'

'Amy, what *are* you talking about?'

'Kate.'

Joe pales. 'Kate?'

'She told me everything! How could you?' I step forward and pummel his chest pathetically, like a bad movie actress, partly because I just want to touch him, even now. All the hours of waiting for him, dreaming of him, heave out of me

302

in big sobs. Joe holds my hands, then my shoulders, and I want to collapse into him, exhausted, spent, but can't because something's clawing inside.

'Kate said what?' he says slowly.

'That you went for walks, without me. That you were close. *Very close*, she said.' I look him direct in his eyes, which are fever bright now. 'Why . . . why . . . were you kissing her arm?'

'Because she was stung by a wasp,' he says gently as if trying to calm a hysterical child.

'You kiss all your friends on the arm do you?' He shifts from one foot to the other. 'She said you tried to go further but *she* stopped *you*!'

'Oh for God's sake. That's a total lie. I swear on Evie's life . . .'

I feel a little assured, Joe would never use those words carelessly. Then I remember another incriminating detail. 'But you said the meeting was cancelled? You said it was work.'

Joe has the decency to blush. 'I did. I lied. Kate begged me to see her on my own. She'd phoned up in a terrible state about Pete, said I was the only one who understood. She was already on her way and I didn't want us all to meet and have to explain.' He squeezes the bridge of his nose with his fingers and looks down, sighs. 'One lie led to another and it all just seemed too complicated to deal with. I behaved like an idiot.'

'Why did you meet her so often?' I'm quivery, as if trying to lift too heavy a load.

'I . . . I . . .' The truth sticks in Joe's throat and he has to cough to release it. '. . . Didn't think I was doing any harm. I suppose I was kind of lonely.' He looks down, ashamed. 'You didn't seem to want me around.'

303

'How can you possibly say . . .' I pummel him again.

Joe grabs my fist. 'Please, Amy, calm down. Let me try my best to explain. Will you sit down?'

I perch next to him on the sofa, goose-bumping in the morning chill, wanting to snuggle up close but too proud to do so.

'You were so preoccupied with the bump. You seemed so down, so tired, kind of weirdly closed off in your body.'

'I was pregnant.'

'But I couldn't reach you. I felt so damned useless, made worse by problems at work.'

'What problems?'

'Big ones. Like I thought we were going to go under. We'd lost two major contracts. But I couldn't tell you because of the baby.'

'What's this got to do with Kate?'

Joe flinches. 'I had to talk to someone. And she was just there. She was always there, saying she was in town, offering to meet for coffee, a quick work lunch,' he hisses. 'I was stupid, really fucking stupid.'

I knot my arms tight across my chest. My engagement ring glints brashly, inappropriately. 'And you knew she liked you?'

Joe grimaces. 'Not really. Perhaps I should have done. She was very unhappy with Pete. We kind of moaned to each other.'

Deep breath. I steel myself. Prepare for the consequences of the question. 'Did you sleep with her?'

Joe grins, a weak relieved grin. 'No! God no!'

'But you fancied her.'

Joe blinks, as if an air-borne object had narrowly missed him. 'Don't be ridiculous.'

'The truth, Joe.'

'Well, the truth . . . is . . . if I'm being totally honest, at that moment in the park I was attracted to her for some reason. There were no other moments like it, I promise, please believe that,' he implores. 'Big mistake.'

'A big mistake!' Is that all? It ruined my birth, my early motherhood. It made me feel about as attractive as a fat-camp evictee.

'She's never let me forget it. She thinks it's proof . . .'

'*Proof?* That you should be together?'

Joe nods wearily. 'I've tried to avoid her since then.' He shrugs. 'I'm so sorry.'

No, sorry isn't enough. Because I close my eyes and the movie is still looping on the blood black of my eyelids, him kissing her arm, over and over again, stop, rewind, stop, rewind. 'You still kissed her arm. That's such a horribly intimate thing to do.'

As I shout, hurling curses like hard red Lego bricks, it suddenly occurs to me that actually, well, we'll probably be fine. This isn't quite as bad as I'd imagined. It's like sitting through *The Blair Witch Project*, expecting to pass out with terror at the ending, steeling yourself and then not finding it so frightening after all. I stop and pause.

'OK now?' Joe looks relieved.

OK? No, actually, not OK. My inner diva is furiously put out. So I shout louder because it's my prerogative and I'm smarting and he deserves this right now.

'Amy, please . . .' Joe's hands are raised, palms open, pleading.

Joe can't expect me to just forgive without a fight. He needs to know it meant something. And *then* we'll get on with our lives, become a had-hard-times-but-we-stuck-together couple. That'll be our story, what we'll tell Evie when she's older. 'So did it happen more than once?'

'Oh come on, Amy. This is all a bit bloody rich considering . . .'

So he hasn't forgiven me then. 'Considering that I fucked up twice . . . no I mean . . .'

Too late.

'Twice?' Joe whispers, eyes screwed shut.

Forty-eight

One word, the tiny hair fracture that reduces everything to rubble. I tried to deny everything but just dug a deeper hole. He didn't believe me. The next day Joe left London, texting to say he was going to work from Leo's ex-girlfriend's holiday house in Cornwall for a while, to get his head straight. He'd call to sort something out about Evie soon. Nothing more, just that. Like we were colleagues or babysitters organising a timetable rotation.

For the last two days I've been sitting here, on my Tracy Emin-style bed, lunching on Wrigley's chewing gum, not sleeping, unable to comprehend any future, only just able to look after Evie. Joe hovers close like an amputee's removed limb, on the right-hand side of the bed, the empty unloved Eames chair, the silence where his thud and clatter should be. And I can still smell him, his aftershave, the plastic keyboard on his fingers, even his farts in the bathroom seem to linger like stale ghosts.

There's a rattle of a key in the lock. Joe? Thank God.

'Only me!' Mum. I hunch into the duvet as she steams up the stairs.

'No more mooning!' She flicks on the light. 'Oh!

'Goodness! Oh Amy! You look terrible. What's happened? Come here.' Mum hugs me to her chest, suffocating me into a crunch of freshly laundered linen. We rock back and forth for a few minutes in silence. 'Darling Amy.' She kisses me, masters her tears, picks up Evie from her cot. 'Let's go out. It'll do you both a world of good,' she says.

Five minutes later I'm outside, squinting in the sunlight. Mum walks so fast, so vigorously, I can hardly keep up. Whatever happened to the bad back?

'The worst thing you can do is waste away inside. You owe it to Evie.'

'Sorry.' I want to scream sorry, sorry, sorry like a demented adulterer on a morning chat show. But I don't, because I woke up from my three-hour night's sleep with an 0898 porn voice and haven't the motivation to project it.

Mum bends down from the waist, like someone twenty years younger, and tickles Evie under the chin. 'Looks a bit peaky. Is she OK?'

Evie grins at Mum. Entertainment at last.

I nod. 'Teething, waking up a lot during the night.'

'Well, that can't help. Still, pulling yourself together is the only way,' Mum continues, grabbing my hand – we haven't held hands since I was a child – and steering me towards the bakery café on the Salusbury Road, opposite the pub where I first saw Josh with his rainbow bicycle and kaleidoscope smile.

We sit down at a large communal oak table scattered with Yoga leaflets and newspapers and tips from the just-departed lunch crowd. Evie sits on Mum's knee and fiddles with her gold bracelet, squeezing the links hard. Mum eyes the prices and rolls her eyes. She'll never understand why anyone would pay £3.90 for a loaf of bread. 'Tea for two please,' she commands. 'Earl Grey if you've got it. Two scones, slightly warm. Jam. Cream, clotted if possible.'

The French waitress, not used to such explicit directions, gives an amused nod.

'Mum, I'm not hungry.'

'You are as thin as a carrot stick. This is taking things too far, Amy. Men like something to grip hold of.'

Men? What men? There's only one man I want and I've screwed that up. 'I've just kind of lost my appetite.'

'You will eat a scone.'

The scone arrives, pale, craggy as a lump of seaside rock. Mum, muttering 'Daylight robbery', butters it, rolls on a thick carpet of jam and cuts it into quarters as if I were a toddler. 'When's Joe back home from Cornwall?'

'Dunno.' I should warn her, she looks so hopeful. 'He may not come back, not back home anyway, Mum.'

Mum's blue eyes, Evie's eyes sixty years on, crinkle anxiously. 'He *will*. I know he will. He is a good man. Whatever went on between you . . . and I wish you'd be clearer but I'm not going to push you – will pass. You'll forgive each other.'

'Hmmm.' If only she knew.

'Joe loves you. I can see it in his eyes. You can't fake that.'

'Not any more.'

'Do you want me to talk to him?'

I shake my head. Mum thinks any problem can be solved by a natter over a cup of steaming Earl Grey. She orders more scones and applies lip gloss. Lip gloss? This is the woman who single-handedly kept Revlon's Matte Rose in demand for twenty years. She rearranges the increasingly heavy love lump that is Evie, one foot flicking up to balance the weight. I notice, even through my self-absorbed smog, that Mum is wearing *flat* strappy sandals (surely her heel-shrunk tendons will snap) which take years off her feet and, combined with her new olive linen kaftan-like dress and relatively undone hair, give her an unlikely bohemian buoyancy. I note these things but don't care about them. I can't imagine ever caring about clothes again.

'That's the problem with love, Amy,' says Mum between nibbles of scone. 'You can't just turn it off. You think you can, but when the initial hurt and anger recede you're left with the love again, leaking like my bathroom tap.'

'You can't know how I feel.' I gulp the threat of tears back down my throat with a dry lump of scone. 'You hated Dad. It's *not* the same.'

Mum's jaw stops mid-chew. 'I did hate your father,' she says quietly. 'For all the things he did. For leaving with that bloody woman. But . . .' Mum nervously strokes invisible crumbs off the edge of the table. Evie copies her. 'I did love him. I loved him for a long, long time after he left. I tried, but I couldn't turn it off,' she says. 'He wasn't a totally bad man, Amy, not in lots of ways.'

'You *loved* him? What, after he left? You told me you hated him!' A flush of muted anger against Mum who, in one breath, has kicked away the certainties of my story: Dad, bad, me, a progeny from a loveless marriage.

'I never stopped loving him, silly sentimental creature that I was.' She twists her tea cup around in her hand. 'Perhaps I should have taken him back.'

'You couldn't. He disappeared.' Out of all of our lives for a long time. Just sent expensive birthday cards, but usually on the wrong day. 'There's nothing you could have done, Mum. He left,' I add wearily, not really being in the mood for a dissection of painful family history.

Something blows behind her eyes. 'Well, not exactly. Um . . .' Mum takes a deep breath. 'He wanted to come back, Amy. He wanted a second chance.'

The words sit in the air like smoke. I watch them, letters just graphics at first. Then they hit. He wanted to come back?

310

We could have been a family again. 'You never told me! You told me that he left. I *hated* him for that.' The waitress stares at us from behind a bucket of baked granola.

'It was impossible to explain to you, so young.'

'Why? *Why* didn't you take him back?' I plead, voice high as a nine-year-old's.

'I had all this anger bottled up inside. The anger poisoned everything.'

'But he was my *dad* . . .'

'He was,' says Mum, thrown back into her chair by the force of twenty-odd years of guilt. 'I know, love, he was. We should have tried harder, your father and I. Sorry.' She grabs the teapot handle. 'Top up?'

'Let me do it. Evie's ready to pounce.' I pour. Evie watches in wonderment. 'But that's so terribly sad. You've been on your own ever since.'

'There's life in the old dog yet!' Mum shrugs and smiles, relieved that I haven't punched her and run howling to the nearest therapist. 'I was young . . .' She stops talking but I can still hear the rattle of her thoughts, the conversation she must have had with herself over the years, as she washed up, took us to school, went to bed alone. I soften a little. 'Divorce felt new then, full of possibility, almost fashionable. Everyone was doing it. No one knew the impact it might have on the kids a few years down the line. We all thought we were doing the right thing and,' she rolls her eyes, 'would happily remarry.'

'More tea?' interrupts our waitress, undaunted by our outburst.

'Lovely,' Mum says, composing herself. 'More tea would be lovely.'

'Why are you telling me this, Mum? Why now?'

Mum smiles. 'Something about forgiveness. You seem to harbour a lot of anger towards Joe.'

It's there all right, sandwiched inside my love for him like a cheap livid jam.

'And I thought it might help you to know that very few men are all bad. Men do silly things. We must forgive them. Am I making any sense?'

No. Nice try, but you're counselling the wrong person. *I'm* the one who needs to be forgiven. I am about to say something to this effect when suddenly, like a hard stale scone flung across the table, a question whacks me on the head: if I'd *known* that Dad wanted to return would I still be the kind of woman who thought all the men in my life would leave eventually, the kind of woman who can't ever believe in the happy ending?

'What are you thinking?' Mum asks quietly.

And if I hadn't presumed the worst, perhaps I would have had the guts to ask Joe about what I saw in Regent's Park. And perhaps I would have felt less vulnerable as a pregnant person, more able to cope when motherhood turned me inside out and made me feel like a howling mono-breasted lunatic.

'Please talk to me, love,' Mum says, voice muffled because she's resting her mouth in the downy nest of Evie's hair.

'Sorry. Just thinking maybe I got Joe wrong.'

She sighs. 'Oh, it's so good that you can say that. You're more mature than I was at your age. I was just furious when your dad left! But I had the weight of seventies feminism behind me. I was the victim.' Her jaw clenches tight and pulses. She's upset.

'Which you were really,' I say quickly, trying to make her feel better. Because I now understand how a family is a magnifying glass. How it turns little decisions made by an individual into raging fires that burn through generations. Josh? An ache between the legs. A longing for a lost identity.

312

Ten years on, he's the reason that Evie will spend alternate weekends in different houses. The reason her world will tilt awkwardly on its axis as she grows up and tries to make sense of boys and commitment and the mum and dad who separated when she was so young.

'I regret not trying again, if just for you and your brothers' sake. I want you to know that.' She sips her tea dreamily. 'Marriage is tricky. If you expect different you'll be disappointed. It's not like the movies.'

'Thanks. I'd never have guessed.'

She clicks her tongue. 'Let me finish. What seems like the end now, well, it's not. Not if you don't want it to be. You've got to fight for the relationship.' Mum's hands grip her cup. I've scared her. She's concerned about me. I'm her baby. 'And yourself.'

'A lost cause,' I laugh weakly.

'Rubbish!' She grips my hands. My nails are still chipped with last month's manicure, which strikes me as strangely macabre. 'I didn't bring you up to roll over and accept defeat and sit in front of daytime TV all day, moping about with unwashed hair. Goodness me, you've got these wonderful expensive highlights, what a waste!'

'Well that's the clincher.' I manage a smile. 'The show must go on, right?'

Mum grins: message received! Because no, she was never paralysed by loss. She put on her make-up, curled her hair and remained the slick engine of the family. She filled the space Dad left. She baked bread for our lunch boxes, negotiated the first sanitary towel, the first condom and secretly followed me on my paper round on dark winter mornings just to make sure I was safe. I don't ever remember her having a lie-in.

More tea arrives. I take Evie. Mum pours and the steam

313

clouds around her face like a wedding veil. Placing the pot down, she readjusts herself on the chair, sitting up straight, as if silently reminding herself of the importance of posture.

'Right. What's your action plan?'

'Action plan?' Other people just live their lives. I lurch between action plans.

'You need to take control again, Amy. Gosh, you've always been the most stubborn, headstrong girl.' She sniffs indignantly at the memory. 'The baby thing knocked it out of you. Now this. OK, it's been tough. But it's about time you got your stuffing back. You've got a job waiting for you, more than I ever had. And Amy, you've got a life to live.'

As she says this, glossed fiftysomething mouth pursing and working, a figure – me, pre-pregnancy – darts across my brain in high red wedges, skinny sequinned scarf flying behind like the tail of a shooting star. She's rushing to a meeting, late, always late, too much going on: boyfriends, mates, work. She sits down breathlessly at the gleaming wenge table next to her colleagues and compensates for her lateness by making jokes and arguing her point against toxic Pippa, winning her point, smiling graciously, steel in her veins. That was me?

When I get home it is quieter than ever. Just the sickening whirr of history repeating itself: I have taken away Evie's daddy. Feeling as worthy as a foot fungus, I bathe Evie. She pops bath bubbles with her fingers, looking up for applause with each successful pop. She is so intoxicatingly beautiful, I could examine her for hours; the pudding-bulge of her belly, the perfect round of her bottom cheeks. Why is it that mothers despise their own fleshiness but can't get enough of their baby's?

Evie begins to dimple like an apricot. I pick her up. She squeals, berserk with pleasure, fat pink legs pumping water all over the floor. Settling her into the cot, I stroke her damp hair and sing lullabies in my terrible tuneless voice, which she adores.

Finally Evie sleeps, eyes pulsing beneath their silky lids, dreaming of nappy-shaped clouds and bottle teats big as air balloons. I sit down on the floor, face pressed against the bars of her cot, watching. An irrational part of me fears that if I leave the bedroom the last precious bit of my life will vanish too, and I'll wake in the morning to find a dribbly baby-shaped imprint on the sheet. So I hover on the landing. Check her. Linger. Then I can't bear to be separated by hard inhuman brick walls any longer, so I pick Evie up, still sleeping, and tuck her into my bed, a habit it took many painful weeks to break. She opens her eyes sleepily, registers her approval of the new sleeping arrangements, slumbers back off.

Ding dong.

I open the door. Mum. 'I couldn't leave you alone tonight. I just couldn't.'

'But . . .'

She wipes away a tear from my cheek with Nivea-scented fingers. 'Come on, you silly thing. Let me in.'

Tonight Mum sleeps in my bed in a peach satin nightie and hugs me (in faux-satin pink nightie) into her doughy arms like a little girl. Evie lies beside us, a soft sighing lump. And I sleep my first proper night's sleep in two days.

Forty-nine

In Joe's absence, it's easier to see who he is, feel my way
around each particular contour of the Joe-shaped hole. It's
a big, surprising hole. Some photos arrived by post yesterday, addressed to Joe, an old roll he must have sent off just
before all this unfolded. The photos are mostly of me: on the
bed; cushioned on the balcony. In all of them I'm asleep.
They're not mouth-open-snoring pictures either, but sweet,
gentle, even beautiful. They break my heart. So does the
lavender and rosemary bath oil he bought me. Did I ever
thank him for it? I don't think so. Nor did I thank him for
fixing my electric toothbrush, or taking my coat to the
menders. Or fishing my hair-ball out of the plughole. No
man apart from Joe ever did the little things like that for me,
without making a big deal out of it, without being asked. I
once thought those things boring, humdrum, anal even. Now
I miss them horribly.

I lie down on the rug, Evie parked on my tummy, and run
over it all for the umpteenth time. But I get muddled about
what he's said and what I've said and suddenly all that matters is that I find him. Mum's right. I need to fight for this.
I've got to *do* something. I can't just let him walk away. This

may be my life, not some piss-poor soap opera, but it still needs direction. OK, Cornwall. Leo's ex-girlfriend's house.

Tucking Evie on to my hip, I open my address book. Evie yanks out two pages and flutters them about like flags. I scan the L section. No. Nothing. I rummage through Joe's boxes. Nothing. But I do have a vague recollection of Leo having had a girlfriend – Sandy? Sara? – who had a house. Penzance? Polzeath? Gut says Polzeath.

The train takes hours. Evie's head wobbles like an antique doll as she squidges wet fingers on the window, trying to catch the fleeting flecks of sheep and cows. She's quiet, a little out of sorts. But fresh seaside air will do her a world of good, paint pink back on those perfect convex cheeks. Passengers come over to coo and I swell with pride. Others give *me* funny looks, stare a little too long, like you might do at a face that resembles a criminal photo-fit. One lady, who's plonked herself opposite, won't stop chatting. A fiftysome-thing lady in a beige Burberry mac, she's not wholly unlike my mother. She does the same thing with her hair, combing it smooth with her fingers, shamelessly using the train window as her mirror. Her presence makes me feel vaguely uneasy because I know Mum would be furious to see me hurtling to Cornwall on a chilly September morning armed with only three jars of baby food, milk and a tube of Pringles.

On the platform at Plymouth station a man with an over-eager head, cocked forward just like Joe's, walks along munching crisps. How I want to see Joe eating crisps, doing something normal. I wipe an eye on my sleeve. The woman offers a tissue. She's heading right down south too. Polzeath, such a lovely beach. I ask her to keep an eye on the pram while I go to the loo.

In the gyrating train toilet I see myself in the scratched

317

square mirror. Christ! A gaunt woman, older than me, nosing her mid-thirties, stares back with hollowed eyes. Hair sprouts at weird angles from her head. Her neck looks like an anatomical drawing. Her cheekbones – cheekbones! – are banana-shaped shadows and, somewhat incongruously, her forehead is as smooth as a shell. Aha, Project Amy! This is the look I wanted! And I look dreadful.

At Bodmin Parkway station I get a taxi quickly, leaving before mac-woman has time to surface from the Ladies and suggest we share one. There are enough conversations going on in my head as it is. Evie has no car seat so I squeeze her tight and gasp every time a truck passes or we take a corner fast, certain our moment is up, imagining the headlines. The driver stops in the Polzeath beach car park. This is as far as we can go without an amphibious vehicle, he jokes. I clamber out into a whipping wind. Assembling the pram is an Olympic wrestle. The tide is out and there is just one slab of blond sand as far as I can see, cupped between low crags of rock, polka-dotted with dogs. The sky is vast, swollen with heavy clay-grey clouds, the sea a crust of black on the horizon.

Occasionally a surfer runs past with a board, bare feet slapping, kicking up sprays of water. The surfers remind me of my brothers. I miss them. My family is too disparate, too complicated. The things that make twenty-first-century life so exciting to the single and childless – cheap air travel, freedom from geographical and genetic ties – aren't that helpful when you have a baby. It would actually be far nicer if my family lived within a one-mile radius and met around an open fire every night over a hog roast.

The pram doesn't move easily, the wheels sinking and jamming in the sand. The best way is to pull it, facing forwards, wind whistling into the bonnet. Evie's hair flutters like lots of tiny wings. She smiles dutifully, as if I've conjured up the seaside as an amusing sideshow for her benefit but, rather disappointingly, have forgotten to cast any sunshine. We scar the sand from east to west, past rocky dunes and back up to the car park. From there I head into the town, if you can call a few surf shops and holiday rents a town. I try to phone Joe on his mobile, gauge his voice for its level of warmth before declaring that yes, I am here, in Cornwall! But it is difficult to get a signal. I eventually get one, swaying on a bench like a drunk, wind fly-swatting hair across my face. His phone is switched off.

We trail a couple of streets. No sign. He could be anywhere, in any of those salt-lashed, modern, rather ugly houses, gazing out to sea. My legs ache with the drag of sand. What next? I cry a little out of frustration, then wipe the tears away crossly. Yes, he'll come to the beach today. Of course he will. I'll wait. I'll surprise him, run towards him, surfy wind in my hair, like a model in a Tampax ad. That'll move him. Then he'll forgive me.

Back to the beach. I drag the pram to a sheltered spot behind a rock, prickling with long thin grass. After draining a bottle of milk, Evie sighs sweetly and stares at the cloudscape above, her lids reluctantly closing as she drifts off. My mouth is dry. I curse myself for not buying a bottle of water earlier. It's easy to forget that I need looking after too. My nostrils are rimmed with a crust of salt like a margarita glass. The sky darkens. The temperature drops. Seagulls roar dementedly. I pillow my head into the rock, it's warmer than the wind. Gosh, I'm tired, so bone-shatteringly tired. What the hell am I doing here? It was Polzeath wasn't it? No, shit, Penzance. Or Polzeath?

My mind skits. So Joe didn't have an affair? All those months of worrying, about him loving someone thinner, all for nothing. So he got close to Kate for a moment. I can cope with

319

that. Because aren't our lives full of such wobbly moments when, for a few heart thumps, someone offers a shinier reality, one that reflects back our funnier, handsomer, pre-parent selves? He wobbled, but he pulled back. Unlike me.

Grass cotton-buds my ear. But it feels like it's scratching someone else. When I close my eyes, only my interior life feels real. Obscure memories and images I thought I'd forgotten engulf me – Dad burying my hamster in a coffin he'd made from a Cornflakes packet; Joe putting a cool wet cloth on my forehead when I had a fever – then retreat, waves of water over a sinking ship.

No, I am not the victim here. Even if Joe did work late or went out drinking or didn't tell me he loved me as much as I needed, he stood by me in those difficult early months, while I retreated into myself, lost in new motherhood, in that lonely twilight zone of leaking breasts and bladder problems and anxious exhaustion, certain my life was over. Truth is, he probably needed a pint or two. I was remote. I was angry and paranoid. I couldn't bear him anywhere near me. And no, he didn't leave. He could have done. Kate would have had him. Lots of women would have had him. But Joe is not my dad. Not all men are like my dad. In fact it transpires not even my dad is like my dad. Oh dear, it's all gone so very wrong.

I reach out and grip Evie's pram, feel it shake reassuringly as she turns in her sleep, and a rush of love for her judders through my entire body like a small electric shock. She is the best thing that ever happened to me. Why has it taken me so long to accept the unalterable reality of life with a baby? Instead I have fought against it, unable to understand that my old life has died, like a war widow who refuses to grieve for her husband until she's seen his dead body.

Fade to black.

*

OW!

Another sharp slap against my cheek. 'Wake up! Wake up!'

'She's conscious!'

Well, I am now! A dog's wet cold nose snuffles my neck. I open my eyes slowly. The first thing I see is my diamond ring, flashing like a lighthouse. Then, a pair of orange thermal socks turned over the top of hiking boots.

'She's OK. Yes, I think she's OK, Sandra,' says a man's voice.

'Thank heavens! Are you all right duck?' A blonde lady bends down to me. The busy-body mac-woman.

'Evie . . . The baby . . .' I manage.

'In her pram,' says mac-woman. 'Fast asleep, warm as toast. It's you we're worried about. You're not wearing a coat. Here . . .' She shrugs a strange-smelling fleece around my shoulders. 'I thought you looked a sad mite.'

'Oh dear, I must have dozed off.'

'We thought you'd fainted! Come on, we'll walk you back . . .' She stops. 'Back to where, dear?'

She pulls me up too quickly, blood rushes from my head. My limbs are so heavy and my head still so light, full of polystyrene beanbag balls. But I must find him. I must find Joe. 'To the town.' I start walking. Oh! The draining whorls in the sand are disorientating, like walking backwards on a conveyor belt. Oh dear, jelly legs. My legs buckle and whoomp! I stumble on to my knees, poised to propose to the orange thermal socks. 'Better make that the train station,' I gasp.

Fifty

4 a.m. London. I wake from a nightmare of being scooped out of my bed in a giant rock-pool fishing net, wielded by Kate. Evie's wailing, forehead hot as a stove. I clear the bobbles of vomit off the sheet and cradle her to my chest. Dear Evie. I spoon her pink Calpol, her second dose. She wails some more. I lie her back down but she won't sleep, tossing her tiny head from side to side as if trying to shake something out of it. Is she really sick, like proper sick? Or did the Cornish wind just give her a cold? She must be exhausted. We got home at midnight. I am irresponsible.

Now, where did Joe leave the thermometer? I scrabble through old soaps and nappy cream in the airing cupboard. Nothing. Her nappy bag. Nothing. Eventually, after a thirty-minute search, I find it in the cutlery drawer. 39.3 degrees. Hot. Then I spot a speckle of pink on her arm. A rash. Meningitis? *No!* I grab a glass tumbler, put the light on. Evie screams. A symptom? As I roll the glass over her arm the rash seems to fade. Or does it? Am I pressing too hard? Evie screams some more. Joe would know what to do. I try his mobile. Voicemail.

Evie's wails get higher and shriller. OK, action. I bundle

Evie into her car seat, face screwing purple. I hardly ever drive the car. Joe always does. But he's not here. I swivel the key in the ignition. It doesn't start. Then the car jolts forward. Evie bawls. I try to reach behind to comfort her but can't do it while driving. It's so fucking difficult on your own. The streets are dark, wet and empty. I jump a red light.

St Mary's A&E. Other people, groaning and bleeding. A man with half his face sheared off, the white of his nose bone visible. A wailing African woman. But Evie is seen immediately. The doctors are concerned. Tests. They prick her with needles. She reaches out to me, but the nurse, a pretty Filipino, holds her tight. I am rigid, cold with dread. My baby, my baby. Please don't let my baby die. The nurse pats my arm. No worry, she says sweetly, no worry. More tests. Wait and see, Miss Crane, says the pink-eyed doctor. I wonder whether he's washed his hands. Do I ask? Too late. Evie is plugged into a cloak of wires, breathing monitored. It's a little fast, they say. I can hear it now, heartbeat like galloping horses. She whimpers and I hold her tiny fat hand. I make a pact with God, just in case there is one.

7 a.m. I have begun to hallucinate with tiredness. The lights and beeps of Evie's cot are a soundtrack to the slideshow in my head, a slideshow of me and Joe having sex on the sofa to MTV, the afternoon we conceived Evie. Then, hospital. A white theatre. Chris Rea on the radio. (This upset me. My birth plan – that fiction – had stated Johnny Cash.) The smell of rubber gloves and cheap disinfectant. Me, wired to machines, beeping like a car-crash victim. The euphoria of the epidural, as the pain leaves my body with an upward whoosh like the soul of a dying man. A green sheet, a wind breaker, hiding my lower body. Surgeon rummaging in my stomach. Rising panic. Joe holding my hand tight. Joe whispering into my ear, 'I love you so much, Amy. You're doing so

323

well.' But I'm not doing anything, a powerless, carved-up lump. Then Joe's eyes and mouth O. An angry kitten sound. Lifted from behind the green sheet is a teeny baby covered in white gloopy stuff, like bacon fat. She hasn't got a willy. She roars. The nurse puts her on my chest. She weighs nothing. Joe is crying, beaming. I smell my baby – metallic, interesting – and wait for that huge foamy wave of maternal love to crash all over me like it says in the books. But it doesn't.

'Miss Crane? It's the doctor.' I crack open my eyes, feeling like I've been out raving all night on bad drugs. The doctor is new, looks about twenty-three. I didn't see him last night. I don't recognise the nurses either. Where is the nice Filipino one? No familiar point of reference now that the cold grey dawn flaps the stained curtains. But the doctor has good news. The doctor says Evie only has a nasty virus. I was right to bring her in. But the rash has gone. Her temperature has dropped. Evie can go home. Keep her cool. Lots of fluids. Come back if she deteriorates.

I thank the doctor profusely. He smiles briskly and moves on quickly in squeaky shoes. And I ache for Joe in a way that I've never ached for another human being. The longing for him is so intense I can hardly walk, but I just manage to shuffle one foot in front of the other, soles tingling, dizzy and weightless like I'm standing on a cliff edge, about to fall. We get to the car.

I have a parking ticket.

Fifty-one

Just when I thought things could only get worse, I wake up feeling a tiny bit better. The disaster movie was rather well directed in the end. I drove the car and parked it without scaling the kerb, albeit in the wrong place. Most importantly, Evie is fine, the virus departing as quickly as it came. (Does this mean I must honour the pact? Visit Grandma in Harrow every week, swap my PR job to work as a care assistant to terminally ill children?) OK, the Polzeath fiasco was anticlimactic, but I went, rather than sitting around and thinking about it.

I also awoke this morning inhabited by an unfamiliar feeling, a strange clarity. It took me a while to put my finger on it. Then I realised: I am not knackered! Evie has slept through for the last two nights. This is without precedent. No 3 a.m. singing for milk. No 5 a.m. raver whooping. Not a peep. Consequently, for the first time in months I'm reasonably well rested. My mood has palpably shifted. The world is a brighter place. My eyes seem less short-sighted. The smudgy muddle has gone.

I feel ready to embrace parenthood wholly, no hankering over the past, for the single life that was. And I know – for the first time ever perhaps – what I really want, ironically, considering I can't get it. I want Joe. And the kind of happy family unit that disappeared from my life, aged nine. OK, I still wouldn't mind Kylie's bottom, but it's slipped a few notches on the priority list. No more miserable cellulite-gazing. No more self-pity. I am just so bloody grateful to have Evie throwing her porridge on the kitchen floor.

I mop the mulch of oats up with kitchen roll. There is a busy ecosystem growing beneath the kitchen units: hard twists of pasta, shrivelled peas, coins, sachets of Calpol. Must be where Alice dropped her handbag. And what's this? A blister pack of pills. Pain killers? Handy. I blindly slide them into my bag.

Half an hour later we're out of the house, no one dragging me, no hare-brain action plan. Just me and Evie, regular mother and daughter, pram ticking north, walking out into our cool city, my head held high, agoraphobia lifted like a lid. Needing to return to my ground zero, after a long walk I eventually push past the Nash buildings, through the horse chestnuts into Regent's Park.

The black water shines like a polished granite kitchen worktop. Ducks and geese paddle towards us, fearless, impatient for crusts of the morning's toast.

''Ack 'ack 'ack!' shrieks Evie, arms waving in evangelical rapture.

An old lady smelling faintly of talc and damp tweed creaks past. She stops, gazes at Evie and, without introduction, stoops down to stroke Evie's cheek with a nostalgic smile. Then she creaks on. Did she once come here as a young mother? Perhaps her own mother, now inevitably long dead, brought her to the ponds. You forget that old people had young mums too. Does she still miss her? How terrible that all mothers and children are separated by death eventually. That we have such a short time to get it right.

'I'm not going to give up, Evie.'

''Ack 'ack 'ack!' Evie points at an exotic red-legged duck waddling towards the willow-shaded benches.

'Ah, I thought it began there,' I say, following her finger, to the little blue bridge where I once stood, gourd-shaped and broken-hearted, past and present cracked in two. To the path where I once ran, panting and humiliated, off into a future I'd dreaded, always expected. 'But it began here.' I twizzle my finger against my head.

Evie looks at me like I'm making perfect sense. ''Ack 'ack 'ack.'

I lift her out of the pram and rain kisses on her ears and nose and eyebrows, feeling a little more like the Amy that climbed that little bridge, not the one who descended it. She's been a devil to find. Because she wasn't scrunched like tissue paper into the toe of a designer shoe. Nor was she in a gap between the thighs. No, I realise that now. I found her in my past, huddled, scared, like a child in a locked cupboard. And it was the birth of Evie that forced her, wailing and shivering, out into the world, and brought all my issues to the surface. I thought motherhood was the end of me but it was just the beginning.

Shame I couldn't have learned all that without pan-frying my relationship. But that's life. That's what I'll tell Evie when she's older. To misquote John Lennon, it's what happens to you when you're busy worrying about other things. I will contain my sadness now, dear Evie, move on, give you the best start possible, nuclear family or not. No more eating out of baked-bean cans.

Evie pats my nose with Pope-like slow solemnity, as if registering the promise. Suddenly, the Regent's Park mosque erupts in a call to prayer, and the greige sky that's hung over London like a wood-chip ceiling for days, splices and splits and sunshine pours over us, making the water dance. Eyes shut, relishing the unexpected warmth, we instinctively turn our heads towards the light.

Fifty-two

'Argh! Amy!' Nicola screams, pulling me through her front door and into a rib-cracking hug. 'I didn't think you'd actually come!'

'No more blow-out merchant,' I promise into her bob.

'I've been so worried about you.' She holds me by the shoulders and stands back, alarmed. 'Oh God, you are all skin and bone. You look awful.'

'Thanks. But the good news is that my appetite's boomeranged back. I am starving.'

'Thank God, thank God.' Nicola ushers me into her kitchen and sits me down at the sticky kitchen table and brings plates of cake, crumpets and pretzels.

We talk about wild-goose chases along windswept Cornish beaches and hospitals and boyfriends while Evie and Thomas develop their immunity on Nicola's kitchen floor. I eat up her laughter and company as hungrily as the food. Two hours feels like five minutes. The day, noticeably shorter now, is beginning to darken. I'm thinking about leaving when Nicola bends double.

'Ow, period pains,' she says. 'Worse than ever. We were told they'd get better after having a baby. Another lie!'

Glad to be the one offering help for a change, I pick Alice's pills out of my handbag, hand them over. 'These should do the trick.'

Nicola flicks the pack in her fingers. 'Where did you get these?'

'Alice left them.'

She slides them over the table. 'They're not painkillers,' Nicola says, matter-of-factly. 'You really do need glasses. Read the pack, Amy. Prozac.'

'Prozac? No way, not Alice!'

Nicola huffs. 'I don't know why you're shocked. Mother's little helpers, Amy. Doctors give them out like free contraceptives to weepy post-natal mums. They don't interfere with breastfeeding and the like. My sister took them.'

'Alice is not exactly a new mum. Nor is she weepy.'

'The drugs do work.'

'I just don't get it.'

Nicola laughs. 'I bet all her gang rattle when they walk. She's exactly the kind of woman who would freak out after having a baby. You know, fully in control of her life then it's all lost in a splatter of shit and screams and possets.'

'Sounds like me.'

'You didn't freak. You just had a tricky start. More cake? Don't worry, I didn't bake it. I buy now I'm working.'

'Go on then,' I say. Nicola dumps another slab of chocolate cake on my plate. 'Well if these pills can turn a lump of misery into five-foot-eight of shining social confidence, maybe I should give them a whirl.'

'Don't you dare!' Nicola says. 'The world doesn't need any more glass-half-full people. Besides, you'd miss being in touch with your miserable-sod side. I know I would.' She bends down and swipes Thomas up just as he attempts to fork the plug socket. 'What's the time? We'd better go.'

330

'Go? Where?'

'Oliver's party! Don't tell me you've forgotten?'

'Haven't been paying much attention to anything other than my own navel recently.'

'Well, you're coming.' Nicola starts packing Thomas's nappy bag. 'You can't hide away any longer.'

'Oh, er . . .' This trip to Nicola's was monumental enough. 'Really I'm . . .' Nicola picks up my handbag. 'Do I have to?' Nicola nods. 'OK, OK, if you promise to rescue me if the inquisition gets too heavy and Hermione starts regaling me about that cashmere booty company.'

'And the scones. Are you in an emotionally fit state to stomach the scones?'

'As long as they don't come with Cornish clotted cream. That might make me regress.' I laugh, not because anything's funny exactly, but more as a release.

Nicola grabs my hand and squeezes it. 'Well done.'

'For what?'

'For pulling yourself up by your old bra straps. It's so good to hear you laugh again.'

Fifty-three

One trainer on Sue's doorstep, one on the paved path. I can't do this. *It'll be good for Evie.* Can't do this. *I need to start getting out more, no more moping.* Can't face the pity. *Mum said . . .* Both feet on the path. Stern look from Nicola. The door opens.

Sue is wearing a fireman's hat made out of red cardboard. She kisses Nicola normally then swivels stage left and with a loud wet sigh pulls me into her gristly bosom. 'How *are* you?' she gasps.

'Fine, better than would be expected.'

'It's all right, you don't need to be brave around me, poor thing.' Sue tries to collude Nicola in A Look, but fails. 'This will cheer you up.' Sue shoves black, triangular, paper pirate hats on our heads. 'Come in my hearties!'

Balloons bang into our faces, twirls of candy-coloured paper catch in the mouth. The sitting room is a riot of screaming babies, cup cakes and exposed nipples. Nicola is immediately pulled aside by Hermione and I'm left wondering who to talk to.

'Alan!' Sue calls out to a blond man bouncing a grizzling Oliver on his corduroy-clad knee. 'Amy, Alan, my husband.'

Pale hazel eyes. Clean-shaven, delicate, with a hopeful

smile, like a children's TV presenter. Pretty rather than handsome. I was expecting someone more roguish.

'Alan, this is my friend Amy . . .' Alan looks blank. 'You know, I told you about . . .' Sue shoots Alan an intense *remember* glance.

'Of course,' says Alan nervously, clearly remembering I'm the loopy one who's Been Left. 'Amy. Nice to meet you. I hope you're, er, feeling better.'

'Much, thank you.' I shake his hand. It is cool and fine-boned. It is a hand that has been in Jasmine's knickers.

'Right, let me get you some tea,' says Sue, seeming to hovercraft jovially over the party litter.

Nicola returns. 'Over there, the Willesden Lane bed-hopper,' I hiss.

Without turning her head too obviously, Nicola peers at Alan through a gap in her bob. 'A bit fem. Sue must eat him alive,' she says.

'Evidently not.'

Hermione appears to my left, fluffy as a soft toy in a pink angora sweater. 'I am so, *so* sorry,' she says in a high cartoon-network voice.

'Er, thanks.'

'Is it awful?' She points her carrot crudité at me like a microphone.

'Not quite what I planned, but hey . . .'

'Oh dear.' Hermione gives me a weak, rather disappointed smile. She was hoping for more details. 'Life really can throw up some nasty surprises. Gosh, I don't know how I'd cope on my own, especially with a little one on the way.' Hermione still doesn't look very pregnant. More like a post-curry bloat. 'Oh, I'm sorry,' she says suddenly, hand to mouth.

'Sorry? Why are you sorry?'

'It must be so hard, well, not knowing if you can have

another one. Not with the same fath . . . Gosh, this is coming out all wrong. I'm really sorry, Amy. I'm not very good at this sort of thing. I don't mean to offend you,' she squirms.

'It's fine. Really. You haven't offended me in the slightest. Please . . .'

Drawn to the fluster like a shark to a flailing swimmer, Sue surfaces from behind a large blue helium balloon. 'Who's offended you?' she demands, offended.

'No one's offended me. Really. Hermione was just saying—'

'Oh, I've put my foot in it, Sue. I made an inappropriate comment, without meaning to, about Joe . . .' Hermione stammers.

Nicola steps in. 'Listen, Amy is fine,' she says emphatically. 'No one has died! Amy is having problems in her relationship, like we all do.'

'It's rather more than that!' exclaims Sue. 'I'd say Being Left by your husband, sorry, boyfriend, when you've got a small baby is rather more than having an up-and-down. You poor thing.' I shuffle awkwardly. I don't need this. 'It is,' Sue continues, 'ab-so-lute-ly disgusting behaviour! If I could get my hands on Joe, what a *pig*!'

'Pig!' chimes Hermione.

'If Alan ever dreamed of doing such a thing, I'd, I'd . . .'

'Please!' I shout over the racket. 'It's not Joe's fault. Don't demonise him. Please. I am fine. Absolutely fine.'

All three start back, worried they've pushed me – an explosive Left person, so obviously not fine – over the edge. Sue reacts quickly to the crisis. 'Here, have a gingerbread man, sugar-reduced.'

'Thanks. One man I can rely on.'

Everyone laughs, exaggerated relieved laughs. Hermione and Sue make their excuses.

334

'Shit, don't you just want to tell her?' Nicola glares at Sue's retreating flank. 'Wet Wipe away that Godawful smugness.'

'You'd think she'd guess. I mean, look at him.'

Alan is standing flirtatiously close to the bloomingly pretty Lisa from number twenty-three, one arm around her shoulders.

'Jasmine's got weird taste.' Unlike me who had good taste but didn't realise it in time.

'Oh, I bumped into Jasmine on my lunch break yesterday,' Nicola says. 'She didn't remember my name of course, those kind of women never do. But I reminded her that I was the least fashionable person in the Westbourne that day. I told her I was going to see you here . . .'

Suddenly, there is a flurry of noise by the door.

'A friend of Amy's? Yes, yes, of course you can come in, no problem. The more the merrier,' Sue is saying. 'And you must be little Martin? Oh, sorry, Marlon. What a lovely name.'

Surely not? I walk into the hallway. But there she is. Jasmine, in an inappropriately exuberant Temperley dress, smiling nervously.

'Hi Amy! Nicola said you'd be here. I was, er . . . just round the corner and Marlon was desperate to play with some other kids,' she jabbers, unable to meet my eye.

'That's just lovely. The more the merrier,' repeats Sue, thoroughly delighted to have attracted another person to her party, and such a glamorous one too. 'Here, let me take your coat. No coat? Please, do have a gingerbread man, still warm from the oven.'

Jasmine refuses, eyes sweeping over Sue – frizzy hair, mumsy shoes – in a quick vicious glance. I'm so stunned to see her here, in a parallel mother galaxy, in Sue's *home*, that I can only glare silently.

335

'Follow me!' Sue says, putting her hand on Jasmine's narrow back. 'Let me introduce you.'

As Jasmine is pushed into the party, fear knots her perfect face for a second. She composes herself, smiles and strides forth in gold sandals. Is she drunk? No, worse, she looks scarily sober.

'Oh God, poor Sue,' says Nicola watching Jasmine accept Sue's compliment about her dress with the detached ungraciousness of someone who has spent their whole life being complimented on their outward appearance.

'What to do?' What would I normally do? Walk away, let it unravel.

Nicola grabs my elbow. 'She's hit her target.'

Jasmine is being introduced to Alan by Sue. Alan's gone pale as milk.

'Come on, we may as well get a ringside seat.'

A heat spreads inside me. An indignant anger. No, Sue doesn't deserve this. No more denial. No more walking away. 'Excuse me, Nicola.' I stride over to Jasmine and pince her by the elbow. 'Jasmine, into the kitchen, *now*.' She smiles frozenly as Sue waves and shouts out, 'Won't tell if you help yourself to more from the oven!'

I push Jasmine against a Formica kitchen unit. 'What the hell do you think you're doing?'

'Giving him a taste of his own medicine,' Jasmine smirks. 'I just found out he's been seeing someone else.'

'His wife?'

'Very funny. Don't worry, I wasn't planning to tell her.'

'No, you're not. Because you're getting out!' I grab her elbow again.

'Hey, what is this? A roar from the mouse?'

'Sue's in my NCT group, it's too close. She's kind of a friend.'

'And I'm not?'

I consider this for a moment. Why should I be intimidated by this woman? I have nothing left to lose. 'It seems not.'

Jasmine yanks her Chloé bag over her shoulder like a rifle. 'You'll make this worse if you create a scene.'

'There won't be a scene. You're going to go in there, make your excuses politely and *leave*.'

Jasmine looks at me, astonished. 'What's got into you?' Her eyes narrow and I can no longer see her cover-girl beauty, just a desperate woman in need of a good feed and a cuddle. 'You know what, Amy? I'm not surprised your boyfriend's left. I never did understand why Alice bothered with you.'

'I wouldn't expect you to.'

'You're really winding me up, Amy. If you carry on I might just confess all to Sue,' she says, floundering a little.

'Leave Sue alone. Pick on someone your own size.'

With a self-righteous sniff, Jasmine strides out of the kitchen to the front door. Sue, spotting her, steers Jasmine-wards. But Jasmine doesn't say goodbye. Jasmine grabs Marlon and slams the door. Sue's mouth opens and shuts silently and the sugar-reduced gingerbread men slide off the plate and decapitate on the hall floor.

Fifty-four

Queen's Park, tea time. I sit on the steps of the bandstand watching children walk – or run or tantrum or trike-jack – home from school across the park, escorted by an assortment of carers: non-working mums in jeans and Converse trainers with playground tans; determinedly enthusiastic working mums in office clothes, the lucky ones, presumably, who have managed to sort some flexible working arrangement; 'freelance' dads; sixtysomething Afro-Caribbean nannies; tired but enchanted grandparents indulging their grandchildren with ice cream. Chattering along a different path, from the wooded area, comes a shoal of brightly dressed toddlers on an outing from the local nursery. They whoop at the older children, straining at the hands of their nursery workers, gentle Muslim women with covered heads. At this moment, London feels like a very benign place, and it occurs to me that, despite their parents' attempts to pigeon-hole with the right schools and rules and diets, children's ebullience resists it. And it is children who civilise a city like London, who give it its humanity.

'Uh oh.' Railing against my sentimentality, Evie spits up her digestive biscuit into my shopping bag. I stroke the crumbs away from her mouth. She looks up and grins. 'It better not have . . .'

I tug open the shopping bags, hauled back from the West End, to check for regurgitated biscuits. Thankfully, Evie needs to work on her aim. My new wardrobe is intact: Zara wrap-around dress – blue jersey, flatteringly hitting just below the knee – smelling deliciously of shop; new jeans, Gap; machine-washable blue boat-necked jumper, the kind of thing Alice would dismiss as 'a bit Jigsaw'; flat-fronted olive-green trousers; silver ballet shoes. I kick a trainer off and slip a ballet shoe on.

'You approve, Evie?'

After a Pinot Grigio-fuelled midnight spring-clean to the strains of *Dolly Parton's Greatest Hits* I reorganised my wardrobe, working out what I don't wear or doesn't fit. Most of the clothes I bought with Alice were in the Don't Wear pile. I find this strange because it isn't as if I don't love those clothes. I do, I really do. It's just that they were bought for a woman who never really existed, some strange lifestyle hybrid of Alice's imagination. And it's not that I want to go back into my leggings and maternity pants. Oh no. But I do *need* stuff – pretty and smart – that fits this new body, which is piling on weight as quickly as I lost it and gradually returning to my pre-baby healthy size twelve. I need heels that I can walk in. Clothes that aren't dry clean only. Clothes that aren't destroyed by a smudge of banana. Clothes that are me, not me trying to be someone else. Clothes that Joe would like.

'Daddy home soon, sweetheart,' I sigh, to myself more than Evie.

Four days. He's back in four days. I can barely contain myself, which is ludicrous because all that will happen, I guess, is that we'll have a sad little conversation about access

339

and money. Gosh, how much I'd give just to see him walk down that path, jaunty in his old-school trainers, head cocked forward, big molar smile. Then life plays a cruel trick, because someone I know does walk towards me on the path, the one that feeds into the copse of wooded trees. But it isn't Joe. It's my mother, wind sweeping the hair off her face, sucking her skirt against her legs. And walking next to her, making her laugh, is a shortish dark man, Moroccan, Indian perhaps, wearing a tailored coat. I can see the release in Mum's body as she laughs. Like that photo taken with my father in the early days of their courtship. A different Jean. They turn slightly. Lord! They are hand in hand!

I feel a rush of protective fury. Who the hell is this man? Doesn't he know that Mum is celibate? Vulnerable? And why hasn't she mentioned anything? Unsure of the etiquette I crouch over the pram, a shaft of hair hopefully shielding me from her view.

'Amy?' Mum calls a few moments later. 'Amy? Is that you? You OK?'

I unfurl and reveal myself. Thankfully, Mother and the man have spared me from the handholding and have sprung apart, red-faced, like teenagers. 'Er, fine.'

Mum tucks her windswept hair behind her ear a little nervously. 'Gosh!' She clears her throat. 'I . . . we . . . were just going for a walk. I was going to pop round later.' I look at the man next to her. There's an awkward pause. 'Amy, this is my, er, friend, Norman.' Mum blushes. 'Norman Srinivas.'

Norman? I imagined Norman to be a middle-aged Anglo-Saxon optician.

'My daughter Amy,' Mum says proudly.

Norman holds out a hand and smiles shyly. 'Honoured,' he says, with a slight Indian accent. 'You could be sisters.' Mum glows. 'Now I will let you ladies spend some time together,' he says apologetically. 'I was just off, wasn't I Jean? Don't let me intrude. I must be getting back to work.'

'No, no, honestly, you have your walk,' I say, desperate to exit the situation. But Norman won't hear of it. He says his courteous goodbye and walks, upright and springy, towards Queen's Park tube. Mum's unable to take her eyes off him. As soon as he is out of earshot I turn to her.

'You never told me!'

Mum feigns puzzlement for two seconds then, despite all her facial muscles straining to hide it, breaks into a wide sunshine smile. 'You've had so much to cope with, I didn't want to give you another thing to worry about. It seemed in poor taste considering Joe . . .'

I brush her off. 'Don't be silly.' So Norman is the secret to mum's new complexion. The lightness of shoe. The bed-head hair. The deeper necklines. Goodness.

'He makes me very happy. I was going to tell you when the time was right.'

Although I'd like to write this off as a fling I know it's not. So suddenly Mum is no longer just Mum. She is someone's lover. That's something to get my head around.

'I'd like you to get to know him.'

'Um, I'd love to. But when I'm dressed properly?' I am wearing a trainer on one foot, a ballet shoe on the other.

'Oh, Norman's not like me. He doesn't notice such things.' Mum laughs, a light soufflé laugh, not the cough-clearance of old.

I shuffle awkwardly from trainer to ballet shoe, not quite sure how to navigate the conversation. My overwhelming feelings are curiously parental: I want to quiz her on Norman's credentials and intentions. But I am thrilled that she's happy and also, rather more selfishly, rather relieved. Finally, the weight of Mum's loneliness has slipped off my shoulders! I always felt that life would be easier, and I'd just feel less guilty somehow, if she'd meet her prince, or at least a half-decent non-psycho heterosexual male who would take her on mini-breaks to Venice and accompany her to garden centres. That she'd then concentrate on her own life rather than mine. That someone would put genuine joy back into her smile. At least one of us got the happy ending.

'And he can fix you up with some glasses,' Mum says brightly, as if this might clinch my affection for good.

Fifty-five

As Mum said, I've got to fight for my life; and a meeting with Pippa always feels like a medieval joust. The skyscraper is taller than I remember, the city dirtier, on a different scale to the upholstered houses and playgrounds that I've spent the last few months of my shrink-to-fit life in. The huge panes of glass reflect a clutter of concrete, cars, lots of cars, and clouds cut like they've been through a shredder. Crossing the main road, people move fast, running late, in heels, slurping impossibly large coffees and looking like they haven't had enough sleep. Office complexions, I'd forgotten those.

I walk to the reception desk and try to look officious. It's hard to pull off when accessorised by a pram. Busy well-dressed women in the foyer eye Evie with an air of amused curiosity. It is obvious I am someone on a maternity leave visit. Not quite in the game. 'Amy Crane, I work, er, used to work here.'

'You have an appointment?' drawls the receptionist, a bored-looking woman with a face shaped like a fifty-pence piece and Starbucks breath.

'Yes, Pippa Price, Nest PR.'

She trawls, painfully slowly, through her computer address

343

book and dials the telephone with salaried complacency. 'Someone will be down to collect you. Please take a seat.'

I try to arrange myself elegantly on the leather corner sofa without ruining the shop-fresh press of my new trousers. I feel strangely proud. Here I am, a functioning human being, sitting on a leather sofa in a corporate building, not wearing a tracksuit, prepared for battle.

After *ten* minutes – when I worked here I only used to leave unimportant people waiting ten minutes – I am summoned by the receptionist and escorted past security to the lifts by a shy work-experience girl. The tummy-curdling journey to the twenty-seventh floor, once so routine, feels like flying.

Returning to the workplace after having a baby is like returning home after a life-changing round-the-world trip. You expect everything to have changed because you have. But it hasn't. Around the door the same awards are still arranged, the best magazine cuttings, framed. The same palm with huge fronds that always reminded me of Joe's hands. The secretary at the front desk is new but the same as the last: young, eager, underpaid. The turnover was always high. I clatter into the main office, my pram scuffing just-delivered boxes on the floor.

Lots of double-takes. 'Amy hi! Hi, hi . . .' A sea of smiling, stressed faces. Quick can't-talk-now waves from bodies glued to telephones. A thrum of old colleagues – Jemima, Sophie, Iris. They huddle around the pram, cooing, and I say that I'm well, really well, and thank you for your kind gifts and cards and yes, I have managed to lose the baby weight, thanks.

Evie starts to grumble. Panicking that she's about to start a fire-engine wail spectacular, I dig out an emergency bribe biscuit which she gobbles triumphantly, then puts her hand out for another. But she's still not appeased. Too much of a crowd, too close. Smile, Evie, smile. She doesn't. She farts. A peal of awkward laughter.

'Oh, that'd be hard to PR!' says a posh, loud voice behind me. I turn around. A tall, gorgeous black-eyed girl with a tumble of Nigella hair. I don't know her.

'Hi Amy, I am Anastasia, your maternity cover.' She offers me her hand, winking with diamonds.

'Oh, er, hi.' I'm suddenly very glad I settled – at my mother's insistence – on the heels rather than the flat ballet shoes. I need the height.

'I've very much enjoyed being you,' she says, then laughs uproariously. Yes, the idea that she could ever be me, or I her, is absurd.

'I hear you've done a good job, thanks very much.'

'A *brilliant* job!' someone booms behind me. Toxic Pippa, hard-bodied as a tailor's dummy in her trademark Dolce & Gabbana suit. 'Hi Amy, nice to see you. Met our Anastasia I see.'

Our Anastasia?

'So this is baby Eva?' Pippa inspects Evie with mild curiosity. Pippa never wanted children. She has four Burmese cats and a Mercedes convertible instead. 'What can she say?'

'Oh, not much, dada mostly. She's not hugely advanced.' I mean this as a joke but it isn't taken as one. Pippa frowns. This is a selling environment.

'And how is her handsome daddy?' shrills Pippa. 'Bearing up to the nappies and late nights is he? Hasn't done a runner yet?'

She can't know? Of course not. 'Um, er, he's fine.' Sound more confident, look her in the eye.

'Well, at least she's a pretty girl, not one of those babies you go, "Oh isn't she pretty" because you have to but who really look like prawns. Do you remember Abby's little girl?'

Sophie and Iris roll their eyes at me behind Pippa's back. So, nothing's changed then. Pippa is as vile and tactless as ever.

'Thanks. She's a much improved version of both of us,' I say, trying to talk in plural, to sound like a family. Being Left isn't going to help my cause.

'Waaaaaaah.'

'Oh.' Pippa steps back. 'That's loud.'

Not now, darling Evie. I feel myself tense, prickles of sweat on my neck. Evie's eyes plead with me to remove her from the assault of this alien air-con environment.

'Why is it crying?' Pippa is offended.

'Um, it's not always a cause and effect thing.' I unstrap Evie and lift her out of the pram. This is like taking the lid off a perfume bottle. Except it isn't perfume.

'Euh! *What's* that smell?' Pippa recoils.

Lamb mash and clementines. A humdinger: where the hell do I change her? The Ladies. Sophie bravely accompanies me. She stares in mesmerised horror as I scrabble on the floor with a sludge of orange poo, Evie's furious feet kicking out at the indignity of the cold, hard tiles, dipping her heels in the soiled nappy. Sophie asks why I haven't been in touch all these months and I apologise and say that I've been knee deep in all sorts of shit. She laughs and says she's missed me and makes me promise to come out for a drink with her and Iris next week. I say that I'd love to and mean it, and feel that finally I'm ready to pick up my social life where I left off.

Anastasia waits for me by the pram. 'Let me take her,' she says, smiling, confident as a Norland nanny. 'Give you a bit of peace. You go and have your little chat with Pip.'

Pip? I reluctantly pass Evie, trailing a poo miasma smell, into her manicured hands. Whimper, Evie. Whimper. But she doesn't. Evie stares at Anastasia's pore-perfect face and grins.

'Don't tell me Anastasia's good with kids *too*?' exclaims Pippa. 'Come on Amy, let's have a chat, quickly, before Evie demands to be adopted.'

I look back over my shoulder. Anastasia has sat down on *my* old chair at *my* desk with Evie on her knee. Funny to think that was where I sat pregnant, swollen feet resting on the waste bin, thinking about baby names and booties and breathing techniques, blissfully unaware.

I follow the flash of Pippa's Christian Laboutin scarlet soles into the glass orchid-bedecked cube that is her office. She nods for me to sit down on her red sofa. I cross my legs neatly, my I-don't-normally-wear-these shoe dangling, some-what self-consciously. Pippa shakes out her shaggy blonde do with her fingers and cracks a tight-lipped smile. She's had her teeth whitened.

'Great to see you looking so unmumsy,' she says, slashing open a stiff white envelope with a blood-red fingernail and checking her mail casually. 'So you're not tempted to do the whole nouvelle housewife bit and stay at home full time then?'

I shuffle on the seat. 'No, not for me.'

'You've been off work a while. Sally was back at her desk after three months you know. And she had twins.' She sighs dramatically, like my presence exhausts her. 'Obviously this job, your old job . . .' It's meant to *still* be mine. 'It's demand-ing. It requires a hundred and ten per cent.' She twists the lid off a 'superfood algae' bottle, tosses two large capsules down her throat and gulps.

'Of course, Pippa.'

'I'm not going to be able to make any allowances for babies. Nursery pick-up times, sickness . . . all that kind of thing. Anastasia has really galvanised your account. She's at the desk until eight o'clock most evenings.' Pippa arches one threaded eyebrow and checks me for signs of surrender. '*If* you do decide to come back, I'd like to keep her on.'

'That's great.' I crack a fake smile and hope the Botox will keep me looking serene.

347

'In fact, because she's more flexible, can do the evening functions etc., I think it best that you report to her.' Pippa nonchalantly waters her orchid with Evian and waits for my reaction.

'Report to Anastasia? You want to make her my boss?' Never.

'I want to make this easy for everyone, considering your change of circumstances. But, of course, if you tell me you are available to do evening functions any night of the week with a couple of hours' notice . . .'

'I will do my best.' Who the hell would look after Evie? I'd never see her.

Pippa throws back her large nose and laughs. 'Oh come on, Amy. That's not good enough. Perhaps your boyfriend will look after her. That seems to be Sally's arrangement. But it's got to be a firm commitment. Can you promise me that?'

'Two hours' notice might be a bit tricky. But that would be exceptional, Pippa, I'd usually get a lot more—'

'Evening functions were always part of your job,' snaps Pippa. 'So what you're really saying to me is that you won't be able to do your job to its full capacity as you did before, which makes me think that it would be best for all concerned if you reported to Anastasia.'

Don't take it. Don't take it lying down. 'I'm not comfortable with that. That's a demotion. I worked extremely hard building my account.'

'Excuse me?' Pippa says, as if she'd misheard. I'm not playing ball, and not having worked here for a while I lack the necessary subservience she instills in her staff through hierarchical terror games.

'I'll do those hours, if that's what the job requires. But,' deep breath, 'I'd like to discuss a three-day week.'

Pippa glances at her Hermès watch stagily. 'Well, that took

five-and-a-half minutes to surface,' she laughs. 'Amy, we both know these ridiculous, sorry, new laws mean you *can* request to work part time. In your case, because you're good, I won't *necessarily* contest it. But it's got to work for both of us. Otherwise negotiating this is going to be a long, drawn-out, bloody business. I don't want another maternity court case on my hands.'

'Which means?' I say, trying to smile.

'Reporting to Anastasia.'

'As my boss?'

Pippa silently pulls together some papers on her desk and opens her diary, mentally moving on to the next task in hand. 'Better contact HR for the next step,' she says breezily. Dismissed.

How dare she? I'm a mother. I won't be treated like this. I've got bigger things to be scared of now. 'Pippa, I will check it out with HR and my lawyer, if you don't mind.'

She looks up at me sharply. 'You're the first woman I've worked with to come back from maternity leave with attitude. *Most* women are pleased to be offered a compromise solution.'

'I appreciate that, but I'm not accepting a demotion, part time or not. I can delegate. I'll make it work, Pippa.'

She glares at me, chewing the end of her pen, weighing up. One maternity court case is to be expected. Two looks careless. 'You better,' she says. And I practically fall off my chair.

Back in the main office Sophie mouths, 'How did it go?' and I give her a thumbs-up. Then it hits me. I'll be here, a soaring twenty-seven floors up, against the thrum of telephones, the self-expanding blink of 360-degree windows, the sound of business being done. No nappies! No park! My days will once again have a beginning, a middle and an end. I can get my legs waxed at lunchtimes, rejoin my yoga class!

There will be someone to notice if I do a job well. And instead of discussing sleep patterns and primary schools, it'll be Kate Moss's love affairs and Sienna Miller's hair. And, most importantly, I will get paid.

'Oh no! Evie!' yelps Anastasia loudly. I swivel round. Anastasia is stabbing at her computer keyboard and staring at the screen in open-pouted horror.

'I don't believe it. Please tell me this isn't true . . .'

I run over to my old corner. Evie's happily gurgling on Anastasia's lap, little fingers coiled around the keyboard wires. 'What's happened?'

'Your baby, she's just . . . just . . .' Words catch on her lip gloss. '. . . SMASHED her fist on to my keyboard and deleted my whole document. Two weeks' work gone, fucking gone.'

That's my girl.

Fifty-six

I see the bicycle first. A streak of rainbow stripes past the living-room window. Evie looks at me quizzically. We exchange glances. No, it can't be. Slamming the door behind me, I thump down the street, rolling back gracelessly on the sloping soles of my MBTs, unsure where I am going, warily pleased about work, sad that I can't discuss it with Joe. A screech of brakes. It is Josh, flushed, tousled and grinning.

'Hey babe, I was trying to find your house,' he says, casually, like we see each other every day. 'Where you going?'

'Just a walk.'

He swings off his bike and wheels it beside me, still grinning. 'You're not going to get anywhere fast with that pram.'

'It's fine. Something jammed in the wheel. Been there for ever, it's the sound of Evie's universe.'

'A bit noisy. Do you want me to look at it? I'm good at things like that.'

I should have known that Josh would turn up when least expected, twist back into my life like a difficult yoga position. I stop and turn to face him. 'What do you want?'

'Just came to see that you were OK. I heard that Joe, it is Joe isn't it? I heard that he left.'

351

'Very big-hearted of you.' I start walking again. Evie gurgles happily from the pram, entranced by the spin of Josh's bike wheels.

'Let's go and grab a coffee or something, have a chat.'

'No thanks. Evie needs some fresh air.'

'O-K. Well how about this little playground here?'

'If I can't get rid of you any other way.'

'You can't.'

Josh carefully sweeps leaves off a graffiti-tattooed bench and gestures for me to sit down. 'Why so glum?'

'Well, the father of my child, my fiancé,' the word sounds even more ludicrous in this context, 'he's left. I'm a bit gutted, as you might be able to imagine.'

'Wanker!' says Josh, rather inappropriately, considering. 'No wonder you look pissed off.'

Tears prick my eyes. Seeing Josh brings the whole nasty episode back. I pick Evie out of the pram and cuddle her on my knee, calming myself with the infinitely soothing smell of her scalp.

'Have you got a channel for it? This anger.'

'Don't be silly.'

'You must release it or it'll warp you inside.' Josh rests a hand on my arm. It sits there like an improbable object, a stranger's hand. There is no buzz. No heat. Josh shuffles towards me on the slatted bench and strokes Evie's hair. I instinctively pull her away. I don't want him to touch Joe's baby daughter.

'Like that is it?' Josh says, looking a little put out. 'I never wanted you to hate me like this.'

'I haven't got the space in my head to hate you right now,' I say wearily. 'I barely even know you.'

Undeterred, he sighs dramatically. 'I've been reflecting a lot.'

352

'That's a start.'

Evie grabs a toggle on Josh's sweatshirt. Relieved to have something to look at, I stare at her busy toggle-rolling fingers.

Josh smiles. 'I want you to know that my feelings for you go way beyond my little deal with . . .' Evie tugs sharply at the toggle. Josh, not quite sure what to do, leans towards her. '. . . Alice.'

'Deal? I'm not with you.'

'You know, our little . . .' Josh slams his hand to his mouth. 'Oh God, you don't know, do you? Shit, shit, I thought she'd told you. She told me she was going to come clean.'

'No, Josh. Tell me.' I start to warp inside.

He squirms on the bench. 'Shit, I can't believe I have to tell you this. Well, thing is, er, Alice asked me to make a pass at you, all those weeks ago, to cheer you up.'

Evie pulls the toggle hard then releases. It pings sharply into Josh's jaw.

'Alice *what*?' I hiss.

Josh rubs his chin. 'She wanted you to feel sexy again, kind of a favour to a mate.'

Oh God. Alice. What a stupid mug. All those 'you'll feel visible' comments from Josh, all second hand from Alice. To think that I thought . . .

'Don't look like that, Amy.' Josh puts his hand on my knee. 'You weren't some charity case. I really fancied you. Honestly, I was more than happy to help.'

I flick his hand off. 'Help?' I take my hand away from my mouth. 'You fucking ruined my relationship!'

'Hey, don't overreact, babe. Alice just thought it'd be a bit of fun, to build your "sexual self esteem" she said. I'm sorry. Joe was never meant to find out. But . . . look on the bright side,' he beams, 'it got us together.'

I push him away. 'I can't believe you're telling me this.'

Josh shuffles closer, still convinced he's got a starring role to play in my life. 'I never stopped thinking about you. About you and me.'

'Oh shut up!' I shout, everything bubbling up at once. 'There is no you and me. There is no me and Joe! It's about me and Evie now.' Despite trying desperately not to, I dissolve into furious sobs against Evie's ducktail of hair.

'Hey, hey.' Josh slides his arm over my shoulders and pulls me towards him. 'It's OK. It'll all be OK, I promise babe.'

I can feel my tears wet on his neck. He bends his head towards mine, cradling my sobs in a cave between our bodies.

'I'll be there for you, I promise. I fucked up before, Amy, even when I knew that you and I had something special. But I ballsed it.'

What is he talking about?

Josh clears his throat. 'I didn't have faith, treated it like just a bit of fun. But it wasn't. It was more than that. And I'm not going to balls it up again.'

I sit back, smearing the tears off my cheeks. 'Again? What on earth do you mean?'

'I think we should give it a proper go, Amy. Me, you and Evie.'

Suddenly the absurdity of the last few months hits me and from deep within my tummy comes a loud, contracting, mad-woman's laugh so explosive that snot flies from my nostrils like geysers. 'No, that's too funny . . .' I breathe deeply into Evie's neck, trying to calm myself. 'It's all too funny.'

Josh looks hurt, mouth slack. 'Funny?'

'Alice. Unbelievable. Now this. Oh, I'm sorry. But Josh, you're not serious? What would you want with us two?'

Josh bends forward, rests his elbows on his knees. 'I've always wanted a family. And I've helped cause some of this shit, so let me make it better again, babe. I don't want any bad karma.'

Is there no end to this man's self-delusion? 'You don't know what you're talking about.'

'I mean it. I don't mean many things, but I mean this,' he says gravely.

A cold, damp wind trembles the leaves. I pull Evie closer and think of our dark little house, its pockets of sadness, ghosts and odd testosterone-free air. I wonder, will I get any more offers like this?

Then I come to my senses.

'It's not as sudden as you might think,' Josh says, defences considered and covered. 'Basically, when you said you were engaged I thought I'd lost you.'

Lost me? Had he been conducting a phantom relationship with me in his head? He never had me, not really. I realise that now.

'And when I heard that Joe had left I . . . I thought maybe I was in with a chance again.' Josh strokes a strand of hair off my face tenderly. 'I could love you. I could fall in love with you.'

'Could?' The laughs are back again, odd intense cackles not spouting from any source of joy. 'I'm sorry. You're sweet.'

Josh looks puzzled, as if he'd anticipated a far more agreeable reaction. 'Will,' he says, adjusting his declaration. 'Will love you.' He strokes my hair again. 'What are you thinking?'

I am thinking that I know, completely and utterly, that I cannot possibly ever love Josh. That even if I had to stay single for the rest of my days I would never be able to love Josh like I loved Joe. He would forever compare unfavourably; his fickleness to Joe's solidity; his shallowness to Joe's depth. He'd be a constant reminder of what I've lost.

Josh squeezes my hand tight and smiles patiently, biding his time for my acquiescence.

'It's not going to happen, Josh. Sorry.'

He looks bewildered rather than upset. 'Maybe in time . . .'

'No really, it's not.'

'It's not the Alice thing, is it? Because that isn't relevant now . . .'

'No, it's not that, really. I just love Joe.'

We stand up from the bench silently. I put Evie back in her pram. Josh picks up his bike and we walk to the gate. He kisses the top of my head. 'Guess this is it,' he says resignedly. 'Goodbye beautiful.' He throws one leg over the saddle and pedals away fast, a flash of rainbow shrinking into the grey street, like a kaleidoscope twisted and twisted until the colour is just a pinpoint against the black.

Fifty-seven

Leaves, the colour of orange Smarties. The grass is chewed and the dry dust of summer that crunched under my flip-flops is now mulch. It's hard to believe I was ever intimidated by this park. Today, a few lone mothers sit at the outside café tables, UGG-booted feet tapping the babies in their prams to sleep. No midriffs, little laughter. It seems strange remembering how terrifyingly glamorous they appeared in the summer heat. How other I felt, an unlikely mother, not quite with the program. Now it strikes me there is no program, just a collection of women muddling along, improvising, huddling together because if they don't there is just the echo of a baby's cry in a rather empty house. I kick the leaves and imagine they're Alice. Silly, controlling, childish Alice. More leaves, up, up in the air. A woman in a fur gilet waves. A familiar face from the sand-pit – we've shared spades – smiles shyly and an unexpected warm rush of belonging spreads through my solar plexus.

'Over here!' Nicola walks speedily up the path from the children's play area.

'Not late!' I say, amazed.

Nicola laughs. 'Work discipline.' She stretches open her arms like wings.

We hug. I notice that she is wearing perfume, a light floral scent, and a new coat, sharply tailored, soft grey. 'Nice coat.'

'Joseph. A treat from Sam, I kid you not. As he is officially The Man With No Taste, I have no idea how he managed it.'

'You, Nicola, are a yummy mummy, a MILF!'

'At last! Who would have thought it?'

'Work suits you.'

Nicola grins. 'A lot easier than motherhood. I needed a rest.'

'Despot editor?'

Nicola tucks a sheaf of glossy bob behind her ear. 'Realises I'm still the best sub on the desk even though I've got working ovaries. I'm now allowed to leave early to pick Thomas up, which makes all the difference actually.'

Thomas picks his nose happily in his pram. 'And how's he surviving it?' I ask with trepidation. Evie and I have got an appointment at our local nursery, Sunrise Smile, next week. I worry about no one picking Evie up when she cries. I worry about untrained nursery staff and Turkey Twizzler lunches and separation anxiety. Mine mostly.

'The master and commander loves it. As he should,' laughs Nicola. 'The nursery is like a second mortgage.' Nicola's eyes zigzag as they follow a yellow leaf whirling to the ground. 'I've stopped beating myself up about it though.'

'You? Guilty? Never.'

'Well, I confess I had a niggle,' she admits. 'It did occur to me I might lack a maternal gene because I didn't want to slip into a Cath Kidston apron and embrace full-time motherhood.' Nicola drums her fingers on the table. 'Now what do you fancy? I'd love coffee and a . . . a . . . Actually *not* a cigarette. Stopped, two weeks so far. Can't pop out for fag breaks as well as leaving early, can I? Back in a sec.'

Evie sticks her finger into Thomas's ear. He pushes her off

with a boy's brute impatience. Thomas looks like he's doubled his body weight since last time I saw him. Gosh, they are no longer helpless teeny babies. Despite appearances to the contrary, life moves forward. Nicola returns, clatters the tray down and tea splashes her Joseph coat. 'Shit, I really am the anti-chic,' she tuts, dabbing with a paper napkin. I pick blueberries out of my muffin.

'News, news . . .' she says, trying to think. 'Afraid I can't top yours.'

We've already analysed Alice – aka the-devil-wears-UGG-boots – to death on the phone and my outrage has dulled to disappointment. Because I did like Alice. And, now I've calmed down a bit, I do think she genuinely liked me. We were unlikely friends and would probably never have hooked up had it not been for the bond of babies, but we certainly had a rapport of sorts, certainly more than I ever had with other accidental baby friends such as Sue. But, sadly, Alice is one of life's meddlers, an egotist, handicapped by a lack of self-doubt. She probably can't help herself. Yes, I can be big about this. Compared to the loss of Joe, and Evie's *ER* audition, Alice's actions seem childishly trivial.

'Missed the last NCT meeting, didn't you?' Nicola grins.

'On Thursday? Yes, couldn't face it, all that chamomile tea with thank-fuck-it's-not-me sympathy on the side.'

'Well, it was probably the last.'

'Surely not? The world as we know it—'

'Yes, the group is splintering into factions! It's civil war, Amy! Hermione has . . . wait for it . . . joined *another* group for her new pregnancy, because of "the different timings". The betrayal! Sue, as you can imagine, is deeply wounded.'

'And Michelle?'

'Wasn't there. Probably busy breastfeeding in the most public place she could find.'

359

So that era has gone, already! The scones, the cradle cap, the assumption that we had lots in common just because we'd reproduced at the same time; I couldn't see an end to it. But that's the thing about life with a baby, you lurch from one phase to another, convinced each will last for ever. 'But how will Sue cope without coffee mornings to pull together?'

Nicola raises a plucked eyebrow. 'Aha! Sue and Alan are officially Trying For Another Baby.'

'No!'

'Yes! She informed us in gruesome detail, exact stage in the ovulating cycle, the special-occasion White Company bed linen . . . I kid you not.' Nicola rocks back on the bench as if recoiling from the image stirred. 'I'm not sure if Sue's trying to catch up with Hermione and use a quick conception as a stepping stone into this new NCT group or whether it's Alan's attempt to rescue his marriage.'

'But Sue didn't know.'

'Something she said, something about another baby being a new start got me thinking.'

We sit in easy silence for a few moments, then Nicola looks up at me, eyes sharp beneath her bob. 'Joe's back, isn't he?'

'You reckon?' I look at Nicola; she shrugs. 'Well, not to *my* knowledge he isn't. But . . .' I check my watch. 'Any minute now.'

'How exciting!'

'Except he's picking up his stuff.' I don't elaborate. I'm a little Joe-talked-out by my mother, who just about survived hearing the whole story ('You silly, silly girl') with a few amendments. I stare silently out at the leaf-stripped trees, the zigzags of trikes and the muddy pram tracks, criss-crossing the park like lines on the palm of a hand.

'I bumped into Alice,' Nicola says abruptly.

'I'm sorry.'

'At the zoo of all places.'

I study my muffin. There seem to be only three blueberries left, buried too far in the dough to gouge out. 'Caged, I hope.'

'She looked gutted actually.' Nicola shifts on the bench. 'Although she behaved despicably, Amy, I do think she's genuinely sorry.'

'Yeah . . . well, whatever.' Got it! I skewer the blueberry on my index fingernail.

'She thinks you hate her. She's too scared to get in contact.'

'So she should be.' I pull the tea bag out of her cup with my fingers. 'So what's happening on Planet Alice then? New shoes? New life to ruin?'

'Oh, you know, deciding whether to import her nanny to the country at great cost, worrying about the local mobile phone mast near the paddock. Yes, I know, the paddock. I imagine it's not some crumbling rural shack.'

I switch the subject. 'How's Annabel? Did she say? I wonder if I'm allowed to visit.'

'Funny you should ask. Alice told me to tell you that Annabel's now fit for public viewing and would love to see you.'

'Great. I'll pop round tomorrow. And how's Milo? Annabel was worried about him.'

'The doctors think he's slightly deaf in one ear. Just one of those things. No one knows why. But he's basically perfectly fine, adorable apparently.' Nicola sips her coffee thoughtfully, sits up straight and fixes me with a direct stare. 'How do you fancy meeting Alice tomorrow, with me? You can talk about all this stuff face to face.'

'You are joking?'

'Well, she suggested it,' says Nicola apologetically. 'I was a bit surprised, I have to say. But she wants to see you

361

desperately, make her peace, thinks it may be easier with me there, someone neutral.'

'She probably thinks you can make me come.'

Nicola's face scrunches into a smile, freckles colliding like stars.

Fifty-eight

I slip the dress off its hanger and over my shoulders, pulling the fabric down with hot fingertips. The silk clings to my tummy like gauze on a round of cheese. But I don't care. Joe loved my tummy. Why should I hate it? This dress is in my DNA. My mother's, now mine. It has been at some of the happiest and saddest moments of our lives, as both witness and participant.

I drag mascara over my trembling eyelashes. Rouge, as Alice taught me, in concentric smudges on the apples of my cheeks. Slip on my soft silver – pancake-flat – ballet shoes.

'What do you reckon, sweetie?' Evie pulls herself up on to all fours and tries to crawl towards me. 'You can do it! Go on, Evie!' She grins and, trembling with the strain, takes one huge determined lurch forward – 'Yeah!!!' – before belly-flopping to the ground. Her first crawl. I could swoon with love and pride. 'Clever girl! Again, again.' But that is enough effort for one day. Evie refuses to move.

'My turn. Watch this!' I twirl and twirl like a ballerina in a box, loving the swish of the dress and the skid of the shoes and Evie clapping her hands clumsily, palms missing each other. Around and around, dizzy and exhilarated as an actress at curtain fall, imagining Joe watching, until I collapse in an umbrella of upturned dress on the floor and realise he isn't.

Portobello. The tattooist. Alice so doesn't deserve this. But Nicola's persuasive, and a part of me needs to say goodbye, confront her head-on. I squint up at the blue neon sign – The Electric – and walk confidently into the café knowing, for once, I'm dressed to deal with it.

A waiter guards the gateway to the back tables.

'Amy Crane,' I say.

His eyes flick over the names on his clipboard. He shakes his floppy fringe.

'It could be booked under Alice Hope.'

Hearing Alice's name, he smiles broadly. 'Ah, Alice! Of course.' More attentive now, he leads me to a little round table, tucked in the corner.

No Alice. No Nicola. Late, of course. Why didn't I think of being late first? Evie grumbles. I put her on my knee and scan the restaurant. To my left is a couple with a very young baby, probably a few weeks old. The parents are trying hard to enjoy themselves, but the father looks nervous and the mother looks exhausted. There is a damp patch growing on her left breast. Their baby, the chaperone, is wedged firmly between them in a car seat, asleep but frowning. The parents eye their baby warily, knowing it could wake and detonate at any moment.

To my right, in contrast, is a pair of young, fashionable twentysomething women. They flick their long blonde hair a lot. They are sexy and free. One of them, who is particularly leggy and blonde and knows it, is smoking, occasionally glancing guiltily at the baby and drawing harder on the cigarette. The other one is bent forward on her chair, rapt by

364

gossip. Funny to think that I'll never be like that again. In the same way I'll never be eight again. Quite a relief actually.

'Dadada,' Evie says.

'Mamama,' I correct, fruitlessly.

The waiter, smirking slightly, slams a bottle of smoking-cold champagne on the table.

'I didn't order this.'

'From Alice.' Typical Alice, trying to buy her lateness off. 'She asked me to give you this.' The waiter passes over an envelope.

Inside is a pale pink sheet of Smythson notepaper. The handwriting is neat, swirly, like a French schoolgirl's.

> *Darling Amy,*
> *Sorry*
> *Love always, Alice xxxxx*

The waiter puts down two glasses.

'Actually, we need three,' I say, wondering whether to accept Alice's pale pink apology.

'No we don't.' A voice behind me. Evie yelps with excitement.

'Joe!'

Joe hovers awkwardly for a second then scrapes a chair towards me and sits down. He is thinner now, cross-hatched and handsomely craggy, like when he returned from a punishing Himalayan trek. Lighting up at Evie's smile, he reaches out for her.

'What are you doing here?' My voice is quick, panicky and unprepared. How am I meant to behave? What am I meant to say? 'I'm meeting Alice and Nicola.'

Joe smiles gently. 'No, I'm afraid you're not.'

'I don't understand.' How very odd it is to have the warm

rock of Joe's flank next to me after all this time, odd because it's so extraordinarily familiar.

'You're here to meet me.' My stomach curdles. 'You've been set up, Amy Crane.'

'But . . . but . . .'

'Nicola and Alice got me here.' Joe leans forward. I can smell his breath. It smells of nothing, merely carries with it the heat and moisture from the engine house of his chest. He talks quietly, almost in a whisper. But his body is so solid, his knee so square, his thigh like a trunk of young, hard wood. I have missed his physicality, his absorption of space. 'They turned up at my work yesterday morning.'

Nothing makes sense. 'But I saw Nicola yesterday afternoon, she didn't say anything . . .'

'Alice told me what went on.'

'Oh.' Game over.

He puts one hand over his mouth and speaks through the gaps in his fingers. 'She said that she got this Josh guy to . . .'

I slump back in my chair, racked by shame. 'It's all right, Joe, I know. Don't go over it.' For a brief moment there I thought, well, what the hell did I think? Of course he won't.

'She said she'd put him up to pouncing.'

I nod, resigned. So he *definitely* knows what happened with Josh that afternoon. Thanks, Alice.

'That he'd just lunged when I walked in and saw you.'

'I . . . I . . .'

'Supernova bitch,' he hisses. 'I should have known. But I suppose at least she had the decency to tell me, even if it was under Nicola's duress.' He reaches for my hand tentatively. His is so big, warm and familiar. 'Amy, I am so sorry that I didn't hear you out and I am so sorry for running away to Cornwall. But I kept visualising you two together. It completely did my head in.'

A weight eases itself off my shoulders. Like when you take off a heavy rucksack and feel like you're floating.

'And I'm sorry for being so crap.' His face knits. 'You were right. I did work too late, sought refuge in the pub too often.' Such minor faults as to be negligible, I wave them away. 'Amy, I want to make it up to you.'

Make it up to *me*? I'm the one who needs to do the making up. And, yes, Joe deserves to know the truth, that it wasn't just that kiss in the studio. How can we be together with a wedge of lies between us like lumps on a bad mattress? 'Joe, there's something I should . . .'

Joe looks up sharply. 'Please, enough. I can probably guess.' He lowers his head, and in that quiet decline I can see that he has a fair idea. 'No more talk of Josh. Whatever happened, it was orchestrated by Alice and, well, I have to bear some responsibility too. I never thought I'd be able to say this, but it doesn't change the way I feel about you, not fundamentally. It doesn't change the fact that we are a family and we still have a future, well, if you want it. We both messed up. But maybe we needed something like this to happen. Maybe this saved us, in a weird way.'

I nod, stunned at what I am hearing. 'Joe, sorry. I'm so sorry for everything. It's my stupid fault, all of it . . .'

'Shussh. I love you, Amy. I'm not going to have my family torn apart.' He picks up a scrunch of my dress fabric and fingers it softly. 'The dress, isn't it?'

'You remember?'

'Of course. Oxford, punting . . .' He looks down at my feet, smiles. 'New shoes? I like.' Joe pulls me towards him, strong arms like cranes. 'Just say we'll work it out . . .'

The waiter skids a bowl of olives on to our table, his physical intrusion creating room for me to catch my breath. Delighted that her two favourite players are back on the same stage, Evie grins and looks at me expectantly. There's a long pause.

Joe slips his face into his hands, eyebrows tufting through his fingers. 'It's not too late? Please don't say it's too late.'

Fifty-nine

The waiter refills my glass and scuttles away fast, removing himself from our table's obvious potential for drama.

'That's all?' says Joe. 'Well I can answer that easily. No. I *never* ever loved Kate. Listen, I fell in love with you the first moment I saw you, way before you loved or even tolerated me. You are the real deal, Amy, always have been. And if you asked me to, I'd happily never see Kate again as long as I live.'

'I may just ask that.'

'I don't think she'll be bothering us. She's happy . . .'

'Now that she's almost ruined everything.'

Joe shrugs and smiles. 'Kate is pregnant. Pete finally managed to get her up the duff.'

The hormonal typhoon pregnant? Thank God. 'The nursery Osborne and Little wallpaper won't be wasted then.'

Joe shakes his head.

'One more question.'

'A deal breaker?'

'Oh yes.' I grin. 'You weren't catapulted into another woman's arms because I grew into a tub of butter?'

'You were *never* fat!' groans Joe loudly.

The mother – the one who doesn't realise she's leaking – glances up anxiously to the source of noise and then checks the baby for signs of waking. Joe, understanding instantly, softens his voice to a whisper.

'You were curvy. I loved your curves. When you were pregnant I thought you were so beautiful, just the most beautiful woman I'd ever seen.'

While her partner studies the menu, the mother pretends to, listening intently to Joe.

'You never told me that,' I say quietly.

'Didn't I?' Joe slides a hand over his mouth. 'But I thought it all the time. You know me, Amy. I'm crap like that.'

'It would have made a difference.'

'Sorry. But you know what? I love you even more now, despite the fact you're still a bit skinnier than I'd like and your forehead doesn't move.' He flutters his long black lashes. 'Can I fatten you up again? I still fantasise about your pregnancy thighs.'

I harrumph, playfully reluctant, knowing that I'd rather Hollywood-wax my head than let him leave again. In fact the realisation that life doesn't always conform to expectation, and that I'm not doomed to repeat the mistakes of my parents and, yes, it's possible to choose a happy ending, makes me dizzy with joy.

'Anything else?'

'One last question. Were you in Penzance or Polzeath?'

'Penzance.'

'Of course.' Laughter froths up, like my heart's been swirled with Fairy Liquid.

'Enough talk.' Joe stretches open his arms, palm upwards, eyes puddling with tears. 'I'm craving broken nights and the smell of nappy napalm in the morning . . .'

Suddenly, in my head, Mum. The late seventies. She's

370

wearing her bad-henna-day gypsy head-scarf and is crying over the kitchen sink, scrubbing the avocado-green plates too hard. Has she just turned Dad away? Chosen not to believe him when he says he still loves her? She tells me nothing's wrong. I go back to Connect Four and wonder why Mum's normal cheeriness has tailed off like the airplane trail haloing her head in the kitchen window.

'Amy?' Joe's eyebrows question-mark.

I try to whisper, 'Come home, we love you,' but I'm drowned out by a cutlery-trembling screech from the baby at the adjacent table. Cue a panicky flutter of muslin cloths and dummies and desperate soothing noises that only serve to inflame the baby more. A set of newly seated diners move tables. The baby's father, red-faced, mouths sorry and the baby carries on screaming until the mother whips out a huge purple boob. After slurping noisily for a few seconds, the baby detaches itself and decides to scream some more. Evie, recognising a kindred spirit, gurgles approvingly. I shoot a quiet smile at the mother, who looks like she'll never dare leave the house with the baby ever again, a smile that I hope says, 'It gets better, I promise.'

Of course, the fashionable twentysomethings don't smile. They wince. The leggiest one recoils back into her chair and exhales a cone of dense cigarette smoke into my eyes. I squeeze them tight. Blood black on the back of my eyelids. I squeeze harder, then rub. No images. For once the park, the kiss, that bad movie is no longer playing. There's just happy yellow light like yolks.

MY BEST FRIEND'S GIRL

Dorothy Koomson

Kamryn Matika has no responsibilities – one birthday card will change that forever . . .

Best friends Kamryn Matika and Adele Brannon thought nothing could come between them – until Adele did the unthinkable and slept with Kamryn's fiancé Nate. Worse still, she got pregnant and had his child. When Kamryn discovered the truth about their betrayal she vowed never to see any of them again.

Two years later, Kamryn receives a letter from Adele asking her to visit her in hospital. Adele is dying and begs Kamryn to adopt her daughter Tegan. With a great job and a hectic social life, the last thing Kamryn needs is a five-year-old to disrupt things. Especially not one who reminds her of Nate. But with no one else to take care of Tegan and Adele fading fast, does she have any other choice? So begins a difficult journey that leads Kamryn towards forgiveness, love, responsibility and, ultimately, a better understanding of herself.

Sphere
0 7515 3707 1

JULIANNA KISS
Hannah MacDonald

Julianna Kiss, gentle and inexperienced, heads to the south coast of England to work on a fruit farm for one cloudless summer before returning to Hungary and her studies. There she falls in love with Matthew, the farmer's son, and for the first time feels some of the passion promised to her by her grandmother. Julianna agrees to meet Matthew in London one last time before they go their separate ways, but a betrayal and a theft leave her living penniless and alone in the capital.

Unable to return to Hungary, Julianna slips into London's dark underworld: working in a restaurant cloakroom at night and mending clothes by day, Julianna survives on the margins of city life. But then she meets Jack, a powerful man who rescues her from the shadows and draws her into the light again.

'This is a timely and engrossing story, which puts its finger on the emotional, as well as the economic, reasons behind the westward move from eastern Europe'
Guardian

'This is a delicate, sad but ultimately uplifting story of a young woman's first experience of love'
Good Housekeeping

Little, Brown
0 349 11956 2

Other bestselling titles available by mail: